Even her wild gypsy blood and wisdom in the ways of rural witchcraft had not readied Sara Pownall for the snares and seductions of Regency London, a London of stark and splendid contrasts—gaming hells and gentlemen's clubs, glittering salons and sweaty sparring rings, country house weekends and crowded cockpits where elegant Regency bucks stake fortunes on the survival of the savage fighting cocks and rub shoulders for the thrill of it with London's criminal underworld of pickpockets and hired assassins.

But queen of the sporting crowd is not to be Sara's destiny—and her first encounter with Lord Southcott's handsome son Harry Summers in the gaming room at Monkey Palmer's marks the igniting of a strange passion that will ultimately transform her life.

"Fascinating."—*Fort Wayne News*
"Absorbing."—*New Haven Register*
"Lusty."—*Publishers Weekly*

About The Author

Brian Cleeve was born in the Essex countryside that is the point of departure for SARA.
Educated at St. Edward's school, Oxford, the
National University of South Africa and the
National University of Ireland, he served in
the Merchant Marine during the Second World
War. A varied career has included stints in
television and advertising and writing both
short stories and novels, among them thrillers
and a series of Irish novels, most recently *For
Love of Cranagh Castle*. SARA, his first Regency
novel, marks a new departure for this estab-
lished novelist. Mr. Cleeve lives in Dublin,
where he is currently at work on a new novel.

Brian Cleeve

SARA

WARNER BOOKS

A Warner Communications Company

Library of Congress Catalog Card Number: 75-38970

ISBN 0-446-89261-0

This Warner Books Edition is published by
arrangement with Coward, McCann & Geoghegan, Inc.

Cover art by Jenny Tomao

Warner Books, Inc., 75 Rockefeller Plaza, New York, N.Y. 10019

W A Warner Communications Company

Printed in the United States of America

Not associated with Warner Press, Inc. of Anderson, Indiana

First Printing: May, 1977

10 9 8 7 6 5 4 3 2 1

*For
Veronica
and
Anne Brady*

Prologue

Spain, 1809

The man rode slowly down the narrow path towards the valley. The burned brown rock at his left hand beginning to lie back, the dark mouth of the gorge opening. Behind the rider, the jagged mass of the Sierra Morena. Below him, a green cup of grassland, a small lake, the dark green of orchards. Orange and lemon groves, and on the hillside olives. The sharp, clean scent of the fruit trees drifted up to him. Beyond the lake and the trees, where the ground rose again into a low crowned hill in the middle of the widening valley, he could see a village. A dozen earth-coloured houses, the dull red of roof tiles.

He reined in his horse and sat with narrowed eyes slowly examining the landscape for movement. He was dressed in a Spanish fashion, round brown hat, brown cloak, that made him invisible against the rocks to any watcher below. A low-built, powerful man, with wide shoulders and grizzled hair under the brown hat, and blunt, plain features. A man who could pass unnoticed anywhere except as a strong-looking fellow. A sailor, or a porter, or a farmer. It was his trade to pass unnoticed.

He leaned forward slightly, wishing he had brought a spy-glass with him, but a merchant's clerk travelling for his master from Madrid to Córdoba to buy wine for the French army of occupation does not carry a spy-glass, and he had to trust his naked eyes. All the way through the mountains he had known that he was riding on the heels of a French patrol, one of the dozen still raking the sierra for the *guerrilleros* who had murdered General René and his family the year before. And if they laid hands on him—

He had spent the previous night in a cave with peasant fugitives who had gloatingly described the deaths of the general and his wife and child, and he still felt sickened when he thought of the details. And of the French revenge. Ever since the insanity in France, twenty years ago, it had seemed to him that men were becoming viler, more drunk with cruelty by the year. And that here in Spain they had reached the seventh circle of damnation. This last year of warfare he had carried his blunt Essex commonsense and humanity like a fragile treasure wrapped in a cloth inside his coat, afraid at every shock that it would be broken and that he would be left adrift in a torrent of savagery with no anchor to hold his mind. Men buried alive to the throat and left in the sun to die.

He shut his eyes for a second, remembering Madame René. "But they were enemies! She was French!" The peasants had laughed. And the one of them who had known him by his real name had whispered, "Have a great care for yourself, Capitán. They will treat you as one of us if they take you."

Capatin Joshua Pownall of His Majesty's Secret Service, and presently of the headquarters staff of General the Viscount Wellington, who was now at Badajoz, much desiring news from Córdoba of the intentions of the French columns thereabout.

The captain touched his knees to his horse and rode down the path. There seemed to be no living thing in the entire valley. Not so much as a horse grazing. He passed the small lake, and skirted the orange grove. Branches slashed down and trampled. They had been this way. He stopped again at the edge of the grove. The village a quarter mile off, above him now. And still no sign of movement. Not a sound. On his right hand the sun was already low above the mountains. In half an hour it would be dark. He thought he could smell burning. Not of a cooking fire but the thick, sour smoke of burned houses and—Not that these mud cabins would have contained much to burn.

He hesitated, half of a mind to ride on down the valley, knowing what he would find if he climbed the hill. But he needed information. And water. And food. There must be someone. Might be. He rode up the dusty track. Not a living soul. Not a dog. He saw the first of the bodies lying in a doorway where it had been shot down. He stooped, looked through the door into the dark interior, and saw another body lying there. A woman, naked from the waist down. Her skirt covering her face.

The captain took out his pistol from his belt, cocked it, listened. Nothing. If they were still in the village he would have heard them long ago. But he sat listening nevertheless, in case one straggler had remained, drunk or sleeping. Only silence. Except for the soft, frightened breathing of his horse, wrinkling its nostrils in fear of the death beside it.

"Easy, Rinaldo," the captain whispered, smoothed his left hand down the warm, dusty neck. "We will go soon."

He slid out of the saddle, pushed the trigger of his pistol forward to set the hair-spring, and went into the single room of the house. The woman, mercifully, was dead. He drew the skirt down and came gladly out into the sun again, went up the narrow, twisting street between the other houses, drawing the horse after him, its head jerking at the reins now, tossing with spasms of panic as the smell of death grew stronger, overpowering.

The village must have been caught unawares, surrounded. Three men crouched against a wall, their teeth bared in a last snarl of rage and fear, one of them still gripping an axe. A woman lay spread-eagled on a dung heap, her red skirt torn aside. A bonfire where the soldiers had roasted meat. Bones and smashed wine bottles. A half-burned door, rags. A thread of greasy smoke still rising from the charred remains. The captain stood looking at it, judging the length of time since the patrol had left there. Three hours? Less?

He sensed rather than saw a movement at the

corner of his vision, swung round and aimed. But there was nothing there. He waited, looking at the shadow between two houses, a narrow throat of shadow between the uneven walls.

"Who is there?" he said in Spanish. "If you move, I fire."

He took a swift step, saw the shadow within the shadow. A child. A yellow dress. She looked at him, her mouth opening, no sound coming. Her eyes wide with terror.

"Do not be afraid of me," he said softly. "I will not hurt you. The wicked men are gone."

She stared and opened her mouth again, and there was still no sound. She made no other movement at all. He realized that he was aiming his pistol at her and turned it away. "Are you the only—Is there . . . no one else?" he said. He looked around them. No movement, no sound. He released the hair spring of his pistol, put up the catch, and set it back in his belt. The child watched his face. "Come," he said. "Come out into the light." Although it was already fading, the street itself full of shadows. He beckoned her, moved back. She stood where she was for a long moment, her face working. "Come here to me," he said very gently. "I shall not hurt you."

She took a step towards him and stood again. He bent down, knelt on one knee so that his face was on a level with hers if she came close enough. "Come," he whispered. "You must let me bring you somewhere safe. You cannot stay here alone." All the time listening, his eyes watching for other shadows that might move. But there were none.

Half step by half step closer to him. A thin, dark child, her black, curling hair ragged with dust, her yellow dress torn, a great bruise already blackening in the middle of her forehead, part of it red with blood where the skin had broken. Her eyes Moorish dark, grown enormous with the fear of him, looking sideways. Searching. Here. There. Swift darts of looking, then fixed on him again. The mouth opening, closing, the thin throat working as if the sounds were locked there.

11

"What is your name?" he said, but she could not answer. Very slowly he reached out his hand. She closed her eyes, her mouth opened, her whole body seemed to grow stiff with terror. He touched her bare forearm with his finger, stroked. So thin his fingers could have closed round it twice over. "We cannot stay here," he said. "You would be all alone. Would you like to ride on my horse?" He drew her towards him, inch by slow inch, her eyes shut. "We must find someone to look after you. Come, let me lift you up."

The body stiffened between his hands, a cry, half stifled, came from the small throat. He held her against his chest and stroked her head, the hair silky under the dirt. So thin she seemed no more than bones, to weigh nothing.

"Which was your house?" he said, and changed his mind quickly, hiding her face against his shoulder. "Come," he said. "Let me set you on Rinaldo's back and he shall bring us away from this place." Holding her in the crook of his left arm, he hoisted himself up into the high Spanish saddle and guided the horse back down the narrow village street, down the open hillside into the now evening-shadowed valley.

One

Essex, 1814

Chapter 1

"We shall be in Urnford soon," the captain said. "And then—"

She smiled, tried to look pleased. The coach swayed, lurched as it passed by a farm cart, the coachman's horn high-pitched in warning, and the fat man sitting at her other side with the large corded box on his knees leaned against her, grunting. Outside the coach windows the green Essex landscape began to take on an evening colouring.

"Do you see the rooks?" the captain said. "Look at them gathering."

She pretended to look. Now and then he held her hand low down against the leather cushion, gave it a reassuring squeeze as though he guessed at least some of what she was feeling. She closed her eyes against the rooks, the pale, northern sky, the trees. *It is only another journey*, she told herself. Tried to believe it.

"They will be so happy to receive you," he had said. "It's so long since there was a child in the house. Forty years almost! If only my father—"

He let go of her hand and she sat looking at nothing, at the woman's basket in front of her, the woman's bonnet, her red face, her mouth open as she slept, her head nodding forward, jerking upright again as she woke for a second, and then once more tilting, falling forward and to one side. Would his sisters be like her? Miss Susannah. Miss Hetty. "They look like me," the captain had said. "Poor dears. Like Father and me. But they have hearts of gold."

"How long shall we stay there?" she had asked him, and he had tried to make light of it.

"Oh, who can say what my orders may be? And as for you, little puss, are you not tired of travelling round with such a grumpy old fellow?"

"You will not make me stay there? When you——"

"Make you? Who is talking of making you do anything? But wait till you are there before . . . they will make you so welcome that. . . ."

The coach swayed, the man with the corded box leaned sideways, the box dug its corner into her thigh.

"Look!" the captain said. "Do you see the spire? That is the cathedral, we shall be home by nine o'clock."

Houses, grey stone, with strange windows and unfamiliar roofs.

"This is the market square! The times I've been here as a boy, on fair days!"

Another street. An inn yard.

"The Bell! I swear that I even know that fellow over there! Oh, Sara, Sara, we're almost home!" Holding her hand as she got down after him, his face alight with happiness, the shadow that had been in it during the last days in London gone completely. Looking around him as though he were already home. She stood with their luggage—not much luggage, one shabby portmanteau—while he found an ostler and went with him to make arrangements about the gig that should take them on to Thaxstone. Even her clothes unfamiliar, foreign. The new bonnet and the spencer that felt too tight under the arms, and the muslin dress that made her legs feel naked, and the strange, stiff boots that did not quite fit. They had been halfway back to the lodging house before she realised that he had left her own clothes behind in that shop, with the old man and the old woman with the painted face.

"But they were rags, child! Rags! Damnation, I am ashamed of my life that you should have stayed in them so long. What was I thinking about to leave you like that?" The black skirt that Señorita Agustina had given her long ago. The red blouse the doctor's wife had given her in Salamanca. As though he had left part of her behind them. Like leaving Rinaldo. Leaving Spain. Until nothing would remain.

He came back to her, the ostler shouldered the portmanteau, and the captain looked at her with such joy that she felt ashamed at not being happy, at the scene she had made about her clothes. She wanted to say to him, "I will be good, I will be truly good," and could not say it, any more than she had been able to explain to him what that patched and ragged skirt had meant to her. Like the time in the Cordillera, when for a whole miraculous summer she had gone in breeches and a shirt, dressed as a boy, had ridden everywhere with him on Ciriclo, the mountain pony Don Manuel had lent them, and she had thought there would never be an end to riding and to freedom. And it had ended, and she had been left in Salamanca all that winter.

"Only another hour!" the captain said. The gig rolling and bouncing over the cobbles, out into the narrow street with the strange houses that leaned above them, into the market square again.

"I wonder if Rinaldo is very sad," she whispered, looking at the brown rump of the horse that was pulling them, looking away from it at the long, ugly building flanking that side of the square. Iron bars over deep-set windows, like a prison. Perhaps it was a prison.

"What put Rinaldo into your head?"

"I just thought of him. I hope that man will be kind."

"Of course he will. Look, look at the fields!"

"Do you think Mr. Hampton will—Do you think he will send for you very soon?"

"Too soon. But we will not think of it now. Look, do you see the rabbit? How many times have I gone snaring them on the Common! And in more forbidden places than that, I promise you. Oh, Sara, if you could know what this means to me!" He put his arm round her shoulders, hugged her with a curious rough gesture, half of delight and half apology, as though he knew her thoughts. And she felt her heart tightening, growing cold with the fear of what was coming—that this time it would not be an ending just for the months of winter but forever. That nothing would ever be well again, there would *be* no more summers.

And as they came nearer to his home, passing a farm house, a clump of trees, a humped bridge over a stream, each thing more familiar to him than the last, he grew very quiet himself and sat with her hand in his, as though he too had that foreboding—that this was an ending rather than a beginning. The ending of almost five years of their companionship.

He left Rinaldo, she thought, and with something like a luxury of bitterness, *he will leave me*. And she closed her hands in her lap, against the sprigged white muslin of the frock she would never love. Never. Never. And for a moment the sun was on her neck, her face; they were in the garden of the house in Saragossa. The señorita kneeling down in front of her, tucking the black skirt up around her waist because then it was too long. "You are like a grown lady now!" the señorita had said, and touched her face. "She's becoming beautiful, Don José, you will have to be careful of her soon!" The two of them laughing, the señorita so truly beautiful that it was like a pain of love and pride to think of her, to touch the skirt and think that it was hers.

"There is the rectory!" the captain cried. And a moment later, "We are home, we are home, there are our trees along the paddock!" The gig coming to a stop beside a flowering hedge, a gate. A house with the same, strange, steep roofs and chimneys, and the small windows. A garden in front of it. She sat where she was while the captain jumped down, threw open the gate, already calling out to no one, "We are here, we are here! Susannah! Hetty? We are here!"

The door opening, a woman standing there, another woman behind her, dark shapes against the lamplight. *I must get down*, she thought. And for another moment held herself back among the shadows. Then the captain was turning to look for her, drawing her forward, saying, "Here she is! Sara, these are my sisters, who will be like two mothers to you! Susannah, my dear, here is my Sara at last! Hetty, what do you think of her?"

Making her curtsey to each of them. *Two strange old women like—like—I must not think anything,* she thought. *I must be good, I must be good.* Like two old sheep, with grey curls under their funny lace caps, and grey taffeta dresses and strained smiles. And then, *It is only for a little while. He will take me away with him again, he must, he must.*

"And this is Mrs. Hobhouse, our cook! And this is Peg!" A fat woman in an apron. A tall, gaunt woman.

"And who is that hidden behind Peg? Someone new?"

"That's Molly," one of the sisters said. "Come here, girl."

Red hair in the lamplight. A round face. Making a clumsy bob to the captain, to Sara.

"What age is she?" the captain said. "What age are you, girl?"

"Fifteen, sir."

"Why, Sara's age exactly! You see, you have someone of your own age in the house, is that not capital? But why are we not going in, why are we standing out here? Susannah, Hetty, my dears! Oh, if you could imagine how it feels to be home again!"

"We cannot imagine anything else, Joshua," Miss Susannah said. "But have the driver bring in your luggage and we shall sit down and get to know one another better." Her eyes on Sara fleetingly. "Is that portmanteau all that you have? And the child? Has she no box?"

"We have not lived a gathering kind of life," the captain said. "And the old clock! Does it still go? And you have a new lamp! Oh, my dears, my dears!"

A small room with a fire burning. To her Spanish eyes it seemed so full of furniture that it would be impossible to move in it. Chairs, tables, rugs, cabinets with glass fronts and china ornaments, lamps, candlesticks, polished brasses winking and glinting in the firelight. Pictures hanging on the walls, miniatures, silhouettes. An embroidered screen. The captain sitting down in the largest chair, his hands on the arms, looking at the chair itself, the fire, the rug, the cabinet beside him with a kind of wonder. "I am home," he said. And caught Sara's eye and said, "And you too, Sara. Is this not to be her home, Susannah? Please, please tell it to her yourself. She still feels so strange here. Tell her this is her home."

"Naturally, everything shall be as you wish it, Joshua. Does she speak English? Do you, child?"

"Yes, señora."

"You may take off your coat and bonnet. Hetty, my dear, perhaps you would take her up to her room? And in a few moments your supper will be ready. I'm sure you're hungry after your journey?"

"Yes, señora."

A small, pleasant room, wall-papered with climbing flowers and green and red birds. A white bed. A dormer window set into the slope of the roof. A view of trees. But she was not willing to be pleased by it. Or anything else. The old woman looked at her, shook her head in admiring wonder. "What a pretty, pretty dress! And your bonnet!" She came close, caught Sara's hands in hers. "Oh, I do so hope you shall stay with us!"

Sara tried to smile at her, to be polite, good. She would have preferred it if the room had been horrible, the old women unkind.

"I do not think—" she began. And stopped.

"And you speak English so beautifully! Did Joshua teach you?"

She nodded, wanted to disengage her hands, made an effort to leave them held. If she could be left alone for even a few minutes. . . .

"And where are your other clothes, my dear?"

"I have no others," she whispered. Looked away. "They—they were left behind." She felt on the point of crying, and clenched her teeth against the weakness, felt a swift spasm of rage that helped her. Why wouldn't he go back for them? Couldn't he understand?

"We'll soon see to that," Miss Hetty said. "Now,

let's brush your hair a little. Oh, such beautiful, beautiful curls! So black! I do, do hope you'll be happy here!"

Downstairs they were all in another room, also with a fire burning, and wall paper, and pictures and ornaments and a clock ticking on the mantlepiece. But not so much furniture. Only a long table and eight or nine chairs, and a sideboard already prepared with supper things.

". . . as obstinate as a badger when she takes it into that black little head of hers," the captain was saying. Leaning back in another large wing chair by the fire, his legs stretched out to the blaze, a wine-glass in his hand, an air of happiness like tobacco smoke wreathed round him. "Oh, don't be deceived by her looks! She would try the patience of a saint sometimes, let alone someone as short in the temper as myself. We have had our arguments, I can tell you that!"

He caught her eye as she came in, gave her a knowing wink. Was he reminding her of the ferocity of her temper about her skirt and blouse, her sandals? She looked away, caught Miss Susannah's considering eye, and looked down at the carpet, her face closed.

"I am sure you've never been impatient with her," Miss Hetty cried. "And I am sure she has been much too grateful to . . ."

"You should hear us fighting, Hetty! Just imagine this now, let me tell you a story of her, the very beginning of our acquaintance—eh, miss, eh, little puss? Do ye remember that sergeant's wife in Badajoz, and the way you ran off from her and followed me?"

She stared down at the red and blue carpet, felt her cheeks begin to flush dark, to burn. *If he tells them that story I shall*—She looked up at him beseechingly, but he has already launched. "I'd failed to find anyone in Córdoba who would look after her—"

Miss Hetty exclaimed in horror at such inhumanity, lifted her hands.

"Oh, you would need to have been there to understand. The ruin of everything after the French pillage of the year before. The people seemed stunned by what they had suffered, even a year afterwards. And the countryside! But no matter—I brought her with me to our headquarters, which was still at Badajoz, although preparing to fall back into Portugal. And found this decent woman to look after her. A sergeant's wife who took in washing for the headquarters' staff. But stay with her? Mercy of Heaven!"

I will die if he tells, she thought. Perhaps he saw her face, or thought better of it, and turned the remainder of the story aside with a laugh. "And we are together yet, as you see. Are we not, little puss?" A thought seemed to strike him, cloud his happiness slightly, and he looked away from her at the fire. "And now at last we are home. Is supper ready for us?"

"Mrs. Hobhouse has prepared a milk caudle for her, Joshua. We imagined meat would be too heavy after a journey," Miss Susannah said. She was told to sit, and they put a kind of white soup in front of her. Out of the corner of her eye she saw the captain's plate of cold meat and pickles and another platter of cheese, and slices of bread and butter. And wine. They had not given her any wine.

"She will love anything," the captain said. "Many is the time we have gone supperless, eh, puss?"

"Do you know," Miss Hetty said, "that Joshua has brought her here without so much as a nightgown or a second pair of stockings? We shall have everything to find for her! I cannot imagine how you have managed to look after her all these years!"

"Indeed, neither can I," Miss Susannah said dryly. She was sitting very upright at the foot of the table, and Miss Hetty had drawn up a chair close beside Sara, as though she had already adopted her. She began urging her to eat up her caudle. Although there should have been no need for urging. It tasted well enough and Sara had realised with the first spoonful that she was starving. Only a sense of injustice about the difference in their suppers made her eat very slowly. If she'd had the strength of mind she would have eaten nothing at all.

"As for her clothes," the captain said, leaning back and lifting his wine-glass to the light. "By God, you should have seen the trouble we had to get her what she stands up in! The puppies they employ in shops these days! Fellows with their cravats so tight they cannot bend their necks to look at you, let alone take a polite interest in a problem. I realised only yesterday that—Well, damme, she had to look smart coming down to ye all, so I thought I'd get her a new dress and bonnet, and upon my soul you'd think it was the crown jewels I was looking for. Not a milliner in London could make her a dress, they said, in less than a week. You'd think we were beggars the way they treated us. And then at last we found this queer little slice of a shop—by heaven, if they'd said no I'd have given up and brought her down to you as she was."

If only you had, Sara thought.

"And how *was* she?" Miss Susannah said.

"Oh, shabby as a rat," the captain cried. "Poor little thing, I'd have been ashamed of my life to let you see her. But in this shop—a French name over the door, no less, Madame something—D'Arblay, was it, Sara? Aye, D'Arblay—and 'Modiste to the Nobility and Quality' and God knows who else. And not a damned thing visible except this dusty old fellow behind the counter. 'Why, yes,' says he, rubbing his hands together as though we were the first human creatures to darken his door for a week past, which we may well have been from the look of the place. 'I think I can accommodate you. If Madame might take the young lady's measure a moment.' And in comes the queerest old bundle of a woman you ever did see, with her face blank white with chalk powder. Wouldn't she give you the frights to look at her, eh, Sara? And not a word out of her, simply looks my girl up and down and sinks herself onto a little gilt chair that I thought would collapse under her and nods her head like a Chinese idol. But, by God, for all they were a pair of effigies, I'll grant them something. They produced her an outfit of clothes by this morning, and a good decent fit to everything, eh, Sara."

"Yes, thank you," she whispered.

"But how did they do it?" Miss Hetty cried. "It is not possible—only from yesterday?"

"They are—second-hand?" Miss Susannah said. "One could never tell—at first glance."

"Some more caudle, dear?" Miss Hetty said.

She managed to say no. As though—as though he had already surrendered her to them. Like that winter in Salamanca. She bent her head over the empty bowl.

"You poor dear," Miss Hetty whispered. "Susannah, do you think I should take her to bed? She is falling asleep over the table and is too timid to say so. Should you like to go straight up to your bed now, dear?"

"If you please, señora."

"You must call me aunt Hetty, my dear. And aunt Susannah. Isn't that right, Susannah, shall she not call us her aunts?"

Miss Susannah hesitated momentarily. "That is something we need not decide immediately," she said. "If you would take her upstairs, Hetty? Good night, Sara, my dear. I trust you will sleep well."

All the good nights. The captain smiling at her, a touch of awkwardness to the smile. *When he comes up to say good night to me,* she thought. He must realise that they—at least the oldest one—did not want her here, that . . . *He must, he must understand. And then in a few days, a week or two . . .* She wanted to be alone to wait for him, to think out everything she must say so that there could be no possible argument. Only this one would leave her alone to go to bed by herself. Fussing with a new flannel at the wash-basin, with the pillows of the bed.

"I suppose you must sleep in the shift you have on, dear." Clicking her tongue as though it was a thing of importance how she slept, what she slept in. She wanted to say to her, "We have slept in caves sometimes when we were alone together. In barns. On the ground rolled up in our cloaks. Anywhere." What *would* she say?

"Would you like to say your prayers now?"

"I do not say any prayers."

"You do not say your prayers? You . . . ?" She threw up her hands in a kind of sheep's anguish.

"No," Sara said.

It was an argument she had fought years ago, with

23

Señorita Agustina, with the doctor's wife, with Padre Francisco.

"You will go to hell!" Padre Francisco had shouted in the end. "You will burn for all eternity! There is a devil in you, a black, ugly devil of wickedness and obstinacy! Suppose I give you to the Holy Inquisitors and they put you to the stake, you will say your prayers then!"

"I will not." Señorita Agustina had had to bring Padre Francisco away.

"How can you be so bad?" the señorita had said. "Do you not love God?"

"No. He doesn't love little children, and I don't love Him."

The captain had come back then and saved her, and in Salamanca it had been the old priest who had saved her from the doctor's wife, about the same thing.

"Leave her alone," Father Curtis had said. "What do we know of children's hearts? It is not only on our knees that we pray." If he'd asked her, she might have said her prayers for him, but he never did. Only pulled her ears and laughed at her.

She stared at Miss Hetty, setting her face hard, drawing in the corners of her mouth and tightening the narrow wings of her nose. Long ago Pablito had told her it made her look very fierce when she set her face like that. The doctor's wife had crossed herself and said it made her look like an imp of Satan.

"Oh, oh, oh," Miss Hetty was saying, as though she was talking to herself rather than to Sara. "What will Doctor Newall say? I must—oh dear, oh dear. Well, this first night let us not trouble ourselves too much about—about anything. I shall—I shall say extra prayers for you myself. Every good child must say prayers, you know. Suppose you were to die in the night? What would gentle Jesus say to you if you had not said your prayers before you fell asleep?"

She did not answer, getting in between the cold sheets in her shift. There was a smell of lavender and tar. Down in the bed there was a hot brick wrapped in cloth. Her feet were cold from the floor, but she kept them away from the brick. She would not even

24

lie down till he came. The old, soft lips kissing her forehead, the hands pressing her back onto the pillow, putting the coverlet up round her chin. "You are so pretty," Miss Hetty whispered. "You must be just as good as you are pretty. Now, won't you be very, very good? I shall say special prayers for you tonight and ask God to look down on our new dear visitor with an especial welcome. Now go fast asleep and wake up joyfully in the morning to God's new day, won't you do that, Sara?"

"Yes, señora."

"Aunt." The old voice whispering. The old woman's eyes full of tears. "Whatever Susannah says," she whispered, "you must call me Aunt Hetty when we are by ourselves, won't you? It shall be our secret. Now say it. Aunt Hetty."

"Aunt Hetty."

She clapped her hands softly together, went away at last with a slow closing of the door. "Don't forget to snuff out your candle, dear."

"No, señ—"

"Aunt, dear. Aunt Hetty, remember."

"Aunt Hetty."

The door closing, closed. She lay staring up at the white ceiling, the candle shadows. He was a long time coming up to her. He must be waiting till the señora went downstairs again. Aunt Hetty. Tía. Was that his footstep? She sat up, listened. But it had been no more than a creaking of the stairs. Aunt Susannah.

They are preventing him from coming, she thought. She waited for what seemed another hour, sitting up in the narrow bed, listening to the strangeness of the house. The quiet. As though the whole house was gone to bed, asleep. And it must be no more than ten o'clock. In Spain. She got out of the bed, the floor like ice under her bare feet. There was a small fireplace in the room, but no fire in it. The room seemed to smell of cold. And another, strange, strange smell, like the sea when they had crossed from France. Could it be the sea? She went to the window Miss Hetty had left open, sniffed at the darkness. The shadows of the trees, a few pale, pale stars.

She went back to the door, opened it gently, and listened again. Voices? She crept down the stairs to the first landing, stood by the banisters, leaned over. They must be in the first room she had seen, the parlour. She went half-way down the last flight and hesitated. The captain's voice, raised, laughing. He had forgotten! Simply forgotten! In another second she was by the door listening.

"Hampton? That ninny of a tailor's dummy? What sort of marching orders should I hope for from him? No, no, I must wait on the general—general did I say? Field-marshal! And marquis! What has he not become thanks to our Spain? No, I must wait until he has a moment free to think of his old officers. There's time enough for that. You are not so anxious for me to be gone yet, I hope?"

"Oh, no, Joshua, no!" Tía Hetty's voice. "It's only that—if there could be time for us all to—to get used —she is so *foreign*, Joshua! We shall love her dearly, I know it—shall we not, Susannah? But, it's just that she will need time to settle—before—"

Sara held her breath to listen closer. Before he went away again? To leave her here?

"She is much more grown *up* than your letters suggested, Joshua." Miss Susannah's voice. Gruff. Almost like a man's voice.

"Why, of course she is! What would you have her do? Stay ten years old till I had time to bring her to you? Indeed, this past two years she has seemed to grow each time I took my eyes off her. Like a garden weed."

"Not a *weed*, Joshua! We never guessed from your letters she would be so beautiful." Miss Hetty. Tía Hetty.

"Oh, she's still child enough for all her tallness, you'll find that out, I warrant you. And as full of mischief as a wagonload of monkeys when the spirit takes her. The stories I could tell of her, if I had a mind!"

"I'm sure you could, Joshua." Miss Susannah. "And I'm sure also that she has had proper instruction in governing her conduct? And that you will perhaps have

26

told her something already of the way that our customs differ from those of Spain?"

"Oh, aye, have no fears on that score, she has been well instructed in all she should know as a young lady. No woman has ever been near her but was teaching her this and that. She has been taught enough, I promise you."

"Joshua!" Miss Hetty. "How can you *say* such a thing? And the child doesn't so much as say her prayers! Oh—oh—I didn't mean—I meant not to speak of it until tomorrow, but . . ."

"Not say her prayers? Joshua!"

"Goddammit! She's no more than a child! What need has she? She took against it for some reason years ago and a priest tormented her about it and made her obstinate. Let her be, Hetty, let her be."

"Indeed, Joshua, let us do so! At least for the moment. When we have not seen you for ten years!"

Sara heard a sound, looked up. At the far end of the passage a door was opening, there was a light. The girl Molly, shielding her candle flame with a cupped hand, looking down the passage towards Sara, her face astonished.

Sara had already moved a pace away from the door and was standing in the middle of the passage. She put a finger to her lips and went quickly towards the girl.

"I was suddenly hungry," she whispered. "I did not eat much supper. Because of the journey."

The girl stared at her. As tall as she was herself. Perhaps an inch taller. Her eyes green in the candle-light, like a cat's. Full of suspicion, of questioning.

"They are in there," Sara whispered. "But I was afraid to knock—and ask for more to eat. Could you —could you find me something? Just a little bread and meat? And—and a glass of wine?"

"Wine, miss?" The girl whispered, her eyes rounding still more, as though the idea of a girl wanting to drink wine was more strange even than her being downstairs in her shift, in the dark, outside the parlour door.

"If it's possible," Sara whispered. "If you could

27

bring it up to my room? Without anyone knowing? I wouldn't like to hurt them, thinking they didn't give me enough." She smiled, turned, and ran softly to the stairs, went half-way up and stopped to listen again. When she leaned over the banister, the girl was still standing there, her candle shielded by her right hand, staring.

Chapter 2

Their friendship began that night. Half of it the passionate, immediate bond of two children, still almost children at fifteen. The other half a strange, guarded, quarrelling exploration of each other, of each other's foreignness. Nothing that they could take for granted, no common experience, so that at times there seemed no stable ground to build friendship on, beyond their loneliness, the hostility, or the impatient, bare tolerance of most of the adults. And for Sara the bitter misery of the captain drawing further and further away from her.

It was as though he was afraid to be alone with her. She would go looking for him and find that he had gone off for a walk by himself without telling her. Or if he was in his room, huddled over the fire that he seemed to need more and more, in spite of the summer, and she went in to sit and talk with him, he would grow uneasy after a few minutes and find an excuse to send her away again. "Maybe you'd run down and get me some fresh tobacco at Stone's, eh?" Or "I wonder, is that the post cart coming? Would you slip out and see has he a letter for me? I cannot think what Hampton is about, not writing in all this time."

Although after the first month or so he stopped asking about the post. "I suppose they've enough to think of now that peace is here at last. I'm wrong to be impatient."

Or he would realise they had been talking Spanish and would break off into English. "They do not like it, child."

She did not trouble to say, "They cannot hear us," because she knew they could, that nothing could happen in the house that was not seen, heard. At least until ten o'clock, and evening prayers, and the soft, careful closing of bedroom doors. Once or twice in the first week or so she had gone to him then, on purpose, when everyone else was in bed, wanting to talk to him secretly, to beg him to take her with him when he had his orders to go abroad again. And he had been so urgent in sending her away, so angrily frightened she had not even tried to argue and had gone back to her bedroom bewildered, thinking she would die of the misery of their separation.

In July he fell ill with the malaria again, and she was not allowed even to go near him.

"You must leave him alone, Sara. He is to be left completely quiet. He doesn't want a young person," Miss Susannah said.

"But I *understand* this fever! I understand it! And you and that doctor—"

"Sara! I will not be spoken to in that tone. Say you're sorry. At once."

"I am sorry, señora."

"That's not the way to say it."

"I am sorry, Miss Susannah."

It had been decided long ago that it was not appropriate for her to call them "Aunt."

Sara found herself needing Molly with a kind of desperation. And even their quarrelling had an excitement to it that made her forget her unhappiness, as though they were two young foxes circling one another, trying to make up their minds whether to fight or play.

Helping Mrs. Hobhouse in the kitchen. Or running errands together down to the village, to Miss Stone's shop, or Mr. Stone's next door. Or bringing a pudding or a pot of jam to old Miss Bowdeker, or Mrs. Gummer, in Over Thaxstone, two of the few exceptions to Miss Susannah's rule that such kinds of charity were harmful.

Molly was sent with her in the beginning to show her the way and because Sara could not make herself properly understood with most of the villagers. And when Sara knew her way everywhere, and had at least begun to get used to the Essex dialect, she still insisted on Molly going with her.

"You're just afraid to go out alone, that's all."

"I am not!"

"Cain't understand this. Cain't understand that. An' all my work still to do. You won't scrub the floors for me when we get back, I s'pose?"

At night they had stolen picnics in Sara's bedroom, still quarrelling. And then there would be a sudden rush of friendship, and they would hold each other, sitting up in the bed, the crumbs of their feast around them, laughing at something that had happened during the day. To fall as suddenly quiet, listening, their eyes wide with fright and laughter in case they had been heard. Until Molly would become half angry again, contemptuous of Sara's nonsense.

"I got to be up, five o'clock. I'll be dyin', and you still snorin' here like a piglet till seven an' after. It's all right for you. I een't comin' tomorrow no matter how you begs me."

But she would come, and they would sit in the bed, wrapped tight in Sara's blankets, sipping wine dregs and eating bread and cheese and flakes of ham scraped off the bones when they were making force-meat, and telling each other stories. Even their stories were part of their circling round each other, trying to impress each other. Molly's stories were most extraordinarily grim, and at the same time matter-of-fact. Hangings and starvation and people frozen to death. Her own mother and a baby brother and a sister had died, all three in one terrible winter. And two more of her sisters had died of something or other a year before that.

"We got put out o' our cottage, our proper cottage, 'cause old Lord Southcott didn't like seein' it so close to the road an' his park wall. He said it looked untidy an' told Mister Cameron to have it pulled down on us and us moved somewheres else. So we went out on the marsh. There weren't nowheres else to go."

"In Spain . . ." But she could not tell her own story, her own equivalent. Even to the captain she had never told it. It was as though there was a heavy curtain between herself now and that child self. And she knew, half knew, what lay behind the curtain, but would not pull it aside, could not. Until it was almost as though she didn't know, had forgotten, and it had happened to someone else, long ago, far away.

"What you goin' to say: 'In Spain'? Something wunnerful, I s'pose."

"It *is* wonderful in Spain." Trying to tell her. About Pablito, about the caves, and the other gypsies, Don Manuel, Doña Ana, all of them. About the pony Ciriclo, "Little Bird," about that summer. And the other summers. And the heat. And Señorita Agustina, how beautiful she was, how brave she had been against the French about the gun.

"Go 'way, ladies don't fire off guns 'gainst sojers."

"She did! She did! Everyone knew she did."

"She'ud fare to get hanged she did that. Go way with your fibbin'."

For Molly, only the marsh was real, the stone floors of the kitchen, cold, and the hunger. "My li'l brother, Tom, he bin hungrier an' colder 'n you ever bin, an' he's only eight year old last Christmas. Pickin' weeds out o' the 'tatie field with the chilblains burstin' on his fingers till he cried. You een't never bin cold like that, you an' your old mountains."

"I have!"

"Go 'way."

She was bigger than Sara, not only in height by an inch or so but in the size and strength of her bones, a bigness of body that had the promise of beauty in it if only she ever got enough to eat and could sleep

31

enough and stop scrubbing floors. A round, high-cheekboned face and a large, full mouth with white, splendid teeth that she never seemed to clean with anything.

"Cleanin' teeth! Raw turnip do clean 'em all you need, you eat enough of it."

And dark red hair with gold in it that Sara thought, in secret, was the most beautiful hair she'd ever seen, thick and burning like a fire. She kept it covered mostly, with an old mob cap of Peg's, by order of Peg and Mrs. Hobhouse. "They'd like to shave it all off me if they had their way."

Sometimes, if they had an errand to Masham's farm, they ran all the way and had time to go on into the marsh, and her father's cottage, to bring the two smallest children a piece of sausage or a slice of white bread. And to see her father for a moment if he was not out as a roundsman, sent out with the other unemployed men to work somewhere at half wages.

"He do get eightpence from who he works for that day an' Dr. Newall gives 'em t'other eightpence."

"But why can't he work for someone properly?"

" 'Cause they do say he's uppish an' won't kneel down an' say prayers o' thanks like old Grimmer do, the old faggot. An' some o' t'others. An' why should old Masham pay 'em full wages an' board an all when he can get 'em for half, an' the parish pays t'rest? Een't you got no sense to see that even? Then they do call 'em a pauper an' look down on 'em like he were jus' lazy dirt. No wonder if he do go poachin'! An' iffen they should catch 'em they'd jus' say it do show how bad he is an' how wicked uppish. Gentle-folk do make me sick in my stomach."

"Is the captain gentlefolk?"

"All of 'um as don't work is."

"Am I?"

"You're worsen all of 'em, li'l lazy-bones, the worst-est of all." And they began to fight in the bed until they were laughing so hard they had to hold their hands over each other's mouths, choking with laughter, and lying like mice until they were sure they had woken no one.

"I'm not lazy! I can run all day if I have to. I used to ride Ciriclo for miles and miles and miles, all day long."

Any 'un can ride a hoss, silly, you jus' sits there, an' the hoss do the walkin'.'"

"That's what you think. How does your father go poaching?"

"I didn't mean to say that. Just you forget what I said or you'll get me in such trouble an' him worse. He'd get put in jail, they catch 'em."

"He wouldn't! The captain used to go poaching. He used to tell me how they went out catching rabbits. And he was only little."

"That een't poachin', silly. That's playin'. Poachin' is with big gangs o' men an' guns, gettin' pheasants out o' the park an' Great Wood. Sacks o' pheasants. And then they sell 'um."

"I'd love to go poaching! If we caught a rabbit—or a pheasant—we could keep it in the garden!"

"Go 'way, stupid. How could you go? I can jus' see you, out in the dark at night, with a keeper after you!"

"I've been out at night. Often. In Spain."

"Spain's a great special place. You goin' poachin'! Wait till I tell me dad, he'll die o' laughin'.'

"I could! I could! I used to go out with the captain, and Pablito, and Don Manuel."

"I do think you're stark mad, sometimes. I'm goin' to bed to do something sensible after all that. I could have been asleep this past hour but for your foolin'."

It was in October that the letter came. Not the letter the captain had hoped for months earlier, from Mr. Hampton in London, with new orders for him, but from Italy. And within the space of time it took him to read it, the captain seemed to grow young, to grow strong again, coming down the stairs holding it, pretending not to be excited, his glasses pushed up on his forehead, his waistcoat undone.

"It's from John Varley. Susannah? Susannah! Do you know who my letter is from? Captain Varley, who came here to visit us that day in '03! D'you remember him, he rode over from Urnford and dined with us? By God, so I am not entirely forgotten, eh? Colonel

Varley now, no less! And sitting in Tuscany to keep watch on Bonaparte across in Elba!"

He pulled his spectacles down onto his nose, re-read a page of the letter. "He says, 'I heard you were lazing your time away in Thaxstone.' Lazing my time! I'll laze him, the fellow! 'But if you feel like exercising your wits, and your legs, and if Hampton will approve it, I'd be glad of company here.' By Heaven! This is what I've been waiting for! Tuscany! Can't you imagine what a turmoil of comings and goings there must be there? Half the rascals in Europe wanting to get in touch with Bonaparte and stir him up again! John Varley a colonel, eh? Who would have thought it when we were in the Vendée together that one day it should be he who should do me such a turn? Sara, Sara, child, get me down my portmanteau from the attic. Ask Molly to help you with it. And run to the village to tell Barling I shall want him to take me to Urnford with him tomorrow morning. And ask Peg if she has my best shirt ironed—and my best cravat— and—and—Run, child, run, or Barling will have his gig filled up with egg boxes and parcels."

"And do you think, Joshua," Miss Susannah said coolly, "that Mister Hampton *will* approve it?"

He stood for a moment looking at his sister, a greyness coming back into his face, a stiffening. And then laughing. "God's teeth, why shouldn't he, when Varley asks for me? I've been remiss in not going up to badger Hampton before this. I've let myself slip out of his mind. But he was so definite that they should be in touch with me as soon as I should be needed that I didn't like—Eh, but this is what I've been waiting for!" Striking the pages of the letter with his hand. "Sara, child, are you not gone yet? Run!"

She ran, with such a pain in her heart that it was like breaking. *He will leave me here. He wants to, wants to leave me here, he doesn't care.* His face had seemed to glow with happiness.

"If he leaves me here I shall die," she said to Molly on the way to find Mr. Barling in the village.

"You dies easy, Sara. Wait till you have somethin' real to die for."

34

And he went, and that night, and the next day, and the night that followed she thought she *would* die. Saw them watching her, saw their thoughts, Miss Susannah's cold acceptance that she would be left with them. Peg the servant's flat slate-coloured eyes bleak with suspicion, almost hatred. Even Mrs. Hobhouse. Only Miss Hetty not thinking of her at all, agitated for her brother, who would be going away again, into danger again—for her all places outside of England being dangerous, whether there was a war or not.

If I make enough of a scene he will have to take me with him, they'll refuse to keep me here. She began to plan what she would do, but the mere fact that he meant to do it, to leave her behind in this house, to go away by himself and leave her, was like being crippled, like having her leg go to sleep, fold under her when she tried to stand up. How could he, how could he? She twisted her hands together in rage, in hurt, thought of what she would break, the lamp, the best tea things, a window. Throw things into the fire. *If he doesn't take me, I shall kill myself.*

But when he came back, she knew the instant she saw him that he was not going to go away, not to Tuscany, not anywhere. He looked not only old again, but withered. Almost shrunk. His face grey and drawn.

She tried to follow him up the stairs, into his bedroom—all thought of everything except his face, his bitter unhappiness, driven from her mind. "What has happened? What did they say to you?" Asking him in Spanish, her voice urgent with longing, to help him, be alone with him.

"Leave me alone, child. Run along." Closing the door against her.

"I will not, I will not! Tell me! Please, please!"

Miss Susannah behind her on the landing, like a cold shadow. "Sara, have I not asked you not to speak in Spanish in this house? It's a grave discourtesy when others present do not understand what you are saying."

"But he understands! What have they done to him, what have they—"

"Sara, go downstairs. At once."

35

It was another hour before she could get to him. She found him sitting by the fire, still in his travelling clothes, staring, staring at nothing. She went and knelt down beside him, took his hand, and held it against her face, her breast, to warm it; it was so cold, still so cold, after an hour by the fire.

"What did they say to you?"

"He told me I am too old. I am grown too old for service, now that there is peace. There are—there are younger men who—" Looking away from her. "It's no matter. I am very well here. There are men who've served their country as well as I and have not so much as a fire to sit by."

"Did he say that to you?"

"Not in those words."

Not knowing what to say, what to do. Only to hold his hand against her body, make it warm.

"Have you been good since I—since I left?"

"Yes."

"I am glad. We are very well here, the two of us, are we not?"

She tried to say yes again, wanted to scream out, "No, no, no! Let's go away, back to Spain, to Don Manuel and Doña Ana and Pablito, and Ciriclo. Find Rinaldo, find Señorita Agustina. Even Madame. Even Padre Francisco. Only let us go away."

"Are we not well and snug here?"

"Yes." Her voice like a thread, the pain hidden.

"Run along with you now. You should be out in the fresh air. Not brooding in here with an—with—Run, child. Leave me alone a little while. I—I am —I must—I will just sit here for a while. I think I caught some kind of chill in the coach from London. I'll just sit here by the fire until I'm warm."

She had to leave him. Went downstairs, feeling her throat locked with the need to scream. Pain for him. for herself. For loss. As though what she'd known for months, all summer, all autumn, had only now become real. That they would never go, never leave here. Never return to Spain. Never. And she stood in the dark of the passage, her throat working, in terror that someone would come, see her, speak to her, make her speak to them.

Someone was coming. She went into the kitchen, past Mrs. Hobhouse, busy at the range, and went out into the yard by the coolroom, where Molly was peeling potatoes into a sack.

"I do hate 'taties, worse'n poison."

"Let's do something. Go somewhere. Anywhere."

"I cain't go now. Look at this great ugly heap of 'taties, and then I got brasses to clean, an' them big pots."

"Tonight. Let's go tonight. Anywhere, anywhere out of here. Let's go to your cottage."

"Tonight? Are you mad?"

"I've got to go somewhere or I *shall* go mad. Please, Molly. If you don't come I'll—I'll go by myself."

"An' go poachin' I s'pose?"

"All right, you think I daren't?" She grabbed hold of Molly's arm. "Let's! Oh, let's! I dare you!"

"I think you're so foolish you don't know what you're talking 'bout half the time. It een't dare or daren't, you jus' cain't. An' I cain't go anywheres. Now nor tonight."

Sara picked up one of the potatoes, held it in her hand, wanted to throw it at something, the coolroom window, the wall in front of her, anything. She let it fall back onto the heap by Molly's feet, Molly's ankles showing above her black, broken boots. "You said Mrs. Goatlake goes poaching. She's a woman."

"I didn't say no such thing, an' don't you go blarin' out people's names like that."

"I didn't."

"You did so. S'pose Miss Susannah heard you, or the captain."

She caught hold of Molly's arm again, shook it so that Molly dropped her peeling knife, stared at her in irritated amazement. "I've got to go out, got to. Please. I'm—I'm—" Almost crying.

"What you got to be miserable about? The captain back an' all for you. First you didn't want him to go, an' now he's back you're still—"

"You leave Molly do her work, Miss Sara," Mrs.

Hobhouse called. "Yapping an' dawdling don't get 'taties peeled and never will. You leave her alone an' come an' pound some more spice for me, you got nothin' better to do with yourself."

"I dare you to come with me!" Sara whispered, and ran in before Molly could answer her.

Chapter 3

The path ran down into the marsh, hid itself among the reeds. The silver black of mud and water, the marsh island lying low and dark in front of them, looked strange, unrecognisable by moonlight, the sullen hummock of the cabin like an ugly rock, ill shaped and crooked. Nothing of it as it had seemed by daylight.

Molly knocked, whispered "Dad? Dad? It's me, Molly, an' Sara."

There was no answer until she knocked again; and then the sound of whispering, shuffling inside the hut, a child's whimper, stilled quickly, a boy's voice saying, hoarse and frightened, "Molly, is't you?" The door opening a crack, Tom's face—white, scared. "Is't you, Molly?"

"Aye, we brought you sausage. Where's Dad?"

The boy said nothing, stared at his sister, at Sara, as though the dark, the unexpectedness, Sara's presence, had taken his wits away.

"Let us in, cain't you?" She beckoned Sara and they went inside, into the choking night smell of the hut, and Sara caught her breath, stayed by the doorway. When they had come here by daylight they had not

38

gone inside at all. Molly lit a candle end. "Een't you got no fire, Tom?"

He shook his head, stared at Sara from under the dark, filthy thatch of his hair. The two small children had hidden themselves in the heap of rags that was the family bed.

"Is he gone out with the others?"

The boy nodded, retreated towards the bed, stood with his back to the uneven wall, and stuck one knuckle in his mouth. He stared at them, his eyes animal-bright in the candle-flame, still frightened by the strangeness of their coming in the dark.

"I told you," Molly said. "I told you there were no sense in it." She knelt down close to her brother, to the heap of rags. "Marthy? Willum? 'Tis me, Molly, don't be feared. Look what I brought you, sausage! An' Miss Sara's here, what'll she think of you, hidin' in there like li'l silly mice? Don't you want a piece o' sausage?" She uncovered their heads, stroked their faces.

Sara tried not to breathe, wished they hadn't come, had simply gone walking along the ridge, or—or anywhere rather than into this stench of poverty, as though it was crying out at her, *How dare you be unhappy, how dare you think of anything but this, this!* Molly's mother, the four children dying here, in this hut. The cold of the marsh creeping through the rotten, mud-plastered walls, like illness.

"Can we not light a fire for them?" she whispered.

"They een't got no wood," Molly said. She turned towards Sara, her voice suddenly shaking with anger. "They put the widow Gotobed in jail for twelve months, jus' for takin' one branch out o' Little Wood. One branch that had fallen on the ground. Twelve months in jail Dr. Newall give her."

"Is there nothing else they can burn?"

"Oh, yes, sacks o' coal. Cain't you see 'um all lyin' round?"

The children whimpered, began to cry at the anger in their sister's voice. "I mus' be stark mad lettin' you make me come here like this. An' now what we got to do? Jus' go back again. Hush, li'l Marthy; hush, Willum, Molly loves you, go asleep now an' dream o' that nice sausage."

She stood up. "You tell our dad we was here, eh, Tom? You tell 'em Miss Sara come to go poachin' with 'em, only she come too late. That'll make him laugh a bit, even if he een't got nothin' else to laugh about. You tell 'em that, eh, Tom boy? You bein' a good boy an' looking after Marthy an' Willum?"

The boy said nothing and Molly tousled his hair and turned away. She needed to bend her head under the sagging roof. "You satisfied?"

"You didn't need to come with me."

"Oh, go on." Pushing Sara outside, dragging the door shut behind her. "I do get silly cross, sometimes. Don't mind me."

They stood in the clean air, breathing. As though Molly too had been conscious of the smell, had grown delicate from her time in Lavender Cottage.

"I'm sorry."

"Een't nothin' to be sorry about. C'mon, let's race. I'm goin' to be so tired come mornin' I won't be able to see the ashes."

I am glad we went, Sara thought, tried to tell herself she was really glad. *I must be grateful. For everything*. But she could not feel it, and it was as though the hut, the children, and the sour smell of misery were only other shadows lying chill and heavy on her mind.

Two days later she was in the kitchen, cutting soap for Mrs. Hobhouse, alone for the moment. And turned to see Molly there, white faced with shock, whispering "I got to talk to you. Somethin' real bad do have happened."

She followed her into the yard, where Molly had been washing bottles. "Mrs. Goatlake jus' come by," Molly whispered. "Oh, Sara, I'm so feared of her, what'll we do? Why'd you make me go with you t'other night? I must ha' bin mad, stark mad."

"What are you talking about? What did she say?"

Molly stared at her. "She knows. She knows I told you 'bout the poachin'. My dad told her you come with me t'other night an' she's so angry with me for

40

tellin' she wants to kill me, she said. She said you'll tell—you'll tell the captain, an' they'll all go to jail. What'll we do?"

"You know I won't tell."

"But she don't. She don't believe it, she says you belong to them an' you'll tell Dr. Newall. An' if my dad do go to jail, what'll become o' Marthy and Willum? Oh, Sara, I could—Why'd you make me do it? I must a' bin mad out o' my mind to tell you anything. An' then go bringin' you. I just thought he'd laugh, just have a good laugh at you—an' now—"

"I'll tell her myself. Where is she?"

"She's gone now, but you can tell her a'right. She wants us to come back to my dad's cottage again an' take our oath on it. Tonight, after dark again. If we don't, she says she'll put her eye on us, make us wither up."

"You don't believe that stuff!"

Molly twisted her hands in her apron in a rage of impatience.

"You're so mortal clever you don't believe nothin' till it come up an' hit you bang on the head. What d'you know about what she can do?" She looked away, her mouth trembling.

"Nobody can do that." But her voice trailed. Doña Ana had had the eye. Although only for enemies. "Nobody can," she whispered.

"Then you won't mind comin' tonight?" But Molly was too frightened to be bitter; she gripped Sara's arm with both hands, beseeching. "You got to come. If you don't she'll be sure you're tellin'."

"Of course I'll come."

Peg opened the kitchen door, looked at them. "There's some as has little enough to do, it seems. Miss Susannah's wanting you, Miss Sara. You get on with them bottles, Molly."

It was close to eleven before they could slip out of the darkened, sleeping house. The night fine and cold. A rag of cloud black-edged against the moon. A dog barking somewhere. A ruffle of wind as they climbed the ridge towards Over Thaxstone before turning away towards the marsh.

41

"We'll just tell her," Sara said. "She's got to believe me." She drew in deep breaths of the night air, was glad to be out in it, the tremor of fear that she had caught from Molly gone with the excitement of escaping from the house, creeping down the stairs, sliding the bolts they'd greased with butter after Mrs. Hobhouse and Peg had gone to bed.

But Molly was still afraid. Not saying anything as they trotted up the path, turned down the far side of the ridge, past the edge of Masham's farm. Now and then catching her breath at something, gripping Sara's arm, making her hurry and then seeming no longer to want to hurry, falling back into a walk. They came to the spongy marsh edge, trodden by Mr. Masham's cattle into deep, sodden holes, the grass becoming sedge, reeds. Followed the path that wound from hummock to reed bank and up onto the island. The oiled paper of the cottage window a small square of dull yellow tonight, a crack of light round the door. Other crevices of light where the walls were splitting. A thin plume of greyish smoke from the hole in the low roof.

"If she looks at me I'll die," Molly whispered. "You promise her, promise her everything she asks."

"I'll promise." She felt her own heart beating. The dark. The silence. Molly touching the door, not knocking, just touching. Then her fingers tapping on it, her voice whispering, "It's us. We've come."

A man's face, dark and twisted, the nose flattened. Beckoning them in, his smile as twisted as his face and nose, thin and savage.

She went in slowly, the same choking smell, worse with the warmth of the fire, the people there. Molly's father sitting on the stone that served as another stool. His face gaunt bones, jutting, full of shadows. The woman opposite, crouched on the one wooden stool, her skirt spread, blackish green in the firelight, her face stooped downwards, only her eyes raised—one eye drifting sideways, staring, showing the white. Looking at them from under black eyebrows, black hair, her face walnut dark, the same thin, twisted shape as her son's. Mrs. Goatlake. Her son, Joseph, looked at them. The three children hidden in the rag bed.

The fire crackled, a heap of stolen wood beside it, beside Mrs. Goatlake. She lifted a stick, held the end of it in the fire, still saying nothing.

"We've come," Sara said. Tried not to be afraid. She felt Molly shaking beside her. Molly's father, Henry Bone, turned his gaunt, slow head, put up one huge, clumsy hand to his chin, rasped at it.

"So you did," Joseph Goatlake said. "And now, what you goin' to tell us?"

"That we—I won't say anything. I promise. I won't say a word to anyone. Never. She didn't mean—she just told me—by accident."

"We don't like accidents, do we, Ma? Accidents is bad for folk." He had taken a knife out of his pocket, opened the blade. He touched the point of it to his thumb, tried the edge, seemed intent only on it. The firelight, the candle glittered on the steel, and it held Sara's eye as though it was threatening her.

Mrs. Goatlake turned her head, as slow as Henry Bone's, the eye drifting, sliding downwards, looking at the floor while her other eye looked straight at Sara, turned to Molly. Sara felt her mouth dry with terror in case the drifting eye should look at her. The dreadful whiteness of it, as though it was coming out of its socket. The old woman drew the stick out of the fire, its end already burning, held the flame up between the two of them so that her eye shone. Like a white stone. Then it stared straight at Sara, as black and malignant as the other.

"What a pretty one," she whispered. She held the stick closer to Sara's face, smiled, her teeth broken, the stumps the same colour as her skirt, greenish black, sickening. "Een't she handsome, Joseph? What a pity if she got spoiled. An' Molly Bone . . ."

She looked at Molly. Sara heard Molly's breath catching, thought she could hear her heart thudding.

". . . An' our Molly Bone grown so fine an' big. All that good feedin', eh, Joseph?" Her voice rustling, like something dragging in wet, rough grass. "Maybe she do have forgotten what 'tis like to be hungry. Eh,

43

Molly?" The stick, its end still smouldering, darting towards Molly's face, almost touching, Molly swaying her head back, staggering, her hair brushing the roof, the rough underside of the turf that covered it, ragged, dirt-crusted, like thick cobwebs. Joseph Goatlake reached out and grabbed her wrist so she couldn't back farther away. The burning stick close to her eyes.

"Let go of her!" Sara whispered, tried to shout, to move.

"Oh, oh," Mrs. Goatlake said. "This een't the time for givin' orders, this een't Lavender Cottage with gentle folk sittin' about. This is here. What you been tellin' that captain o' yours? About us? About what Molly here been tellin' you?" She moved the stick, quickly, like a snake darting. The heat of it against Sara's cheek. "What you been tellin'?"

"Nothing. I swear, nothing."

"An' what you goin' to tell? Dr. Newall comes to take tea with your ladies an' says, 'Them poachers, them wicked poachers, I do wish I could have 'um took up an' sent to jail.' What'll you say then, sittin' an' listenin'? 'I do know who they are, I do know where they go and when, with their faces painted black; I do know how they sells their gainin's. 'Cause Molly Bone did tell me.' Is that what you'll say?"

"No. No."

"Give us your oath on that, eh? You oath me now you won't tell?"

"I swear I won't."

"Oh, not lady's swearin', not Bible oath. *My* oath. That I'll give you. Will you swear that?" She lowered the stick, the end of it now no more than a dull eye of red, dying. Her own eye swerving away to the fire, showing the white glisten, blind.

She breathed, "Yes, I'll swear." Her own eyes fastened on that whiteness. Beside his mother, squatting on his heels, Joseph Goatlake slowly honed the blade of his knife against the heel of his palm. Henry Bone said nothing, his hands like slabs of knotted wood hanging again between his knees, his face expressionless.

44

"You kneel in front o' me," Mrs. Goatlake whispered. "The two o' you. Say this after me. 'If I tell what I knows o' Mrs. Goatlake, or any o' hers, or any o' her doings,' You say that after me now. 'If I tell . . .' "

Kneeling. Not wanting to obey. But kneeling as if she had no will. Whispering the words after her. Their two voices.

". . . may my throat close an' leave me dumb . . ."

". . . leave me dumb . . ." Molly's voice almost crying, thin with fear.

". . . may my eyes be blinded . . ."

"No!"

"You say it after me, Molly Bone, both o' you say it."

". . . may my eyes be blinded . . ."

". . . like hot coals o' fire, an 'may my heart wither in me till I drags about blind an' fumbling my path. Say it."

The fire burning. And yet the hut cold. ". . . my path."

". . . and here's my blood on it, for my solemn oath."

". . . my solemn oath."

And before she could move, the knife had touched her wrist, cut skin and flesh. Hers, Molly's. Joseph held both their wrists; the knife dropped on the earth floor. A thin ooze of blood on her skin. And he put his mouth to her wrist, his lips wet, cold wet, sucking, like a toad. Her wrist, Molly's. Her whole body shuddering from the cold wetness of his mouth, the shock of the knife blade. He picked up the knife again, a red smear of blood on the tip, mixed with dirt. He put it against his tongue, licked it clean, his eyes still watching. Molly's breath crying in her throat.

"An' that een't the end of it," Mrs. Goatlake whispered. "I'll be watchin' over you, day an' night." The eye swivelled, stared full. "You hear li'l tappings at your windows in the dark, I'm there, I'm there. I'll know if you tells. Such pretty ones. Such a pity to go blind, eh? Eh? You feel your eyes a bit sandy, your throat go sore a bit—then you think o' me, eh? You say to each other, 'She's thinkin' on us, she's watchin' over us.' You do that, an' you won't be tempted to tell stories. Jus' a li'l pain'll come to you, an' you'll think, 'They took my blood, they took it, for an oath, an' she's workin' on it, workin' to do me harm.' Now you 'member all that an' go 'long back to them nice warm beds o' yourns. But don't look round too quick as you go, 'case I'm follyin'——" She cackled with a sharp, cold laughter, showed the blackened stumps, the red throat, the whitish lump of tongue, reached up her hand with its black fingernails, earth-coloured fingers, to touch Sara's arm, her body. "Such a pretty one. Send 'um away now, Joseph." She stood up, reached out, touched Sara's eyes and throat. "Blind an' dumb," she whispered. "You 'member that. Blind an' dumb an' fumblin' about in the dark forever. Jus' you 'member. An' my eye'll be on you to keep you a' mind on it."

They stumbled to their feet, out the door into the moonlight, Joseph behind them, his hand at Sara's neck, on her shoulder. "You 'member," he whispered. The knife in front of them, point upwards, the moonlight on the blade. Then they were running, their breath gasping until it hurt to breathe, and the sweat ran into their eyes, stinging.

"I cain't go no more," Molly gasped, fell on her knees in the grass, lay flat. Sara knelt beside her, tried to pull her up again.

"We've got to get home."

They got home at last, holding their breaths, to the familiar dark of the kitchen. Up the stairs.

"Can I stay in with you?"

Lying in the narrow bed, holding each other, long shivers of fear running down Molly's body, as though nothing would warm her. Sara lying awake, listening, now shutting her eyes against the moonlight, and then opening them quickly as she heard a sound, the creak of timbers, the rustling of a mouse, something. "It's all lies," she whispered. "She can't do anything." Molly's arms tightening round her, clenching, half asleep in nightmare.

Almost asleep herself, Sara saw the old woman's white, staring eye like the moon, her skirt spreading black across the room, over her. Pushing out her arms against it, against the dark. The clock striking four. Was she asleep? One minute yes, then awake again, listening. Half asleep. The nightmare of the bone-white eye. Mixing with other nightmares, screaming. The sound of screaming, the soldiers—

"Wha'—wha'—"

Both of them sitting up. Dark. The moonlight gone. Pitch dark.

"I cain't see," Molly whispered. "I cain't see."

Chapter 4

The sky hung livid, a sickly, leaden colour, threatening ill weather. Autumn had become winter overnight and the leaves of Great Wood were already blackened. They ran, hugging their parcels, two stolen bottles of claret wine, a pudding that should have been delivered to Mrs. Grimmer.

"Wait for me," Sara called, Molly ahead of her. "Wait for me." Still trying not to believe in Mrs. Goatlake of last night, in Mrs. Talbot, whom they were going to see now. "Will it be enough? What we're bringing?"

"It'll have to be, it'll have to be. An' we can promise her money from when we gets it. Come *on*."

Along the ridge, the dark mass of Lord Southcott's Great Wood on their left, like a wall, and the marsh to their right, below them. Flat, sullen, stretching to the far horizon. Steel-shimmering of water. Black reeds, black mud, the vivid green of marsh holes gathering the remains of daylight into them, a skein of birds far out, black arrowheads. The horizon already threatening night. No wind blowing. A heavy stillness, cold falling from the air, settling.

"There it is," Molly whispered. "She do live down there all alone with no one. Jus' her cat."

Mrs. Talbot. Just a name in Lavender Cottage, not well thought of, but just a name. Old John the gardener's half-sister.

"Oh, no more than gossip, child," the captain had said. "A poor old woman who lives alone, there's always some sort of gossip."

A tongue of land below them, pushing out into the marsh. Lapped on three sides by water, mud banks, the water shallow, green with weeds and cresses, one thin stream of blacker, deeper water twisting among the reeds, touching the narrow point of land. And there, built almost on the water, the cottage. Square, heavy, blacker even than the water. Built, like Henry Bone's hut, of old boat's timbers, canvas turf. But stronger, better made, with a brick chimney and a chimney-pot, smoke rising, losing itself against the grey sky. There was even a garden, a narrow strip of colour, still a handful of autumn flowers sheltered between the black cottage and the black timber fence, the gate.

They went down the path, not running now, slower and slower as they came near. A cat sitting on one of the posts. A large tabby cat with amber, narrowed eyes watching them come down the path towards him.

"That's him," Molly whispered, and made a kind of bend of her knee, a ducking of her head as she went by, pretending to be settling her parcel under one arm before she knocked at the door. And as she knocked, the door opened, an old, tall woman was standing there, staring at them. As tall as Molly. Thin. Her hair snow white under a black satin cap. Her nose thin and straight, her eyes grey and commanding, her whole bearing one of command. Staring at them as though she knew who they were, why they had come, everything.

"We—brought you somethin'," Molly whispered. Held out her parcel. "We got somethin' to—ask you. Oh, please, you got to help us, we're in such trouble, we—we don't know what to do."

The old woman still said nothing. But she stood aside and they went in, Molly so slowly Sara needed to press her forward in case it seemed rude. A smell of herbs, of tar. A candle burning, the soft hiss and whisper of the fire. Like last night. But nothing else the same; even the fire was of sea coal, not of wood, the flames whispering, content. The candle in a pewter candlestick, set on a table. The floor swept. A chair. Spectacles lying on the table, and a book. And behind the table, shelves full of china jars, glass bottles. Bundles of brown herbs were hanging from nails in the black timber walls. The light caught the green glass shoulders of the bottles, the white china.

The old woman went behind the table, stood there still looking at them, waiting. Molly set her parcel down, and Sara hers. Not knowing whether to open it.

"Jus' some wine," Molly whispered. "An'—an' a puddin'. An' a bit o' money. It een't much, but we'll . . ."

"Tell me what is the matter." Her voice sounded harsh and at the same time educated. Nothing like Molly's voice. Or Old John's. The gossip that she was Lord Southcott's half-sister, by Old John's mother. The old lord's daughter.

"Just wretched, ugly gossip. Villages are full of such malice, puss. There was never a lord, but people claimed he was father to half the neighbourhood. Why do you ask me? Whatever has put her into your head all of a sudden?"

"Nothing. I just—Someone was speaking of her."

Beside her on the wall the shape of a bat, pinned against the timber. A real bat. Mouse head, sharp, papery brown wings. Bead eyes. She couldn't look away from it. Forced herself. And in a clear glass jar behind the old woman's head two snakes were coiling. The fire brightened, turned them to jewels, blue, silver, amber.

"Mrs. Goatlake," Molly was whispering, "she told

us—" Whispering the story. Stumbling. Repeating. And the old woman listening, her face showing nothing, her eyes fixed on Molly, turning once or twice to Sara. The snakes coiled, drowning in the alcohol jar. The brown shadow of the bat. The sharp smell of herbs, of tar, the warmth of the sea-coal fire, tiredness. She felt half asleep, swaying.

"Show me your wrists," the old woman said. Her fingers were cool, like ivory, and yet the tips of them were rough. Drawing their wrists towards the candlelight. She had put on her spectacles, bent her head a little to see the small cuts of Joseph's knife, no more than red lines a half inch long across the blue veins. Molly's hand, red from scrubbing, large, powerful. Sara's, thin and brown, her fingers as long as Mrs. Talbot's.

The old woman let go of Molly's hand, spread Sara's out until it lay flat, the fingers bending backwards. She traced the lines on it with her forefinger, closed the fingers up, reopened them, said nothing. Took Molly's and did the same thing with it. Spread it out, tried to make the fingers lie flat as Sara's. But they curled upwards, made a cup with the palm.

"You have strange hands, the pair of you. Many things will happen to you both." She sat down, looked at them unsmilingly. "Why should I help you? Why should I make an enemy of Mrs. Goatlake for the sake of—" She made a gesture of such contempt towards their offerings that Sara felt her face burn. "If you keep your promises, she'll not harm you."

"She will, she will!" Molly cried, leaned over the table towards her. "I feel it already." She half lifted her hand towards her throat, her face, and took it down again as though even the gesture might bring evil.

Mrs. Talbot sat for a long time, no longer looking at them, seeming to be considering, looking at something far away.

"If I should help you," she said, "there would be a price. But not in money."

"Anything!"

The old woman looked at Sara.

"What sort of price?"

"I do not know yet. Do you want me to help you?"

"Yes, yes. Oh, please, missus, please. We'll give anything, anything."

"And will she?"

"Yes, oh, yes. Tell her Sara, say you will."

"If I can," Sara whispered.

The old woman smiled at that, and was suddenly beautiful, as she must have been long ago. "That is a good answer," she said. "Show me your wrists again."

She held them, peered close at wrists and hands through her spectacles. Her own hands somehow courteous, touching delicately and yet very strong. "It will hurt you," she said. "Those scratches must be burned away. Will you be able to stand that? And to bring the burns back to me untouched?"

"Burned?"

"Yes. With a hot iron. Are you brave?"

"I don't know."

"I een't brave, but I'll do anything, anything if it do—if it—"

"Go tomorrow to the smith, to Mr. Lightharness. He'll know why you've come. But you'll have to be very brave." She took the shillings that Molly had laid down on the table beside the wine. "Take two of these, one each, and give them to him before he begins."

"What will he do?"

"I told you you must be brave. He will burn your scars away with iron."

Molly staring at her wrist, her throat working, swallowing. Sara standing beside her, the cottage, the old woman, seeming a long way away, the sharp smell of the herbs catching her breath, choking. The warmth of the fire. To burn the scar away with iron. She tried to imagine it, wanted to shut her eyes against the thought of it. And saw the bone white of Mrs. Goatlake's eye, felt Joseph's mouth on her skin. As though he had put poison there and she could feel it working. Her wrist throbbing. It had throbbed this morning, the skin reddened around the scratch. She looked down at it. Angry red.

"Will you go?"

She nodded, tried to say yes.

"An' tonight?" Molly breathed. "If she do know we ha' come to you—an' een't safe yet? Please, een't there nothing you can give us for tonight?"

The old woman stood up, reached down a bunch of herbs, and another, tore off a part of each, put the parts together, and re-divided them. "Keep these close by you," she said. "Under your pillows. And lay this on your window-sill and this by your door. You will be safe. She cannot reach you across these tonight." She gave them the small sprigs of dried brown grasses, dried flowers. Stood up. "Run home now. And come to me tomorrow night."

They went out into the evening stillness, almost dark already, the cat gone from the gatepost, the flowers colourless in the narrow garden. They held their bunches of herbs close against them, dry and prickling, already warm in their hands. The door shut behind them, the grey mass of the ridge above them, the dark line of the wood.

"We best hurry," Molly whispered. "They'll kill us we're so late." Running, up the narrow path, along the ridge, until they could see the cottages of Over Thaxstone below them to the right, Thaxstone itself down away to the left, the spire of the church, the houses a mass of shadow. And far beyond it the sea, a line of leaden darkness under the edge of the night.

Down the ridge path, onto the roadway, breathless from running, the rectory elms still stirring with the rooks, the sky still crimson behind them, burning. Lavender Cottage, the chestnut trees, the paddock, the kitchen garden.

"They'll kill us dead," Molly whispered. "What'll we say we bin doin' to be so long?"

But the kitchen was too full of bustle for anyone to waste time on questions. Mrs. Hobhouse merely scolded at them. "Dr. Newall comin' to supper, an' Dr. Malthus with him, an' you two dawdlin' an' playin' somewhere these hours past. Wait till Miss Susannah gets a hold o' you! She been looking for you this past hour to get your good gown on and help with things. An' you, Molly Bone, you good-for-nothing, what's that you got behind your back? Bits o' grass! And Peg an' me here with everything to do."

"A good switchin' she needs!" Peg said, coming behind Molly's back, tugging at her hair. "Stayin' out all times. You ccn't Miss Sara, nothin' to do all day."

Sara ran, met Miss Hetty on the stairs, almost ran into her. "Where have you been? And running like a mad thing! Susannah is so vexed with you! Quick, quick, quick into your company gown and come down and make your excuses to her. The doctors will be here on top of us before you're dressed even. And your hair, look at your hair!" Following Sara into her bedroom, seizing the hairbrush, making Sara sit down and have her hair made presentable before anything else. And she too wanted to know what Sara was holding, made Sara open her hands and put the herbs down.

"Why, it's betony! *Stachys macrantha!* Where did you find it all dried up like that? And *Angelica sylvestris!* I didn't think you'd become a botanist, Sara. Have I interested you at last? After supper I shall show you their pictures in my book, and proper specimens that I've pressed out in my album, not like these poor crumpled ruins. Why didn't you tell me you were gone out looking for wild flowers? I should have told you much prettier ones to gather. Oh, the tangles in your hair—and Susannah is so vexed—and poor Joshua worrying that you were lost somewhere. Oh, dear, oh, dear, shall I ever get you ready in time?"

Downstairs the guests had already arrived, Dr. Newall standing chubby and rose-cheeked in front of the parlour fire, lifting his black coattails to the blaze, his bald crown pink and white, his spectacles glistening silver like his old-fashioned shoe buckles. His friend and cousin Dr. Robert Malthus from Littleton in the captain's chair, stretching out his long, elegant legs to the fire, his hands, which long ago Miss Hetty had thought beautiful, linked under his chin.

"Ah, Miss Metty!" Dr. Newall cried. "And Sara!

Our young scholar! You should hear her reciting her lessons, Robert, you'd be astonished at her progress. Although, with such teachers, we shouldn't really be astonished at anything, eh, Miss Hetty?"

She made her curtsey to Dr. Malthus, the captain eyeing her uncomfortably from where he sat on the other side of the fire. Miss Susannah frowning. The room full of tension, of the high-pitched chattering of Dr. Newall, Miss Susannah saying in a low, icily controlled voice, "You may tell me afterwards why you are late and where you have been."

The conversation turned back to what it had been before she came in, to labourers' wages and the machine breaking. "In Suffolk too, I heard yesterday. And rick burning. I told Lord Southcott but last week: if the government doesn't take measures soon, we shall see it spread everywhere. It is plain Jacobinism, and nothing else. These radical agitators go among them, setting their heads on fire. What do you think of it, Captain?"

"I? I've been away too long to understand it," the captain said. "When I was a boy, men were glad to put up ricks for sixpence a day. And now they can earn three times that and more, and they burn the ricks down in gratitude. I think sometimes the world has gone mad."

"It's not really so mysterious," Dr. Malthus said. "With the war ended and the new, improved machines for harvesting and threshing, a few men and boys can do the work of a hundred. There are too many labourers. And so they rebel against the machines, poor fellows. It cannot come right until there are less labourers."

"And until wages come down," Miss Hetty said timidly, looking as though she had surprised herself by speaking.

"I see you remember my cousin's teaching." Dr. Malthus raised his wine-glass and sipped approvingly. "Wages must fall, and they must therefore have fewer children, or none, if they do not wish them to go hungry, and all will be balanced again. These troubles are a temporary thing. Purely temporary."

"I wish I felt so calm about it, Robert. A man with his ricks burned feels nothing temporary about that, I imagine."

"Then it must be our business as magistrates, Edward, to set their wages lower. You give them too much relief, I've told you often. And it's a poor kindness to them in the end."

"I wish that *we* might set servants' wages lower," Miss Susannah said. "They've gone beyond all bounds. Do you know, we must pay even the kitchen girl twenty shillings a quarter?"

"I tell you, it's a false kindness," Dr. Malthus said, shaking his head. He lifted his wine-glass again in emphasis. "What happens? Exactly the reverse of what we have just been saying ought to happen. She takes those wages home to her parents and at once, thinking they're rich, they have more children. And what happens then? Those children grow old enough to work, but find none, for the wages are too high and they are too many. Too many either to find work, even should the wages be lowered, or to be supported in idleness by the sacrifices of the charitable. For as you'll remember, the supply of men multiplies in geometrical progressions, but food no more than arithmetically. So then, cold and hunger, misery and vice must take their toll of the surplus and restore nature's balance that our profligacy had disturbed. It's a simple but perfect illustration of my cousin's theory."

"Dear me, dear me," cried Dr. Newall, "such sad talk in front of ladies. What will they think of us? Let us talk of something else, more appropriate to the excellent supper that my olfactory organ detects in the preparation. Suppose we hear Miss Hetty's pupil recite her latest achievement of scholarship? How are we upon the Roman emperors today, Miss Hetty? Have we mastered them yet?"

"Oh, yes!" Miss Hetty said. "She knows them, every one, right down to Romulus Augustulus, do you not, Sara? Come, stand up and recite them and show our visitors how well you are learning!"

Chapter 5

The forge was like a black cave, full of the noise of hammering, the hiss of white-hot iron in water, smoke from the charcoal fire. The smell of iron, harsh as blood. The smith's face dark, sweating, the sweat rolling in silver snail paths onto his naked throat, onto his enormous chest, itself sweating, the black hairs curling above the ragged, greasy edge of his leather apron.

He shaped and hammered at the horseshoe with tremendous, effortless blows, the hammer like a toy in his fist, the tongs holding the shoe, reheating it in the furnace, turning it, while his bellows-boy strained at his blowing, teeth grinning with the strain of pumping at the leather lung of the bellows, his yellow thatch of hair as blackened as his master's, his eyes red-rimmed, weeping from the fire smoke.

The two girls waited outside, holding hands, Molly's hand trembling in Sara's, while the great brown cart-horse was backed and whoaed into the forge for shoeing. "Easy there, Brock, easy now," until the vast chestnut rump was by the anvil, the hoof lifted, the shoe struck on.

"Only a li'l burn it'll be," Molly whispered. "Like touchin' a coal. That's all it'll be." Her hand trembling.

"Easy now, Brock, out a' there now, boy." The ploughboy guiding the enormous horse, stamp of feathered hooves, a shaking of the great head, jingle of brass. Out into the road beside the girls, the plough-boy watching them, hoping to be watched, admired as he caught at the harness, pulled himself up onto the mountainous back. "Whoa now, Brock!"

The smith beckoned them, his eye red as the fire. The bellows-boy looked at them and looked away, as though he too knew why they had come. He had a strange, soft, foolish smile that he turned on everything —the bellows, the fire, anyone who came—as though all were one to them. He was deaf and dumb, and simple.

Slowly, and then with a quick movement that almost spilled the coins onto the black earth floor, Molly put their shillings down, side by side on the anvil, bright as white eyes in the dark, the firelight. The smith nodded to the boy, who took the shillings, dropped them into a pocket of his leather apron, smiled, at Molly, at Sara, at the dark. The smith made a gesture with his fingers, and the boy took two horseshoe nails from a box and laid them where the coins had been. When he had done that, he went out into the road.

"He'll tell us if someone comes," the smith said. " 'Twon't take long."

He took the nails in the long pincers, held them as delicately as finger-tips could, thrust them into the fire. They watched, Sara's mouth growing dry, her throat closing with the terror, the charcoal fumes, as the smith worked the bellows with his lame foot, his shortened leg, pumping them up and down, up and down, the flames hissing, the nails reddening, glowing, becoming as crimson as the fire itself. Sara wanted to close her eyes against it and was afraid to, could not look away, could not breathe.

The nails grew white, burned with a white light in the fire, unbearable. And still she could not look away from them. The smith took smaller tongs, a smaller hammer, and with an extraordinary swiftness gripped one nail, began to beat it with quick, short blows, the hammer dancing on the burning iron, curving it, curving it, until the nail became a ring, the white glow dulled to red, began to blacken, was re-

57

plunged in the fire and grew white again, was hammered, hammered, laid aside, and the second ring formed as swiftly, white glow dulling to red and blackening, burned white again, laid with the first, and then both heated red, smouldering and dull like burning eyes on the black surface of the anvil, where the white shillings had laid.

"Do ye still want them?" the smith said.

Sara swallowed, managed to whisper, "Yes."

"Hold out your arm, girl." He came close, grew huge, black as midnight, and she shut her eyes against him, holding out her arm. And there was a sudden pain in her wrist, on the inside, where Joseph Goatlake's knife had cut, the pain terrible. She tried to shriek, her throat locked with the agony, with the burning could only gasp and feel her knees giving, Molly gripping her, the smith's hand closing on her wrist, dragging it down, plunging it into the bucket of water beside the anvil. There was a hissing sound, and the ring was in the bucket with her hand, burned her knuckles as it sank, turned black instantly, sent a curl of steam up from the shimmering surface of the water.

Molly whispered, "Hold me, Sara, hold me," and Sara threw her arms round her, hid her own eyes against the sight of Molly's bared wrist, the second ring. She felt Molly's body shiver with the pain, heard her gasp in her throat, her jaws clenched against crying out, and then whimpering, "Oooh, oooh," as the smith bent her forward, plunged her hand and wrist into the water.

They stood shaking, holding each other, and the smith took up the two rings, tossed them on the horn of his palm. "You take them wrists to her tonight," he said. "An' don't you show 'em to no one till you do. Nor these." He gave them the still warm rings, made them close the fingers of their hands over them, held their hands tight in his. Stared into their faces. "You've got friends now," he whispered. "Will have, when you do with those as she tells you. Against her you're afeared of and else besides. So long as you don't talk." He held their hands so tight that Sara thought her fist was crushed, the ring driven into her flesh. The furnace whispered, the charcoal seemed to have its own soft language as it burned and glowed. The dark of the forge closed round them, there was no daylight, there was no day outside. Only the forge and the black shape of the smith and his eyes, like glass, red-burning with the firelight.

Then he let go of their hands, said harshly, "Keep them wrists covered, mind. And get to her quick as you can or 'twill be no more than a burn, an' all for naught. Get along home now."

The boy came in, made signs with his hands, and set himself to the bellows. The smith took up a bar of iron, said in a louder voice, "You bring that old pony down to me one o' these days an' I'll see to 'er. She do need shoeing all four feet, I do reckon." And then to the carter who came in, "Aye, master, a half hour, 'bout, I'll have that tyre ready. You fetch me a quart o' ale an' it might be less, too."

Sara and Molly had already pulled their sleeves down over the burns and picked up their baskets, and they went out into the road as though the daylight was blinding them, as though they'd been a year inside the darkness.

It was midnight before they reached Mrs. Talbot's cottage, panting against the gusts of wind, with the fear of being missed from the house, of what they were doing. Their wrists still hurt with a sharp, raw pain as their sleeves touched the burns. They had twisted rags round them, but the rags kept slipping down as they ran and in the end they had thrown them away. They had their rings tied tight in their handkerchiefs, and gripped them against the shadows, the sounds of the night. The weight of shadow of the Great Wood, an owl drifting overhead, the desolate crying of a night bird in the marshes ahead.

They were over the ridge, and below them they could see the light of a candle in Mrs. Talbot's window, the black shadow of the rook against the water.

"So it's done, eh?" Mrs. Talbot said, drawing them in, a subtle difference about her manner from the previous day. She examined their burns by the candle-

59

light, pursed her lips over them and took a small earthenware jar from the table, opened it. "This will hurt, too, mind. Just for a moment and then you'll feel no more of it." She put her forefinger into the dark red ointment, paused for a second. "After this," she said, "the mark won't leave you. Ever. You've still time to change your minds?"

"Please," Molly whispered. "We don't want to change our minds."

"And you?"

Sara shook her head. The burn throbbed on the sinews of her wrist, like a pulse.

"There's more to do, I warn you. And no going back."

They both stayed silent, looked at her. The cat was by the fire; he stood up and arched his back. With a sudden leap he was on the table-top, beside the book, the spectacles, the pewter candlestick, the jar of ointment. He composed himself, curved his tail over the open pages. Sara saw without thinking it strange that the book was not printed, but in manuscript, the letters rusty with age.

"Aye, Robert," Mrs. Talbot said. "Do ye want to see them close?"

On the timber wall with its glimmer of glass jars, its jewelled adders, its shadow bunches of dried herbs, the bat seemed to quiver as the candle bent its flame. The hut felt cold as ice. "What else we got to do, missus?" Molly breathed. "I cain't do much more, I think."

"You must go to Shuck's Wood and find a place I'll tell you, and sit there for a little. No more than that. And put your rings into the pool you'll find there. To seal our bargain. Bargains have to be sealed."

"We cain't go to Shuck's Wood," Molly whispered. And then, not as though it was the real argument, "There are traps in there. We'd be killed."

"You wanted to go poaching."

"I didn't. 'Twas her." She caught her breath. The cat looked at her and yawned.

"We'll go," Sara said. She gripped Molly's arm. "I'm not afraid." Mrs. Talbot took her hand, the finger-tips rasping her skin, and yet gently, drawing her wrist out of her sleeve again. "Now!" she said. The ointment touched the burn, and it was as though she was being burned again, as though the red hot metal was being driven into the flesh and held there. Then there was nothing but a pleasant warmth, a dizziness of pain gone by, of pleasure. Sara felt her head swimming. Her wrist was cold, cold as ice, and then warm, the warmth spreading up her arm, throbbing. She felt her heart pound.

Beside her Molly cried out, clutched at her with her free hand, dug her fingers deep into her arm, hung there for a moment. Mrs. Talbot was smearing more of the ointment onto two clean strips of rags. She bound first Sara's, then Molly's, wrists, tied flat knots and smoothed them down. "There. Sit on those two stools a minute till your heads clear." They sat, and she told them where they must go in Shuck's Wood, which lay half a mile to the north, along the marsh's edge, like an outpost of the Great Wood, separated from it by half a mile of the rough, rabbit-burrowed turf of the ridge.

"There is a keepers' path," Mrs. Talbot said. "It begins this side of the wood and winds in. Twenty paces along it there's a trap, and ten paces more another. After that there's none."

"How d'you know so certain sure?" Molly whispered, her voice dying away with the fear of questioning what they must do. And yet having to question.

Mrs. Talbot smiled gently. "Robert does tell me things," she said. "When he chooses." She looked at Sara and it was impossible to tell whether she was serious or not. "Now, listen to me. And remember. When the path comes out at the marsh, be very careful. There are marsh holes there. You must turn left and keep close against the bank and follow it along until you find the mouth of a small stream. Then turn back into the wood along the bed of the stream and you'll come to where I'm sending you. It looks no more than a green mound from the outside, but when you get to the top, you'll find it's hollow. And below you you'll see a small pool among big stones. Go down and put your hands and the rings into that pool and promise to be good friends to us, and wait a little. Only a little. Then come back to me. After that Mrs. Goatlake will no more threaten you than she'd threaten me, or Robert there. You can sleep like babes."

She smiled, and again Sara thought she became young for that instant, became beautiful in such a way that it was frightening, there was so much power in it. As though for that second she held Mrs. Goatlake in her cupped hand like a poor insect, black and ugly and yet helpless.

"Now go."

They went, still faintly dizzy, the bandages warm and comforting on their wrists, their arms throbbing.

"I near fell down," Molly whispered. "But 'tis nice now, eh?"

They walked fast, ran along the firm slope of turf, the marsh shimmering on their right. Now black pools of water, now the silver of naked mud, now clumps of reeds like black combs or a long bank of reeds and grass tussocks that looked solid enough to walk on. And all spreading as far as the night reached, to the horizon, to the sea, desolate.

Shuck's Wood before them, a dark tangle of ancient trees and oak shrub and ash and hawthorn thickets, binding itself round. They found the entrance to the keepers' path.

"We need a stick," Molly whispered. "To feel for traps. Suppose—suppose—" She had stopped and was looking at the wood, her eyes half frightened, half dazed by the ointment. "They do say—they do say—"

Sara freed herself, listened. She could hear nothing, and then a thousand sounds, all the small whisperings of the wood, of the night. She felt for a dry branch she could snap off from its tree.

"We could get put in jail for what you just done. You know that?" Almost laughing.

Sara had begun prodding at the path ahead of them and Molly followed, laughing now as though drunk, and yet still afraid, shivering with fear. Sara felt her head burning, her heart pounding. Pounding so much that she had to stop and lean on the stick. How far in had Mrs. Talbot said? Ten paces? She pushed the end of the stick into the dead leaves. A bird woke and cried and she thought, *I must be quiet, I must be very quiet*, and she too wanted to laugh. As though her feet were above the ground, as though she could fly if only she lifted her arms and tried. How stupid to walk along this path. She waved the stick ahead of her, began to run.

"Sara!"

She stumbled, tried to save herself, fell headlong, the stick running ahead of her, its jagged end skidding among the leaves, digging into the leaf mould. There was the chink of metal, a sharp crunch and clang of iron, and the stick was torn out of her hand—shivered upright, broke, and fell, ten inches of it severed by the jaws of the trap. She lay on her stomach looking at it with stupid eyes. Black shimmer of iron, wet and shining, leaves sticking to the curved jaws, the locked teeth. She reached out and touched it. Cold as ice.

Behind her, Molly had fallen on her knees, was whimpering, "You all right? You all right? Oh, God have mercy."

"I'm all right," Sara said. She found she still wanted to laugh. It was very funny the way the stick had jumped out of her hand like that. If she lay here she would go to sleep, she would have such dreams. Or she would just fly away. Just fly away.

Molly was tugging at her. "Let's go home, I'm so feared I could die."

"We can't go home," Sara said. She stumbled to her feet, stepped over the trap. What had Mrs. Talbot said? Another trap? She'd just jump over it. Just—Molly was shaking her, both hanging on to her for support and shaking her.

"I feel sick," Molly whispered. "I'm going to be sick."

"We've got to go on," What had Mrs. Talbot said? She had enough sense left to pick up the remains of her stick, to prod ahead with it, but it seemed very funny. There was a shadow beside her. There seemed to be shadows all round her, jostling her, holding her up, making her walk straight. "Leave me alone," she whispered. But they only tugged at her, would not leave her alone. Her cloak caught on a thorn branch, tore a thread from it. The second trap, the sound of it muffled by crushed wood. She tugged at her stick, and the teeth held it upright. She left it there, caught Molly's arm and dragged her by. They ran then, stumbling with drunkenness, with the effects of the aconite and hemlock and belladonna in the ointment, their hearts pounding, pounding, now very fast, now slow. Their feet seemed to skim the ground, not even to touch the dead leaves. They were flying, flying, like shadows, surrounded by shadows. And suddenly the wood opened, they were among low, twisting scrub, the last trees, the marsh spread at their feet, a shimmer of water pools, of mud banks and silence. A bright trembling green of cresses, waiting for any living thing to set foot on them, to suck it down. A narrow strip of gravel, of firm mud, under the low bank of earth that framed the wood's edge.

They began to walk along it, sobered a little by the change of landscape, by the open sky and marsh, the wind, which came softly whispering across the reeds. The mud sucked at their heels, and they took off their boots and carried them, the small stones hard and round under their feet, and then sinking away. It was extraordinarily pleasant to walk like that, feel the wet cold of the mud squeeze up between their toes. They squelched and held each other against falling, laughed.

"I do feel so queer," Molly said. "Like I'm drunk. I don't fear naught anymore. Keeper come, I'll shove him into the marsh." She laughed so much she had to stop where she stood, flapping her arms. Sara pulled her along. Their feet were in running water, thin mud and leaves against their ankles, the water cold as ice and silk soft and gentle. They turned up the stream, now gravel, now rotted leaves under their bare feet, the wood closing round them again, arching low above them, so low they must stoop, almost crawl in the running water. And then they were in the open, the mound in front of them like a grey shadow, fifteen, twenty feet high, curving back away from them on either side, the stream coming out from the mound itself, from between two great leaning stones, fallen against one another like the pillars of a ruined doorway.

The trees had turned back, left a clearing around the mound, as though the trees were watching it. White thorn and juniper and hazel, ash and oak and holly. A thick wall of trees. They scrambled up the sloping turf, hampered by the boots they were carrying, pushing each other upwards. Came to the top, a broad rim of turf and scattered bushes, and looked down into the hollow of the mound. They could see water, and more stones, like fallen men, lying sunk in the ground. Grey shadows. More bushes, but not many, and one thorn tree, dark with its red winter berries.

"There's someone down there below," Molly whispered, her voice strange and rasping, her breathing so loud and heavy that Sara wanted to hush her. "It's him!"

"There's no one," Sara breathed, her own voice strange to her. "Come on down." She began to slide and scramble down the inner slope of the mound. Molly behind her, whispering hoarsely, "Wait for me, wait."

Slithering against a stone beside the pool, lichen rough under her palms, like something—something she knew—Mrs. Talbot's hands touching her, rough and cool, gentle. She felt a peacefulness, a quiet. Lay down on the long, flat boulder, put her cheek against it, against the roughness of the lichen, a soft pad of moss. If she reached down, she could touch the water. She remembered the ring, knotted inside her handkerchief, pinned safe in her apron pocket. She took it out, slid the coldness of it onto the first joint of her forefinger. Reached down. Pushed her hand deep into the water, let it soak into the bandage round her wrist, cold and clinging.

She cupped her palm, drew up water and drank it, realised her throat was burning, cupped both hands together, and lay with her face close down to the surface of the pool; drank and drank until she could drink no more and still lay there, her hands cupped in the water, her face above it like a dark mirror, shadows in the pool, the shadows of her hands, her face, Molly's face beside her, still lapping at the water, breaking the surface, the reflection. She moved the small iron ring from her forefinger onto the third finger of her left hand and it slid into place as though it had been made to fit there.

But when she lifted her hand out of the pool to look at it, it was difficult to see. Two hands there, two rings. Difficult to see Molly's face, everything seemed to have its shadow, to be twice there. Two Mollys. Even the stone under her. She lay down, the pounding of her heart grown slower, like the slow pounding of the smith's hammer, far away. Far away. Lay drugged, half sleeping, heard the pool whispering to her, the stone whispering. If she listened harder, she could hear what they were saying, telling her marvellous things, old, old, caressing things. The thorn tree whispering, bending down over her, touching her hair.

"We got to promise," Molly whispered. "Remember?"

"I am promising," Sara murmured. "I promise, I promise." She held the stone, clung to it, the lichen scratchy against her cheek, her mouth, like the rough beard of a man. She lay quietly, surrendered, the shadows whispering, her mind drifting, a tumbling of shadows, of old voices. Wanted to be naked, to lie there naked on the stone and hold it to her, feel the cold tendrils of the wind caress her skin like water.

"Oh, my love," she whispered to the stone. "Oh, my dear."

They want back by way of the stream and the path, still carrying their boots, stepping over the sprung traps, their minds dazed and wandering, as though their bare feet guided them, the trees guided them. They sat down on the turf of the ridge and pulled on their boots and sat for a long moment holding hands.

Chapter 6

The winter hardened. Ice gripped the marsh, lay in the ruts of the road. Grass crunched under foot even at midday. An old woman died in a ditch and was found next morning by a carter, stiff and bent as a stick. When Sara and Molly went on errands, their breaths hung on the still air, the cold was like iron.

Once or twice Mrs. Goatlake met them and gave them a sickly smile, her eyes sliding away from them, towards the ground. "Such pretty ones, so pretty an' good. But time may tell, eh? Nice pretty maidens."

The captain huddled in his room all day now, never left it. The fever hadn't come back, but he still shivered as though it were there, in his bones. Nothing would make him warm. But he'd pretend that he felt well, that tomorrow, next week, when the wind changed, he would go duck hunting. "Oh, you can't imagine it, the great cloud of 'em flying in. And lying there in the punt, with our guns, me and Jack Bowers—oh, he was a friend. Poor, poor Jack. He died at Trafalgar on Nelson's own *Victory*. But not so bad a way to have died, eh?"

Just before Christmas a beggar came, thin, one-legged, hobbling past the cottage, half a dozen village children screeching after him, throwing stones. Sara ran out and cried, "Stop, stop that!" And the children ran.

The beggar's face was yellow with sickness, gaunt

as a skull, and he leaned on his crutch and smiled at her. "Merci, Mam'selle. Thank you."

"You are French?"

He was a French prisoner, making his way home. He had been ill a long time in a prison camp somewhere in the north and all his comrades had gone long ago. He did not look as though he would reach the coast.

"I'll get you something," she said. She took a loaf and cheese and four slices of mutton off the joint, and some ham and a bottle of wine, and brought them out to him wrapped in a cloth. He looked at the bundle and at her, and began to cry. Silently, tears running down his gaunt cheeks.

"I'll try and find you money," she said. She ran in again, and the captain gave her five shillings and some tobacco.

"Quick," the captain said. "Before they see him."

The soldier stood looking at her, leaning on his crutch, the silver in the palm of his hand, the dark tobacco. "Go now," she said. "I hope you get safely to your home." She wanted to cry herself. He limped away and she stood looking after him.

"Did you give that man anything?" Miss Susannah said. "You shouldn't run out like that to speak to a beggar."

"He was a French soldier. I gave him—the captain gave him a little money. He looked very ill."

"A French soldier! What should he be doing here? A vagabond like that should be whipped, not encouraged. My brother—" She turned away and Sara escaped up the stairs.

Sara's real life was no longer in Lavender Cottage, but in Mrs. Talbot's.

They went to her whenever they could steal an hour or two during the day. Or at night, slipping out like foxes in the dark, no longer frightened. Not very often at night, because Molly was so tired the next day she could scarcely wake and stumbled round the kitchen all morning. But when they could. On Saturday nights in particular, when Molly could sleep in, the next morning, until half-past six or even seven.

And they would come to the small squat hut by the marsh as though they were coming home. Even Robert seemed if not to welcome them, to accept them, to look at them with a kinder eye.

They could scarcely have said what it was they did there to make it so pleasant. Mrs. Talbot would make a pot of tea—not the shop-bought China teas Sara drank in Lavender Cottage, but herb teas of Mrs. Talbot's own making, which filled the room with a strong, wild scent as though they were in a wood, in the spring. And she would give them small flat cakes to eat with their tea, and then a glass of a cordial that tasted a little like ratafia. It was dark green and sweet, and left its taste in their mouths long after they had licked the last drops out of the bottom of the glass.

Mrs. Talbot would tell them stories, not sitting down to tell them properly by the fire, but in half sentences, her voice harsh and almost indifferent, as she moved about, taking down a jar from the shelves, grinding the dried herbs into a powder in one of the small stone mortars she kept on the window-sill, boiling a pot on the fire to make an ointment, consulting her manuscript book now and then, her spectacles reflecting the fire, the candlelight. She told them about a voyage to India, the sea like a fire of stars behind the ship at night, fishes that flew, palm trees and coconuts and brown-faced men in turbans. Holy men standing all day naked on one leg, their blind eyes turned to the sun. An elephant carrying a golden house on his back, and an Indian king inside it.

"All gold?" Molly whispered.

"All gold."

Or old stories, of savage men who came in long ships to murder the Thaxstone people and drove them into the marsh to drown. Of times when all the people gathered at the Ring Mound at Candlemas and May Eve, and Lammas, and All Souls', and stayed the whole night there, dancing and feasting.

"And did He come to 'em? Old Shuck?"

"Aye. He came." She stirred the fire under the ointment pot and a great horned shadow danced for a moment on the far wall. But it was Robert, Robert's ears that threw the shadow.

"Don't He come no more?"

"Who can tell?" Mrs. Talbot said harshly. "Show me your marks."

The burns had died away into small pale scars, almost invisible, a faint red ring of colour, so faint that a stranger would have needed to be told it was there before he could have found it. "Aye, they're well enough." Their rings hung round their necks on leather laces Mrs. Talbot had given them, knotting them herself. "Never take 'em off. Never show 'em unless you mean to. And if they're seen by strangers who ask questions, say they're a keepsake. Just a keepsake. Does Mrs. Goatlake trouble you anymore?"

"No," Sara said. "Except that she mutters at us sometimes."

"What does she say?"

"Only that we're pretty ones, and that time may tell."

"That's true enough." She took both their chins in her fingers, turned their heads. "I could've had grandchildren your age if I'd—You'll have to be my grandchildren." She had a strange laugh, sharp and fierce like—like Robert coughing, Sara thought. "And time tells everything. Near everything."

She sat down, held their two hands across the table-top, looked into their palms. "Tell us our fortunes," Molly breathed. "Please."

"Fortunes!" Mrs. Talbot said scornfully. In that small, tar-smelling, shadowy room she looked sometimes like a fierce hawk caged up, her head turning as though she were looking for a way of escape, looking with savage arrogance and contempt at anyone who gaped between the bars at her imprisonment. She let go of their hands and took out a silver mirror from a narrow drawer in the table, above her lap. She polished the surface with a corner of her apron, handling it with a sudden tenderness, looking down into it for a long moment before she laid it on the table-top between the three of their bent heads. "You first," she said to Sara. "Tell me what you see."

70

She saw only her own face, her eyes looking back at her from the cloudy surface, wondering what they should see. The candle bent its flame in a draught, stirred the shadows. She stared and stared, narrowed her eyes until her face became no more than a paler shadow in the surface, grew small, indistinct. All the mirror was full of shadows, and she thought that she could see—she did not want to see; she wanted to shut her eyes, shut out the picture that came to her, the village street, men running, women. Mrs. Talbot gripped her wrists, held them, preventing her from pushing the mirror away. "Tell me what else you see," she whispered. "Quickly."

The picture faded, the red skirt was no more than shadows.

"Look, look again! Look deep!"

A room. An old man. An old man like an idol, his face ivory yellow, wearing a padded gown, sitting alone in the bare room. Staring. Staring at nothing, his eyes blind.

"What is he doing?"

"Nothing. He's blind." Depth on depth of blackness. Staring down into it, into the cold. Such cold. As though it were reaching up to her. Like terror.

"Look closer, closer!"

"No!" She forced herself to look away, forced her head up from the mirror, the sweat running cold on her face, her throat, her heart beating with fear. "What are you making me see?"

"No matter," Mrs. Talbot said. The room was close, stifling with its tar smell, the herbs, the fire. And yet a moment ago it had been icy cold.

"What fortune's that?" Molly said. "That weren't a fortune."

Mrs. Talbot looked at her, seemed almost surprised, smiled at her. "My dear," she said. "My big, dear Molly. Look for yours." She pushed the mirror towards her. Molly stared down into it, frowning.

"I don't see naught," she whispered. "Only shadows.'"

"Make your mind quiet."

"What you mean, quiet?"

71

"Empty and still." She touched Molly's hands, smiled. Sara thought sometimes that she treated Molly with much more kindness than she treated her.

"I see somethin'," Molly whispered, stared up at Mrs. Talbot with her eyes huge. "Me! And dressed so fine!"

"Aye. You'll have fine dresses to wear, I think. And now that's enough nonsense for one day." She took the mirror, wrapped it in its cloth, and put it away in the drawer.

Sometimes there were other callers, women, girls, sometimes a man, looking sideways at Sara and Molly, shamefaced and nervous, saying nothing until Mrs. Talbot sent the two girls out of the cottage to fetch her something or look for Robert or to go home.

Once Jim Lightharness came and sat holding the little glass of cordial between his fingers, like green fire, his face still black from the forge, his lame leg drawn under him on the stool. Watching them. But saying nothing, and after a few minutes Mrs. Talbot told them to run outside.

Beyond the gate they found the Smith's boy lying in the stiff, frost-brittle grass as though it was summertime, playing with Robert, who pounced on him, patting his dumb mouth with a paw, leaping over his dark yellow hair with a sudden kitten-jump of excitement. And the boy's eyes glittered with the same amber cunning as the cat's. Until he saw the two girls coming out of the cottage and rolled over onto his knees. They tried to talk to him, make signs to him to go on playing, but after a moment he ran away into the marsh, ice crackling under his bare feet, jumping from hidden firm place to reed tussock until he vanished against the night shimmer of black water and silvery reflecting mud and the reed shadows and the sky.

"We best go home," Molly said. And they ran home in the bitter cold, holding their cloaks round them until they grew warm, both of them feeling, without need to tell each other, that after all their time with her they knew nothing about Mrs. Talbot. Nothing about anything.

The next time they came there Mrs. Talbot said, "I

have something for you both." And when they were going home she gave them a large pot of ointment, which looked and smelled like the one that had healed their wrists, although not so dark a red. "Undress by the fire," she said, "and smear this on. Everywhere. Everywere, mind. It'll not hurt you like the other. And put this fennel seed in the keyhole and lay this along the window-sill, and go to bed."

It was already a familiar journey, running home in the dark, or the moonlight, the wind on the long ridge lifting their cloaks behind them like wings, fastening their skirts against them, now holding them back, now driving them forward, lifting them as though they were flying, down the slope towards the rectory, towards Lavender Cottage and the road, their faces glowing with the cold.

They ran and ran, stopped to catch their breath, and crept into the silent garden, the silent house, easing the bolts home. Crept up the stairs to Sara's room, each of them carrying wood from the kitchen, stepping over the stair that creaked, standing like shadows on the upper, narrow stairs, listening for sounds. Nothing but the house sleeping.

"What you think 'tis *for?*" Molly breathed, holding the jar of ointment in one hand as they knelt by Sara's fire. Sara blew softly on the embers; coaxed a flame, and they laid their sticks and the two split logs carefully in place, until the fire was blazing; there was a circle of warmth about them in the icy chill of the room.

They undressed, knelt naked for a moment in front of the fire, feeling the warmth of the fire meeting the freed warmth of their bodies, which seemed to dissolve on the instant of their nakedness. Molly's body already a woman's, dark green shadows on the slight curve of her stomach, under her breasts, pale shadows on her throat as she lifted her arms, linked her two hands behind her neck, offered herself to the fire. And for a second Sara felt almost jealous, almost angry that Molly was so much more grown than she was; and then oddly pleased, she began digging her fingers into

73

the coldness of the ointment, took out four fingers' full, and clapped it against Molly's stomach.

"Oooh, 'tis cold!"

They both filled their hands with it, faced each other, rubbed in the ointment from their shoulders, their throats, down the length of their bodies to their laps and thighs, held each other, the ointment vanishing as they rubbed, seeming to melt and soak into their skins on the instant, leaving no more trace than a velvet moistness, the beginnings of a glow of warmth as they rubbed and rubbed, Sara standing up for Molly to rub her knees and shins and calves, and then Molly standing and Sara kneeling. Each turning round and feeling the other draw the long smears of coldness down back and hip and over buttock, down to the hollows behind their knees.

The coldness became warmth, glowing. Except where their hands and legs had been scratched by thorns. There it burned with a sting of pain, seemed to work its way into the flesh, like fire.

"We got to go to bed now."

The sheets ice cold, moist with the ointment, clinging to them, holding them tight, bound together so it was difficult to move. The warmth was inside them, like fever, and Sara felt her heart beginning to race, to beat harder and harder, pounding until the throb of it was in her head, her ears, deafening her. She couldn't breathe, her heart was bursting. They had drawn back the curtains when they laid the fennel on the windowsill and the window was filled with moonlight, with a white fire of light. It glowed, pulsed, reached towards her. She had a fever, she was sweating until she felt the sweat run down her stomach, her legs, mix with Molly's sweat, Molly's whole body slippery with sweat, clinging to her, Molly whispering, "Lord, have Mercy. I'm dying, what have we done?" But her voice lost and half asleep, half-drugged asleep, unconscious.

Sara felt terror, terror of the moonlight, of slipping out of her own consciousness, of dying as she lay there; she tried to throw off the sheets, throw off Molly's arm and leg that held her pinned, helpless. Her heart seemed to stop, hesitate, and race again; she tried to move her head, could move nothing, not her hand, not a finger; she lay sweating and dying and the moonlight reached to her, the fire burned in her. She thought she was lifting out of her body, she wanted to cry with terror and could not make a sound, the moonlight was drawing her towards the window. She clung to Molly and Molly was not there. And then she was no longer struggling, she was in the dark, among a multitude of shadows. Now moonlight, now dark, and the land below them, houses, trees, the shape of the Great Wood, the endless shimmer of the marsh—flying, flying, their cloaks like dark wings and Molly crying out, "Where are you? Sara, Sara!" And the Ring Mound below them, and Shuck's Wood. Whirling down like leaves out of the sky on the night wind.

He was waiting, waiting, waiting, and she twisted with terror in the dream, terror and longing, as he stood waiting with his lame leg and his great hammer and his soot-dark face. The dumb boy rolled in the grass at his feet, played with the torn edge of his master's leather apron. The smith lifted one hand to gather her down out of the air. The ice coldness of the leather apron against her naked skin, under her flying cloak, and the cloak falling, covering them both. So cold. So cold! And she cried out with the cold of it and woke and she was lying naked, the fire died down again in the hearth, the moonlight gone, Molly's cold body against hers, still holding her, the sheet under them damp with chilled sweat, the bedclothes slid away onto the floor.

She dragged them up again, wrapped them both close, and clung to Molly in spite of the cold of her body, clinging to her in terror against the nightmare. "Wha'? Wha'? Is it five yet?" Molly whispered in her sleep and buried her face against Sara's shoulder and the side of her neck, her breath warm and soft. "I'm so cold," she breathed. "Cold inside me." The fire flared on a knot of wood, threw shadows on the slanted ceiling. Sara closed her eyes against them, shivered, was afraid to sleep again and dream, and yet longed to go back to the Ring Mound, to things that had happened there that she had already forgotten. The whole dream sliding, fading, dissolving in her mind as she tried to hold it, to recover it.

Until suddenly it was long past five o'clock and Molly sat upright in the bed with her eyes tight shut and said, "I'm awake, I'm awake, Missus," and staggered out onto the floor to bury her head in Sara's basin of cold water, let it run down her naked body, to lap it like a dog.

"I do think I'm dying," she whispered, her voice hoarse with the burning of her throat.

Chapter 7

They scarcely said a word to each other about their dreams of that night. And there was almost nothing Sara remembered for her to have told about. Only a sense of shivering excitement, of longing, and then—then nothing she could really remember, nothing she wanted to talk about, even with Molly. And Molly only shrugged and looked away, saying, "Jus' queer dreams, I don't remember 'um rightly."

And Mrs. Talbot asked them nothing. But it seemed to Sara that from that night they were on a different footing with her. As though she no longer regarded them as children. Almost as—assistants? They were allowed to help her now, pounding the dried herbs, the berries, rendering down ointments under her careful eye—more careful than Mrs. Hobhouse's.

"When the spring comes I'll let you help me with

gathering. Do you know what that one is? That one there?"

"Herb Robert."

"Aye, Death Come Quickly. And that grey feathery one?"

"Woundwort."

"What is it for?"

"For healing wounds?"

"And fevers. If you should give that in a strong brew to your captain it would cure his fever better than any of the surgeon's bleedings. And his rheumatism. Molly, what is this one?"

"I don't know."

"Foxglove, girl, foxglove. Can I teach you nothing? But maybe it's as well if you do not learn what that one does."

But Sara still felt at times that of the two of them Mrs. Talbot loved Molly the best, was easiest with her, ruffling her red hair and shaking her own head over Molly's forgetfulness of everything she was trying to teach her. While she would look at Sara with a strange, judging look, as if she were weighing her in a balance, unable to make up her mind about something. Two or three times more she brought the mirror out and made them look.

"It makes me frightened," Sara whispered.

"What do you see? Tell me!"

"A grey house." Trying to see Spain, Pablito, Doña Ana. But only the grey house, the old blind man.

She tried again to make the captain tell her about Mrs. Talbot, coming at the question sideways, by way of Old John the gardener, Mrs. Talbot's half-brother. "All he'll say about her is '*Her!* I never held with her. Uppish from young.' He's so funny." But the captain seemed genuinely to know nothing about Mrs. Talbot, beyond the gossip, and not as much of that as Sara knew. Not nearly as much. She thought at times the captain knew far less about the real Thaxstone than she did herself.

"Heavens, child, what more should I know about her, the poor old creature?"

She had to hold herself back from crying out in protest at that description of Mrs. Talbot. "But when she was young?"

"How the devil should I know? Except that Lord Southcott, not this fellow now, his grandfather, yes, his grandfather, took her into the hall as a servant, as a maid to his own daughter. It was that that started all the gossip, of his being her father. Goddammit, the malice people have! A kindly action, and there was his thanks for it!"

"But maybe it was true?"

"Sara! A man to take his—his—such a child—into his own house to—to mix with his lawful children? You don't know what you're speaking of! Thank God you don't! And I am very wrong to be talking to you of such things. If they should hear us. Come, read the *Gazette* to me again. Farmers' riots? God above! What do farmers have to riot about in Heaven's name? I think sometimes the world has gone quite mad."

She felt an added tenderness for him these days. Not only that he was grown so ill, but that it had made him so helpless against Miss Susannah. She treated him more and more as nothing but a privileged guest, a valued lodger, who must be well cared for and considered always—but who had no real part in the house, no roots in it, even though he was its owner; even though she made an elaborate, cool parade of treating him as its master.

And she made it even more clear that Sara, too, was only a visitor, and only by reason of the captain's wish. Not that she herself wanted to be anything else, and she was almost grateful that Miss Susannah made no charade, like Miss Hetty, of drawing her into the family, making her one of them, however junior. But she made it so patent, at least to her, that her future lay outside the family, outside these four walls, that it created a constant uneasiness.

Even Miss Hetty with her botany lessons, enchanted to find Sara could recognise flowers and herbs after only one telling, although she could never remember their Latin names ("No, no, dear, we do not call it *that!* That is only a foolish country name, Devil's Bit Scabious! It is *Scabiosa succisa pratensis*")—even Miss

Hetty let it be understood how valuable an accomplishment botany might be for a young woman with her living to earn. "Of course, dear, as Susannah says, there's not a doubt in the world but you will be married, but one can never tell. In these days men look first for such things as dowries, I'm afraid. For so many things other than mere virtue, or even beauty. But you are so young yet, what nonsense we are talking about marriages! Now, child, what is this one?" And she would turn the page to another brown, pressed flower and its name in copperplate Latin and its particularities. Although none of them the particularities Sara had already learned from Mrs. Talbot.

But there always seemed to be a curious undertone to the hints of marriage, as though there was something else that lay behind them.

"I shall never marry," she said to Molly. "They are always hinting and pushing at it, as though they think that is the only way they will ever get rid of me."

"Go 'way, you silly, it's not that! They do be scared stupid you could up an' marry the captain, an' be mistress here an'—Oh, Lawd, have mercy, what a joke that'd be. I can see Peg's face, an' Miss Susannah, an' even Miss Hetty. She may like you better'n Miss Susannah do, but she don't fancy calling you Mistress Pownall, an' you keepin' the keys an' all! None of 'em don't fancy that!"

"Molly!" Looking at her more amazed than horrified, trying to take in what Molly had said, what she meant. "Marry the captain? But—but you must be mad!"

"I'm not thinkin' it, but they are. Day an' night, I reckon. They do look at you times—"

"But he's—he's like my—my—It's horrible, horrible."

"He's not so old as all that. Just sick a bit, with the fever, an' so cold here after bein' out to Spain an' hot places. He's not so old as Lord Southcott, an' he did marry his second lady when she were only sixteen, just a li'l bit more than us."

"They *couldn't* think it! They couldn't!" Yet it stayed in her mind like poison, and even when she was sitting with the captain, reading to him or letting him tell her of old times, Sara thought she could feel their hostility, their fears, reaching through the door to them, listening, watching. It drove her away from him, away from the house, so there should be no least suspicion that anything so dreadful was in her mind. And only Molly, and Mrs. Talbot, made her life endurable.

The snow that winter lay thick only for a week or two, turned grey. The snowdrops came, the crocuses, and then the daffodils Old John had planted under the chestnut trees in the paddock. At Candlemas, while the snow still lay thick as fleece on the ridge, and they had had to struggle kneedeep in it to reach her cottage, Mrs. Talbot gave them the ointment again. This time they had knelt very quietly by the fire and smeared it on each other's bodies gently, without joking or playing, their hearts already pounding before the action of the drug began, as though they were frightened and at the same time longing for what would happen.

And again they lay and dreamed, locked together, the sweat running on their shoulders, on their breasts, their breath gasping, shuddering with the ecstasies of their dreams, their legs twitching as though they were trying to dance, to run, the covers wrapped round them like clutching hands, like lovers, until Molly cried, "Oooohh," in a long whimpering gasp of love and lay limp as a doll, and Sara's head rolled, lay on her shoulder, her arms clinging to her, until they both woke in the small, small hours with that shock of cold. The covers fallen away, their skins pricked with graveyard shiverings.

In the kitchen Peg seemed to avoid them now, almost to be afraid of them. "She's not pulled my hair in weeks," Molly said. "I do think she knows!"

"There's nothing to know," Sara said harshly. "Nothing." And it seemed to both of them she used Mrs. Talbot's exact tone of harshly scolding voice as she said it, and Molly stared at her in astonishment.

It was a month or so later that the news came of Bonaparte's escape from Elba. A man rode by on the way from Urnford into Thaxstone and stopped at the gate crying, "Boney's escaped! The old Devil is 'scaped off Elba and is landed to France, an' 'tis war ag'in." He rode on like a man who knows the world is waiting for his news, the captain leaning out of the window crying after him, "What is that? Escaped? Bonaparte escaped, you say?" And even the women of the house were excited.

For another month it was as though the captain was grown strong once more, as he had when Captain Varley's letter came. She found him one day cleaning his pistols, and he looked at her over them half shame-faced and half excited and said, "Who can tell, child?" He didn't ask whether the post had come, but about the time it should arrive he took to walking in the garden, and he began talking to her of Spain, instead of the old, good days in Thaxstone. Of the times he'd spoken with the duke, long before he was a duke! "He chose me himself, you know, for Spain. 'Give me Pownall,' he said. 'This one and that one too, but make sure Pownall is among 'em.' Maybe he'll remember me. If he has need of that kind of service."

He talked of other kinds of service as well, of going to London and asking Mr. Hampton if he could obtain him a commission in one of the line regiments. "God knows, child, it wouldn't be much to ask, after thirty years?" But he didn't go. Dr. Newall came, and Dr. Malthus, and sometimes Mr. Cameron from the hall, a thin, hollow-cheeked Scotsman with sparse hair and a lawyer's look rather than a steward's. They talked of politics and strategy and the czar instead of poor relief and the rates and for once the captain joined in as a full partner, and told them what Bonaparte would try to do and how the duke would stop him, and what the duke had done at Torres Vedras and how he had forced the Pyrenees.

But although the two clergymen and the steward listened to him politely, it seemed to Sara they were a shade impatient with him, as though even his knowl-edge of war was long out of date and they knew much better than he did what the duke would do, and Blücher, and the czar, and Bonaparte.

And no letter came, and the two pistols were locked away in the captain's desk. It was May, and then June, and just before Mid-summer's Eve the same messenger, or a man so like him as to be his brother, went galloping by Lavender Cottage crying, "Victory, victory, Boney is beat and the duke has won! The French are beat, lads! 'Tis victory!"

All the church bells ringing.

The captain went out to listen to them. The bells of Thaxstone Church, and even of Crouch five miles away, carrying to them on the summer wind, and in imagination even from Urnford, even from London. All the bells of England ringing for that great victory, and the guns sounding. Sara found him not in the roadway but in the paddock, under the trees, the old pony near him, nuzzling at his coat.

" 'Tis all done now," he said. "There'll be true peace at last." He held some withered, shrivelled horse chestnuts in his hand, and was looking down at them.

"We used to thread these on strings when we were boys," he said, "and have great fights with them. Jack and I." He threw them down into the long grass, sighing.

"They're making a bonfire on the green," Sara told him. "Can we go down and see it tonight?"

"Aye, aye. Oh, aye, yes, we must. There will be great happenings tonight. We must all go and join in the fun."

But Dr. Newall visited them that evening and there was no more talk of going.

"They're behaving outrageously already," Dr. Newall said, his rosy, kindly face tight and almost pale with anger. "I told Cameron he was mad to give them so much ale, no matter what Lord Southcott may have ordered. They're bad enough with what they'll buy of themselves, without Cameron's free casks. I tried to remonstrate with them, but they're past all bounds of respect long since. It will be days before there's a man or woman of them fit to work again, to say nothing of attending divine service."

"Leave them be, man," the captain said. "When I was a lad, it needed less than such a victory as this to set the whole village feasting and dancing till they fell senseless in the grass. A cricket match would be enough."

"I trust we've progressed somewhat since those days," Miss Susannah said. "And indeed, their wages must be far more than sufficient if they can afford such extravagance. You are too kind to them, Dr. Newall."

"The price of bread is so risen," Dr. Newall said defensively, "almost to a shilling now—but we—I am trying to abate their wages. And I shall speak to Cameron very strongly after this disgraceful episode, and to Colonel Sampson and one or two more, and we shall take strong steps, I promise you."

Sara went out to help with the supper preparations and whispered to Molly, "We must go down to the green after they go to bed and see what's happening," and it seemed to her that supper had never been so long in being eaten, and talked over, and that Dr. Newall had never delayed so long before drawing out his gold repeater from his waistcoat pocket and saying, "My goodness, 'tis past nine! What hours you do make me keep with all your good talk and hospitality!"

But at last the house was quiet and bolted, and they were able to creep down to the back door, Peg already snoring. Out into the kitchen garden and then the roadway, which was still almost light, the last of the evening sky like turquoise, the hedges full of summer flowers that were still half open, spilling warm scents among the shadows. They ran like the wind, afraid all would be over, but half-way to the village they could hear the sounds of voices, drunken singing, the banging of a mallet against an empty barrel for a makeshift drum, the thin sound of a flute, and they could see the light of the bonfire blazing.

On the green, outside the Dragon and Horseman, next to the churchyard, they had set out trestle tables for a hundred and fifty, two hundred people. Everyone for miles round who could walk and drink had come, and half of them were already past walking, lying scattered on the ground, grinning at nothing, snoring, still trying to sing, rolled onto their faces under benches, under the tables, lying against the stone wall of the churchyard still clutching their quart pots. On the tables the remains of the feast lay scattered, broken crusts of bread, ham bones and mutton bones and beef ribs torn from the two oxen Mr. Cameron and Colonel Sampson had given, which had been roasted whole over the bonfire, with half a dozen sheep and piglets. Cheese rinds and onion skins and apple cores, survivors of last year's apple crop; jugs of cider lying empty, and the hardy drinkers still staggering towards the barrels with their pots to refill and drink again and sing and shout with laughter and cut another slice of beef from the wrecked and smoking ruins of the roasted carcasses. Dancers trying to dance, swaying opposite one another, falling into one another's arms and hiccuping with laughter. Joseph Goatlake climbing onto one of the tables, staggering among the leftovers, his mother laughing up at him, clapping her hands.

The two girls were recognized, dragged towards the bonfire, ale mugs pushed into their hands. "Drink pretty ones, drink to us! Up Thaxstone forever!" Mrs. Talbot, not drunk at all, but laughing, as if she was young, leaning on Jim Lightharness' arm, watching three couples trying to dance, seeing the two girls there and smiling at them in welcome. The flames of the bonfire leaping, falling, filling the green with light and now with dark. A woman shouting "Eh, bor! Eh!" as a man tried to tear her dress down from her shoulders, running from him, laughing like a mad thing, her hair falling, the man staggering after her, clutching. Couples disappearing into the shadows, arms round waists, and kissing, the boys' hands already fumbling at bodices, looking back to see if they were out of sight of the tables.

Sara and Molly drank their ale. Two men came staggering and caught them, swung them round, and Molly pushed her man so that he tottered back five yards and fell on his back crying, "Give me a kiss, li'l pretty, 'tis my right o' victory!" Sara slid out of her attacker's arms, breathless, half with laughter, half with the beginnings of fright, and ran and was caught by Molly's father, speechless drunk, standing like a tree with wavering branches that he clapped round her as she stumbled into him. "Ah, ah, ah," he mumbled, staring at her with eyes like blind pools of rain. "Ah, ah, ah." She tried to free herself, the fright gathering in her throat, becoming real, and he seemed bewildered, as if he didn't know he was holding her, why she was pushing at him, hammering against his chest with her fists.

" 'Tis Sara, 'tis Miss Sara, Dad!" Molly shouted at him, managed at last to pry his arms loose, and he turned round and round with his arms wavering again while they ran away from him. A couple lying in a depth of shadow far beyond the bonfire, clasped together, the woman's face a sudden pale glisten of joy as a flame lifted, threw its light on her, the man's back humped over her, half naked.

"We'd best go home," Sara whispered, stunned by the savagery of passion round them, as though it had escaped from their dreams, become real and terrible and monstrous.

"Just look at 'em," Molly whispered. "Right to brim they are, maybe we best go after all."

But up on the churchyard mound there were other dancers, and the flute playing, only shadows in the dark there, beyond the light of the bonfire, and as they went to look, hands caught their sleeves, voices whispered, "Come and dance with us, quick, come and dance," and they were drawn into the chain, the flute playing ahead of them, a small, thin tune that made the blood shiver and the skin prick.

Into the churchyard, round the gravestones, round the old cross with no arms, in and out, the flute playing, the chain swaying, bending, each dancer holding the shoulders or the waist of the dancer in front of him, in front of her, until with a skipping of his feet the flute player was on the sloping roofstone of a half-buried vault, squatting cross-legged like a tailor, and as she danced by him, round him, Sara recognised the bellows-boy from the forge, his eyes glinting, reddened, his head nodding, the pipe lifting and bobbing.

One of the women hooded, Mrs. Talbot. She knew her by the green gown, the leather girdle, the tallness of her, holding out her arms, turning round and round. "Hoodman blind! Hoodman blind!" The dance breaking, like a flight of rooks on the wind, here and there among the gravestones, in and out, in and out, touching Mrs. Talbot's shoulders, tugging at her skirt, and her arms groping, turning, as she stepped among the graves, a flare of light from the bonfire lifting, throwing shadows, dancing shadows, and then falling, leaving all in darkness, shadows upon shadows, the gravestones like white fingers in the dark and the dancers running, the flute still playing, swift and wild.

Making a circle round Mrs. Talbot, round and round, crying, "Hoodman, hoodman, choose a one!" Mrs. Talbot's arms outspread. And behind Sara someone pushed her, hands flat against her shoulders, the small of her back, and she went stumbling into Mrs. Talbot's arms. In terror for a second, the blind hood, the tallness, the groping arms that folded round her, held her, as though it were not Mrs. Talbot, but a strange woman, and this not a game.

The hands felt her face, her hair, the familiar rough finger-tips, and yet unfamiliar, cold.

" 'Tis Sara," Mrs. Talbot cried, her voice muffled. " 'Tis Pownall's Sara!" She pulled off the hood and it was over Sara's head, the folds warm with Mrs. Talbot's breath, and she was in pitch dark, stifled, groping with her hands, twisted round and falling, stumbling, tipped by hands that held her up, pushed her sideways, the ground slanting under her feet, the sound of the piping muffled, distant, now near, now far. Hands at her hood, her skirt, tugging and pulling, her own hands reaching, grasping, finding no one. Until again someone came behind her, twisted her round, pushed her, and she stumbled forward, arms outstretched, touched a body, closed her arms on a man's shoulders, held him as he tried to run away.

She heard through the folds of the hood a quick gasp of breath, touched a face, a mouth, eyes, with her finger-tips, knew who it was, and shuddered with a kind of terror.

"Guess who 'tis, Hoodman, guess who 'tis!"

She didn't want to say and said in her harsh mimicry of Mrs. Talbot, "Joseph Goatlake. The hoodman chooses you."

She pulled off the hood and he stared at her, his eyes reflecting the fire and his face almost pale, twisted with something that was trying to seem mockery. And that glitter of the firelight in his eyes like fear. Then his mother was at his shoulder. She tore the hood out of Sara's hand and pulled it on her own head, pushed her son away from her, tried to grasp Sara, and Sara ran and ran, all the dancers running, hiding behind the gravestones, only the bellows-boy still keeping his seat on the sloping stone of the vault, his music mocking, teasing. Behind a gravestone hands grasped Sara against an enormous chest, crushed her against shadow, and Jim Lightharness kissed her, his lips so cold they were like the gravestone her hand was touching. She could not move, not stuggle, not breathe.

He let her go and she fell; he supported her, brushed his huge hand over her face. " 'Tis only sport," he whispered. "Only sport, girl. No more." But it was not only sport and she wanted to scream for Molly, for both of them to run, escape out of the graveyard, run home to safety. And Mrs. Goatlake's shadow lifted enormous against the wall of the church, shrank down to a humped monstrosity, vanished, and she was groping, reaching, and the terror of being caught closed Sara's throat. She thought then, *She's trying to find Molly, she wants Molly*. She didn't know how she knew it, why, but she knew it, and began to run, hunting for Molly among the dancers, among the stones, and found her crouched behind the bellows-boy, the music maker, and knew that she was frightened too, so frightened she couldn't speak, only look at Sara with huge eyes, hold her hands.

"Let's run," Sara whispered, and they ran and Joseph Goatlake caught at them, cried out, "They're running away, here, here they are!" Sara pushed him, his heels catching on a buried stone, throwing him off balance for a moment and they were over the wall and running. When they looked back, they saw the dance continuing, the flames dying now in the bonfire, the shadows of the dancers almost lost in the darkness of the graveyard, the music a thin thread of echoes, nothing, only in their minds.

The next day no one worked in Thaxstone except those who were too educated to have gone to the bonfire celebrations. Labourers stumbled round, foggy with hangovers, or tottered into the Dragon and Horseman for revivers, or stayed at home groaning. Women dragged themselves to the pump for water and had to sit on their upturned buckets half-way there. Girls went slowly about the place with sleepy eyes and fulfilled and sauntering bodies, and stood for long minutes staring at nothing or at the still-smouldering scar of the bonfire on the green, at the litter of bread and bones and bottles and refuse that covered the grass where the tables had been, or at some more hidden corner that held memories for them. As though not the duke's victory but mid-summer had touched Thaxstone for a night and transfigured it with pleasure.

Dr. Newall threatened to have the green ploughed up, as he'd had the cricket field ploughed up years earlier, because of the scandals cricket caused. He let it be known that the names of those who were not at work were being noted, and woe to any of those names that came looking for poor relief next winter. He also let it be known that the whole monstrous affair had shown him once and for all that wages were too high.

All that autumn a sullen argument smouldered as to wages, between the farmers and the labourers, the news of Bonaparte's flight and exile no more than a far-off echo against the price of bread and corn. The farmers rioted widespread against the import of cheap corn, and the labourers began to gather themselves against the selling of expensive bread. In November Colonel Sampson's flour mill at Thorpe was attacked. The flour was brought out into the road and given to anyone who came with the means of carrying it away. And a fortnight after that Dr. Newall's barns were burned to the ground. A notice pinned to the church door read:

You may except wurs next time for you ar a

dam bad un that preech slaverie to All and drinks and eats heartie wile poer people is starving an ha no worke to doe but must go on the parysh an hav charitye. Go an preeche that the meschiens be dun awaye with an por peeple get Work an Bread. An rite wages for work, not giv as Releif. Iffen we doent get cheep Bread ther shall be Bloode and burnyng all round an a great bussel agen all you gentlement to brake your skulls and kicke yr brains about. Find out whoe dun this if you have the witt.

A troop of yeomanry rode in from Urnford and for two days was quartered in Thaxstone, finding nothing and riding away again to the bitter pleasure of the poor. There was worse trouble farther north, in Suffolk and Norfolk and Cambridgeshire, and the yeomanry were needed elsewhere. The *Gazette* was full of stories of ricks burned and machines and mills broken, of farmers attacked in their farm-houses and dragged out to sign agreements concerning wages. Of millers and bakers threatened with burning. Of discussions in Parliament about the corn laws, which would keep up the price of grain for farmers and drive the price of bread still higher.

"It is the men come back from the war," the captain said. "Fellows like this Daniel Blogg and his cousin John Porter." It was as though the victory and midsummer had never been and the winter came on Thaxstone with a creeping hunger, as visible as the white frost on the paddock, as the black films of ice on the marshes. It seemed to Sara, without knowing how she knew it, that the village was gathering itself for a purpose, for one tremendous effort to break out of its misery. She felt aware of it even in Lavender Cottage, in the conversations at supper, the discussions of the news—or when Dr. Newall came, or Dr. Malthus, or their other occasional visitors. Conversations in which the misery was never recognised, only the outrages, the ingratitude, the extraordinary fact that peace after twenty years and more of warfare should bring such troubles.

She felt almost a sense of disloyalty to the captain, as if they were choosing sides in a great, coming

89

struggle, and she couldn't choose his side. *He doesn't know*, she thought miserably. *He doesn't know anything about them.*

"It is a conspiracy," Dr. Newall said. "I've written to Lord Sidmouth himself to warn him of it. A widespread plot. I've seen lights burning at night in huts far out in the marshes where by all decent reckoning they couldn't afford candles for longer than to go to their beds like Christians. I tell you, Pownall, it's more than my barns that are threatened."

He'd grown pallid and sickly since the burning of his barns and his hand trembled as it held his wineglass. The rosy flush had gone out of his cheeks and their plumpness had fallen into flaccid, half-empty purses, as though he had aged ten years in a few weeks. "We need some exemplary hangings," he said, a wine drop spilling on his black knee-breeches. "The devil's abroad among them."

"It is this fellow Blogg," the captain said. "Oh, I grant you your conspiracy, Newall, no doubt of it. But that makes it the more urgent to crush it everywhere it shows its tentacles. The local ringleader here is Daniel Blogg. Arrest him and, at least as far as Thaxstone is concerned, you have the thing by the throat. And you may learn much else of what is being plotted in a dozen other villages like ours."

"Aye, aye," Dr. Newall said, his hand shaking more. "But one must have a reason, Pownall. Some legal proof of his ill-doing. You and I know full well the brute is guilty of a hundred crimes in the few months he's been home. And John Porter with him. And the Goatlakes. And that they may well be in touch with God knows what other ruffians throughout the county and farther afield still. But what proof have I, that would satisfy his lordship? We magistrates lack proper powers, we are tied hand and foot, Pownall."

"Mr. Cameron tells me that poaching has gone beyond all bounds," Miss Susannah said. "It's like warfare, he says."

"Aye, that too!" cried Dr. Newall. "They begin as poachers and end as murderers, and in no long time. Now that Lord Southcott is become a minister, perhaps we shall see new laws against poaching. The poor man has suffered enough from their depredations. No more than six months in prison for a first offender, unless he uses violence! It's a holiday for them, they laugh at it! And if he's caught again, why, even then a mere two years of so-called hard labour and a whipping. They think nothing of it. Unless any poacher can be hanged, or at the least transported for life, property can't be safe. First they take up a sack of pheasants, and next they burn my barns, and after that, who can tell what dreadful abomination may come?"

The strange thing was that whereas Dr. Newall seemed to have grown old with his fears and his lost stores, the captain seemed this time truly to have got back his vigour and his health. He talked eagerly of how conspiracies must be combatted, how one finds spies and agents to break the secrecy, how one sets one leader against another until the conspiracy falls of its internal divisions, as the great mutinies had done, and the Irish Rising of '98, and his own attempts, his and Wickam's, to create a rising in the Cevennes against the Directory. He talked again of going up to London, and held councils of war with Dr. Newall and Mr. Cameron, who came to Lavender Cottage for the occasion.

"I have advised my lord and her ladyship that they shouldn't come to the hall for the Christmas festivities," Mr. Cameron said. "But I'm afraid her ladyship is not a young noblewoman to be advised on such matters."

In fact she came to the hall the next week, with three carriages loaded with her trunks and portmanteaux, and her maid and her hairdresser and a little black page who rode in the light, closed phaeton with her ladyship, his chocolate face and rounded eyes staring out the window. And two days after that Sara and Molly on their way to Mrs. Grimmer's saw her out riding, like a gold and lilac arrow on a black horse, her face pale white, her hair a cold fire of gold under the tight tricorn hat, the lilac skirt of her habit spreading flat along the black glisten of the horse's flank.

Two grooms rode behind her, galloping to keep pace

with their mistress, and in a few moments all were by and gone, no more than three silhouettes against the dark bulk of Little Wood, the sounds of their hoof-beats thudding and fading.

"Ohhhhh," Molly whispered, staring after her. "They do say her stepson fare to be older 'n her! Imagine that! An' he calling her Ma!" She looked at Sara. "I told you. That's what they do be afraid of with you, Miss Susannah an' all of 'um."

"You'll make me angry if you talk about that again," Sara answered harshly, and they said nothing more until they reached Miss Bowdeker's cottage, and Mrs. Grimmer's beside it.

They went on from Mrs. Grimmer's to Mrs. Talbot, and sat by the fire while she made them tea and Robert stared at them with his amber, considering eyes.

"Why did you come back here?" Sara said. Hardly knowing why she asked it, why she asked it then. As though the sight of Lady Southcott had put the question in her mind. She had tried many times to get Mrs. Talbot to tell her more of her life when she'd been away from Thaxstone, but all she had ever learned were those half stories of the journey to India, hints of other travelling, of the Welsh mountains, of France before there was a war or a revolution. Of Italy. But never of who she might have been travelling with, whether she had ever been truly married. Her village title of Mrs. was no more than Mrs. Hobhouse's, merely an indication of respect.

"Where else would I go?" Mrs. Talbot said, her voice impatient. "I belong here." She gave Sara her tea and one of the small flat cakes. "You have to go back where you belong."

"I belong in Spain," Sara said.

"Do you?"

"Of course I do." And then, almost hoping Mrs. Talbot would take out the mirror. "Shall I—Do you think I shall go back there? One day?"

"Maybe," Mrs. Talbot said, not looking at her. And then impatiently, with that harsh, half-angry voice, "How should I know?"

"I cannot stay here."

"Some are born for long roads."

"Doña Ana said that," Sara whispered. "She said that I was like them, like the gypsies, that I was born to follow the road."

"Will I go anywhere?"

"Oh, you!" Mrs. Talbot said, reached out, and touched her. "You! Aye, you'll go. You'll not find all those fine dresses here with us. You'll go all right. And forget everything I've ever taught you." Her smile strange, almost hurt as she said the words, and yet so fond it was as though Molly was her child, her grandchild.

"And—shall I forget everything?"

Mrs. Talbot looked at Sara, the smile gone, frowning. "You will forget nothing. Nothing. Ever."

Sara put up her hand slowly to her throat, tried to laugh.

Mrs. Talbot looked away from her. "Such nonsense! Clear up these things and get home with you before it grows dark."

It was after another visit to her, at night this time, that they saw the captain. Barely a hundred yards from Lavender Cottage, coming out onto the road from the gateway of a field, turning to his left, away from them, and walking swiftly down the road, in the shadow of the hedge. Only like a darker shadow himself, at first, simply a man. Sara had gripped Molly's arm, made her stop. The moon came into a gap of clouds and filled the road with light. And they saw that it was the captain, striding there ahead of them, the familiar, solid figure, the low-crowned hat and broad shoulders, and the heavy cudgel he used as a walking stick.

"What's he doin' this time of night?" Molly breathed. Sara guessed but said nothing, kept her hand on Molly's arm. The captain was almost home, the path hidden below the wall of the kitchen garden, black with shadow. They heard the garden door open and close.

"He'll bolt the back door!" Molly whispered. "What'll we do?"

They were at the garden door, listening, heard

nothing, and crept in. The chickens stirring. The house dark above them.

"Is your window open?" Sara said against Molly's ear. Molly's own garret was at the very back of the house, above their heads, above the roof of the back house room and the coolroom, its window no more than a skylight let into the slope of the roof.

"I 'spect it is," Molly breathed. "If I leaves it shut old Peg do open it just for spite. I 'spect 'tis open. But what good's that?"

"I'll climb up."

Molly clung to her. "Are you mad? You cain't climb up there! You'll break your neck."

"I won't, and we can't stay down here." She took off her cloak, gave it to Molly, and felt over her head for the rain gutter. She thought again and took off her boots; then with a swift wrench of pleasure she pulled off her frock as though she were dragging off a year of slavery in one scornful movement. She stood in her petticoat and shift and stockings, and would almost have stripped herself to the skin but for the cold, as if she wanted to throw off everything that belonged to this house.

"Sara!" Molly whispered. "Don't try! You'll fall for certain sure and kill yourself dead."

Sara gripped the gutter again, felt for a window ledge with her toe, was up onto the back house roof, onto the higher roof of the coolroom, hearing Molly gasping with terror. She whispered, "Ssssshhhh." Imagined Mrs. Hobhouse, Miss Susannah leaning out of a back window and seeing her shadow, screaming, "Burglars, thief! Help!" She felt savage with joy, with the sense of danger, the slates rough and then slippery with frost under her stockinged feet. She hooked her elbow over the ridge of the coolroom roof, pulled off her stockings and wound them round her throat like a scarf, feeling the icy slates with her bare feet as though they were mountain rocks. She wanted the climb to go on forever, up and up. Even the cold was beautiful, the breath of the wind against her body.

She found the down pipe from the highest gutters, from the valley of two slopes of roof, climbed it, had

94

her hand on the gutter, was up into the valley, could see the open skylight of Molly's attic above her, almost within reach of her finger-tips. She inched her way up the slates, held the edge of the skylight frame, and pulled herself level with it. Two minutes later she was easing back the bolts of the door beside the scullery, letting Molly in.

"I thought I'd die," Molly whispered. They stole up the stairs, a rim of candlelight under the captain's door. Held their breath, were safe. "Lord have mercy, Sara, just like a monkey you must be, I thought we were done proper."

After that they took the precaution of leaving a downstairs window unlatched. She realised the captain was going out almost every night and usually staying out much later than they ever did. The first time she kept herself awake to listen for his coming home she heard the clock strike three before there were the sounds of his careful tread on the landing below, the soft shutting of his door. She put on her nightgown and slippers and crept down to him, her heart beating. He was by the desk, putting away his pistols and taking out pens and a sheaf of writing paper, the candle and a chair set ready as though he intended to write immediately.

"What are you doing?" she whispered, her heart beating so loud he must hear. She put up her hand against it.

He had swung round and was staring at her, his face almost guilty and at the same time lit with pleasure, and she knew he felt exactly as she had felt climbing the roof wall half naked. Tried to be glad for him, to think, *It's like it used to be.*

"What the—Damnation, child! Why aren't ye asleep?"

"I heard you come in just now. What have you been doing?"

"I—Nothing, nothing child. Go back to bed. At once!"

She had closed the door behind her and went now to the almost dead fire and began to chafe it into life, laying splinters across the ashes and placing two small logs above them. Trying to behave as though it was quite natural for her to be there, for the two of them to be alone like this in the sleeping house. The flames caught and licked and crackled in the stillness. "Will I make some punch for you?" she whispered.

"Do you want to wake the whole house going down to the kitchen? Go to bed, I tell you." He had come over to the hearth beside her and bent down to catch her by the shoulders. "Suppose they heard us!"

He drew her upright and she stood looking down into his anxious face, the anxiety drawn like a curtain over the pleasure, the excitement. She was by now a half-head taller than he was, and it gave her a strange feeling of distance from him, as being an adult. And at the same time, fear. Of what she had done, of the things Molly had said, so stupid, so terrible. She wished she hadn't come down to him, and yet was held there by—She could not tell what she felt, her heart beating, a nerve seeming to keep time with it at one corner of her mouth.

"They'd think . . . ." he whispered.

"What should they think?"

He looked away from her. "Goddammit, do as you are bid, child. Go to bed. You—you will catch cold, you will—" He had let go of her, turned away to his desk, touched some papers there, and swung round on her again. "For God's sake, go!"

Two nights later Mrs. Talbot said to her, "Your captain is taking a dangerous path, I'm afraid. They are talking of him as a spy and of teaching him a lesson such as they taught Dr. Newall." She gave Sara a hard, frowning look that seemed to say more than her words.

Sara caught her breath, whispered, "You don't think . . ."

"No," Mrs. Talbot said harshly. "I do not think that. And what could you tell him if you would? That there are fools about who will come to hanging soon enough, whether your captain spies on them or no? He knows that already." She had drawn the silver-backed mirror out of the drawer and was staring down into it, frowning, her whole expression fierce with

96

anger. "There is nothing any of us can do," she said.

"If you could warn them," Sara said. She hesitated, not knowing what it was best to say. That the captain was writing his reports to London, to Mr. Hampton, and to the government? And have the house burned down for it? "If you could make them leave him alone," she breathed.

"How can I make them do that, girl? This isn't like Mrs. Goatlake's business."

"I know, I know. But she is in it? She and Joseph and—and Molly's father and—"

"Aye."

"Could you not—not tell them that—Oh, please, please, don't let them hurt him. He is—he is—he doesn't understand." And even that seemed like betrayal.

Molly listening, her face closed against revealing anything. As though what was coming had laid its shadow on all of them, divided them already.

"What can I tell them?" Mrs. Talbot said angrily. Sara caught at her hand, turned it over. The red mark glowed faintly on Mrs. Talbot's narrow wrist with its blue veins and thin, hard sinews.

"You said that if we—if we asked one another anything . . ."

"What do you fear, child? What should they do to him? Poor labouring men?" She jerked her wrist out of Sara's grasp, stood up, and swept the mirror into the drawer under the table. "You'd best be going home, it's late."

"But you said they're talking of—I am so afraid for him," Sara whispered. "Please—"

"You don't know what you're asking," Mrs. Talbot said. "If I were to—"

"If—"

"If I were to try to persuade them . . ." She looked down at Sara, the fierceness gone out of her expression, a kind of resignation in it as though Sara had persuaded her not only against her will but against something deeper still. "I may need to ask something very hard in exchange. Of you."

"Anything."

"I wonder." She frowned again and put away her book and spectacles beside the mirror. "I shall remind you of this when the time comes. Have I your promise?"

"I swear it."

"Then I will do what I can." She sat down, looking tired and old. "Now you'll be twice over in debt to me," she said. "Twice over. Remember that."

Chapter 8

The sense of trouble coming grew like thunder building in the air. News of worse rioting in Norfolk, in Cambridgeshire, spreading down into Suffolk, towards them. More ricks burned, more machines broken, flour mills attacked, farmers dragged out of doors and threatened, mobs gathering outside the bake houses, crying, "Bread or blood." A wing of Sutton Hall, which belonged to Lord Southcott's cousin, Lord Dartry, was burned to the ground and the damage reckoned at thirty thousand pounds, And that happened no more than twenty miles to the north of Thaxstone.

"God's teeth!" the captain cried, a brief letter from Mr. Hampton crushed in his fist. "He tells me, 'Lord Sidmouth is well informed of the situation and gives no credit to rumours of a widespread conspiracy. And as far as the Thaxstone district is concerned, His Lordship does not feel the circumstances justify the kind of preventive arrests you have advocated.' Blast and damn them both for their folly. Rumours! I write to them of what I've seen and heard, and they yawn of 'rumours.' And arrests not justified! Have they forgotten the Nore? Do they think these poor country simpletons would dare what they are daring if there weren't hidden forces moving them? God knows what may yet happen by reason of their blindness."

He banged his fist on the breakfast table and Miss Susannah shut her eyes, small red patches of anger on her flat grey cheeks. She said coldly, "You have been so long retired now, Joshua, they think perhaps that you imagine these things."

"They should all be hanged!" Miss Hetty cried, patting her mitten together like rabbits' paws. "To think of Sutton Hall! Poor, poor Lord Dartry! Such terrible destruction! Why didn't Lord Dartry's steward shoot the villains?"

"There's my Hetty," cried the captain, brought back to a semblance of good humour. Sara gathered up the dishes and put them on the sideboard ready for Peg and herself to carry away. She had given up all attempts to talk to him about any of the realities of Thaxstone. They used the same words and meant different things, and if he spoke of someone in the village, it was as though he was talking of someone she had never seen: not of the tall, red-headed ex-soldier Daniel Blogg, with his smile distorted by the sabre-cut he had got at Waterloo, and with his sudden hearty laugh and his fury at being sent out as a roundsman by Dr. Newall—sent from house to house like a child asking for a day's work here and a day's work there, chopping wood, sweeping, digging weeds, so that he might have his seven shillings a week relief money and keep his pregnant wife from starving. And his cousin John Porter with him. The other roundsmen went slouching along like sheep, dulled with hunger. But the cousins marched as though they were still in scarlet, in step, their heels ringing on the frost-bound road, their faces savage with humiliation.

"That red-headed devil Blogg and his cousin have joined the poachers now, I'm sure of it, and taught them still worse criminality. Cameron was telling me that a dozen of them set on five of his keepers the other night and beat them half senseless. It was sheer chance that one or more of the keepers weren't killed."

"Oh, mercy!" Miss Hetty cried. "We shall none of us be safe in our beds soon."

"And that old fool Newall still giving them parish money to spend on beer!"

"Joshua!" Miss Susannah said warningly, her eyes indicating Sara. "Dr. Newall is our friend and a clergyman."

"Then he should stick to his prayers," the captain said furiously, "and not try to be magistrate too. He's an old fool, Susannah. An old fool, I say. Hetty there would do better. Since his damned barns were burned he has no more spirit in him than a corpse."

It was later that same morning that Sara first heard of the plans for her going as under-governess or companion into a family. "Shall you like that, dear?" Miss Hetty said. "Dr. Malthus has promised to enquire for you and to recommend you. Although we—I—shall truly, truly miss you. Oh, dear, oh, dear, how sad life is—but—but—" Her eyes filling with tears.

Sara had stared at her, unable to answer, and without a word had turned and run up to the captain's room, where he was writing one of his endless, fruitless reports to Mr. Hampton, to Lord Sidmouth himself, to old acquaintances in the service. "Miss Hetty says that—that I am to be—"

She realised that he knew. She felt suddenly cold, stiff with a kind of shock, so she could not continue. "You want me to—I am to be sent away?"

The age had come back into his face. He was an old man, turned round from his writing desk, facing her but not meeting her eyes. Staring over her shoulder at God knew what. "Sara," he said in a strange, croaking voice she didn't recognise. "Child." And then, "It's best. What should you do here?"

"They are *making* you send me away," she cried, and wanted to fling herself against his knees, hold him. But she couldn't move, was held stiff by shock, by an agony of pride and betrayal. "Do you want me to go?"

"It's best for you," he said again in a dull tone. "You—you must meet people—must have—see—

100

Goddammit, Goddamn and blast Hetty for a blabbing wretch. I didn't mean that you should—"

"You didn't mean me to know in advance?"

"Not like that, child. Don't twist my meaning. These things are best done quick," he said, his voice falling to a whisper, looking down at the carpet by her feet now. He looked up suddenly and met her eyes. "If it were up to me, you should never go, I swear it. But I'm a selfish old fool and they know best for you, I recognise it. You must have young people about you, must have a chance of marriage." He held out his hands. The same image in both their minds. The road out of Badajoz, long ago. In moonlight. The captain riding east towards Mérida and Madrid. And looking back to see her running. Running after him. A small, lost shadow on the road. Running. Stumbling.

And he had ridden back towards her, taken her up onto Rinaldo's back, held her there. Small, thin body trembling with exhaustion, soaked with sweat, filthy in the yellow cotton dress. She remembered the sense of triumph, the pain of breathing, his hands lifting her. Long, long ago. And now . . .

He held out his hands to her and she wanted to take them, wanted again to fall on her knees at his side and kiss his hands and beg him not to send her away. But she couldn't do it, and she turned and went out.

That evening the rioting began. Over a donkey and two thin cows and a pig. Their owners had turned them out along the road to find what grass they could by the sides. And Dr. Newall and Mr. Cameron drove by in Mr. Cameron's gig and saw the animals and had them driven to the pound. An hour later Mr. Cameron sent a plough team to plough up the roadsides so no other vagrant animals should find a meal there. It might also have been in his mind that their owners would then give up keeping them, together with such pretensions to independence as a cow or a pig or a donkey might give a labourer.

That night the pound was attacked, and the pound keeper had his head broken. The church windows were smashed and a mob formed on the green to march to the rectory and burn Dr. Newall in his bed.

Sara and Molly watched them from behind the graveyard wall, half terrified, half trembling with excitement, some of the mob already drunk, staggering one against another, cudgels waving, bill-hooks endangering a neighbour's skull, here and there the muzzle of a fowling-piece jutting up from the dark mass of men and women.

"Burn the old bastard, burn 'em alive, lads!"

Daniel Blogg came out of the Dragon and Horseman waving a sheet of paper in his hand. "Friends! Comrades! Brothers and sisters! Listen to me, listen! There is word from Crouch! They're coming to aid us if we'll but wait for them and do this right. And more from Burleigh and Littleton and farther off still. They've sent us a proclamation that has been printed out in Ipswich for all the labourers of England. It is rebellion, lads, rebellion! We shall have justice if we but go about it right."

"Read us the proclamation, read it to us, Dan'l! Shout 'em out, boy."

Daniel Blogg standing bare-headed, his hair like the fire of the ricks, tall and scarred and furious with excitement. "Right friends, here it is. 'We the free labouring men of England have been robbed of our rights. Our common land, which was ours since Adam, has been taken from us and fenced against us and it is prison for us if we set foot in it, and lift up a fallen branch from the ground, or take a rabbit to feed our children. Even the labour of our arms and bodies is now taken from us by insensible machines and we are put out to charity or let starve to death in corners.

" 'We say to you gentlemen, and to you farmers, who have robbed us of our very lives, that we will have bread or blood. That we will have a fair wage for fair work and no charity nor scorn. Let the machines and mills be done away with so we may work for our bread.

" 'We say to the millers and the bakers that we do also mean to have that bread at the old rate and flour at two shillings and sixpence the stone, so that we who do grow the grain may have our share of it. We have starved too long and become slaves and now mean to be free again. On which we set our oath this day at Ipswich, the ninth of April in the year of Our Lord 1816. Amen.' "

The mob roared, "Hurrah, hurrah for the Ipswich men." "Hurrah for Thaxstone." "Hurrah for Crouch." The landlord of the Dragon and Horseman and two of his men came struggling out with a barrel of ale and a trestle, his wife following them with a vast burden of mugs held together by a string through their handles.

"Come drink, lads!" the landlord cried. "Hurray for Thaxstone."

"Listen, listen, men," Daniel roared. "All must be done right. Drink now and hearty, but tomorrow, come dawn, be here with clear heads and strong hearts and we shall teach the gentlemen such a lesson as shall set our names up in the history books and bring us our desires. We must form strong columns, each with its officer. While you drink now, elect the officers who shall lead you tomorrow, and I shall instruct them how we are to act. Those who have no weapons, run home and get what you can. Pitchfork or bill-hook or cudgel, let each man get something. And each woman too. And sheaves of straw for burning, and each officer to have flint and steel. Listen to me, listen."

They were already round the ale cask, the mugs overflowing. Strong ale, not the weak beer they drank at harvest in the fields. Ale like brandy with a mule's kick in each mug.

"Hurrah for Dan'l!"

"An' for John Porter!"

"An' Joseph Goatlake! Hurrah for the poachers!"

Daniel Blogg striding among them like a burning tree. "Listen to me! Those with fowling-pieces are to share themselves out among the officers. And if the yeomanry come—"

"T'hell with the yeos! Damn 'em forever, blast and curse 'em."

A mass of men and women round the barrel, women with their hair loosened, men shouting, mugs upturned to empty their dregs into gaping mouths and throats.

103

"There's Missus Talbot!" Molly whispered. They saw her pushing her way through the crowd. "Talkin' to Mrs. Goatlake, ain't she?"

Daniel Blogg, still shouting, trying to make himself heard and heeded. ". . . the men with fowling-pieces in the rearmost rank. Rest your muzzles on the shoulder of the lad in front of you. And those with pitchforks kneel down before and jut 'em up at the horses' bellies. . . ."

"And there's my dad! Ooh, what they all going to do, Sara? 'Tis the end o' the world coming!"

Men came and went, more ale was brought out, the crowd began to spread over the green, an air of festival rather than of riot gripping some of the drinkers. A girl and a man locked together, swaying their mugs in the air, staggering towards the churchyard wall.

"We best go quick, Sara, lest they catch us peeping."

They crept away and ran, the noise of the mob dying behind them, and woke early the next morning to hear it again, closer now, the rumble of a loaded cart, the sound of shouting, "Bread or blood! Burn the old bastard, burn 'em!" The whole house awake, the women running, clutching their nightgowns round them—Miss Susannah, Miss Hetty, Peg, Mrs. Hobhouse, Molly, the only one already dressed, Sara, pulling on her gown, running down the stairs to the front door.

"What are you doing, Sara? Are you gone mad?"

She stood with her hand on the bolts, came slowly back to the foot of the stairs, Miss Susannah at the head, the captain just behind her, his hair rumpled, pushing his two pistols into his waistband.

"I was going out to look."

"Going out?" Miss Hetty screamed. "To unbolt the door! We'll all be murdered, murdered alive!"

The rumble and crunching of the cart-wheels, the thudding of marching feet. Sara ran into the parlour to the bow window and saw them passing, pitchforks sloping this way and that, a fowling-piece, another, Daniel Blogg's hair flaming, their heads just visible above the neat box hedge of the garden. Some of them shouting, "There he is, the spy. There's the spy-captain, burn 'em too."

The cart rumbling, armed with a giant duck gun, its muzzle slanting like a narrow cannon above the great haunches of the cart horse, shining chestnut in the morning light. A creak of wheels and harness.

"To Dr. Newall's, to the rectory, burn 'em alive!"

"They'll murder Newall!" the captain was crying. "I must go out and stop them, the devils. By God, they'll burn the poor wretch in his bed." Miss Hetty clung to him, whimpering, "They'll kill *you*, they'll murder us all!" But the crowd was already by, except for stragglers, and the captain broke away from her grasp.

"They'll not come here again, why should they? If they're looking for me as well as Newall, they'll find the pair of us together." He ran for the back door, through the kitchen, and was gone before any of them could do more than cry after him, "Joshua! Joshua!"

Miss Susannah stood for a moment in the hallway, her eyes shut with the effort of controlling her anger, Miss Hetty with trembling hands putting up the door chain that Sara had taken down, testing the bolts, still whimpering, repeating again and again, "The wretches, the villains, we must get word to—" But no name came to her mind.

"We must fasten all the shutters," Miss Susannah ordered. "Peg, Mrs. Hobhouse, see to the back door, and the windows there. We must put furniture against all the doors. Sara! Look to the parlour windows. Every last window must be shut and fastened, and the shutters—be sure that the bars are well pushed home. Molly, what are you doing? Go and see to the breakfast." She looked round for her sister. "Hetty? Let us get dressed. He didn't think to leave us so much as a pistol to defend our lives."

"A pistol!" cried Miss Hetty, wringing her soft old hands in despair and terror at the mere thought of such a weapon; her grey false fringe of curls shook under the edge of her white muslin night cap, her blue flannel dressing gown was wrapped round her like an ill-made parcel. "They'll cut our throats! Oh, how could Joshua leave us like this?"

"It's no more than I should have expected of him," Miss Susannah said. "Are all the upstairs windows fastened, Sara?"

"I'm going up to see."

They took breakfast as though they were in a fort in the Americas, Miss Susannah getting up every minute or two to listen at the shutters for the sounds of the mob returning, Miss Hetty refusing to sit down at all, her cheeks flushed with fear, trembling as she sipped her tea and nibbled at her toast, her sheep's eyes haunted by the expectation of butchery.

And they were still in the dining-room, as though unable to make up their minds to leave its safety, when there was the sound of running, a woman's voice crying, "Help, help!" and a banging at the front door. "Oh, help me, let me in. Oh, dear Miss Pownall, save me, let me in!"

"They've come back!" Miss Hetty screamed.

"It's Miss Stone," Sara said. "We must let her in."

"No, no, no. It may be a trick to capture us, Sara!"

"Of course we must let her in," Miss Susannah said. "Come, Sara." They went to the front door, Miss Susannah putting her hand on the chain and calling, "Miss Stone, is it you?"

"They are robbing and stealing and threatening; they're in the shop and will kill my father. Please, please, I shall die of fear."

Miss Susannah unfastened the chain and Sara drew the two bolts, top and bottom, and unlocked the door. Miss Stone came tottering in, clinging to the handle as though without its support she would have fallen at their feet. She was crimson in the face with running and with breathlessness and fright. "May Heaven preserve us all! They've gone mad, mad! Have they come this way?"

"Half an hour since."

"And where is the captain? If he'd only save my poor father! They've stolen all his hatchets and billhooks out of the shop, and the hams and cheeses and all the money in my box. They demanded five pounds."

"And did you give it to them?" Miss Hetty whispered from behind Sara's shoulders.

"I told them I had only three, and they took that and went off, and I fainted behind the counter." She threatened to faint again, and Miss Susannah and Miss Hetty supported her into the dining-room while Sara rebolted the door, locked it, and put up the chain.

"They are mad with drink and sedition," Miss Stone said, and collapsed into the captain's chair. She tried to hold a teacup in two tiny fat hands that threatened to spill the tea all over her mauve satin lap. She had run out without hat or bonnet or shawl or coat, and her buttons were wrongly fastened as though she too had been awakened by the noise of the mob and dressed with trembling fingers. "I saw one dreadful gang of them armed with a cannon going towards here and I thought, 'Oh, the dear, dear Misses Pownall will be murdered. Murdered dead!' " she cried, her accent dropping back into its native Essex for a moment.

"*One* gang?" Miss Susannah said. "Are there more of them?"

"Oh, a thousand, a thousand more. They are like an army, you cannot imagine the wickedness. That dreadful Daniel Blogg!"

"We saw him go by at their head just now."

"But there are others. John Porter was crying out like a—like a *Jacobin*—that they would burn Southcott Hall while Daniel Blogg and his ruffians burned the rectory. And there were others too, men I've never seen before. And they're going about the houses demanding money and food and saying they will break all the machines and burn down Colonel Sampson's flour mill and I don't know what. They're run mad. They will kill the king! Oh, oh, oh."

"If only the yeomanry were here again," Miss Susannah said. "They'd teach them a lesson."

"The dragoons!" cried Miss Hetty. "To put them all to the sword! They mustn't spare one of them, not one, the villains."

"Sara, go and make sure everything is secure at the

back, and then go up to your bedroom and look out and see if you can see or hear anything."

"Look out of the window?" Miss Stone cried. "Oh, mercy, don't let her."

"We have all the front windows of the house fast shuttered. Sara, run quickly."

She went down to the passage to the kitchen, and found Mrs. Hobhouse and Peg and Molly in much the same kind of conference as their mistresses, tea and bacon and bread on the table and an air of terror shot through with excitement.

"We are to go upstairs," she said to Molly, "to keep a lookout."

Peg watched them, her flat, slate-grey eyes seeming to accuse them both, to be saying, "I know what I know. I know what brought such evil down on us."

" 'Tis fierce sport, ain't it?" Molly whispered. "I did hear that old Miss Stone screeching like a pig. Do her good if they got her an' rumpled her petticoat a bit, the old sow."

"She gave them three pounds to go away."

"I wonder what old Dr. Newall'll have to give 'em afore they leave *him?* I seed my dad going along with Daniel, did you see 'em? Fare to makin' a soljer he looked, with a fowlin'-piece an' all, wherever he got it. Off o' Joseph Goatlake, likely. They do all have guns now, the poachers. Ohh, I wunner'll they come back?"

They hung out the window, straining their ears, their bodies squeezed together in the narrow opening. "They're all scared sick downstairs," Sara said. "Oh, I do wish he hadn't gone out. What do you think they'll do to Dr. Newall?"

"Give 'em a good roasting, likely. Serve 'em right, too, preachin' an' preachin' about God on Sunday an' sendin' folks to jail all the other days o' the week. I hate 'em an' his black breeches an' his li'l appley face. An' that old Mr. Cameron, I do hate 'em, too, like he's made o' dust or somethin'."

Half an hour, more, went by.

"Listen!" Sara whispered. "They're coming back!"

"No, no, they ain't, 'tis far off. Look! Look! They're burnin' the rectory!"

Over the distant elm trees they could see smoke rising, a thin column, no more than chimney smoke at first, then thickening as old timbers caught, bellied a great mouse of smoke into the cool sky above the trees. "The captain!" Sara whispered. "What have they done to him?" She began to struggle back out of the narrow window.

"They won't have caught him that easy," Molly said. "He ain't goin' to stay put for 'em to burn 'em alive. Nor Dr. Newall neither. They fare to have run off to the hall, surely, to Mr. Cameron. Don't you worry for 'em."

They stayed watching the smoke climb and thicken, billowing into a dark grey cloud, the bottom reddened by the flames. They could hear the shouting of the mob, a roar of triumph as part of the roof, a mass of timbers, fell into the fire's mouth, shooting flames a hundred feet into the darkened sky.

They were so absorbed in watching that the returning men were almost at the house before they saw them, at the bend of the road just beyond the paddock and its thorn hedge. Danial Blogg again, and Molly's father, and ten, twenty more. The straggle of the mob must have stayed to watch the fire or guard the cart and horse and punt-gun.

"Cap'n Pownall!" Daniel Blogg shouted. "We know you're in there. Come out to us like a man and face us, 'stead o' spyin' an' skulkin' like a damned rat."

"He is not!" Sara shouted down. "Daniel Blogg, Daniel Blogg, look up here, at this window!" She waved her arm and he turned about and moved farther back across the road to see her properly. The others with him stared and pointed and called, " 'Tis Sara, 'tis Pownall's Sara! An' Molly. Henry Bone, Henry Bone, 'tis your Molly up there, look at her wavin'!" The men waved back at Molly. The burning of the rectory seemed to have filled them with good humour. Some had bottles in their pockets and they took them out now and drank, up-ending them with a flourish and tossing them over their shoulders into the ditch. "Come down out o' up there an' join on with us, Molly. An' Sara too! Come down to us, prettys."

"Tell your captain to come out to us and bring out Dr. Newall," Daniel Blogg was calling. "We'll not touch his sisters but we mean to have words with them two."

"They're not here, I swear it," Sara cried. Behind her she heard someone coming up the stairs calling out, "Sara? Sara? What is it, what's happening?"

"They've come back," she cried, turning towards the room and the open door, Miss Susannah coming in, Peg behind her holding the dining-room poker above her head as though she expected to find the mob in Sara's bedroom. "They're looking for the captain," Sara said in a lower voice. "They promise they'll not touch you." And as an afterthought, "They're burning the rectory."

Miss Susannah put her hand up to her heart.

"Tell 'em to come out to us!"

"I swear they are not here! You may come in and search if you will."

"Sara! Are you gone mad?"

"Tell the old faggots we want money!" someone shouted.

"An' beer!"

"An' somethin' good to eat!"

More men joining them, some women, the cart with its gun. Joseph Goatlake in charge, riding in the cart like Caesar, his mother beside him.

"An' some o' that wine o' theirn," Henry Bone roared, "an' a couple o' their hams. You fetch 'em out to us, Molly." He turned to his comrades, his face still amazed with last night's drinking, his eyes staring. "They do have famous wine, Pownalls do, Molly do bring me a bowl now an' then."

"Dad!" Molly screamed in anguish. "They do be listenin', you'll get me killed dead. Shut that foolish mouth!"

But the roar of "Give us money, an' meat an' ale" had drowned both their voices. It became a chant, men were pressing forward, there were crashing, splintering sounds at the front of the house, out of Sara's view, as though they had already broken down the trim box hedge that Miss Hetty clipped so carefully every fortnight of the summer, and were in the small front garden.

"We must give them something," Sara said. "If you give them a barrel of wine and a few guineas they will go away content."

"She's right," Miss Susannah said. She looked round her. "Mrs. Hobhouse, Peg, go down to the coolroom, fetch out a keg of the elderberry wine, the one that's spoiled. Hetty, there are some bank-notes and three guineas in my purse. Fetch the guineas to me. Molly, run down with cook and Peg. What are you doing up here? Sara, tell them they shall have wine and money."

Sara shouted from the window, could no longer make herself heard, and ran down to the captain's room, began to open the casement and the shutters. Miss Hetty was already behind her crying, "No, no, Sara, they'll murder us. Oh, Susannah, come quickly, prevent her, she'll have us all killed."

The mob was trampling the flower beds, the lawn; the hedge broken down, the trim white gate smashed from its post, the gateway jammed with rioters. When they saw the shutters open and Sara at the window, they raised a cry of "Hurrah" and "Pownall's Sara" and "Shall we have ale?" In the roadway, beyond the cart and horse, there were the less urgent rebels, and beyond them, sitting on the brow of the ditch, eating bread and cheese and bacon that perhaps they had got from the rectory kitchen before they set fire to it, were three women and a man and a half-naked child, eating patiently in the morning sunlight as though this were a holiday and they were waiting for what other pleasures it might bring.

"I'm in here!" Sara called over her shoulder, hearing Molly and Peg, Mrs. Hobhouse and Miss Susannah behind her, Miss Susannah guiding the cask of spoiled elderberry wine. "Here's wine for you," Sara shouted down to the rioters, to Daniel Blogg. "And Miss Pownall will give you money if you'll be good and leave us alone."

111

She made way for Peg and Molly, who levered the small cask onto the window-sill, holding it balanced until Daniel Blogg, stretching up like a ladder, took it from them as easily as though he were carrying a filled mug, and gave it to Henry Bone behind him, who had leaned his fowling-piece against the broken hedge in order to take the burden.

"There's my Molly!" Henry Bone shouted. "Give us wine, she have! Old faggots!" He staggered towards the cart, leaned against the side of it. "Thaxstone forever! Hurrah!"

"Quit!" Daniel Blogg roared. "Quit all!" He looked up at the window, at Miss Susannah, who had the three guineas in her hand to throw down to him, hesitating whether two would be enough to send them safely away. "Where's the cap'n, missus?"

"Gone to fetch the dragoons!" Miss Hetty cried from behind her sister. "You shall all be hanged!"

"Be quiet, Hetty," Miss Susannah hissed. "Do you want them to burn us alive?"

But in the garden they'd heard what she said, and the word "Dragoons" was running like the wind in the trees. "The old bastard do be fetching the dragoons to kill us all!"

"It's no such thing!" Miss Susannah cried. "He did but go to save Dr. Newall from you. Here are three guineas. Take them and go to your homes, haven't you done enough wickedness today?"

" 'Tis no wickedness to demand our rights," Daniel shouted. "If the dragoons come, we'll face 'em, eh, lads? And if there's Essex lads among 'em they'll join us surely." He forced his way out of the garden onto the road, holding the money aloft in his fist, crying, "Three more guineas for the treasury, lads, three more golden guineas." He handed them up to Joseph Goatlake on the cart, who handed them to his mother. She pushed them into a leather bag that already seemed heavy and sat on it again, staring up at the opened window as though she were looking for Sara and Molly, behind Miss Susannah.

"Now for the hall!" Daniel roared. "Tom Hassett, Jos Mainer, run to find my cousin John an' the others,

112

they'll be to Masham's likely, an' bring 'em to meet us at the hall."

"Burn the hall, roast old Cameron amidst o' it!"

"Thaxstone forever!"

Daniel marched ahead, turned the corner of the garden onto the side road that led to Over Thaxstone and Southcott Hall beyond it. The crowd began to follow him, poured out of the garden, leaving it crushed and ruined, the spring flowers trampled into rags of colour, the lawn scarred with mud, an empty bottle lying in the middle, the hedge broken and gapped. On the road the horse leaned into his collar, the cart groaned, creaked forward, the punt-gun wavering its muzzle, jolting up and down, Mrs. Goatlake holding on to the side of the cart with one hand and her son's shoulder with the other. She threw a last glance of triumph at the window, turned the corner, and was gone, followed by the stragglers, all pretence of a formed column vanished out of their heads, only the pitchforks and the bill-hooks, the cudgels and one last fowling-piece showing that this was no holiday. Last of all, the three women and the man and the small child, getting up wearily from the ditch at the far side of the road, cramming the last morsel of bread into their mouths, trudging after their comrades.

"Are they gone?" Miss Stone said quaveringly. "Oh, mercy, I do be wringing through."

"If they find Joshua now, they'll kill him," Miss Susannah said. "You realise that, of course, Hetty?"

"Oh, oh, oh!" Miss Hetty cried. "They would not dare! Oh, what shall we do?"

"He'll be at the hall," Miss Susannah said. "He'll have taken Dr. Newall there for safety, I'm sure of it. If only we could warn him."

"I can go," Sara said. "Molly and I, they'll not harm us even if they should see us. We'll run now." She caught Molly by the arm, pulled her out of the room past Miss Stone, Miss Hetty crying behind them, "She'll be murdered, they'll kill her. Oh, stop her, Susannah. Sara, come back."

Out of the house, the garden. Ahead of them, up the road, they could see the tail of the mob, the three women, the child, the cart's dark outline, shouts and singing drifting back on the breeze, and far ahead of all the tall shape of Daniel Blogg, the great staggering figure of Henry Bone behind him, waving his fowling-piece against the sky.

"We best keep to this side of 'em," Molly panted, "we can run faster than they're goin' an' we can pass 'em by, but what'll we do then, Sara? We cain't stop 'em. An' the cap'n won't run away from 'em, that's sure."

"I don't know."

"My dad's so foggy drunk he don't know what he's doing. I do hope he don't get into no trouble for all this. You think the dragoons'll come to catch 'em?"

"Them or the yeomanry. Maybe he's really gone to fetch them."

"You tell him not to be real angry with my dad, Sara. He don't know which way he's looking, my dad don't. He'll fall flat on his face shortly an' sleep till morning."

They ran like hares, keeping below the brow of the rising ground that the cart track followed, the still-burning rectory a dull grumble of smoke to their left, behind its screen of trees. Above them to their right, the mob, spread out now in a long uneven line of silhouettes, seemed darkened by the brightness of the morning; the horse still leaning hard into his collar to drag the heavy cart up the slope; the sound of trampling feet, the voices, the rumble of the wheels, the protesting screech of the axle, softened by the distance into no more than country sounds.

And looking ahead of them again towards the familiar, misshapen Over Thaxstone cottages, crouched under their blackened thatch, their small windows glinting like eyes—Mrs. Grimmer's, old Miss Bowdeker's, Jos Mainer's, the others—they saw the captain. Striding, half running, his blue coat tails flapping, his head bare. There was still a quarter of a mile between him and the mob; they had not seen him yet, or he them, the ground, the road, rising between them. But Sara and Molly could see both. She cried out to him, uselessly. She ran until her heart was bursting, the pain in her side was a wound, and the captain heard her, turned to look this way and that, searching the falling ground to see where her voice was coming from. She stumbled on a rabbit hole, turned her ankle, ran on with the pain of it burning, twisting like broken glass. And in that same moment he saw the mob ahead, breasting the brow of the ridge, and they saw him, recognised him.

" 'Tis the spy! The spy! Fetchin' the dragoons to us! Shoot 'em, Dan'l, shoot 'em dead, lad!"

Running, stumbling, her ankle going from under her, seeing it happen as though it had already happened, unfolding slowly like a dance. The captain stood in the track, held his two pistols levelled, cried out, "Stand or I fire!"

"Shoot 'em, Henry, level your piece at 'em, lad. Down with the spy!"

Daniel halted, no more than thirty yards between him and the captain. Henry Bone wavering, trying to aim his ancient gun, men jostling, shouting insults, women crying, " 'Tis the dragoons, the dragoons!" The cart still rumbling forward, until it was almost at the column's head, the long barrel of the punt-gun aimed like a black finger at the captain.

Molly screaming, "Dad, don't fire at 'em, *Dad!*"

And the puff of smoke, the sharp barking explosion of the charge.

The captain standing, one arm raised, and then first one and then the other of his pistols falling, his knees buckling, the thick, strong legs still trying to hold him upright.

She reached the track as he fell, almost caught him falling, was holding his head and shoulders, kneeling, hearing someone, someone screaming, "Dad," hearing voices, shouting, nothing, holding his head, the front of his clothes already bloody, blood welling dark out of the great gape where the rusty nails and the duck shot had torn cloth and flesh, mangled them together.

He was trying to whisper, looking at her astonished, his eyes amazed with pain. "Ahhh." Someone was beside her, kneeling beside her, touching the wound with her hand. Mrs. Talbot. Mrs. Talbot tearing strips from her underskirt, padding them against the wound. But the strips grew crimson as she touched his body with them; the blood was covering their hands. Sara wanted to scream, to crush him against her, hold him back from dying.

"Oh, my dear," she whispered, not recognising her own voice.

But the amazement was already fading from his eyes.

Behind them the mob was hesitating, wavering, half a dozen of the stragglers already running away, a dozen more backing slowly from the huddle of figures on the track ahead of them, the fallen man, the two women, Daniel Blogg trying to rally them, Henry Bone still aiming his gun, his face bewildered, dreaming, staring at what he had done. How had he done it? How had it happened?

Daniel was crying out, "Stand fast, lads. He has his desserts. He were a spy, a spy." But even his voice was uncertain, he who had seen so many die at Waterloo and in other battles. This one death. A woman crying, "Murder, murder," and gathering her skirts and running, flying after the forerunners. A dozen more, the whole mob breaking, flying, until only Daniel and a few others stood their ground against the dead man. And the cart with its gun stayed there, the horse trying to bend down its head far enough to crop the grass.

The horse lifted his head, neighed. The sound of hooves, of galloping, a drumming of hoofbeats, a ringing of harness. A voice yelled, "The dragoons!" Another voice cried out, "The yeos! The yeos! Run, lads, for your lives!"

All running now, only the dead man lying, and Sara and Mrs. Talbot kneeling by him, and Molly crouched behind them. And the cart still standing, empty except for its useless gun. The cart horse lifting his head towards the coming horses.

Swords naked in the sunlight, a voice crying, "At the brutes! Cut them down!" All the side of Thaxstone ridge scattered with flying figures running, stumbling, falling on their knees, crying out for mercy, and the horsemen riding, slashing, striking at men and women.

Three horsemen stopped beside them on the track, one jumping down to see who they were, to see the captain lying with his head resting on Sara's arm, to recognise him.

"He's not dead," Sara whispered. "Only hurt. He's only—only hurt—"

They could not separate her from him, and she held him all the way down to Lavender Cottage, crouched beside him in the cart, the punt-gun thrown out of it to make room for them, her dress soaked with his blood like a crimson apron.

Chapter 9

She woke each morning from dreams in which he was still alive, and behind them nightmares in which she held him again in the cart, tried to prevent his head from rolling, rolling with the unsteady heaving of the great wheels over a rut, the sudden lurch into another.

For half a moment as she woke she would think, *He's still alive, it was only dreaming, only a* . . . And reality would come and she'd lie quite still, wanting to cry out loud in desolation. And then she would have to get dressed and go downstairs, and behave as though this was another day, simply another day of mourning, of living. Have to say, "Yes Miss Susannah. No. Thank you."

Even she and Molly could scarcely talk to each other, looking at each other with stunned, stricken eyes. Miss Susannah had wanted to send Molly out of the house at once, but Dr. Newall had said, "No, she had best stay if they would make themselves—force their natural instincts of horror to—In short, dear ladies, she will be needed as a witness, a most important witness and—You understand, I'm sure. If she were to—to run off . . ."

Dr. Malthus came to assure the Misses Pownall of his deep, deep sense of tragedy, his sympathy, his—his—and he put his handkerchief to his eyes with a sweet gentleness of shared sorrow. Mr. Cameron came, grey and dry with banked, deep anger, assuring Miss Susannah and Miss Hetty that the villains would be hunted down and hanged to a man. And woman. He looked at Sara with bleak dislike as though it griped his stomach to include her in the sympathy, but he managed to take her hand and murmur a word about, "Your guardian, Miss Sara."

The dislike spread round her, and she almost welcomed it, did welcome it as a kind protection against her real wound. A dislike without form or obvious reason except that she was an outsider in this tragedy that was not simply a family tragedy but one that knitted half a community together in horror, in a sense of sacrifice. From Southcott Hall to Miss Stone's shop, from the rectory to Masham's farm, to Colonel Sampson's mill and his house at Thorpe, all bound together in hatred and vengeance against the labourers. The *Gazette* wrote a long account of the tragedy, one to make every loyal heart shudder at the depths to which ". . . foreign influences . . . radical sedition . . ." And an almost equally long account of the captain's splendid career. Not much of it accurate, since most of his service had been secret. But no reader could be in doubt that an English officer had crowned a life of heroism with the ultimate sacrifice.

Forty-seven of the rioters had been arrested, on charges ranging from murder to arson and extorting money with threats of violence. And among the forty-seven, Mrs. Talbot. The yeomanry, originally, regarded her as someone helping to save the captain's life and had allowed her to go home. But among the

118

first rioters taken had been Joseph Goatlake and he'd denounced her, along with twenty more names he offered in hope of being allowed to turn king's evidence and so save his and his mother's life. His mother, in fact, was not arrested. The whisper went that one of the fire agents—or, according to others, one of the Bow Street runners hired by Dr. Newall—had caught her in Urnford on the way to London and had let her go in exchange for her leather bag of extorted guineas, together with the treasury of the Thaxstone Box Club and the money received for the last consignment of poached game sent to the London market.

"I hear they've taken that dreadful woman," Miss Susannah said.

"Mrs. Goatlake?" Miss Hetty said, pouring out her tea. "The thought of such a creature!"

"No, not yet. But Mrs. Talbot. They've taken her at least."

"That can't be!" Sara whispered, as though the name had reached her from a long way off and she was not really answering them, but speaking to herself. "She—"

"She's one of the worst of them," Miss Susannah said dryly. "Why should you think it can't be, Sara?"

"She had nothing to do with it," Sara said. "She tried to save him."

Miss Susannah tightened her mouth in anger.

"Poor, poor Joshua," Miss Hetty said, beginning to cry. "How *could* they? So kind and gentle always, so —so—Oh, oh, oh, oh."

Sara looked down at her plate, her cup and saucer, looking at the patterns of flowers, unable to feel anything at all except that deep heaviness of pain. Even Mrs. Talbot's arrest. She thought, *They will let her go when they find—I shall tell them when I—*She even lifted her tea-cup, went through the motion of bringing it to her mouth, and set it down again without tasting it.

Miss Susannah stood up, said something in a distant voice about Dr. Newall, tomorrow, preparing. They were to go to Urnford to make their depositions. Miss Susannah; Miss Hetty; Sara; Miss Stone; Dr. Newall's

119

housekeeper, Janet; Mr. Stone; Mr. Rumbelow, the landlord of the Dragon and Horseman; Molly; Mr. Masham; half a dozen others. A coach was to bring them, and they were to stay the night. Mr. Hampton, the under-secretary, would be there himself, Dr. Newall said.

Sara went out into the paddock and stood under the chestnut trees. Chestnuts lay in the thick, rough grass, and she picked one up, turned it between her fingers, wondered why it stirred something in her mind. A blackened, shrivelled thing. She threw it away. In the kitchen garden Old John was bedding plants, his back stooped as though his work must go on no matter what should happen. Mrs. Talbot was his sister. She wanted to touch his shoulder, console him, have him console her.

"John," she said. He got up slowly, up from his knees, his joints creaking, then straightened as much of his back as would straighten, and at last lifted his head, turning his whole body towards her, his feet shifting, his breath rasping, "Aye? Aye, miz?"

"Your sister," she said. "They've taken her." She wanted to say, "It's a terrible mistake, I shall tell them so, nothing dreadful can happen to her," but she said none of it, only looked at him hoping for some kind of consolation.

"I've never held with 'er," he said, staring at her out of blank, pale eyes. His face an old lump of brownish, greyish earth; his two days of beard a thin, silvery bloom of decay on the brown, weathered skin; his teeth black stumps. "I've never held with 'er," he said again. "Uppish from young. Naw, I never did." He held the dibber in his tortoise hand, the shallow basket of green plants by his shapeless boot.

She turned away and he stared after her for a long moment and slowly turned round again, knelt down, and thrust the point of his wooden dibber into the brown earth. "Aye," he said to himself. "Uppish. Always uppish she were. I've never held with 'er."

Sara went out into the side road that led—She didn't want to think where it led, had led, stood with her eyes shut against the sunlight. A hand touched her foot, and she looked down. The smith's boy, lying in the ditch, half hidden, half taking his ease. He smiled at her, smiled and nodded and patted his ragged coat, took out a fold of paper, looked this way and that up and down the road, and gave it to her.

"What is it?" she said uselessly. He smiled, touched her foot again, and nodded and worked his mouth, urging her to read. She, too, looked round to see if anyone was watching them, and opened the paper. "I am taken up. Come to me in Urnford jail when you can. Go first to my cottage and bring me what you shall find in the drawer of my table. All of it. There is not much for you to carry. Above all a packet that is there. Do not weep for whatever shall happen. It must happen. Remember your promise to me. Your loving frnd: Marg't Talbot."

She folded the note again, put it into the neck of her dress, against the ring, held the ring for a second in her fingers. At her feet the bellows-boy nodded and smiled. "I'll do it," she said, then nodded down at him elaborately. He pointed up the road, still urgent.

"Now?" she said, mimicked the question. He came up from the ditch and caught her hand, his own hand like old, cracked leather, rasping her fingers. He drew her up the road, pointed, croaked his poor sounds. She began to hurry and he ran beside her for a moment, urged her on with his hand, was running behind her. She thought he was still there and looked round and he was gone. Was nowhere. She went on, still hurrying, thought, *Here is the place, in a few more yards, there.* Felt the sickness of it and turned away from the beaten, rutted track before she came to where he had been killed. She began running across the turf. Her ankle was still bandaged from twisting it that day and she thought, *She could have cured it for me*, and tried not to think of anything. Because of her ankle she couldn't run very far and fell into a walk, the ground rising, bringing her above the cottages of Over Thaxstone, past Little Wood, past all the familiar landmarks, towards the marsh. And she thought she would die. As though she knew already that nothing would be left, nothing at all. And there was almost a cruel pleasure in the pain of it, as though to have something left would have been worse than to have nothing.

The Great Wood to her left, and the marsh stretching out ahead of her and away to the right dark with reeds and silence, the pools and winding water glistening here and there like steel, the mud banks silver. A bird rising into the sky from a clump of reeds, singing and singing, small and black as a cinder against the pale green-blue immensity.

She saw the hut on its tongue of land, the water, the mud, the reeds behind it, the coloured garden, the fence. Nothing changed. And she went slowly down to it, her throat tightening. She called out, "Robert? Robert?" But there was no answering movement in the garden, in the grass. She found the key under the flat stone and went in, the smell of tar close and choking, the shadows heavy against the sunlight from the doorway, the one small window. The bat pinned to his wall, the coiled adders, the jars. The manuscript book lay open on the table. She looked at it, but the letters were so old, so cramped and clasped that she could not make out more than a word here and there. She pulled open the narrow drawer. Mrs. Talbot's spectacles. The silver mirror. The packet. She held the sealed paper in her hand, felt it. As though it held dry seeds. A leather purse with a drawstring. Nothing else.

"Robert?" she whispered. The ashes dead in the hearth. The kettle, the black iron pot. In the cupboard the cups, the glasses, the bottles of cordial, knives, and plates. She did not need to open it. She knew they were there. "Robert!" she called again. The name died in the silence. She found a cloth and made a small parcel of the things she must carry, knotting the corners of the cloth into a bundle and looked round, thinking, *She will be back in a little while, it will all be explained, it will all . . .* And the thought died in the shadows as Robert's name had done. She knew she would never stand in this room again, breathe the herb smell, the scent of tar, sit at that dead fire.

She put her hand to her throat, drew out the small

iron ring, and held it tightly. "Please," she whispered, "please." She shut her eyes against the jewelled shining of the drowned snakes in their glass jar. *I must take something else to her*, she thought. *The book. The cordial. Something.*

She heard voices and went to the doorway. But she could see no one. "Is there anyone?" she whispered. Wanted to call it aloud and was afraid. She stood half in sunlight, half in shadow. "Is there someone there?" Only the still garden, the sound of insects, a rustling of wind far off in trees. The path rising towards the dark shape of the wood. She drew the door shut, locked it, hesitated with the key in her hand, and put it into her dress pocket. If there were people near, spying, watching her? She went out of the garden, pulled the gate to, and called softly for a last time, "Robert? Robert?"

She looked round her, the glare from the marsh making her shade her eyes. No one at all. She went up the path, hurrying and limping, carrying the bundle against her side, to stand at the top of the ridge, where the path turned, and look back. Nothing. Only the squat black shape of the cottage, the chimney. She went on, half running, hobbling, her heart so heavy it was like death. And behind her she heard a strange, sharp cracking, a pistol sound, like flames crackling. She stopped and turned and saw a column of black smoke twisting up from where the cottage was, hidden from her by the ground. She began running back, the smoke thickening, shot with flames, a tongue of red and orange fire licking up into the already dense, tarfed smoke.

She came to where the path turned downhill, saw the cottage burning, the three figures outlined against the marsh, then hidden, then visible again, jumping round as though they were leaping with excitement. One turned to look up at the ridge, saw her, shouted something, and all three stood for a fraction of a minute staring up at her. Then they ran, vanishing behind the burning mass of the hut. Another moment and she saw their flat, marsh punt slide out of hiding, into red water that itself seemed burning. One of the men poled, seeming to be hiding his face from

123

her, although he was too far away from her to be
recognised. The others crouched low. The cottage
burned like a torch; there was another sharp, explo-
sive cracking as the flames snapped across the last
corner of the tarred canvas on the roof. Something
inside the fire—the snakes in their jar of alcohol?—
exploded; coloured fire leapt and died; the smoke
coiled thick and greasy, now grey, now black, like
entrails, stained red with blood, coiling. All a furnace.

The book, she thought. *I didn't save the book.* And
then, "*Robert! Robert!*" The punt had slid behind a
high clump of reeds, showed again for a moment, the
men staring at her. One of them shook his fist. The
man poling turned them into another channel. It was
hard to see them among the dark reeds and mudbanks,
against the sun. She started to run down the path and
stopped again at the uselessness of running. A roof
timber wrapped in flames fell, slithered across the
narrow garden, burned among the spring flowers. And
another.

She stayed and watched until the hut was only a bonfire with the blunt chimney standing like a massive
stake. Then part of that fell, sent sparks whirling,
smoke. Nothing but smoke and dying flames. Even
the garden blackened, the grasses burning, the flowers.
She turned away and climbed the path again, slowly
this time, the bundle still held against her side.

At Lavender Cottage she had been missed. "I have
been looking for you," Miss Susannah said. Since her
brother's death she seemed to have grown even colder.
And at the same time to have lost something of her
strength. She did not ask what was in the bundle, or
where Sara had been. "Dr. Newall wishes to speak
to you about tomorrow."

About her evidence. The doctor had grown thin
with anxiety in the last days, with a trembling ferocity
of hatred, as though day and night his mind was filled
with dreams of hangings and gave him no ease. "You
realise, child . . ." He had already asked her the same
questions, urged the same answers half a dozen times
since the funeral, and the announcement of the special
assizes. This name and that. Who had fired the shot.

"But you *must* have seen it, child, you *must!* Was it Joseph Goatlake? Daniel Blogg? Who, child, who?" As the nearest magistrate—in fact, the only magistrate for miles round—he felt that all depended on him, to uphold law, justice, the safety of England against this monster of sedition. "Who else was there? They'll want names, Sara, names! They'll not be satisfied with prevarications, I warn you! Your own guardian dead! Murdered! And you seem reluctant to point out his murderer! I tell you, Sara, it has a very strange appearance!" But he scarcely meant what he said, was no more than striking blindly about him with his little plump hands. His cheeks like shrunken wattles trembled with nervousness at the thought of the assizes, that vast weight of his responsibilities; of the judges, and Mr. Hampton, Lord Sidmouth, Lord Southcott —as though the bench and the government would stare at him with one tremendous eye like God, demanding an account, and would find him wanting. "We must have names, names!"

He was still goading her when they got down at The Bell in Urnford. The men, except for Dr. Newall, had travelled on horseback and were there ahead of them, and the inn was a scurry of expectation, of maids running, fires lighting, meat roasting, and a cluster of passers-by gathering in the street to see the witnesses, whispers running, "The murder, the riot, the assizes, them from Thaxstone."

Sara had to share a room with Miss Stone and stared out of the leaded window while Miss Stone chose which bed she would have and groaned over her portmanteau and wondered again whether the assizes would pay for all their expenses. "As though we haven't lost enough already! To have to close the shop today and tomorrow! And such a price as this will be!"

An old, narrow, leaning street, the houses reaching towards one another above it. At the far end of it Cathedral Square, the jail. Sara couldn't see the jail door, only the wall, some of the narrow, barred, windows. Remembered their passing it. So long ago. A long, low, heavy building, meant for the dozen or so prisoners usually held in custody for the regular assizes. Crammed now with the rioters.

"What are you looking at? I am sure our supper must be ready soon and you're not even unpacked."

She had to endure supper, more talk of tomorrow. It was eight o'clock before she could escape them, saying she was going to her room for a moment and slipping out the inn door as though she were already a criminal. Molly had been lodged with the inn servants, but even if she had known where to look for her, Sara wanted to be alone. She had the leather purse and the mirror and the spectacles in her reticule and by some instinct had put the sealed packet inside her bodice. What was in it? Touching it again to make sure it was safe, feeling the dry seeds move and rustle together under her fingers. Ringing the bell at the jail door, studded with iron, a spy grille set into it, a small wicket door cut into the great one that was large enough to let in carts with their loads of prisoners. Two passers-by stared at her, whispered. Heavy footsteps. The wooden shutter behind the grille rattling. She gave her name and Mrs. Talbot's and pushed a half guinea through the narrow space between two bars.

The door opened and a turnkey in unlaced breeches, his shirt open on a fat, hairy stomach, jerked his thumb for her to come in. The door clanged behind her. They were in a tunnel beneath the upper level of the prison. "Come with me," the man said. He had been eating his supper and held a lump of bread in his left hand. *I should have brought food*, Sara thought. *She will be hungry*. Another archway, another door, steps leading down, and still another iron-bound door, a creaking, heavy lock. A smell of damp, of filthy straw, of bodies, of rancid air. Through an iron gate that took the place of a cell door she saw men, saw Joseph Goatlake, John Porter, Daniel Blogg, twenty, thirty men—a dozen of them, men she knew by sight to talk to—Molly's father. They saw her, began crowding towards the bars. Molly's father staring at her. A clanking of iron round their ankles. The turnkey held her roughly by the arm as though no one who came

126

visiting such a place deserved respect, not even for half a guinea.

Another iron gate and this time women. Not so many women. But the same fetid stench of straw, of bodies, of stale air, catching at her throat, choking. Mrs. Talbot sitting beside a straw pallet, a woman lying face down on it, shivering. Others eating, licking out tin bowls, crouching in a thin finger of sunlight that slanted through the bars above their heads.

"There she is," the turnkey said. Mrs. Talbot stood up, held out her hands, and said as though it were an ordinary day, "Why, Sara!"

Still handsome in her green gown with its leather girdle and black apron and white collar and cuffs, although they were no longer white. One sleeve was rolled back and she held a cloth with which she had been trying to clean the sick woman. "I wish I could have asked you to bring me something to ease her," she said.

"I should have brought many other things," Sara whispered. Tried not to look at the woman lying there. At the others. Some of them were Thaxstone women and knew her and whispered, " 'Tis his girl, Sara." The Urnford women, there for other crimes, stared at her with blank eyes. Sara held out her reticule and the turnkey leaned forward and snatched it away before Mrs. Talbot could take it.

He rummaged through it with thick fingers, pulled out the purse as though by instinct his fingers discovered gold, weighed and felt it. The coins clinked.

"Some are for you," Mrs. Talbot said. She took the purse from him and emptied the guineas and half guineas onto her palm. "Two are yours now," she said, "if you will bring me something I shall need for that poor woman. And more later. May I have the rest of my things?"

He gave them to her without further examination. Sara had eased the packet out from the neck of her dress, was holding it concealed. And as though Mrs. Talbot had seen exactly what she was doing, she held out her own hand with ten sovereigns in it. "Please take these," she said. "You may need money soon."

Slowly, not wanting to take the money but needing to take the hand, Sara closed her fingers over Mrs. Talbot's, and then, as though seized by an impulse of emotion, she took Mrs. Talbot's hand in both of hers, held it tight, and said, "But you will be home again." And thought of the burned hut, and of what she was at that moment doing. Knew then with absolute certainty, knew what she had known from the moment the smith's boy gave her the note and she had read, "Above all a packet that is there. Do not weep for whatever shall happen." Had known when she took it from the drawer, felt it. Twenty or so belladonna seeds. She wanted to cry, "No, no," but Mrs. Talbot had already taken the sealed paper, left the sovereigns in her hand.

"How is Robert?"

"I couldn't find him," she said. She wondered whether to tell about the hut.

"Robert will look after himself. And so must you. Now go, child. This is not healthy air." She smiled, as though that were a joke. Her voice had kept its familiar harshness but lost its arrogance, as though she no longer needed to be arrogant. She seemed to have grown almost gentle, to be amused by what had happened.

"It's all only a terrible mistake," Sara whispered. "I am to give them my evidence tomorrow. I shall tell them so, I shall tell them that you—"

"They will not listen to any of that," Mrs. Talbot said. "So long as you know that I tried to save him. I knew I could not, but I tried all the same."

"It's gettin' late," the turnkey growled. He jingled the coins in his pocket, his voice almost kindly.

"And you cannot save me. But there are other friends. You will remember? Always?"

"I will remember."

"Not only here. But you must go away when all this is done. Far away. You know that?" She smiled, tried to make her smile happy.

"I'll never leave you. Never. It will all be—all be—"

Mrs. Talbot shook her head, touched Sara's face,

and Sara clung to her, as she'd never clung to her in all the time she'd known her. "Don't," she whispered. "Don't!"

"I must, child. Would you have it any other way? They must have their blood, they will not let us go. And my way is very easy." She held Sara's head against her, and they stood like that for a moment while the turnkey grew impatient and growled again that it was late, that all must be locked up.

"Now go. Go in peace." She kissed her mouth, held her for another moment, and put her away from her, Sara's eyes half blind with crying. "And take this," Mrs. Talbot said. "I've had it a long time and shall like to think it will see young eyes again." She held out the silver mirror and Sara took it in both hands, obediently, not knowing what she was doing or what Mrs. Talbot was saying. The turnkey pulled her by the elbow, drew her away. There were a hundred things she wanted to say and she could think of none of them.

"I shall look for you at the trial," Mrs. Talbot said. "Have no fears of anything. I have known for a long time that—"

The iron gate opening, closing, doors, stone, the air, the sky. The square in front of her and the dark bulk of the cathedral, people walking, taking the pleasant evening at their ease. Still twilight. Shops. She felt her way blindly along the street towards the inn, holding the mirror, the ten sovereigns, not knowing she was holding them. In her room she lay down on the bed and thought, *It isn't true. She said, "I shall look for you at the trial." She doesn't mean to, doesn't mean to, doesn't . . ."* And knew as she tried to think that it wasn't true, that she was lying to herself.

Chapter 10

In the few weeks before the assizes began Sara felt as though she were living with a thick veil between her and reality, a veil that distorted everything she saw and heard—brought it now very close and frightening, its meaning altered, heightened, drumming inside her head like a nightmare, and the next instant far away, so far away she felt it had nothing to do with her at all. Sometimes at table Miss Susannah or Miss Hetty would say something and she would look at them politely and decide they could not possibly have been speaking to her. They were so far off.

Only with Molly she came close to reality. And still they could not talk together. Merely stand and look at each other with haunted eyes. But there was no veil then. "He didn't mean to do that, Sara, I oath my life he didn't. Oh Sara." And they held hands for a moment and could not cry.

They had questioned Sara for four hours that day of taking the statements, and had called her back for questioning again ten days later, until she scarcely knew what she had said, what she had signed. Putting names before her, now kind, now shouting, threatening, then kind again. And she had sat while their voices came and went, sometimes not even catching the sense of what they were saying so they had to repeat themselves. And images grew and swelled in her mind, became terrible, unendurable. The captain lying against her arm, that apron of blood covering him. And

Molly's eyes. And Mrs. Talbot getting up from beside that shivering wreck of sickness, in Urnford jail. As though all were one. One cruelty. Whose?

"Do you not wish to see your guardian's murderers punished? Come, come, girl, is this not a most unnatural attitude? Was it Henry Bone? *Was it? Answer me!*"

Once she had fainted.

She thought she would faint now, even before the morning began, the trials began, even before the judges took their places on the new-made bench in Urnford town hall, refurbished for the occasion. The benches and enclosure for the grand jury, for the attorneys, for the witnesses. Sitting crammed against Miss Stone, with Dr. Newall's housekeeper, Miss Janet Fosdyke, on her other side. Behind them the weight and heat and clamour of the crowd, shuffling, the grinding of chairs and benches, calls to make way, coughing, whispering. As though every whisper were aimed at her. "That's her, the one with black hair, foreign. He were her guardian. An' you know she don't want to testify against 'em? Unnatural girl." She could not hear what the whisperers were saying, only imagine it. And then seeing Molly's eyes, Molly sitting four places along the bench from her, her face white with despair, her eyes blank like mirrors. The heat growing, stifling, and then cold.

The prisoners were entering the dock. A long column of chained men and women, like dangerous animals. Daniel Blogg, his scar a ragged crimson line in his white face, gaunt with prison. John Porter, William Deakin, Henry Bone, Mrs. Blogg, and Mrs. Talbot, walking in her chains as though she were walking into a private room, staring contemptuously at nothing. She saw Sara, smiled slightly, and looked away.

She hasn't done it, Sara thought. *Thank God. I'll make them believe me, make them. They must let her go.* Although, three weeks ago, when all their statements of evidence had been taken, they had not believed her.

"Is it not very strange you should remember so

clearly *her* share in the matter? You remember no one else's, not a name, not a fact. But of Mrs. Talbot's share, or rather, as you are claiming, of her *lack* of share you have no doubts at all. Is that not strange?" Again and again and again. "We have other information, reliable information, that she was among the ringleaders, a chief organiser."

"It's a lie, a lie, they hated her." Trying to reach their minds across the softly shining table in the room where Mr. Hampton and the lawyers were building their case. But their minds could not be reached. Surely here, now, there would be someone who could understand?

The judges entering, three old men in scarlet, with long grey wigs. All standing, a ceremony like church, and the shuffling and the silence. Oh, yea, oh, yea, His Most Gracious Majesty . . . The King's Peace . . . in that on the twentieth day of April in this year of our Lord eighteen hundred and sixteen . . . the prisoners did conspire and compass to bring about the death of Joshua Pownall, Esq., of Thaxstone in the county of Essex, and that they did also conspire and compass the burning by arson of . . . and they did conspire and take secret oaths . . . they did by night . . . they did riotously assemble for the said purpose . . . they did demand money by menaces of violence . . . they did steal . . . and of these counts they do now stand accused before you. . . .

Daniel Blogg, Henry Bone, John Porter, Margaret Talbot, William Deakin, Katherine Blogg—all the roll-call of their names. But not Joseph Goatlake's name, who would come separately to give evidence for the king.

All the whispering, the hushing, the strange, black-robed, dusty men, the rattle of documents, the murmuring voices using words that seemed to mean nothing, to pass like insect murmurs in the shafts of dusty sunlight from the town-hall windows. All the prisoners led down now except Daniel Blogg.

"You do stand accused. How do you plead?"

Murmuring. A sudden lifting of a black-robed voice. "Witness! Witness! Sara known as Sara Pownall."

132

Hands beckoning, Miss Stone pushing her, whispering, "You are to go up."

"Take the book. I do solemnly swear . . ."

Her mouth dry with terror, the words unfamiliar, meaningless. The truth? The truth?

"Did you on that day see the prisoner?"

Her voice whispering, trying to articulate.

"Speak up, girl!"

"My lord, I am told the witness has an affection of the throat. Her voice is always low by reason of it."

Whispering, "Yes," because they had made her come to it through those hours. And so many others would say, "Yes."

"What was he doing?"

All again. All that they had made her tell. And Daniel Blogg staring over her head with his soldier's eyes, his scar, his flaming hair, which alone had kept its colour. Until her story was done, and the other stories, and the formalities of guilt were satisfied, and he was at last led away. And John Porter and then Henry Bone, and the same witnesses, the same stories, her own whispering, "Yes," until they came to that moment when he fired and she cried, "No!" and the court murmuring, the murmur rising to shock, to horror that she had said, "No," that she had not seen this monster kill her guardian. Nor anyone. No! No! No!

Until at last they were forced to let her go. And Miss Stone tried to draw herself away from contact, and Janet on the other side.

Molly whispering in the same way, "No, no." But they had more pity for her, being her father's child, and let her go.

One after another of the prisoners, each to have his separate trial, his chance for justice. And then as that first day was ending, Mrs. Talbot.

"You are Margaret Talbot, known as 'the herb woman' or as 'Granny Talbot'?"

"I am."

Grown gaunt, bone thin in prison, her skin a leaden grey from the foul air and the diet. But she had managed somehow to wash her collar and her cuffs.

133

She stood like a dying hawk, staring at nothing. Half smiling.

"The witness, Sara Pownall." They had given up the nicety of "known as Pownall."

"She had nothing to do with it."

And Mrs. Talbot looked at her and smiled and almost shook her head in pity.

"She was trying to save the captain."

"Witnesses have deposed—"

"They are lying. *Lying!*"

As though she herself were in the dock. "It will be stated by other witnesses that you were the intimate pupil and apprentice of this woman in her superstitious practices. That under her influence you—"

"She was my friend," Sara whispered. Felt her knees giving, had to hold the side of the witness box to save herself from falling. "*Is* my friend." And the hornet murmur of the crowd.

"I fear that from the moment of our beginning to gather statements this witness has proved most refractory, my lord."

"Sara, you are not a child. The court has had great patience with you." An old, kind voice. So kind she felt she could weep. "But there must be a limit to patience in such a case as this. Do you understand what your oath means?"

"Yes, my lord."

"Do you understand the meaning of the phrase 'contempt of court'?"

"No, my lord." His voice, his figure very far away. The sunlight had vanished. The court was grey with twilight. She had not eaten anything since morning. Nor then. Nor last night. Had she eaten last night?

That kind old voice. "So now, do you understand, Sara? I fear you stand in some peril. Fortunately for the course of justice your evidence isn't essential to identification. But you must beware of . . ."

The thin, grey, mouselike man who seemed the only one on the prisoners' side, standing up, looking as though he were afraid of the judges, afraid of the counsel for the prosecution, afraid of everyone. "You have said that the prisoner wished to *save* your guardian. How did she propose to do that?"

But by the end of his nibbling questions, his bobbings, and "If your lordships please," and his coughings and mumblings, he seemed only to have made it worse, the thick-set man, the one with the red face, coming back with his false, fat smile to say, "So you knew your guardian lay in danger? Did you warn him?"

"He wouldn't be warned."

"Did the prisoner warn him?"

"She tried to prevent the others from—"

"Aha! So *now* we come to it! There existed a prior intention, and the prisoner and you were aware of it? An intention to murder? Did you carry your knowledge to Dr. Newall, the magistrate?"

"No."

"Why not?"

And the old, kind voice interposing, saying, "We must advise the witness at this point, Mr. Graveney, that she is not obliged to answer your questions if the answers might tend to incriminate her. Do you understand that, Sara? You are not obliged to answer that question."

Until at last Mr. Graveney let her go, and she stumbled back to her seat to her loneliness, and from a great distance heard Joseph Goatlake say that Mrs. Talbot had been one of the chief inspirers of the murder, had spoken of it to his mother, who had done her utmost to dissuade her from such a dreadful purpose.

"It's a lie," Sara cried. "He's telling lies. He has told nothing but lies since he began."

"Tell that young woman that if she interrupts the trial again she will be removed from the court. She stands in great danger. Great danger, I may say."

Perhaps only her illness saved her from that danger, from taking her place with the others in the dock. She stepped down from the witness box, and the floor seemed so far down that she could not reach it, and then seemed to be rushing up towards her, and someone cried out, and there were faces, hands. She

135

was being lifted, the captain was lifting her, and his hands and face and body were masked with blood and the blood would cover her, and she could not breathe. His hands gripping her, his eyes—and they became Molly's eyes, Molly's voice crying, "Sara, Sara," and going far away again.

"She tried to *save* him," she whispered.

She was in bed. Miss Stone there. Miss Susannah. Someone else. Holding her wrist. The thin cutting of the knife, the cold rim of the bleeding bowl. Everything fading again. Then the fever.

She lay ten days without really knowing where she was or what had happened. She talked to them in Spanish. To Mrs. Talbot; to Molly; to Henry, Molly's father; to the captain. They came and saw her and bent over her and sometimes changed into Miss Stone, or the surgeon, or Miss Susannah.

She tried to tell them things. About Pablito, Señorita Agustina. But no one would listen. "You stand in great danger." And sometimes she was very small and lay beside her mother, and her mother whispered to her, not in Spanish but in another language. "Sleep, my small one. It is only a bad dream; sleep, my darling." Her mother's secret language, which no one else in the village could understand. Not even Papa, who grew so angry when he heard them whispering together. "Speak Spanish! Spanish! I forbid you to teach her that—that wicked talk. You swore you'd leave all that behind you when I took you, you swore it."

Like Miss Susannah. It was funny. Papa and Miss Susannah. Both so angry. She tried to laugh.

They bled her so much that she came close to death, came so close to it one evening that she saw herself dying, seemed to hover above her own body, watching them while they bled her, her wrist like a white bone above the bowl of blood, her face whiter than the pillow. Miss Susannah, Miss Stone, the surgeon, someone else, a boy in an apron stained with blood, holding a small tray of knives. *What are they all doing*, she wondered. *Why are they there?*

And yet perhaps the bleeding saved her, because

that night for the first time she came back to a weak reality, lay as helpless as a newborn but knowing where she was, what had happened, even guessing that more than one day had gone by since she collapsed. But not ten days. Miss Stone told her that.

She moved her head and looked at them, and the inn servant brought in the broth and Miss Susannah held it to her lips, her hands coldly efficient, her eyes bleak with accusation.

"You've been ten days like this!" Miss Stone said. "Imagine that!"

"It's well for you that you were," Miss Susannah said when the servant was gone. Sara wondered why they were troubling to look after her, the dislike in their expression was so clear. "Dr. Newall has been at great pains to save you from being charged with knowing of the conspiracy and not revealing it. But we'll not speak of that now. Drink your broth."

"They are all condemned!" Miss Stone said. She went to the window. "Every one of them."

"Mrs. Talbot?" Sara whispered. Miss Susannah's face contracted, her blunt nose pinched in at the nostrils.

"You mustn't trouble yourself about anything," Miss Susannah said. "The doctor has feared for your life."

"Tell me! Tell me, please! She is—"

"How can you speak of her?" Miss Stone cried. "That dreadful, dreadful creature! And to have cheated justice so!"

"What has happened?" Her voice like a thread.

"She is dead," Miss Susannah said. "Now, no more talking, or all the doctor's care of you will be for nothing."

"Dead?"

"She killed herself!" Miss Stone said, turning round with a kind of vengeance in her face. "They found her this morning."

Miss Susannah took Miss Stone out of the room.

Sara lay so weak that even to think was an enormous effort, to take in the meanings of words. Dead. Cheated justice. Dead. Ten days. Mrs. Talbot came slowly into the room and held out her hands. "Where is my mirror, child?" She tried to take Mrs. Talbot's cold hands and warm them and couldn't move. Couldn't hold her there. And the captain whispered, "You turned away from me. You turned away."

She was too weak to cry. Could only lie still, watching them, as they faded out of the twilight, became shadows, nothing. Dead.

She must have slept for twelve hours. When she woke, it was full morning, the sounds of traffic, of distant hammering, people moving along the street, their voices raised in some kind of expectation, of excitement, holiday. The sense of holiday reached her through the closed window, the drawn curtain. The sunlight made the curtain bright. She looked at the furniture of the inn room with a slow, questioning surprise, lay there a long time. What were they hammering?

Miss Stone came in, opening the door only slightly, then fully when she saw Sara stirred her head.

"And how are you this morning?"

"Better, I think."

"They're building the new gallows! Do you hear the noise? They're to be hanged twelve at the one time!"

"You said Mrs. Talbot—"

"She was to be one of them. One of the nineteen they were to hang tomorrow. But she hanged herself, the creature! And now there will be eighteen only. She didn't even confess."

"Hanged herself?" Sara whispered. She tried to sit up, stared at the fat white shadow of Miss Stone's face by the door.

"So they say. Although I heard from one of the servants here that the bars she is supposed to have hanged herself from were scarcely four feet above the floor. How she could have done it no one knows. And with a string no thicker than the lace of a boot, or a stays. They're saying it is the devil came for her." She tried to laugh at that and failed. She went over to the window instead and drew back the curtains. "Why, you will be able to see from here. I can see three

138

of the gibbets. But perhaps you'll not be strong enough to come to the window." She opened it and the hammering grew so loud it seemed to be in the street below them. "Just imagine! Twelve at one time. It quite makes one shudder."

"Is Molly's father . . ."

"Henry Bone? Why, I should think so! He first of all!" She turned to Sara, her eyes still with that look of shock in them—that life could be so dreadful, that people could do such things—and at the same time an excitement, greediness to know more of it, to know more of evil. "How could you have tried to defend them? Oh dear, how angry you've made poor Miss Susannah! It's taken all her Christianity to allow her to attend you. She's a saint. She wouldn't hear of you going into the hospital. And quite certainly you would have died if you'd been taken there. It's a dreadful, dreadful place. 'I must do this for Joshua,' she said. 'In spite of everything, Joshua would have wished it.' And you defended them!"

Sara closed her eyes.

"If you hadn't become ill just at that moment I can't think what might have happened."

The hammering, louder and louder. If she could only become ill again, lose her senses, her hearing. Molly. "Where is Molly?" she said.

"Miss Susannah wouldn't allow her to come near you. She's been sent to lodge in another part of the town. Indeed she may have gone away for all I know. Now that the trials are over. Indeed I'm sure she must have gone, for how could she stay anywhere at her own expense?"

"Her father—"

Miss Susannah came in with the surgeon, but she wasn't bled that day when she would have welcomed it, welcomed the sense of drifting away. He rebound her arm where he'd made his cut and said with a reluctant complacency that she was upon the road to recovery. She was glad when he went away, when they all left her. The day. The night. And the hammering that went on and on until long after dark, and after that in her dreams. And it was morning, and she was given broth, and again that air of holiday in the servant, in Miss Stone—even in Miss Susannah, with a cold anticipation in her face—and the deep, murmuring sound of the crowd from Cathedral Square, of a slow movement of many people down the street beneath the window.

She did not ask if they were going to watch the hangings and they didn't tell her. She didn't ask them about Molly, or for the names of the others. She did not want to drink her broth, and found after a few minutes that she had already drunk it, that the cup was empty. Four feet from the ground. A string no thicker than a lace. She stared at the doorway, where an angle of the room made shadows. Could see her hanging there. What had she done?

And as she stared the door began to open, slowly, slowly, and she thought, *It is her*, and put up her hand to feel for the ring that hung at her neck. And it was not there, and she was still feeling for it when Molly came in, stood for a second holding the door-handle, and then with two quick steps was kneeling beside the bed, holding one of Sara's hands, burying her face against the coverlet. Neither of them said anything, and she touched Molly's hair and then felt again for the ring. *If it is lost*, she thought. Molly's head heavy against her.

"They're going to hang him," Molly whispered. "I think I'll die." She was crying, her hands gripping at the coverlet, clawing at it. "They kept me away from you, said I were a murderer's—Oh, Sara, he didn't mean it, he didn't, he didn't."

"I know."

They stayed like that and heard the crowd grow still. Heard a voice reading prayers. Another. Now and then a shout from the crowd, sharp rising and as quickly silent. And the prayers ended and a long groaning from a thousand people, a great sighing groan of expectation. Twelve at the one time. Twelve at the. . . .

She heard a voice shouting, couldn't catch the words, and the crowd-groan quieted for a long moment and then came again, as deep as horror, a huge and

140

terrible sighing. She held Molly, bent over her, held her head against her as though she were trying to prevent her from hearing it. She looked at the window, imagined she could see them, the twelve gibbets, the bodies dangling, dangling, their hands and feet chained, their necks twisted sideways. And there would be six more. She tried to shut her own ears, shut her eyes against the bright square of the window, bent down until her face was against Molly's hair.

Chapter 11

Her room at home seemed more strange than the room at The Bell Inn in Urnford. The house. The garden. As though it were merely somewhere she had stayed before, where she must stay again, unwillingly, for a brief time.

Why didn't I die? she wondered. She tried not to see the door of his room when she went downstairs, not to look at his chair in the parlour, not to think at mealtimes as Miss Susannah took the head of the table, *He sat there.*

She scarcely spoke to them and they left her in her silence, only Miss Hetty with small, horrified whisperings, trying to get from her, "Why? *Why* had she defended them?" The meals quickly, uncomfortably over. Mrs. Hobhouse, Peg, turning their heads aside when she came near, trying to have no occasion to speak to her.

Only Old John spoke to her as if nothing had happened, as if he hadn't heard of anything. Weeding, tending, muttering about "them earwigs, them wood-pigeons," as though the captain had never lived, let alone been murdered, as though he knew nothing of his half-sister on her knees in Urnford jail, the lace drawn tight round her throat, her hands quietly folded in the lap of her green gown. "The devil come for her. Bad wicked from small, she were always."

Sara grew stronger, could feel them waiting, a dreadful patience in their eyes as they watched her. And she wanted to cry out at them, "I am strong enough. Send me away now. Now!" But she did not say it. She hoped Molly would come to her, but the days went by and she did not. And she could not think of the future, could not think of anything but those half-dozen moments of the immediate past.

Up there, on the rutted, narrow road to Over Thax-stone, seeing them again and again, like silhouettes. The cart, the gun, the men and women marching. And his blue, square figure, standing in front of them, crying out to them—what had he cried out?

The sound of hammering. And that deep sighing of the crowd.

Why hadn't Molly come to her? And she thought sometimes, *I must go to her*, but she could not summon up her mind to it. Through the stuff of her gown she felt the ring they had given back to her that evening, when she asked for it. "What a strange, ugly thing for a keepsake! Who gave it to you?" Miss Stone had said. Wanting to tell her how they had died.

"And that Daniel Blogg! Shouting in the very moment he was about to meet his maker face to face 'To Hell with your prayers!' Can you believe such wickedness? My blood ran cold. They threw him off very quick, I can tell you, before he could say any more, and the others, too."

She tried to think what she should do. Held the shape of the ring through the cloth. Go away. Go far away. But where?

They told her that night. Dr. Malthus was there, in the parlour, and Dr. Newall and Miss Susannah, Miss Hetty making herself painfully busy elsewhere. Dr. Malthus smiling with a distant tenderness, Dr.

Newall not yet recovered from his fears, all his weight of anxiety. His clothes seemed loose on his body, his hands to have grown shaky as he took his snuff and spilled it. Since the rectory had been burned, he was staying in Mr. Cameron's house, but even that seemed not to have made him feel safe.

"Why, she looks taller still!" Dr. Malthus said. He smiled down at his white, slender hands, refolded them, looked up expectantly towards Miss Susannah.

"Do you feel well enough to discuss your future, Sara?"

Miss Susannah standing. Dr. Newall also standing, his back to the empty fireplace, his snuff-box tightly held as though he were afraid he might let it fall. Only Dr. Malthus sitting, in the captain's chair, the captain's long churchwarden pipe with the amber mouthpiece still lying on the small table beside him.

"Yes," Sara said, looking at them as though they were strangers. *Now I shall be able to go away*, she thought.

"Dr. Malthus? If you would tell her your plan?" As though even this much contact with Sara gave her pain.

"Pray sit down, my dear," Dr. Malthus said. "If Miss Susannah doesn't mind my offering a chair in her parlour?"

Sara sat at the round table where Miss Hetty had left one of her albums, touched it with a finger.

"You will remember that some weeks ago we spoke of a family . . . under-governess . . ." His voice drifting away out of her hearing. She had to make herself listen. "I'm afraid that you must realise that the events—the trial, the notoriety—your behaviour hasn't been, shall I say, easy to understand, Sara?" His voice drifting away again, lost. What was he telling her? "We could hardly expect that a private family. . . . But I have been most fortunate in hearing of an apprentice house in Lancashire where they are in need of an assistant. Do you know what an apprentice house is, my dear?" She shook her head. "It's an institution to which poor children, orphans, are sent when they're of an age to gain their livelihood, at seven or eight, to work in the cotton mills. Naturally at such a tender age they must be cared for, so they are lodged in such houses, where they may be under supervision when they are not at work, until their apprenticeship term is ended and they may care for themselves. You would be a kind of assistant housekeeper there. Wouldn't you like that, Sara? Miss Susannah speaks highly of your abilities in that direction." He smiled gently. Miss Susannah stared bleakly at the mantelpiece, Sara tried to think, *He is speaking of me, of where I am to go.*

"It would be a great responsibility for you, my dear," Dr. Malthus went on. "As many perhaps as a hundred children, some near as old as yourself. And you'd have to keep them in order, you know! Be quite the disciplinarian! And at the same time a mother to them!" He seemed carried away by the thought. "Best of all, scarce a word of your—of the recent—Why, it's so far off they aren't likely to have heard of any of our troubles. Now, I've told you all. What do you answer me? Oh, but what am I thinking of? Naturally you would be paid a wage! Twenty pounds per year, with your board and lodging! You'd be quite independent! In a way much more so than had you been going to a gentleman's family to care for his small children. Quite, quite independent."

She said nothing, and after a moment Dr. Newall said sharply, "Well, miss?" His mouth twitched, gave him a petty old-womanish look. *I must answer him. I must say—say what? Suppose I were to say I didn't wish to go?* She almost smiled. *Or that I wished to think—to think—think of what?*

"Dr. Malthus is waiting for your answer," Miss Susannah said.

"He is very kind," Sara managed to say. It seemed someone else who was speaking.

"So you agree?" Dr. Malthus said, folding his hands together as though they were precious things that he was gently touching.

"Have I a choice?"

Miss Susannah drew in her breath.

Sara wanted to say to her, "Why did you not let me die, there in Urnford?" So much cold charity.

"If you put it to me in such blunt words," Dr. Malthus was saying, "why, what can I answer you? There are so few things a young lady can do. And in your—your particular situation—"

"I understand," Sara said. "Of course." She wondered whether they would give her anything that had belonged to him. That pipe. Anything. And even to ask that much seemed to tighten her throat.

"So!" cried Dr. Malthus. "A happy outcome after all. What a great adventure it will be for you! And twenty pounds per year!"

"We, of course, shall provide you with your travelling expenses," Miss Susannah said.

"When must I go?" She wished she had not said "must."

"The sooner the better!" Dr. Malthus cried. "A clean break with old unhappy—" He stopped himself and said, "Off with the old, on with the new! We thought the carrier *can* bring you to Urnford tomorrow and. . . ."

She was no longer listening, looking at the window, the drawn curtains, thinking, *I shall not see them again.* She wondered if she was glad. Doctor Malthus came to an end.

"I found this in my brother's desk," Miss Susannah said. She picked up a fold of paper from the table beside her, held it out. Even then she looked not at Sara's face but at her hands.

Outside the door Sara stood holding it, in the dark of the passage, and it was as though he was upstairs, in his room, and she need only go up and he would be sitting there by the fire, the *Gazette* beside him, looking up at her as she came in. She went slowly up to the landing, stood outside his door, put out her hand to touch the handle.

"What are you doing, Sara?" Miss Hetty, standing there in the shadows, a kind of terror in her voice.

"Why, nothing. I—" Wanting to say, "*I* am to go away. Tomorrow." Almost wanting Miss Hetty's tears, although why, why?

"Sara, there's something, something in your room." What was she talking about, what was the matter with

145

her? "Oh, what have you done? You—you haven't—? There is a purse of guineas!" Her voice whispering with terror. "And a silver mirror with Lord Southcott's crest on it! Oh, Sara! You haven't stolen? If you—if you wanted money you could have—"

She scarcely understood what Miss Hetty was saying, only heard the terror in the old, soft voice, only understood she had been in her room, touched her things, the mirror, the purse.

"They are mine, they are mine!" she said. "Why were you—" She stepped so swiftly towards the old woman that Miss Hetty threw up her hands in a kind of defense, took a step backwards on the narrow landing.

"Sara, you must tell me the truth."

"Let me alone!" Sara whispered. She pushed by Miss Hetty, ran up the stairs, breathless, with a sudden fear that the mirror was gone, that the old woman had taken it. But it lay where Sara had left it, in the drawer of her washstand, only the scarf unwrapped from around it, the drawer itself not completely closed again. The purse lying beside the mirror. Miss Hetty's fingers probing, searching. Why? Couldn't they even leave these things to her without—without—

She stood looking down at the drawer, so like the drawer in Mrs. Talbot's old wooden table. "I'm going away," she whispered savagely. "Going away, away, away. I'll never see them again." She remembered the folded paper in her hand, stood for a moment looking at it, her name written there. *Sara.* Trying to feel through the surface what it held. A letter? To her? Knowing that he—fearing that—There was no letter at all. A scrap of yellow cotton, torn from something. A bill of goods from a shop. *Madame D'Arblay— Modiste to the Nobility and*—that shop in London. A list of the clothes he had bought for her, the prices. On the back of it, as on the outer fold of paper, her name written again, in the captain's careful, old-fashioned script, with many cruls and scrolls, as though he'd sat at his desk writing it with long care. *Sara.* Only that. A list of clothes.

She looked at the piece of yellow cotton, held it,

felt its thin nothingness between her fingers, no longer needed to look at it. The yellow dress. She lifted her eyes and stared into the dark mirror in front of her, into the past that was always there, hidden like a crouching animal. "No," she breathed, "No!" She shut her eyes against it, crushed the cotton in her hand, held herself so tight her nerves screamed inside her head. *No, No, No,* and the echo of that scream, a woman screaming, *No, No, No,* and the sounds, the sounds. She had to support herself on the edge of the shabby washstand, bend her head down. She smelled the burning, the gunpowder, the blood. And that scream that had turned to an ugly, broken moaning there in the yard, and the panting of the men.

Her eyes still shut, she folded the yellow cotton and the bill together, folded them with careful fingers into the paper that had held them, put them into the drawer, and closed it. She put on her cloak and went down the stairs and out into the garden, not even noticing Peg, Mrs. Hobhouse, who looked at her and away with closed faces. She stood in the kitchen garden for a moment and went out onto the road, with nothing in her mind except to be out of that house, to be free of them. To be free of that memory. Free of everything. It was only when she was outside that she thought of Molly, began to run.

The hut, Henry Bone's hut, which was Molly's now, black against the marsh. No light. No smoke. *If she isn't there, if she's gone away*, She had fallen to a walk, and then run again, as though all her soul depended on finding Molly, as though the thought of losing her, of that last loss, would be too much to bear, would break something that could not be mended, ever. She banged her fist on the door, called, "Molly, Molly! Are you there?" There were sounds of waking, stirring, a child's voice, Molly crying out, "Sara? Is't you?"

The door opened, the stench of the hut caught at her, and yet it was almost familiar, almost dear, Molly still half asleep, amazed, big and naked-seeming in her shift, straw clinging to it, a sense of warmth from her body, from her breath as she held her, the

147

door still open behind her, the children stirring and rustling in their bed of rags and straw.

"You got thin," Molly said. "Silly thin, you got. Oh, my dear." She closed the door, drew her in. "Tom, find that candle stump an' put a light to it. 'Tis Miss Sara come."

The stump of tallow made its uneasy crocus flame, showed Tom's face, the dirt yellow hair, the deep-set, suspicious eyes.

"Tom's a great lad, now, ain't you, Tom? The man o' the family now, and Willum an' Marthy, oh, them are brave too. Working for Mr. Masham like big people an' earnin'. Scarin' off the crows an' weedin', oh, they're big as big now, they ain't crying just cause Miss Sara is come, eh, Marthy?" She cossetted the almost invisible small girl, came back to Sara, set the stool for her, pulled her gown round her. "Fire's gone out," she said apologetically. But there were no ashes there.

"I have to go away," Sara said. "To Lancashire. To work in an apprentice house."

"Lancashire?" Molly said wonderingly. "Is't far off?"

"Yes."

They sat and said nothing. Tom had crept back into the bed.

"Have you—have you found work?" Sara said.

Molly shook her head. She looked to have grown thin herself, her eyes shadowed, her big, handsome mouth gaunt. But it might have been the candlelight.

Sara gripped Molly's hands. "Why did it happen?" she whispered. She scarcely knew herself what she meant.

"I don't know." And then, "They do want to pull this down on us. Mr. Cameron said we don't have no right to stay here, 'twere only a kindness to Dad he let 'em build this. And what Dad done—"

"Pull it down? They can't."

"They can."

"What will you do?"

"I don't know. The little 'uns can sleep at Masham's I 'spect. There's sheds there. Won't be no worse for 'em than this." She let go of Sara's hands. "Better, really. We ain't had no fire since—"

"What will *you* do? Can Mr. Masham not give you—"

"Missus Masham won't let 'em. I'll go on the road, likely. Find something far off." She smiled. "Lancashire maybe."

"Come with me," Sara said. "I've got money. I've got eleven guineas and they're going to give me—"

Molly stared at her. "Go with you. How could I?" Her eyes faded. "They wouldn't let me. An' what'd I do there to get my bread?"

"They couldn't stop us," Sara said. And thought of Dr. Newall, of Dr. Malthus, of Miss Susannah. "And when we got there . . ." Her voice trailed.

"I'll find something," Molly said.

"Let me give you . . ." But she hadn't brought her money with her. "I have to be ready to go tomorrow afternoon," she said. "Could you, would you, come to say goodbye to me? I would like to—to—"

"They wouldn't let me near," Molly said. "When they put me out I told 'em things. What I thought of 'em. That's why Missus Masham won't let me work aside the little ones an' Tom. She wanted Mr. Masham to put them out too an' said Miss Susannah had told her how wicked I was. We'd best say good-bye here."

They held each other again for a moment. "At least they didn't hang her," Sara said. "She cheated them."

"Aye. She did that."

"I'll come back," Sara said. "You must have her money, I don't need it." She was in a sudden haste, a fury with herself for not bringing the money with her, for not thinking, knowing . . . She was afraid she was going to cry and pushed herself away from Molly, was at the door.

"What money you talking about?" Molly said. "I don't need no money."

But Sara was gone, running and running until she was home again.

"Miss Susannah's bin looking for you," Mrs. Hobhouse said, not quite turning round, not quite looking

149

at Sara's face, busy with her candle, with a cupboard door in the dresser.

Sara went into the hall, saw the parlour door still open, a lamp still lit. "Is that you, Sara?"

She went in. Miss Susannah. Miss Hetty. Miss Hetty's staring at her in terror.

"My sister tells me . . ." Miss Susannah said.

Miss Hetty looked away, her eyes beginning to fill with tears.

". . . that you have a large sum of money in your drawer, and a silver mirror that must belong to Lord Southcott. Where did you get them?"

"They're mine."

"That is no answer, Sara. Where did you get them? I must know."

She wanted to say so much, and a dozen furious words died on her tongue with a kind of heaviness, of despair. "They're mine," she whispered again.

"If you persist in saying only that I must imagine you obtained them in some wrong way."

"Oh, Sara, dearest, you must tell the truth. I was so sad that you must go away that I wanted to—to —And then I saw them, oh, oh, oh. Do you not understand what stealing means, child?"

"I got them . . ."

"Yes?" Miss Susannah said. The light of the oil lamp falling in soft yellow tones on the flowered carpet, on the chairs, the tables. His pipe still there.

"Someone gave them to me." She stared at them. She thought, *I'll die before I tell them. If they kill me I shall not tell them.*

"Who?" Miss Susannah sat waiting, her square grey face, the blunt hook of her nose like an ugly remembrance of the captain. The grey wisps of hair under the edge of her lace evening cap. Her dress like black iron rather than taffeta, her big, mannish hands locked together. Only the whiteness of the knuckles showed her anger, her tension. Her voice as flat and emotionless as always, as coldly questioning.

"I do not wish to believe in your guilt, I assure you. I owe it to our brother's memory not to believe you capable of—at least of that. And for that reason I haven't so much as gone to your room to look at your drawer for myself. But you must satisfy me beyond all doubt as to where you obtained the mirror, and so much money."

"I shall not tell you," Sara said. She felt rage beginning to shake inside her, something quite new and terrible, as though she could kill, like a fever, and at the same time almost a triumphant pleasure. She imagined taking that lamp and smashing it against the wall, picking up the china ornaments, the clock, the candlesticks, and smashing them to pieces, grinding them under her heels.

"Then I must put the matter to Dr. Newall tomorrow morning," Miss Susannah said. "We cannot send you to Lancashire with such a possibility existing. If you haven't told me by breakfast, then I shall be forced to send word to Dr. Newall. Do you understand that, Sara?"

She stared at them both, felt the hatred grow in her like poison, like a fever.

"If you don't understand me, then you must take the consequences. Now go to your room."

Even to do that was like submission, like confessing something, but she could not stay there either, and she turned and went out, began to slam the door and then drew it softly behind her as though nothing so simple, so childish as a banged door could ease her fury. As though in those seconds she had finally grown up, was a woman, as though all that had happened in the last weeks had been held back like a dam across a river that holds back a flood and then breaks.

"They mean—they mean—" And all the possibilities of what they meant, possibilities of vengeance, came against her like a physical thing, there in the dark of the passage. She had to cling to the newel-post for a moment, catch her breath against the realisation. Mrs. Talbot gave them to me. Run back, crawl, say that to them? And she could see Miss Susannah's cold stare of disbelief. Or belief. "And where did Mrs. Talbot get such a mirror, I wonder?"

She went up the stairs as though she were ill again, gathered her things, threw them onto the bed, made

151

two piles of them, those that he'd given her and those they had had made for her, left all those aside with a shiver of fury. Put on the dress he had given her, that was too small, too short, even though the hems and seams had all been changed and altered. Forced on the slippers she'd worn when she came, put on the short jacket, felt almost clean, almost free, took the silk reticule he'd given her, the mirror, the guineas, the folded paper with its cotton and its list of clothes, and ran down the stairs again and through the dark kitchen, and let herself out into the yard, the kitchen garden, the road. Ran.

Molly opened the door of the hut, astonished out of her sleep for the second time that night, lost for a moment. "Wha—what's 'a matter, what's happened?"

"I've run away," Sara said. "They're going to accuse me of stealing the mirror. And the money." Molly drew her in, lit the candle stump again, rubbed her eyes. The children were so fast asleep they only groaned and whimpered in the depths of it, like puppies. "I'm going to go to London," Sara said. "And then—and then—" She gripped Molly's hands, knelt on the mud floor in front of her, Molly still dazed with sleep. "Come with me. Tom'll take the little ones to Farmer Masham's tomorrow. You can send him money, we'll leave him money now, just come."

"To London?" And then, as though that were the important thing, "He don't need money, Tom don't. They got their wages an' food."

"Come with me. We can be in Urnford by morning, and take the coach. We'll get work, we'll—"

"What kind o' work?"

Sara shook her with impatience, with a fury to be going. "What does that matter, what kind of work? What will you find if you go tramping by yourself? Come with me. You're—you're all I've got left. Please, please come."

"Aye?" Molly said, seemed to be turning it over in her mind like a puzzling object in her hand. She laughed suddenly, a rasping hoarseness of laughter like savagery, her teeth glistening, no kind of amusement

152

in the laughter. She turned on the stool, began to shake one of the heaps of rags, went on shaking it until Tom pushed out his head, blinked and stared at her, then recognised that it was his sister and not the overseer on the farm about to cuff him. "I'm goin' away with Miss Sara, Tom. You got to be a big boy an' look after the little ones altogether, now. Tell Mr. Masham I have gone off somewheres an' you want to sleep at the farm 'cause you've nowheres else. Will you tell 'em that?"

She had to repeat it before he was awake enough to understand.

"I'll give him some of the money," Sara said.

"He'd only lose it or they'd take it on 'em. If they're talking about stealing, they'd say how did he get a guinea piece? And hang him too." She said that with such ferocity that Tom, who'd half fallen back to sleep, woke up again and began to cry, and she had to hold him. "No one'll hang my Tom, Molly won't let 'em touch you, my love. Molly's goin' to London to get rich and buy you fine big boots an' a new shirt an' a dress for Marthy an' something wonderful for Willum. She'll come back to you carryin' such wonderful things an' a great bit o' bacon to eat, an' a plum puddin'. Won't you like that, Tom? You're too big a grown-up man to cry, my love."

She stood up, found her stuff dress, and pulled it over her head, felt for her boots on the floor and pushed her feet into them. Her cloak was hanging on a nail behind the door. "I'm ready," she said. She went back to the bed and knelt down and held the children, still asleep, stroked their heads. Sara went outside and Molly joined her, pulling the door shut. "It might as well be London as anywheres," Molly said. They began to walk.

Two

London

Chapter 12

They reached The Swan in Holborn at one o'clock in the afternoon, getting down from the Urnford coach into the inn yard, ostlers, grooms, passengers, inn servants, the great black bulk of the coach above them like a ship, the horses stamping, the cobbles slippery underfoot, a servant girl hanging out of an upstairs window, looking at the arrivals, at the coachman in his vast green coat climbing down from the driver's seat.

"Luggage, miss? Your boxes?" A man in a striped black and yellow waistcoat, black breeches, staring at them, his eyebrows raised, respectful readiness altering to another kind of interest as he summed them up. "Ain't got no luggage, eh?"

Sara turned away from him, hugging her small bundle of belongings, tried to think where to look, where to go. A man carrying a great leather trunk, bumping into her, shouting, "Can't 'ee look out?" And then seeing it was a passenger, mumbling, "Mind yerself, Miss, mind yerself."

"Where are we?" Molly whispered. "Is this London?"

The man in the striped waistcoat followed them, took Sara familiarly by the arm. "Just up from the country, eh? Anyone meetin' yer?" His eyes assessed them, knew that no one was meeting them, that they had nowhere to go.

Sara pulled her arm away from him, said, "Yes,

someone is meeting us, we must hurry," and pushed Molly towards the entrance of the yard. She had thought they would hire a room wherever the coach set them down, imagined somewhere like The Bell in Urnford, tried to remember what she'd seen of London with the captain. But it had not been much. The coaches arriving and leaving, inn yards like this, the lodging house, a quiet street, the ugly, grimed window, and the roofs of houses. She had thought she would recognise something but she recognised nothing. Even the inn yard, the people seemed different. And she thought, *If he was here* . . . And she gripped Molly's arm and pushed her towards the street, the man calling behind them, "If 'e don't turn up, you come back 'ere an' I'll fix yer up with something."

Crowds in the street, traffic, coaches, carts, men shouting, cracking whips, the grinding of iron tyres on stone, people hurrying, jostling them, shops, houses towering four and five stories above their heads, the smell of smoke from chimneys that seemed to hang over them like a cloud, reach down into the street. Smells of cooking from open windows, a baker's shop and the smell of bread, the sudden overwhelming familiarness of new-baked bread; a man in a white apron and brown paper hat at a counter, sorting loaves and buns and kinds of bread they had never seen.

"I'm starvin'," Molly said. "Could we buy somethin' to eat?"

They went into the baker's shop and bought two buns. The baker stared at them the way the man in the yard of The Swan had and gave Sara her change slowly, shilling by shilling, as though he had it in mind to keep them there as long as possible.

"Do you know how we can get to somewhere called Glovers' Row, please?" Sara asked. She had written out Madame D'Arblay's address and showed it to him. When he had told them, they walked down the street eating their buns and trying to keep out of the way of passersby, hesitating for long moments before they trusted themselves across the roads, beginning to shrink closer and closer together, to hold each other against the enormous weight and size of everything, the rush of it as though they had thrown themselves into a river, an enormous, bursting river that was threatening to drown them at any second, hurling them along.

"At least you bin here before," Molly whispered, and had to shout it to be heard.

"Yes," Sara said. "I'm sure I'll recognise somewhere soon." Trying to remember what the baker had told them, along this street for so many crossings, then turn left, then right, then—They found a woman standing in a shop doorway and Sara showed her the address. The woman stared at her: at her bare head; at her slippers; at her dress, which was too small; at her spencer, which was too short. She seemed to take her in from head to foot with one flick of the eye and in the next summed up Molly in her broken, down-at-heel boots, her worn, mended cloak too hot for the summer street and her servant's washed-out blue staff gown beneath it.

"Never heard of it," the woman said, and wrinkled up her nose as though they had insulted her by asking. "Gypsy sluts," she said as they turned away. Molly stopped and would have turned back if Sara had let her.

"Who's she calling gypsies?"

"Come along, for pity's sake," Sara said.

"Ignorant old faggot. Ignorant old faggot!"

They had to ask three people before they found their way again. "I thought you knew about London," Molly said.

They turned a corner and it was Glovers' Row. They walked along it slowly and Sara felt something rising up in her throat that she recognised as terror. She had hardly thought beyond this moment, beyond finding this street. Suppose Madame D'Arblay had no work for them, knew no one who had, how long would eleven guineas last? For both of them? Yesterday it had seemed enough for forever.

A China warehouse. A narrow, almost hidden doorway and a dark, narrow window. Two steps down into the shop. A gilt sign, the gilt rubbed, faded. "Madame D'Arblay, Modiste." The old man at the counter, look-

158

ing up as their standing in the doorway cut off such light as was reaching him.

"Yes, ladies? Come in, come in." Bending over the counter towards them, smiling. An old, stoop-shouldered man with grey hair and long yellow teeth that smiled at them.

Sara stepped slowly down into the shop, Molly behind her. "Is Madame D'Arblay here?"

He had seen their clothes and something of the yellow smile faded, altered: the small brown glassy eyes, became somehow alert, birdlike. "And what might you want with Madame D'Arblay?" he asked. He did not seem to remember her. He looked at the paper in Sara's hands with the address on it, looked at her clothes, her face, her hair, with the same swift taking-in as the woman in the shop doorway a quarter of an hour before. Looked at Molly, at Sara again. The smile came back.

"We were—we're looking for work," Sara said. "Just for a little while."

"Ah, I see. I see. And you've just arrived, eh? From the country?"

"Yes," Sara whispered. And then said, "Yes" louder, more at her ease. He seemed a pleasant enough old gentleman.

"And may I ask who gave you this address?"

He had come round to their side of the counter and still seemed to be considering them, his old, knuckly hands rubbing each other slowly, his head bent forward, extraordinarily like a bird's.

"My guardian. We—he brought me here once, once before."

The smile seemed to lose a fraction of its kindliness.

"Ah, indeed? And who might your guardian be, if I might enquire?"

"He was Captain Pownall. He bought me some clothes here once. Two years ago, if perhaps you wouldn't remember."

"Ah, ah yes! Captain Pownall, eh? And how is the gentleman?" The hands rubbed slowly together, the smile hesitated. "Did you say, 'was'?"

"He's dead," Sara said.

159

"What a tragedy, what a tragedy! And left you alone in the world to make your way? So you've come here. And this young person, is she all alone too?"

"Yes," Sara said. "We're together. We only arrived just now."

The door in the wall in front of her opened, the inner door, disguised by the long mirror. The same fat old woman came in, dressed in black. The same strange, white mask of a face under the black curls, the black lace cap. The same two bright red circles on her cheeks, like crimson patches. The black snapping eyes.

"And here *is* Madame D'Arblay," the old man said. "Such a lucky stroke of fortune that the pair of you should come here today of all days. They're seeking work, my dear," he said turning to the old woman. "This young lady was our customer two years ago. Do you remember her? With her guardian? Who has just died, alas, leaving her quite alone in the world. And this young lady with her is in the same sad case. Is that not correct?" He turned back to Sara.

Madame D'Arblay had sat down on a thin, gilt chair, and was breathing heavily as though she'd climbed stairs, or as though the effort of coming into the shop had made her breathless. Sara tried not to stare at her. She wore a black silk dress that seemed to change its shade of blackness as she breathed, to shimmer in the light. The old woman said nothing, looked at them, expressionless.

"But we must know a little more, my dears, before we come to terms. So many young people seek work from us, you know. We must ask questions and make sure that we give work only to the most deserving. Now, no doubt you have at least some friend in London? Someone you are to lodge with? Who might speak for you?"

"Speak for us?" Sara said. "But we know no one here."

"Oh, dear," the old man said. "Or at home, for instance. Now, there must be someone where you've just been living. Someone anxious as to how you shall get on in London? Of whom we could enquire about

160

you both? Just a reference, you know: one must be so careful, I'm afraid." He peered sharply at her, seemed to probe into her with those bird-bright eyes, the hands washing each other with a faint cracking sound of knuckles.

"There's no one," Sara said. "No one at all. No one." She wanted suddenly to get out of the shop, away, before he got the word Thaxstone from her Miss Susannah, everything that had happened, held them there. She took a step back, bumped against Molly, and the old man had caught her by the arm, was smiling, smiling, shaking his head sadly but smiling at the same time with those long yellow teeth turned black at the roots.

"What a sad state of affairs," he said. "No one in the world, and no one at home who cares for you? Well, I never! Can you believe the heartlessness of the world, my dear?" He'd turned to the old woman again, his hand still holding Sara's arm. She wanted to wrench free and tried to do it gently. But he drew her forward to stand exactly in front of the old woman, caught Molly by the elbow and drew her forward too, clicking his tongue against his teeth.

"It's against all our rules," he said. "We only employ young persons with the highest of references, only the most respectable young persons. But in this particular case, my dear, what do you think? Could we bend the rules just this once? Such poor, unhappy young people. Please, my dear, let us make an exception just this once."

The black slits of eyes looked at them, the white face above its short, frog-thickness of neck and throat seemed to bend forward a trifle, either to see them closer or to nod assent. The old man must have recognized it as assent because he said, "Oh, thank you, thank you, my dear, I'm sure we shall not regret it. She says, yes! Yes! And such a handsome young pair, I couldn't have borne it to let you go off into the streets and think of you without a friend or a place to lay your heads. I must call Doris and tell her she will have you for companions. I must call her at once, and we will go downstairs and talk

161

about your work and your wages and such things as that."

He seemed genuinely excited and let go of their arms to rub his hands again before opening the door with the mirror set on it and calling, "Doris! Doris! We've two young people to join us, straight from the countryside!" And turning back to them, he said, "Oh, you'll like it here!"

"But what work is it?" Sara said. Even though he'd changed his direction and was asking no more questions, the feeling of wanting to get away from this place had stayed with her like an uneasiness. She had to crush it down, make herself stand there in front of the silent old woman with her dreadful face.

"Oh, the lightest and pleasantest of work. A little sewing, a little helping here and there about the house, a mere trifle." Another woman was in the passage behind the opened door. She seemed to fill the passage with her fatness. A youngish woman but with rolls of fat that ran down from her chins to her thick body, her bare, massive arms, like mutton—purplish red and white like great uncooked legs of mutton. She too wore black silk and had the same black, snapping eyes. Like mother and daughter. When she said, "Yes?" she showed a front tooth broken short; the "yes" came hissing through it.

"Here they are!" cried the old man. "Now, let's go downstairs and be comfortable! Show them the way, Doris." He had taken hold of Sara's and Molly's elbows again and was pushing them forward. And the fat woman, Doris, reached out for them, her hands so fat they were like balls of suet, yet with a look of strength about them, in the hooked fingers, the thick, monstrous wrists. And something about the movement, about everything, the gentle pressure to have Sara go forward, through that door, to be taken hold of by that fat, waiting hand —she did not even look like a woman, like a fat grotesque of a man disguised. Something set the alarms ringing in her mind, redoubled that urgency of wanting to escape, to get away from here, and she held back, jerked her elbow free of the old man's hand, tried to take a step back, catch hold of Molly and pull her away too.

The old man caught at her again, gripped, began to drag her forward, and she cried, "Let go of me! Let go! Molly!"

"Don't be foolish, my dear, we're your friends! Doris! Take her by the hand!"

The fat, soft hand closed on her wrist, seemed to lock there spongily, like wet leather, pulled her towards the passage. She began to fight, heard, sensed a shadow behind her, the old woman standing up, Molly struggling, the old man soothing, urging, and in the doorway of the shop the silhouette of someone else, a bonnet, a skirt, and she cried, "Help! Help us! Let go!"

The woman, the girl rather, who had just come in came down the two steps, saying, "Whassamatter! Whassup? What yer doing, Darby?"

The old man, Doris, stayed frozen for a second, and Sara wrenched her arms free, caught her bundle as it was falling, her reticule still hanging safe on her wrist by its string, backed away, cried, "Molly!" and Molly freed herself from the old man's hand, was beside her, beside the girl who had just come in, and who was looking at the old man with a peculiar, jeering smile.

"Nothing, my dear, nothing, just two young girls coming to work for us. Come along now my dears or Madame D'Arblay may change her mind. Doris—" Advancing towards them, reaching out. "Molly, run!" Sara hissed at her and ran herself, was up the steps, into the street, Molly slower behind her. The old man shouting, "Stop thief! Stop thief!" They were in the street and running, passersby staring, turning, the old man's voice, other voices shouting, "Thief, thief, stop thief!" and a carter turning the corner, hearing the shouting, standing up on his footboard and flourishing his enormous whip, the lash curling towards her, catching her across the shoulders like a sword cut that sent her staggering. Running feet, a hand grabbing her arm, tugging. She tried to jerk free and stumbled again, and the hand held her, pulled her forward. A girl's voice panted, "This way, down 'ere." Tugging her down an alleyway, into sudden shadow. She looked for Molly, saw her pounding behind them, her cloak flying, and then the cloak vanishing off her shoulders like a conjuring trick as someone grabbed it from behind and it fell away, wrapping round the pursuer, making him fall headlong. Seeing all that in the turning of her head, the girl beside her running as fast as she could run herself. Across another street, into a still narrower alleyway, through an arch, up steps, round corners, cobbles underfoot, mud, rubbish, a wooden door in a wall and the girl kicking it open, pushing her through into a dirty yard, bottles, a pile of straw, the stink of horse manure, a horse in a stall with the half-door swung open, pulling her towards it.

"Molly!"

"I'm here."

The three of them in the horse's stall the brown flank against their faces, the horse turning his head, tossing it, stamping his hooves in the straw. Across the stable-yard the back of a tall, narrow building, other buildings, windows, some of them bricked up. Her shoulders burning where the carter's whip had caught it, a sudden agony as she leaned against the timber wall. Out in the alleyway, beyond the wooden door, a voice shouting, "Which way? Three pickpockets! Which way'd they run? Three girls!" More voices, running feet going by, someone pushing the wooden door, looking into the yard. They stayed like shadows, holding their breaths. And the horse stared at the man in the doorway who took another step into the yard, saw no hiding place, and went out into the alleyway again. Ran on.

Silence. Only the sounds from the houses, the distant streets, traffic. The horse's snuffling breath, the shuffling of a hoof.

"Gawd!" the girl said. "The old bastard. We better go inside." She had gold ringlets under a fashionable leghorn bonnet, and a long, tip-tilted nose in a broad, pink-and-white face. Much shorter than either Sara or Molly, picking her way daintily among the tawny pools of horse-stale towards the house, a back door set at the head of three broken steps. They followed her because there seemed nothing else to do. She lifted up her skirts of lavender satin, showed white leather boots.

They waited on the steps, the girl knocking in an odd rhythm, one-two-three, one-two, and repeating it. The burning in Sara's shoulders seeming to spread down her back until her whole body was on fire. The door opened, a pale boy stared at them, recognised the girl, and jerked his head. " 'Oo're your friends, Snipe?"

"I'll tell you inside. Didn't you 'ear the rumpus just now?"

He shook his head and let them into a dark passage, packed on one side with wooden boxes. There was a smell of roasting coffee, and drains, and rotting wood. The boy shut the door and the girl gave a long sigh of relief. "Anyone comes," she said, "we bin 'ere the past two hours, see? Tell your father. Darby 'ad these two 'ayseeds, these sawneys in 'is shop and was kickin' 'em through to Doris when I comes in. You're a lucky pair," she said, turning to Sara. "You a gyppo?" Sara looked blank and the girl said, "A gypsy, a chai?"

"No."

"Just as well."

"I don't understand any of this," Sara said.

"I know you don't."

"We ain't no thieves," Molly said. "What did he mean shoutin' 'Stop thief' like that?"

"Oh, Gawd," the girl said. "Let's go in an' 'ave a drink. Bring us a pint, Toby. An' I'll 'ave a pie; I'm near dead all that running, it ain't good for you. I'll explain inside." Toby led them down the passage into a kitchen where an older man was tending a large oven, a great smell of meat and baking as he turned to look at them, the oven door open on a brown expanse of baking pies.

"Could we have a pie, too?" Molly said.

" 'Allo, Snipe," the man at the oven said. "Trouble?"

"Not really trouble."

"I 'opes not." He straightened up, thin and tall and bony in his cook's apron, looked at Sara, at Molly, raising his ragged grey eyebrows above deep sunken eyes. "Pickpockets?"

"No, no, no," the girl said. "Just you give us three pies an' three pints o' claret an' remember we bin 'ere 'arf the morning. You 'ad enough from Jim in your time to do me a favour." She pushed Sara and Molly in front of her into another short, brighter passageway and through a doorway, past Toby, who'd opened the door for them, into a pleasant coffee-room with bright diamond-shaped windows looking onto a street, and tables and chairs and a handsome fireplace set with logs, and an air of quiet. A man was sitting at a table writing, surrounded by a scatter of papers, an ink-well, a pounce-box, half a dozen quill pens, and a quart tankard. Two others were reading newspapers by the farther window and in a darker corner three men were smoking pipes and talking in low voices that died away as the girls came in. She led them to a table beside the fire-place, in a kind of alcove made by the deep bulge of the brick chimney breast and the corner of the room.

"All's well as ends well," she said, composing herself carefully on the leather seat of her chair as though she'd been out for a morning's shopping. "My name's Beth, but they call me Snipe. On account of my sneezer." She touched a delicate finger-tip to her nose. "An' what may you two be called?" They told her, and she considered them, a depth of amused compassion and sad contempt in her round blue eyes. "You poor 'ayseeds."

"We ain't hayseeds," Molly said. "You hadn't come in then an' we all run like that, I'd 'a give that old villain such a thump."

"We're very grateful," Sara said quickly. She looked round the room, looked at the girl again, tried to sum her up, felt a hundred memories of Spain come back, of secrecy, of knocks on doorways, of safe houses.

"If I 'adn't come in," Snipe said, "you'd 'ave been stretched flat by now down in Darby's cellar, waiting for 'im to sell you to a kip-'ouse. Fifty quid each 'e'd 'ave got, at least. 'E ain't going to be pleased."

"What's a kip-house?" Molly said. Snipe stared at her in amazed pity.

"A flash-'ouse, stupid. A brothel, an 'ores' parlour."

Molly stared in her turn. "Whores? Us? He couldn't—" She opened her mouth to say more, could think of nothing to say and shut it again. Toby came with the pies and three bottles and glasses on a tray. The man at the window table nearest them stopped his writing and began to read to himself in an undertone, punctuating his reading with long pulls at his tankard.

"How could he," Sara began.

"You just up from the country? Don't know no one?"

"Yes."

"An' you went in there for what?"

"To look for work."

"Oh, my Gawd! Into Darby! For work! 'E'd 'ave found you work all right. On your backs down in Aldgate, or along in one o' Danser's 'ouses, an' someone like Doris keepin' 'er eye on you to knock you flat if you tried to make a fuss. Take all your clo' off of you when you ain't working an' leave you locked up naked. That was what 'e 'ad marked up for you two. Gawd's truth 'e's going to be 'opping mad." She laughed, a small, hoarse rattle of laughter like pebbles in a box.

"But *you* went in there," Sara said.

"I'm one of 'is suppliers, 'e wouldn't dare touch me or 'e'd wake up with 'is head stove in. 'Ere's to us." She had filled the three glasses and tilted hers and emptied it at one swallow. "You can run, the pair of you, I'll say that for you." She filled her mouth with pie, eating noisily and catching the crumbs in a delicately cupped palm held under her chin. "Dead cats 'e puts in these, I swear it. Your back 'urting, love?"

"Yes," Sara said, trying to ease it as she tasted her own pie. Molly was eating with an earnest solidity

167

of hunger, holding the pie in both hands. " 'E caught you a right smack, that carter, I saw it."

"I do think it was proper silly to run away like that," Molly said. "What'd folk think, seein' us run, except we'd done something awful? We should have told 'em what that old villain were tryin' to do, 'stead o' runnin' off like rabbits."

"Oh, should you? Well, I tell you something, if that mob 'ad caught you just now, you could tell 'em down in Bow Street 'ow innocent you was till Kingdom come, an' the best you could 'ope for'd be twelve months in Newgate. Show us your ridicule." She twitched Sara's reticule from off her wrist and opened it before Sara could stop her. The purse. A handkerchief. Oddments. A black jet brooch set with seed pearls. Sara caught her breath at the sight of it.

"Anything there that ain't yours?"

"That brooch. I never saw it before. I swear I—" She looked up into the mocking blue eyes.

"I believe you, but thousands wouldn't. I even know that prop myself, it's Ma Darby's." The eyes narrowed suddenly to cat slits. "You ain't on dip? You ain't pickpockets, the pair of you? 'Aving me on?" The eyes and face relaxed. "I believe you. Nobody but a born fool'd try an' nick anything off of Ma Darby. She must 'ave stuffed it in your ridicule while they was tryin' to get you inside the passage. So if anything went wrong, they could say they caught you stealing. 'Ow about you, Moll?"

But Molly had no reticule, nothing. Even her cloak gone.

"You 'ad your cloak on inside there. A quid to a 'a'penny they'd pinned something inside it, an' they've got it now an' are telling the watch to be on the lookout for you." She weighed the brooch in her hand and smiled, her small, rosebud mouth wicked with enjoyment of the joke. "She can pay for our dinner anyway, the dirty ol' draggletail. They owe me an 'undred quid, near about, those two old bastards, leastways they owes it to my feller, Jim. I was going to try an' collect some of it just now. Toby!"

Toby came, with his tray and napkin, his white,

tired face and knowing eyes. "Show that to your father," she said, palming the brooch into Toby's hand. "Bring me the change."

Sara tried to think of something, to say, to do. She had the feeling she was being drawn helplessly along, down a path she did not want to follow. She stared at her money on the table, the handful of gold and silver left from her eleven guineas, her handkerchief, a blackened chestnut from the paddock, the fold of paper with her name on it, and the yellow cotton and the bill inside it. The piece of yellow cotton. The pebble. From the beach where he and she had gone once, to be alone together, to walk. When had that been?

The man at the window table had raised his voice. "And I believe in the prince regent, lord and giver of places, who together with the ministers, we should worship and glorify."

Sara turned to look at him. He was lifting his tankard, saw her movement, and held the tankard up in salute. "Hey ho, my pretty doll," he said. "So you appreciate my catechism?"

"Don't mind 'im," Snipe said. " 'E's drunk. Bloody scribbler."

"Who says I'm drunk?" the man said. "Snipe? Is it you hiding there, my lovely one? Let me read you my new confession. The Munrovian creed, to replace all the outmoded old confessions of faith. A creed for our times." He had come over to their table, not quite lurching drunk, but unsteady, and not in a state to be argued with. He was large and plump and high coloured, with steel spectacles balanced askew on his snub nose, his cravat untidy and far from clean, and his buff waistcoat powdered here and there with snuff and stained with wine droppings. "A creed for our times!" He announced to them, leaning his thick-fingered, ink-stained hand on Molly's shoulder to steady himself, waving the other hand over their heads, a sheaf of paper clutched in it.

"Whosoever will be a sinecurist, his first duty is this: that he divide with the ministry, and be with the ministry in a majority. Neither confounding the persons . . ."

"Go away," Snipe said in a low, furious voice. "I'll call Toby."

". . . nor dividing with the opposition. For there is one ministry of Old Bags, another of Derry Down Triangle—"

"Go away!"

Toby came over, grasped him respectfully but firmly by the arm, and drew him back.

"Now, now, Mr. Munro, don't be bothering the young ladies."

"Young ladies?" cried Mr. Munro. "Are they young ladies? Why, Lord save me, I have made a mistake. I thought it was Snipe and two of her fellow fluffy ones. Let me apol'gise to them, let me kneel down and tell 'em—"

The other customers were already staring, craning round to look at the disturbance.

"I'll have to call Father, Mr. Munro, 'e won't like it."

"Let's get out of 'ere," Snipe said. " 'E's a lunatic, 'e'll 'ave the watch in next." She stood up and Mr. Munro called, "Snipe, Snipe, d'ye forgive me? Oh, Snipe!"

"I'll kill 'im," she said viciously. "I swear I'll kill 'im one day." She led them out through the back, the three men who'd been sitting with their tobacco pipes and wine looking at them, full of amusement and enquiry. And something else less pleasant that struck Sara's mind even in that nervous half-second of leaving. A kind of greedy speculation that she'd seen already that morning, in the eyes of the servant at The Swan, in the baker's eyes when they bought their buns, in the eyes of men passing by, a mental licking of the lips. They were in the kitchen again. Toby's father dusting bottles, a woman in an apron and mobcap setting the fresh-baked pies out on a warming rack to keep them hot.

"That Mr. Munro," Snipe said. "You shouldn't let 'im in the place. 'E'll get you a bad name."

" 'E shouldn't let you in neither," the woman said

without bothering to look round at them. "'As Jim gone yet?"

"Next week, I think." She pushed Sara and Molly into the rear passage, out into the stable-yard. And they let her push them as though they had no wills of their own, as though she had taken possession of them. They stood by the manure heap, looking at the horse. "My man, she means," Snipe said. "'E got booked for a passage. Fourteen years. Bloody bastards. They got the 'ole mob of us except me an' the boy. Well, what we going to do with you, eh?" She looked them up and down, standing in front of them like a small golden bird, her head tilted upwards, her eyes narrowed, the little rosebud mouth pursed. "You got nowhere to go?"

Sara shook her head.

"No friends? Nothing?" She waited, and Sara shook her head again. "An' you wants work? But not 'oring? Or thieving?" She smiled as though she knew so much more than they did that it wasn't worth trying to explain. As though she were an adult with two small children lost in the street. And Sara felt as though she *was* lost, stunned by all that had happened in the past few hours, clutching her thin bundle of clothes, the silver mirror, a pair of slippers, all wrapped in her shawl, as though it was all that was left to her of certainty. An echo of the old man's questioning in what this girl was asking her, a sense of danger. Yet she'd saved them already from—*from God knew what*. The cut across her back had stiffened in the warmth of the coffee-room and now it burned again as she moved, stood in the chill shadow of the dank little stable-yard. As though they were hunted things. Foxes. The men's eyes.

"Well?" Snipe said. "Come on, Gyppo. I can't 'ang round all day. You don't want to whore nor go nicking with me? What else can you do?"

"I can scrub," Molly said hopefully.

"Oh, Gawd."

"I can cook a little bit," Sara said. "Or sew."

Toby came out to them. "Father said 'alf a quid."

He tossed the half guinea in the air and caught it, a small glitter of gold against the grey yard.

" 'Alf a quid?" Snipe said furiously. "For a prop like that? Pearls?"

"Take it back then," said Toby. "An' pay for the drink an' wittles like a lady."

"I should 'ave took it to Ikey," Snipe said. "Or Monkey even."

Toby spun the little gold coin again, and with the quickness of a bird pecking, Snipe caught it out of the air above his hand and dropped it into a pocket inside her skirt. "Bloody dead cats in those pies, you tell 'im from me." Toby laughed at her, screwing up his tired, watery eyes, showing his teeth. "Come on out o' 'ere," she said, opening the door into the alleyway, looking and listening with those bird movements of the golden head, the lavender silk bonnet, the lavender skirt lifted mincingly above the straw and horse stale and manure. Even her tiny white boots seemed to have the knack of staying clean no matter what they were treading on.

"All clear." She beckoned them and they joined her, and she began walking at an astonishingly swift pace up the alley towards another street. "If Darby makes a fuss about that prop an' whatever she pinned on Molly, you two 'ad best stay out o' sight for a bit. Unless you wants a dose of Newgate. Could you wait on tables like Toby back there? Without dropping things on the customers' 'eads?"

"Oh, yes," Sara said. "We're used to something like that. But where are you taking us?" Again that memory of Spain was there. But not the captain. And she realised that in those times it had been a game, a child's game she had scarcely thought of it as a strange fashion of living. Only as the way they did live. The two of them. And that solid, comforting assurance always there, swinging her up onto horseback, riding ahead in the twilight, sitting like a rock in shadow by the fire, the sky full of stars, the smell of coffee boiling, pancakes frying, his slow careful fingers rearranging the burning sticks. There when she fell asleep. When she woke. And now—

"I'm taking you to a friend of mine. Monkey Palmer. The best flash-case in London. You'll be safe as lice in a blanket with Monkey if 'e takes you on. An' 'e was lookin' for table girls. Even Darby won't touch you there."

She went ahead, the white boots twinkling, the lavender skirt dancing its frill above their low heels, her bonnet and her shawl seeming by the way they sat on her head and shoulders to convey a watchful self-certainty, like a fox in a dangerous wood full of snares and gamekeepers. But a fox that has saved its life a thousand times and eaten a thousand pheasants and means to go on doing it.

Molly caught Sara's arm and shook it. "What's a flash-case?"

"How do I know?"

"You always know so much. I do think we oughta run like mad an' go somewhere a bit quiet. I don't like London."

"Go where?"

Snipe was beckoning them impatiently from a corner and they hurried forward, Molly still holding on to Sara's arm. Snipe diving ahead of them through the crowds, dodging under a horse's nose, the coachman shouting at her. Wheels grinding, voices shouting, men jostling. And then another lane, a woman crouched in a doorway holding an almost naked baby, holding it up to them as they came by her.

"A penny for the love o' God!"

"Come *on!*" Snipe hissed at them, dodged back, and grabbed them by the wrists.

"That woman . . ." Sara said.

"What woman? 'Er?"

"She wants a penny."

"Don't be soft. She 'ires that bloody kid by the week. Come *on.* D'you want to get nicked, the pair of you?" She dragged them away. When they were a safe distance down the lane the beggarwoman screamed after them, "Bloody whores! Draggletails! Scabby sluts! I 'ope I sees you 'anged!"

173

Chapter 13

" 'Ere we are," Snipe said. They were in a narrow street full of traffic, old-looking houses, some of them half-timbered, plastered, like houses she'd seen in Urnford, the upper stories leaning out over the pavement as though trying to touch the houses opposite. At street level, bow windows, the panes small and green, impossible to see through. Steps up, steps down. Above the doorway that Snipe had brought them to a sign read "Jno. Palmer. Prop. Est'd 1797." A larger, gilded board above that read PALMER'S PRIME CHOP HOUSE.

"Don't mind what 'e looks like," Snipe said. " 'E was a boxer an' got bashed a bit ugly. But 'e won't bite."

She went in first and they followed her, and for a moment Sara could see nothing. She stood lost in a fog of tobacco smoke, of noise, of thick shadows that the light, filtering greenish through the windows, falling from the doorway behind her, seemed merely to thicken. Fifty, a hundred people sitting at tables, talking, shouting, laughing, banging mugs for attention, rattling knives and plates—a man in an apron holding a tray at head height, struggling through the crowd; a girl with a cluster of filled mugs in each fist, trying to do the same thing.

A great shadowy figure with a bald, shining head, its back to the doorway, bent over a long charcoal grille, the red light from the burning coals glowing upwards, dancing red and ivory on the sweating baldness of the huge, naked scalp and the bulging, rolling fat of the neck. Smell of meat grilling, the hiss of burning fat. Snipe forcing her way through, turning to beckon. Some of the noise dying, fading, a kind of quiet spreading from where Snipe was, heads turning, even the waiter, the girl with the filled, tilting mugs stopping for a second to look towards the doorway.

In that moment, if she could have run, Sara would have run for her life. And yet why? Why? No more than an inn, a tavern, like a thousand taverns in Spain. Molly behind her, also hesitating, dazed by the dark, the sudden difference of indoor clamour after the open street. The eyes watching them, the noise taking up again, but with a difference, as though all the talking was of the two figures standing near the door, looking so lost.

"Come *on!*" Snipe called. The bald head had turned, the face still shadowed, away from the firelight. Sara went slowly forward, Molly behind her whispering, "Sara? What are we doing?"

Fumbling their way past tables, shoulders, eyes watching, voices whispering, and gradually the rhythm of talk recovering as though they were no longer the centre of the talk, the interest. The man by the fire stood waiting for them, Snipe on tiptoe beside him, whispering. What was she saying? *I'm mad to follow her like this,* Sara thought. Held her bundle against her ribs, tried not to move her shoulders as she sidled through towards them. The man stood like a column. Bald head, bald sweating face, even the eyebrows gone, thick sweating neck running down into the enormous chest under the open shirt, the white, grease-spattered apron wrapped like a sheet round the massive body, the invisible legs. Enormous arms, hanging down almost to the level of the hidden knees, covered in a black fur of hair, even the hands, the knuckles. An iron fork in one hand. The burning of the fire behind him, the shapes of the steaks, the chops, the kidneys broiling on the iron grilles.

"This is them!" Snipe shouted. "What d'you think of 'em?"

The man stared, his face a melting mask, a bloodstain from a piece of meat smeared on one cheek. He stared at Sara, his eyes like charcoals pushed into a great lump of fat. Expressionless. His nose flattened shapeless against the shapeless suet of the face. He lifted the hand holding the fork, jerked it over his shoulder, said something Sara couldn't hear, then roared *"Ben! Ben! C'm 'ere!"*

A small, thin man, also wrapped in a white apron, came scurrying from somewhere behind the chimney breast. Took the iron fork from the huge man's hand, began immediately stabbing at a lump of meat, turning it over. Snipe caught Sara's hand, pulled her round the corner, through a doorway behind the chimney and the open grille, and they were in a kind of inner kitchen where the thin man must have been. A woman at the range turned to look at them. Molly, following Sara; the thick, white shape of the man behind her; Snipe saying, "This way," as the noise of the tavern faded.

Through a door into a passage, no light at all, a sense of stairs leading down, and panic taking Sara's throat, choking her. But before she could hesitate, Snipe's hand was pulling her, not downwards, but up, up a stairs, light now from a window above their heads, more stairs both down and up, another door to their right, and what seemed like a flood of light, a vast room filled with light and emptiness. Windows at both ends and a long row of chairs down the far wall. Nothing in the middle but an enormous square platform, surrounded by ropes. Posts at the four corners held the ropes like a chain fence round a garden lawn. A smell of sweat and dust and sunlight. Snipe pulling her into the room and all the impressions of it striking her at once, incomprehensible.

Molly saying furiously, "Don't push me, you!"

"Shut your face," the man said. His voice was a thin piping, so extraordinary from that bulk that Sara turned to see who else was there. But it carried authority, and Molly stayed quiet, moved beside Sara, not even muttering under her breath. "They look all right," he said. "Can they work?"

" 'Course they can work!" Snipe said. "Look at 'em. Fresh as butter."

176

"Is that all the clothes they got? I couldn't use 'em dressed like that."

"They'll pay you out o' their wages. Go on, Monkey, do us a favour."

"What you care about 'em?" The little sunken charcoal eyes looked at Sara, at the childish, too-short dress, the bundle clutched under her arm. He reached out, the movement so quick that she had no time to move before he'd gripped her chin between fat, greasy finger and thumb, was turning her head this way and that before she could jerk away. "A gyppo?"

"She says she ain't."

"'Ow much they want?" He might have been speaking about two horses, buying them.

"A quid a week an' tips. An' no dolly-mopping, mind. I promised 'em."

"A quid? Are you mad? For two gyppos what 'asn't even got clothes to work in? I'll give 'em five bob an' their vittles an' kip, and if they ain't no good they're out tomorrow."

"You're a trump, Monkey!" Snipe hung on his arm, standing on tiptoe as though about to kiss him. "An' you won't let anyone touch 'em, eh?"

"'Oo wants to touch 'em?" Monkey said. "What you so worried about 'em for? Got your eye on 'em for a new mob?"

"I'm sorry for 'em, that's all. An' you won't know 'em when they're dressed up, they'll do you proud, Monkey. Can we show 'em up top?"

"I suppose." He jerked his thumb again, turned away. Snipe beckoned them, her face alight with pleasure, and suddenly for that light of pleasure, her smile, Sara trusted her, thought, *She's good, whatever else she is, she's good, she wants to help us.* And followed her out of the room, feeling oddly like a child with an adult who means to be kind.

"What's that thing?" Molly whispered, pointing at the ropes, the platform.

"I don't know," Sara said impatiently. "Come on."

"I hope you know what we're about. I don't think we'll ever get outa here, God's truth I don't."

"Oh, shut up," Sara said.

They climbed more stairs, came to a narrow landing, a door with a Judas spy-hole in it, a sense of heavy weight and strength. Monkey turned a key, pushed the door open, and Molly clung to Sara, tried to pull her back, whispered, "Don't go in there, they're goin' to kill us."

But behind the open door there was only a wide, shadowy room, long tables, a faint smell of scent, of stale wine. Monkey walked in without bothering to see if they were following him, Snipe with him, turning back to beckon them. Sara went forward slowly, uncertainly, shaking Molly's hand away. The tables were covered in green baize, the curtains drawn. Snipe went to a window and pulled the curtains back, letting light fall on the nearest table. Cards on it. A wooden and ivory stick with a crosspiece like a tiny garden rake, markings on the table, red and black and gold. Other tables beyond it. A curtained archway. Carpet underfoot, a sense of luxury.

"Some o' the time you'd work up 'ere," Monkey said. "Serving drinks. Can you mix punch?"

"Oh, yes," Sara said. "I've often done it."

"You don't 'ave to take cash up 'ere, just serve. The drinks is free."

Sara touched the cards, felt the slither of them under her fingers.

"You know what this is?" Snipe said. "You knows what gamin' is? Anything you see 'ere you don't talk about to no one, mind."

Sara picked up the pack, let it slide together, opened and closed it like a fan.

"Gawd," said Snipe, "you've 'andled cards before. You sure you ain't a gyppo?"

"A gypsy taught me," Sara said. She put the cards down.

"Do that again," Snipe said. "Monkey, look, she knows 'ow to 'andle a pack."

"Do what?"

"What you just done. Open an' shut 'em like that. Watch 'er, Monkey."

"They're beautiful cards," Sara said. She let them

178

run up her arm in a ladder. Snipe caught her breath. Monkey stood still.

"Gawd," Snipe said again. "You're a real sharper. Look at 'er." Sara let the ladder fall, slide down into her hand. Monkey reached forward, gripped her wrist, the cards falling in a slippery scatter on the green table-top.

"What's the game?" he said. He closed his hand until it seemed he was going to break her wrist and she cried out with the pain of it.

"There ain't no game," Snipe cried. "Let 'er alone, Monkey, you're 'urting 'er."

" 'Oo sent you?" Monkey whispered. "The Parson? Frenchy? 'Ow'd you like to go back to 'im with no ears? You whoring spy!" Snipe was beating at Monkey's shoulder with both her fists, shouting, "Let 'em go, let' em go! I tell you I found 'em at Darby's, getting took! Let 'em go!"

The hand slowly loosened on her wrist, let go of her.

" 'Ow'd she learn the cards like that then?" Monkey said. "If this is the Parson, I'll—"

"You 'eard 'er telling you. A gyppo taught her."

"What gyppo?" he said, looking at Sara.

"A boy," Sara whispered. "A long time ago."

" 'E did, eh? You know any gyppo words?"

"A few."

"Go fetch Dido," he said to Snipe. "Bloody sharp." And as Snipe hesitated, he thudded his fist on the green table like a hammer, sending the cards sliding, and Snipe ran.

"You let us go!" Molly shouted. "We ain't done nothing."

"Shut your face," Monkey whispered. "Or I'll shut it for you," and as Molly began to move, he pointed his fist at her and took one odd, shuffling step forward. She ran and Sara ran, and they wrenched at the door handle. Nothing happened, the brass ring twisting loose in their hands like a swivel.

"I told you to stop still," Monkey said. He came towards them, one long, gross furry arm reaching for them.

179

"Don't touch us!" Molly screamed, and the handle turned behind them, the door opened sent them sprawling against Monkey's body, not softly fat under the apron but like stone. The two monkey arms gripping round them, twisting them to face the door. Snipe was there with another man, as dark as Sara, a gold earring, a red and yellow neckerchief, black hair curling on a low forehead, a broken twisted nose. A young man, thick-set, looking at them, at Sara, at Monkey.

" 'Ave a look at this one, Dido. Tell us what you think. Is she one o' yours?"

He shoved Sara forward, and the pain across her shoulders burned again, as though the cut had re-opened. "Shut the flaming door, Snipe." He dragged Molly back into the middle of the room, put her hands away as she tried to claw his face and half pushed, half threw her from him so that she fell against another table. "You try any more, I'll break your neck. Well, what you waiting for, Dido? Look 'er over, can't you?"

Dido was already looking at her, walking round Sara with cat steps. *They are going to kill us*, Sara thought. She felt suddenly tired, as though it didn't matter very much what happened, so long as it happened quickly. As though a long time past something had broken inside her and it was only now she realised it. She looked at the locked door, at Snipe's frightened face, at Molly picking herself up, at the dark young man examining her as though she were wild game in a snare. He was of her own height as he stood in front of her, but so broad and heavy in the shoulders that he looked much shorter. He touched her face with a brown, powerful hand, tilted her head.

"Is she a gyppo?"

"D'you *jin the pooker, Rakli?*"

She shook her head.

"But you bin with a rom?"

"I knew gypsies in Spain," Sara said. "I spent a winter with them. That's where I learned the cards." She felt her courage coming back. So long as he talked, didn't touch her; so long as the fat man stayed where he was. How would the captain have talked his way out of this room?

"What else did you learn?" the gypsy said. "Can you count? *Yek? Dui?*"

"*Trin, sistar, panche.*"

He smiled suddenly, his teeth white in the brown, sharp, battered face. And a strange sense of countryside about him, of hedges and woods.

"Don't be frightened, *Rakli*," he said softly. "If you're telling the truth you won't get 'urt."

"I *am* telling the truth."

The gypsy turned to the fat man, to Snipe. "She ain't any English gyppo," he said, "whatever she is. She don't count like us, not quite."

"I don't care 'ow she counts," Monkey whispered, a strange, hissing whisper as though he had a hole in his throat. "Make 'er 'andle the cards an' tell me is it gyppo 'andling."

The gypsy nodded towards the nearest table, the scattered cards. "Show us, *Pen*."

She went slowly, trying to think what was best to do, to pretend to be clumsy or—She gathered up the cards. The gypsy smiled at her, encouraging, and again that sense of out of doors, of running water. As though the night wind had found its way through the grey windows into this stale room. She made a great mass of the cards, three or four packs that had been lying scattered there, spread them in a sudden fan across the table, thinking of Pablito, the cave, the smell of cooking, the mountain. Like remembering happiness. Freedom. Fanned the cards and closed them, broke them in two and sprayed them up in two fountains, caught and folded them together, her eyes half shut, as though by conjuring she could bring that freedom back, free them from the snare.

Monkey had come close, and Snipe, and Molly, murmuring threats and hatred under her breath, the murmuring stilled as she saw what Sara was doing. The colours shimmering, climbing in a swift sleeve, a ladder up Sara's left arm and down again and into that great curving fan in front of her that had been Pablito's first scornful lesson "for a girl, a baby." She

181

lifted the first card with her finger-tip and all the cards lifted, one after the other in a water ripple round the whole curve of two hundred cards, until they lay face upwards on the green cloth. She touched the other end and the ripple ran back again, the cards lay face down.

"Gawd's truth," Monkey whispered, impressed against his will. "The Parson didn't teach 'er that, not in a 'unnerd years. Nor Frenchy." He looked at Dido. "Is that gyppo work?"

"Could be," Dido said. "I've seen near it. Tellin' fortunes. Could be."

"Let's 'ave a look at your fingers," Snipe said, catching one of Sara's hands and pulling it towards her, folding and unfolding the fingers, turning the wrist. She shook her head, sucking her breath softly. "Gawd, what a dip you could be. Born for it, dead born for it. Give me a week to show you this an' that, an' there ain't a pocket made you couldn't dip better'n I could. Monkey, you *got* to keep 'er, she's a natural. Dido, make 'im see sense."

But Dido had also taken her wrist, was holding it with the small red burn mark uppermost. He rubbed his thumb on the veins, pressed slightly, and the faded ring glowed darker. He eased his thumb away, turned her hand over, seemed to be doing no more than follow Snipe's admiration.

"Well?" Monkey said.

"She ain't the Parson's. She ain't anyone's. She's telling you the truth." He let go her hand.

"I told you, I told you!" Snipe cried. She ran to Monkey and hung on his arm, cajoling. "Tell 'em you'll take 'em on." She began to dance up and down. "Imagine 'er as a croup! Gawd, fanning the cards like that. You could dress 'er up as a gent! Just imagine it, Monkey! Look at 'er, look at 'er! What a gent she'd make! Give 'er a pair o' breeches an' a swell tog, an' there ain't a girl what comes 'ere wouldn't double 'er stakes jus' to see 'er wink at 'em. Dress 'er up, Monk. She'll be the best croupier you ever dreamed of!"

Monkey shook her off like a cat, thumped his black

182

hammer of a fist on the table and hissed, "Shut up, you stupid slut!" He came shuffling towards Sara. "So she's all right, is she?" he said to Dido. Dido nodded. "I 'opes you're right." He peered into Sara's eyes, his own expressionless as charcoal. "If you wants the job you can 'ave it. Wait on the tables downstairs. Serve up 'ere. A quid a month an' your vittles and a bed. Your friend the same. 'Oo you sleeps with is up to yourselves. But this ain't a brothel an' no one gets robbed 'ere, see? Except *I* do the robbing." He touched her chin with his knuckles, the black fur like a huge spider brushing against her face.

"I don't want to sleep with anyone. Except Molly."

"Sapphos, eh? I tol' you, that's up to yourselves. Just no robbing. You pick a customer's pocket 'n I'll kill you, you'll end up with the Gravesend twins, floating. Treat me right an' work 'ard, I'll be like your father. Well, what you say? Stop 'ere or go?"

Beyond him she saw Molly's face, knew Molly was begging her to say, "Go," to get out of here. But where? Go where?

"They can't go nowhere," Snipe said, "they ain't got nowhere *to* go. Why won't you dress her up, Monkey? Can't you see—"

"This ain't a flaming circus. Shut up, for Gawd's sake, before I give you a 'eadache. You brought 'em 'ere for work an' they can 'ave it, take it or leave it."

"We'll take it," Sara said. Molly caught her breath, whispered, "Sara!" her voice despairing.

"Show 'em where they sleeps, Dido. You get 'em some clothes, Snipe. Take 'em to Ma Casey for some fancy stuff. 'Ave 'em back 'ere in an hour for Maggie to teach 'em the ropes while we're slack."

He was gone and Molly was beside her whispering, "You're mad, you are, Sara. What you say we'd stay for?"

"If you don't stay 'ere," Snipe said, "you'll stop somewhere worse 'fore morning. I tell you, you're safe 'ere, ain't that right, Dido?"

Dido was looking at Sara with a strange expression, and said something to her in Romany she couldn't understand, only catching a word or two. But one of them

183

meant witchcraft even in Caló, in that almost forgotten language her mother had—had—He took her by the arm, not familiarly, but with respect. "Let me show you, *Hani*. An' you." He beckoned Molly. They went up another twisting flight of stairs, and down a corridor, Sara feeling against all reason that she trusted him. Molly came nervously behind her, Snipe holding her by the arm, hanging on her, laughing about Monkey's fury, and calling ahead down the corridor to Dido, "What you think, Didy? Wouldn't she make a smasher of a gent? 'E ain't got a brain in 'is ugly skull, Monkey ain't."

"No one'll 'arm you," Dido said in a low, reassuring voice. "You're as safe 'ere as in your own tent. I promise you. An' your friend." He opened a low door. Inside, there was a small attic room, the ceiling sloping on one side to floor level, a brick chimney running at a dog's-leg angle up the one straight wall there was. A skylight, grey with dirt. Bare boards. A mattress.

"There y'are," Snipe cried triumphantly. "Snug as a duck in a ditch. Throw 'em in some blankets and a pillow an' I'll take 'em to get rigged out." She pulled them out into the corridor and down another stairs, Dido following until he turned away into one of the maze of turnings; they went on down into a stone passage with an underground feel to it, a smell of damp, of sour earth and a sickly-sweet stench of rotting drains that choked in Sara's throat like fog. Snipe tapped at a door that rang iron. A man opened it and they were in a cellar, stone arches and vaulting above their heads, beyond it another cellar, only a glimpse of it in a kind of twilight, a shaft of dusty light falling on what looked like sand, a sand pit, and shadowy rows of seats rising up in tiers.

" 'Allo, Jim," Snipe said. "We wants to go out the back way." He was a hunchback, holding a broom and leaning on it like a crutch, his head sunk into the distorted shoulders, his face green white as though he never saw daylight. " 'Ow are the rats?"

"Chirping, chirping away," he said. "Come 'n see 'em tomorrow."

"Get away! 'Oo's dogs you got?"

"That Lord Pretty Mug is bringin' 'is Billy, for one. A lot o' money'll change 'ands, I promise you."

"Bloody rats. I got a livin' to earn. Come on, you two."

The hunchback limped and hobbled towards another door, unlocked it, led them out into a basement courtyard, up stone steps slippery with damp, and unlocked another iron-lined door. They were in a narrow lane. The door clanged behind them, the locks turned, smooth-oiled and quiet.

" 'E only loves 'is rats. Breaks 'is 'eart when they gets chopped."

"Rats?" Molly said, shivering. "Where?"

" 'E collects 'em. For the dogs. It's 'orrible. C'mon, we better 'urry or Monkey'll start shouting again. Don't tell this old bag we're going to that you got any money or she'll want it on the nail." She hurried in front of them, still delicately mincing and animal-wary, the small golden head in the big, coal-scuttle bonnet turning this way and that as though every corner, every doorway, concealed a danger. Molly clutched Sara's sleeve.

"Let's run for it."

"Run *where?*" Sara said, her voice too loud, suddenly furious, with Molly, with all that had happened, with herself.

Snipe darted back to them, stood with her hands on her hips, two red spots of anger on her cheek-bones, her mouth tight with rage. "All right," she hissed. "Run. Run where you bloody like, the pair o' you. I been trying to 'elp you and there isn't many in London that would, I can tell you that. All right, bloody run an' I'll go an' look after my own business instead of yours."

"She didn't mean it," Sara said. "She's just afraid, that's all. Weren't you ever afraid here?"

Snipe looked up into her face, the anger dying out of her cheeks, her mouth, a sad smile taking its place. "You think I still ain't? Every morning I wakes up? But it ain't no good being scared. If you was born to

185

swing at Newgate, what can you do except 'ave a good time till it comes? Now, are you comin' to Ma Casey's or ain't you?"

Chapter 14

They began work that evening in the gaming room, carrying trays of drinks, champagne, punch, sherry wine, blackstrap, and later, as the room filled, only champagne and small game pies and hot sausages and sandwiches, learning to lean their way between the gamblers' shoulders, lifting the trays over their heads balanced on one hand with outspread fingers, to smile and smile.

"Sport your Charlies a bit," Snipe had said at Ma Casey's. "Show 'em off." And had pouted her own meagre bosoms and winked and smiled and twirled herself seductively.

"I couldn't do *that!*" Molly had whispered, round-eyed, and Ma Casey had laughed so hard she had had to stop finding clothes for them and sit down on a trunk and wheeze with laughter till she cried.

"Where you find *them*, Snipe? Up the garden?" But she'd seemed a kindly enough woman behind the wheezing, asthmatic voice, the endless grumbling. "I don't know where I can find anything for a couple o' bean-poles like them. Comin' in 'ere, sayin', 'fit these out for us,' as if you was buyin' a loaf o' bread. No warnin', nothing. What you think I am?"

"Don't ask me," Snipe had said, "or I'll tell you. Rig 'em out, Monkey said. Real swell."

Ma Casey's house, a narrow tenement in a dirty back street, was an Aladdin's cave of clothes—every room, every passageway crammed with boxes, trunks, hanging cupboards, racks of men's and women's clothes on hangers, row upon row of coats, pelisses, pelissettes, spencers, gowns, dresses, bodices, skirts, underskirts, chemises, camisoles, petticoats, stays, embroidered drawers; boots and half-boots and slippers; men's black ebony and mahogany-shining boots still on their wooden jacks; hats, bonnets, shawls, scarves, archery dresses, and riding habits—as though the whole of London must come to this one dusty, twilit house to buy its clothing. Or sell it.

"Where do they all *come* from?" Sara had whispered, and Snipe had laid her finger along her nose and winked and said, "From the petermen, o' course. They use 'ooks to pull 'em out of passin' coaches. Near new, too, everything you can see 'ere. All the rags she sends to one o' the Jewmen. She only keeps the fancy stuff, she's a real lady."

And Ma Casey finding them dresses—satin, with lace capes and short puffed sleeves, rows of lace trimmings round the skirts. "The latest thing," she wheezed. " 'Ardly in the *Ladies Monthly* yet. Or this 'un. Fit you to a tee, ducks." She held it up against Sara, fluffed out the drapery over the sleeves. "Princess Charlotte's they calls that. An' look at them little tassels an' roses. You look like a duchess yourself. With satin slippers to match. A crested coach that come off, cross my 'eart. Let's 'ave them rags off of you and see 'ow this looks." She had pulled the spencer down and back off Sara's shoulders and saw the long red welt of the carter's whip underneath, with its dried blood. She hissed through her gapped teeth.

"A bloody carter 'it 'er," Snipe said, "the bastard. Gawd, look at that tog!" She had a man's evening coat off its hanger and was holding it up. "If I was as big as she is," she said, nodding at Molly, "I'd dress up as a gent, just imagine being a man, doin' what you like, swinging your cane."

"Your man ain't doing what he likes, Snipe. You

was the lucky one. When's 'e booked out for Australy?"

"Next week, if he ever gets there. At least 'e didn't get hung. 'Arvey did, an' Jacko."

"I know," Ma Casey said. She had Sara's dress in her hands, was looking at it scornfully. Sara pulled the new dress over her head. Not completely new because there was a faint, expensive perfume still clinging to it. The satin fell round her like a caress; the gown was cut very low over the breast except for the transparent Princess Charlotte drapery, the Cobourg ruff round the neck. Ma Casey fastened up the back, patted the primrose satin over her hips, arranged the fall of the skirt, turned her round, and stepped back to admire. "Like a duchess!"

Snipe had put on the blue evening coat, had tilted one of the new style of top hats on her head, holding it up so it didn't fall round her ears like a candle-snuffer. "If only I was big." She came over and tried to adjust it on Sara's head, but it was too big for her as well, and Snipe tossed it back onto its shelf with a sigh.

They'd spent an hour and more in Ma Casey's, lost in the wonder of the wealth of silk and muslin, satin and cashmere and cambric, Brussels lace and French ribbons, paisley and Shetland, trying on half boots and slippers and sandals, clocked and embroidered stockings, fringed shawls and scarves, hats and bonnets, until other customers came in and Ma Casey began to lose patience with them and chased them away.

"You wouldn't think she had any sort of a shop at all from outside," Molly said, overwhelmed with her new clothes, needing to stop every few yards to look at her reflection in a window, touching her dress with unbelieving fingers, and then stopping Sara to be able to look at her again.

"Come on, come on!" Snipe said. Monkey'll kill us you been so long."

"*We* been so long? An' you tryin' on those breeches an' weskits this past half hour. How much we owe her?"

"About twenty quid. Come *on*."

"Twenty quid?" Molly said uncertainly. And

then, guessing what Snipe meant. "Pounds? Twenty *pounds?*" Her voice rising to a scream of outrage.

Even Sara felt shocked, tried to calculate five shillings a week in her head to make twenty pounds. Eighty weeks? Eighty!

"For Gawd's sake!" Snipe said. "What you think you got on you? Slops?"

"But how will we ever pay?' Sara said.

"It'll take you about a couple o' weeks. Unless you upset Monkey again. You can get two or three quid a night upstairs if you're quick an' 'appy about it."

"Not—not—" Sara whispered. Passersby jostled them, stepped aside to look at the three handsome girls standing in the middle of the pavement gossiping. An elderly gentleman raised his beaver, smiled, made a suggestive half-bow, his eye running from Snipe to Molly to Sara and settling on her, from her feathered Austrian toque to her little red boots.

"Jesus Christ, King o' the Jews," Snipe said. "I don't know why I'm bothering with the pair of you." And turning to the elderly gentleman. "What you staring at, Grandpa? Lost your crutch?" The elderly man's smile faded and he walked on, exaggeratedly not hurrying. "No, I don't mean on your back," turning to Sara again. "Slinging the drink is what I means. Serving. Food. 'Elping 'em stuff themselves. You do it right an' they give you something. Five bob. Half a shiner. Even the skinny ones give you a shilling. You don't know what money *is*, you two. 'Ow much did they give you down in your 'aystack, Moll?" They were walking on again, Snipe tugging them ahead.

"Four pounds," Molly whispered, ashamed.

"A month?"

"A year." The whisper still lower.

"Gawd love you, I'm only teasing you. I know what it's like. I started at twopence a week up north in the mill. An' cane bread with it to keep us awake. You know what me an' Jim an' the mob could pick up in just one day? Not workin' too 'ard but just a bit lucky? Three 'unnerd quid I've seen us take. Starting round twelve o'clock outside the bank, and just goin' on easy till round midnight. That's money—that's what we call

189

rhino, that is. Wait till I show you 'ow it's done, you'll be amazed."

In Monkey's chop house when they came back in through the front entrance no one took any notice of them, beyond ordinary glances, as though their new clothes had blended them with the surroundings.

"What they want them 'ats for?" Monkey said. "They ain't goin' to work in them, for Gawd's sake."

"Girls 'ave to 'ave 'ats. You leave 'em alone. You scared 'em enough for one day."

In the attic Dido had found bedclothes for them and a chair, and had hammered nails behind the door and with an old curtain had made a kind of hanging space in the recess between the chimney and wall. By the time they'd spent two hours with Maggie, the woman they'd seen in the back kitchen when they first came in, learning where things were and what they'd have to do, there was almost a feeling of belonging, a strangely pleasant excitement about what they were doing, only broken now and then by a quiver of strangeness, of fear, like a whisper of chill air in a wood on a summer day.

An air of purpose to everything, a running to and fro, a hurrying to serve, to cook, to pour, to please. The hunchback staggering up from the cellars with a great basket of dusty bottles, Maggie filling quart tankards out of one of the huge barrels in the tap room, showing them how it was done, how not to spill the head in a slippery pool of liquor on the trays. Up in the gaming room, a sense of waiting, the croupiers coming in yawning, two to a table, rubbing their fingers together, dull eyes as though they had slept all day, six of them, nothing in common between them except an air of silence and knowingness, picking up their rakes, their cards, flexing their fingers, shuffling.

"None of 'em ain't a quarter as good as you, Sara," Snipe whispered. She had stayed with them, pretending to help and getting in Maggie's way—Maggie, large and raw-boned and Scots, with hands like washboards and a knack of carrying four quart mugs in each of them without spilling a drop.

"Get out o' ma road, you wee slummock," and

Snipe would hang on her elbow and threaten to shake it, and spill a gallon of ale on the floor. The only other girl who came upstairs to the gaming room to carry drinks was Maggie's daughter, Janet, a large, soft-looking girl with pillow breasts, a yearning mouth, and her mother's large hands. She had greeted them kindly enough, but she clearly thought their purpose in coming there was to save her from working. Even when the room grew crowded and busy, Janet spent most of her time admiring one of the croupiers, or downstairs in the kitchen, sitting straddle-legged on a stool and saying she was dead.

"I know what killed 'er," Snipe said. "She never stops. Like a rabbit. An' she don't even charge for it, she's stark mad."

Snipe nudging them, whispering, "Over there, that gent in the green coat an' the brown curly 'air. 'E runs the Oxford Street mob. Take 'im your tray and give 'im a smile."

The room filling with men and girls, almost all the girls young, pretty, fashionably dressed, moving in clouds of scent, their faces powdered, painted, their lips scarlet, black paint round their eyes, cheeks chalk-white and red-patched with rouge; the men almost as young, scarcely a man there over thirty. And boys, some of them no more than children; with smart-cut clothes, their cravats set with even more care than the men's, their hair curled and oiled, gold and jewelled fobs on their watch-chains, taking snuff with the world-weary air of dandies. They tilted their child heads to look down their noses at the gaming with narrowed eyes, each of them with one or two of the girls fussing about them, petting them, staking counters for them.

The croupiers calling, "Black is two. Red four. Black wins." Raking in the ivory counters from the red enclosures of the table. Or crying, "One après!" And all the stakes pushed into the gold enclosures. And on the roly-poly table the wheel spinning, the white ball dancing and clicking, the gamblers leaning closer as the wheel slowed, and the soft sighing of breath as it came to rest in its cell. "Twenty-four. Evens. Black pays."

Carrying the heavy trays, running up the stairs, down. Stopping with Molly for a moment on the landing, leaning against the wall, then straightening herself again to ease her back.

"D'you get any money yet?" Molly whispered.

"Some."

"I got eleven shillings!" Molly said, her whisper an astonishment of joy, of unbelief. "Six weeks I'd work for that back home. Six weeks! An' we only been here half a night! I give you best, Sara Pownall, you do have downright clever notions, now an' then."

Maggie coming out of the gaming room, shouting, "Where are ye, ye lazy bones? Where's the champagne?"

Molly crying, "Comin', missus, comin'."

They ran till their legs no longer seemed to belong to them, smiled till their smiles were like masks, carried the trays with hands and arms that had lost all feeling. Janet disappearing with the Oxford Street mobsman, not coming back until an hour later, her eyes sleepy with content, her bodice wrongly fastened. Maggie cursing Sara and Molly, jollying them, patting their heads with her paddle hands as though she were a schoolmistress with willing pupils. Snipe gambling and losing, getting slightly tipsy on champagne, laughing her little gravelly laugh as another girl commiserated with her about her Jim.

"You let 'em pinch you and they'll book your passage after 'im. You must weigh your forty pound by now, Snipe, an' a lot besides."

"I know a girl did that," Snipe said. "She thought she'd get seven years like her man. Only they 'anged her for an example, instead. No thanks."

Midnight. One in the morning. The room thick with scent, with heat, the smell of wine and punch and pies, little cups of pastry filled with lobster sauce and shrimps, fresh baked and smoking hot. Monkey in his tail-coat, his squire's buff waistcoat, his head sweating under the chandelier, his small black pits of eyes summing up the stakes on every table, the crowd, who was

192

gambling, who was merely drinking the free drinks, the women, the young boys with their cunning old-man expressions, Sara, Molly, Maggie, Janet with her white velvet breasts and sleep-crumpled face. As though nothing in the shadowy, stifling length and breadth of the huge room escaped him for a second.

He had been in and out all night, and when he came in, it was like the entrance of a king, a circle of deference forming round him. But a king at ease, without formalities, clapping a friendly hand on a shoulder, joking with a girl, a boy, calling him "Young master," laying a bet for him.

"The swells'll be coming soon," Snipe said. " 'Ow you doing, the pair o' you? Got much cash yet?"

"Thirty bob!" Molly whispered, her eyes alight with the wonder of so much money, with the wonder of everything that was happening.

"Ain't it easy?" Snipe said. "I told you. 'Ow about you, Sara?"

"About the same, I think."

"I've lost more'n that on the bloody roly-poly." She moved toward the door, where Dido was standing now, as doorkeeper, also dressed in a long coat and breeches, a "mailcoach" cravat pushing up his brown chin, his curls fresh oiled and glistening in the candle-light, his shoulders threatening to burst his coat in half.

"There must be nobs coming now, some o' the real swells. Dido's waitin' for 'em. This is where you picks up a couple o' quid if you're clever."

"Nobs?" Sara said.

"Gents, upper customers. Monkey only lets a few in 'ere an' only if 'e likes 'em an' they sports enough blunt, spends their cash proper, that is."

Three men came in as she said that, one older, two very young, all dressed in a way that made the smart-ness of the mobsmen look flashy and slightly cheap and overdone. A curled magnificence to their lapels, a white foaming to their cravats that seemed to have been put on their necks no more than ten minutes earlier; their hair combed and brushed and set and arranged as magnificently as any woman's but with a casual carelessness. The shoulders of their collared coats fit without a wrinkle, a crease, and the three of them wore not breeches but pantaloons that moulded their legs, their narrow black boots glistening with champagne and cream polishing, as though valets had only that moment removed their loving hands and dog bones from the glove-soft, ebony toes.

Dido bowed to them, Monkey came shuffling, royally condescending, a king greeting ambassadors from another power. One of the young men lifting his quizzing-glass, staring round, saying in his high-pitched, Eton voice, "Damme, Monkey, there ain't a Cyprian left on the Haymarket, ye've got 'em all in here losing their blunt."

"Not losing it, milord. Winning, most of 'em. I'm near ruined with 'em. What's your fancy tonight, gentlemen, roly-poly? Faro? Roog-y-nwah?"

They went to the rouge-et-noir table, threw down a handful of gold coins, quizzed the room again as though indifferent as to how many ivory counters they might receive. One or two of the girls ogling them, one or two of the mobsmen nodding a respectful greeting, but most of the crowd treating them with polite indifference, as merely three more customers, members of the club. Monkey beckoned Sara over. "Bring three glasses o' the special champagne," he said. "An' some shrimp pies. Just fresh made, milord, Maggie's best."

"New girl, Monk?" The quizzing-glass lifted, the three looking at her with cool and insolent stares, the oldest curving his eyebrow up, setting his mouth in a considering smile as though in that second he had undressed Sara and found the result mildly interesting, but no more. She felt herself flushing, her breast and throat and face burning.

"Blushes pretty," the man said. He had dark chestnut hair and weary eyes, and the other two had an air of taking their cue from him, as though they would admire nothing until he had pronounced it admirable.

"Dammed black," one of them said, pouting his boy's mouth. Sara turned, wanting only to hide, to run, furious and ashamed. "Is she foreign?"

"Spanish, milord. But speaks English good as you an' me. Snipe found 'er."

194

She was out of earshot, out of the door past Dido, hurrying down the stairs to the kitchen, her face still flaming. She found Molly there, eating a game pie and drinking ale, her feet stretched out towards the oven, Janet half asleep behind her, her head resting on her arms on the table-top.

"Am I the only one doing anything!" Sara shouted. "A bigger crowd than ever and you're sitting down eating pies." She slammed her tray on the table beside Janet's elbows, and Janet lifted her head, stared at her irritably, and cradled herself more comfortably. Molly stood up looking guilty.

"I was only havin' my supper. I got to eat sometime."

"Well, they want the special champagne and more pies."

"The special's in the ice-box down them steps," Janet said, her voice muffled by her arms.

They fetched it up, two frosted magnums running with melting ice from the ice-cellar, wrapped the gold-foiled necks in napkins under Janet's languid directons, filled two silver buckets with crushed fragments of ice, set the magnums in the centres, and carried them up the stairs, Janet slowly following them with a small tray of pies, yawning.

" 'Ere's the other 'un, Mr. Hunter, fresh as butter I said when I saw 'er, still smell the grass on 'er." The two younger men were already gaming, barely condescending to look round. But Mr. Hunter arched his eyebrow, gave Molly his slow, narrow smile, while Dido, who had joined them, poured the foaming, chilled champagne into three tankards, offered Mr. Hunter one, took the others to the young men at the table.

Mr. Hunter waved Janet and her pies away without looking at her, felt in his waistcoat pocket, and tossed Molly a coin, a quick glint of gold. It fell against her breast, slid down into her bodice. She caught at it, felt the cold metal on her skin, sliding down between her breasts, and laughed with joy. Sara's face flamed again. Mr. Hunter looked at her as though he knew what she was thinking and smiled gently. Monkey

195

put his long arm familiarly round Mr. Hunter's elegant shoulders and guided him towards the table.

Molly had put down her bucket, fished out the coin. "A guinea!" she whispered. "A whole guinea!" A girl peered round her shoulder at it, laughed and patted her arm. Mr. Hunter looked back at her as though he'd heard her whisper, smiled not with the knowing, Corinthian's curled lip of previously but with a genuine amusement and pleasure.

"I'd like to kill him!" Sara said. They carried their buckets to an empty table, set them there, continued serving. Two o'clock. Half-past. The crowd, which had been changing its components all night long, thinned, grew yawning-tired, only a few clusters round the roulette wheel, and at the faro table in the alcove, beyond the archway with its dark red velvet curtains and golden tassels, a last four at whist. The candles guttering. Janet had disappeared long ago. Maggie was rubbing her deep, bony eye-sockets. Mr. Hunter and his two young friends also long gone, obsequiously ushered out by Dido and Monkey with loud promises of, "Tomorrow, your lordship's dog'll 'ave the biggest rats Ben ever caught, I promise you!"

Molly sitting down on a chair in a corner, spent. Surreptitiously counting her money, knotting it into a handkerchief. Sara thinking her back was broken, her knees giving way. Last trays of glasses down to the kitchens, tankards, empty bottles, traysful of broken pie crusts, congealed sausages.

"The skivs do the rest in the morning," Maggie said. "You go up to bed, my dears." Monkey nodding with distant approval. Dido touching Sara's arm as she stumbled up the stairs, saying "Good *Hani*." And then, holding her elbow for a moment, "Bring me good luck—the *kushti bok*, eh? Call it for me?"

"What did he want, that Dido?" Molly said, swaying as she undid her dress, let it fall in a shush of satin round her feet.

"He wants me to bring him good luck," Sara said.

"I think we've got a load of it ourselves," Molly said, yawning like a cave. "A whole guinea at a time, just for a li'l sip o' wine! A quarter's wages! Oh, I'm

196

tired dead. I wonder where Snipe went?" She fell down on the mattress in her petticoat, lay stretched. "Look at my placket!" she said. "All li'l flowers! 'Tis a sin no one can't see it but you."

Sara knelt down, collapsed beside her, felt sleep coming like a tide rising in her bones, her mind. Full of shadows. Snipe, the old man in the shop, the clothes ranked on rank in Ma Casey's hidden rooms like ghosts, Dido, Monkey, the captain. She eased her shoulders against the pain, turned over, and lay face-down, her cheek pillowed on Molly's arm.

Chapter 15

She woke, startled, not knowing where she was, thinking they were still at home, Molly beside her in the little narrow bed. She moved and it was as though someone had drawn a hot iron across her back. She hissed with the pain of it, and Molly sat up, her eyes fast shut, saying, "I'm comin', missus, I'm comin'." And then, "Where are we? Sara? *Sara!*" Feeling round for her, gripping on to her. "I had such a dream. Whuh? Whuh? We're in London." She tried to jump up from the bed and hit her head on the sloping ceiling. "Oh, my head! My legs!" She stood up more carefully, all his muscles stiff. "I thought I were dreamin'. Oh, I didn't work so hard since I were little, hoeing at Masham's. Oh, my back."

"*Your* back!" Sara said. "I think mine's broken where that carter hit me." She tried to ease herself up, groaning. A fist banged on the door.

"Come up away out o' your pallets, girls. D'ye think you're on holidays, the pair o' you? It's past nine."

"Nine o'clock!" Molly screamed. They scrambled out of bed, put on the daytime dresses Ma Casey had found for them, and the daytime boots, Molly holding her feathered toque for a moment as though she were thinking of wearing it to work, and sadly putting it back on its nail.

Downstairs in the kitchen Maggie gave them oatmeal porridge and small beer. There was no sign of Janet, but two middle-aged women in sacking aprons were washing the glasses and the plates, scrubbing the slate floor round the girls' feet as they ate their breakfast and Maggie was already carrying in steaming coffee-pots and tea and piles of soft new-baked buns she called baps, into the chop room beyond, Ben already drawing ale, fetching bottles, carrying empties down to the hunchback's cellars.

The morning began, seemed to go on forever; food, drink, tea, coffee, tobacco pipes—remembering what men or girls in the chop room had ordered. Not many girls that early in the day, only beginning to wander in around noon, looking as though they were still asleep. One or two of the sharp boys, some of the mobsmen. Cracking jokes about Molly and Sara being new, being up from the country, where was their haystack, what it was like wearing boots the first time, did it hurt them. But kindly jokes, here and there and patting their behinds as they went, saying, "Let's see your Charlies, duck."

"Mind I don't pour something over you," Molly said. They pinched Molly more than Sara, watching Sara with a different, less immediately accepting eye, as though her darkness made a difference. And after Dido came down, about eleven o'clock, and sat eating a bap and a slice of fried bacon, there were no more pinches at all and even the jokes quieted. In Monkey's absence Dido was obviously prince regent of the house, and he seemed to expand and receive an atmosphere of homage, of admiration, sitting at his ease in his shirt sleeves and breeches, the knee laces

198

hanging down against his shins, the calf muscles bulging the breeches as though there were ships' knotted cables under the tight black cloth, his frilled cotton shirt open to show the smooth brown chest, the thick brown column of his throat.

Dido went back into the kitchen and vanished somewhere. The morning wore on and the customers came and went. The chop room subtly changed its atmosphere, half hour by half hour, from morning to midday. There seemed a developing excitement about it, about the customers coming in, full of chatter, gossip, greeting one another, wanting chops and steaks and kidneys now instead of baps and bacon and coffee. Maggie's famous baps and bacon, as they learned afterwards, famous from the Strand to Holborn. And Monkey's broiled steaks in oyster sauce. And roast pheasant for the real flash customers.

"Where'd you get them?" Molly had whispered, seeing one of the pheasants hanging, waiting to be plucked.

"Up the market, o' course," Ben had said. "Where d'you think?" And he had laid his finger to his nose and winked, and for Sara and Molly it was as though Molly's father had walked through the door in a chill wrap of shadow, carrying his long gun and his snares and his game sack, Joseph Goatlake behind him, and all the others. They shivered and hurried back to the chop room and the warmth of life.

By two o'clock and half-past, and three, even with Janet come to help them, and the day girl, Sophy, a pug-faced girl with fat red arms and brassy hair, they seemed to have been working forever. Until the crowds slackened and Maggie called them in to eat their dinners, one at a time, three grilled chops each on a pile of potatoes, a mug of thin claret and, as a treat for their first morning, a cup of thick sweet coffee and a glass of blackstrap.

"My *feet!*" Molly whispered.

"Well, ye can go up an' rest 'em till eight o'clock. The gambling dinna start till late tonight."

"What you ever do before we come, missus?" Molly had her boots off and was caressing her bare feet with

199

her hands, or resting the soles on the cold slate of the floor like an ecstasy. Sara was lying back with her eyes shut, sipping the blackstrap and screwing up her face at its sickly sweetness that yet became pleasant in her mouth.

"What did we do? Ma wee Janet had to stir her bones a bit, that's what we did," Maggie said. "An' we had another wee girl that took sick. The French sick," she said, looking at her daughter.

"Oh, shut up, Ma," Janet said. "My head's bursting."

They went slowly upstairs, an effort to climb each tread, and fell on their mattress again.

"I got another nine shillings," Molly said. But she was too tired to count them out.

"We'd better find a hiding place," Sara said. She hung her dress on a nail and stood there as though even to let go of the nail was too much effort.

"I'm goin' to spend mine soon as I get the chance," Molly said. "I won't need a hidy place."

Sara came back and knelt on the mattress, facing her. "But we've *got* to save."

"Why've we got to? I saw a tippet there in Ma Casey's took my eye like it were speaking to me, sayin' 'Molly Bone, you do ought to take me home with you.' Real fur! Only I were afraid to ask Snipe if I could have it."

"If we save up enough we can—" She broke off, hardly knowing herself what she meant. In the very back of her mind the thought of Spain. How much would it cost to get there? How could they go? And when they—if they got there—"if we saved up enough," she said, "we can do what we like."

"What I'd like is to buy that tippet," Molly said. "How much you think we might get tonight?" But she was already asleep and Sara lay down, pillowed herself against her, and tried to sleep too, was half asleep, the sounds of traffic in the streets, the sounds of the house mixing with her dreams. *Pablito dealing at the long green table, spreading out the fan of cards. One après. Twenty-four wins. Here's a guinea. And the captain stamped into the gaming room, lifted a quizzing-glass, and cried, "Sara? Sara?"*

She sat up, not knowing whether it was night or morning. The same chill twilight filtering through the grey glass panes overhead, the same shadows in the room. The house oddly silent. Night? She went to the door, opened it onto the narrow landing. No one there.

"Sara? Where are you?"

"I'm here. What time is it, do you think? We have to start at eight."

"They'll tell us, come back to bed, you're making it all cold."

She listened, seemed to sense a murmuring far down in the depths of the house below them. The heavy slam of a door that came up the intervening stories and flights of twisting stairs like an echo.

"I'm going to see where everyone is," she said. She began to pull on her dress and slippers.

"I'm goin' to go on sleepin'," Molly said, turning facedown and wrapping the blanket over her head. "They want me, they'll come."

Sara shivered, felt her whole body tightening not so much with disgust as with a shock of fear and horror. She went running down, lost her way on a landing with two stairways leading from it, was in a part of the house she'd never seen before, a corridor with a row of doors, then down more stairs, and she was at the head of stone steps, leading down and down. The murmur she had guessed at rather than heard had become a reality now, a bee-swarm sound of voices, people, somewhere below.

She hesitated, heard someone coming behind her, and ran on softly down the stone steps, into a large stone passageway, cellar archways opening on either side of her, the shapes of wooden casks, racks of wine bottles, a smell of damp, of dust and stone and that sweet, fetid stench she had noticed yesterday. There was a candle in a saucer on an upturned barrel, its light flickering yellow, no more than a puffball glimmering. A scuttle of claws in the shadows, a small grey shape running. She caught her breath with horror, turned, forgot which way she'd come, where

201

the steps were. Only the sounds of people to guide her. She ran like the wind towards at least that much familiartiy and was at a door, her hands against wet-feeling iron, and the door was locked. Her other hand finding the small Judas window at the level of her eyes, pushing the plate aside. Ready to call out for help, for the hunchback Jim, for Ben, anyone.

She was looking into the cellar they'd seen the day before. But crowded now. The tiers of seats filled, mostly men but some women, all the faces alight with excitement, expectation, a shouting of voices. "Two to one 'e breaks twelve minutes! Two to one!" "I'll give you threes, I'll give you threes in guineas!" Suddenly, right in front of her, standing up on a bench she saw Snipe, waving a bank-note in a tiny fist. She thought she could pick out her voice from the hundred others, screeching, "Five quid! A fiver!" A man took her money, slapped hands with her, and they both spat on their palms. Down in the sand ring Jim the hunchback was holding a great sack by the corners, and opposite him Dido was bent down, gripping a dog between his knees. Monkey behind him, holding a fistful of money, bank-notes like a pack of cards and a leather bag. A young man was forcing his way down the tiers of seats, square built and scowling, his low-crowned hat pushed back on thick chestnut hair, something oddly familiar about him. Mr. Hunter with him, tapping his shoulder, pointing at something, laughing. The two young dandies in the front row by the ring, one lifting an eye-glass to quizz the dog.

But what held her eye, gripped it with a growing sense of unbelieving horror, was the sack. The sack was moving. Was alive. She knew what must be in it and could not let herself believe it, think the words. She only stared at it, her mouth dry, unable to pull away from the iron door, the Judas grating. Dido changed his grip on the dog, a low-set bull-dog with a long, powerful muzzle, his thick body quivering between Dido's knees, his jaws drooling, one torn ear flapped down, the other pricked, his eyes red-wicked like a murderer's.

"All bets made!" Monkey shouted, his piping,

whispering voice bringing silence as if he'd blown a whistle. "All your bets in 'and?" Looking round, holding up his thick bunch of bank-notes. "On the count of three Jim lets go the rats, an' Dido lets go o' Billy. I 'as the timepiece 'ere ready!"

In his other hand a thick turnip watch.

"One, two . . ." The dog shivering with effort as though he, too, could count, could recognise the promise of the counting, Jim twisting his hands round, readying the sack for opening, Dido gripping his knees together, his hand round the dog's massive throat. ". . . three!"

The sack upturned, a grey flood of rats, a squeaking, twittering riverfall of living things, striking the sand, scrambling, spreading, running for their lives, and the dog in midair, sprung from Dido's knees like a catapult, jaws reaching catching a rat before his forefeet had touched the sand, catching it as it fell, a snapping, a toss of the flat, brutal head, the limp grey body flung like a glove, and another following it, the dog buried in the squeaking mass, snarling, snapping; and after the first snarl no sounds at all except the chopping of the jaws, and then the rising scream of the crowd, "Billy, *Billy*! Kill 'em, kill 'em!" The dandyish young man with the quizzing-glass trying to look bored, as though he were indifferent to his dog's success or failure, and the dog like a rushing storm of killing—rats flying, scuttling, trying to climb the steep, greased sides of the ring, to bury themselves in the thin covering of sand, turning to fight, eyes glittering with fury, flinging themselves at their monstrous murderer, hanging on his ears, his throat, lips, cheeks, and flanks, until he shook himself, shook a rain of rats in the air and chopped them as they fell. His white skin was stained with tiny blood marks, chisel scars, his good ear was torn now, his mouth a foam of rat blood, and the last rats were running, cowering, fighting, a rat corpse quivering, the last rat dead, and the shouting rising to a roar of triumph. Monkey raised his ape arms, Dido grabbed for the dog, hauled him back from the pile of bodies. Mr. Hunter stepped down into the ring and slapped his young friend on the shoulders, who was still trying to look bored. Snipe jumped up and down on her bench screaming, "I won, I won, I won." And Monkey managing to still the uproar enough to call out the time.

"Ten minits, forty-nine seconds, ladies an' gents! A record go!"

Sara turned away and was sick on the floor, the claret and the blackstrap and the chops and potatoes coming up in a thick and horrible bile of nausea. The candle still guttering behind her on its upturned barrel, its soft crocus flame stirring the shadows. She hung against a stone pillar, retched again, and felt slightly better, her forehead cold wet with sweat from vomiting. She leaned it against the stone, heard the confused shouting behind the door, was suddenly afraid that it would open and that they would see her there, and went unsteadily past the candle. She found a stairs and climbed it and was in the kitchen, Maggie rolling pastry, Sophy, the day girl, sitting at the table eating, trays of glasses she'd been polishing set out in front of her.

"Where you been?" Maggie said, turning round. "Ye look green as grass."

"The rats," Sara whispered. "They was killing rats." And yet she'd stayed watching all that time, as though she needed the horror. Needed to know its face.

Sophy filled her mouth with cheese, shook her brass ringlets. "Men," she said. "The things they do." Maggie turned her pastry over and scattered more flour on it.

"Since you're awake," she said, "you can take the glasses up. Are they finished down there?"

She took the glasses up to the gaming room and went to wake Molly, and the evening began as though they'd lived like this for half their lives.

Chapter 16

It was three days before she could sleep without dreaming of the rats, waking to hear the mouse-scuttlings, the creaking of timber, of the wind in the chimney, and thinking that the rats were coming, imagining them pouring up the stairs in a grey tide. And then, as that horror faded, as she lay awake, the deeper horror of them being killed that way, of the blood and terror, the tiny, squeaking death cries as the dog smashed their bodies with his jaws. And all for what? For Snipe to win five pounds, for the others—

She tried to tell Snipe what she felt, and Snipe stared at her as though she were mad. And Molly only shuddered at the thought of seeing them and then laughed.

Gradually the work became, if not easier, at least familiar, and it began to seem natural to sleep twice a day and never long enough, and she began to understand how Molly had felt in Lavender Cottage, staggering out of bed before dawn to rake the fires and reset them, her chilblains burning. To go to bed with her legs quivering with tiredness, the muscles of her shoulders aching from carrying the heavy trays over her head; her feet feeling as though the soles had been beaten with a stick.

She began to think of nothing except sleep. But Molly insisted they had to see London now they were there, and after they'd been a week or slightly more in the chop house, they went out during the afternoon, calling in at Ma Casey's to pay a part of their debts and to buy Molly's tippet.

"What a lovely pair," Ma Casey wheezed at them, fitting the narrow fur cape round Molly's shoulders, taking a small green velvet pelerine and holding it up for Sara to admire. "You're the most 'andsomest pair o' girls I ever saw in this 'ouse, I promise you that." She came closer to Sara, patted the velvet round her bare shoulders, smoothing her soft, fat old hands on them, fondling. "Monkey's ain't the place for girls like you. All them poxy sluts an' thieves. You wants the swells to see you. Now, I got a friend what keeps the nicest 'ouse you ever saw, an' she's such a lady, never 'its 'er girls, never robs 'em, treats 'em just like 'er own daughters. An' the gents what comes there! Lord This and Sir That, members o' Parliament, bishops! It's an education for a girl to live in that 'ouse."

"No, thank you," Sara said. "We're happy where we are."

"You don't know what I'm off'ring you. Jewels. Clothes. The best o' vittles an' champagne every night."

"We get champagne every night where we are," Molly said, admiring herself in a cheval-glass.

"That stuff o' Monkey's?" Ma Casey said scornfully. " 'E makes that 'isself in the jakes. Now, my friend 'as 'er stuff brought from France by a' ambassador in 'is luggage."

They escaped from her at last and went walking, Sara wishing she was in bed and Molly staring at everything with her face so full of wonder that a half-dozen men in the course of an hour stopped and asked if they could help the young ladies find their way or do them any service.

"For God's sake, stop gaping so," Sara said, pulling Molly past a shop window. A man stood in their path again, lifting his hat.

"Go away!" Sara said furiously. "We don't need . . ."

"Snipe's little friends! Or rather, her big friends. Your servant, ladies!" The man from the coffee-house. The drunken man, Mr. Munro. He loomed in front of them, holding his hat across his chest, his eyes

206

twinkling happily, his cheeks flushed, his cravat slightly astray, and one of his collar points broken and tilting away from his cheek. "And how is my dear Snipe?"

"Leave us alone!" Sara whispered.

"Leave you alone? In the street? Never!" cried Mr. Munro. "A gentleman leave two young ladies alone in the street? What might happen to you? What dreadful fate might befall you? And how should I forgive myself, lying awake in my bachelor bed, thinking, 'Ah, wretched man, but for your brutal indifference those two lovely creatures would still live and breathe, be happy, beautify the earth!' No, no, I'll never leave you. We must go and have a drink together, mingle our souls in wine! Come." He fitted himself between them, took their arms, drawing them along with him and supporting himself on them at the same time. "And what may you be doing with yourselves these days?"

"If you don't let go of us, we'll call the watch."

"The watch?" cried Mr. Munro. "*Watch, Watch!*"

People turned and stared and, seeing a large, more or less gentlemanly dressed man with two young girls apparently hanging on his arms, merely stared in puzzlement. But two or three assumed that two whores were robbing a drunken man and came quickly towards them, saying, "What's the matter, sir? Are they trying to rob you?"

"No, no, no, no," Mr. Munro said, letting go of Molly long enough to wave his hand in the air. "We are friends." He grasped Molly's arm again and said almost soberly, "Are we going to have a drink together?" He turned his head, winked at Sara, and it was impossible to tell whether he was drunk or quite sober and merely pretending. And yet he was hanging heavily on her arm. He turned them down another street, and they were outside the coffee-house where they'd first met.

"My club!" he cried delightedly. "My second home! My office of work! Let us slake ourselves at the fresh springs of Father Luke's appalling slops that he calls claret. Or would you ladies prefer tea?" He crooked his fingers and pronounced "tay" in such a genteel fashion it reminded Molly of Miss Hetty calling for her Bohea; she laughed so ringingly that Mr. Munro transferred his hand from her arm to round her waist and squeezed her against him. "Let us go in! Let us not dawdle in the forecourts of the Temple, but enter the Holy of Holies. Toby, you dog, wretched boy! Bring us three stoups of wine!"

He made them sit, contriving that they were against the window and beyond hope of escaping unless they climbed over the table. Toby came with his soft, tired tread, his face as white and knowing as before, his eyelids drooping, smiling slighlty at seeing them again, and there was a sudden extraordinary pleasure in the familiarity of everything, the quiet, handsome room with its panelling and its fire-place, its newspapers on the rack, the few customers here and there in corners, smoking and drinking and reading. Sara sat back, glad to be sitting anywhere, even with Mr. Munro leaning across the table, patting her hand and saying, "A pie? A trifle of apple tart?"

"If I could have coffee instead of wine," she said. "We get enough wine where we are."

"I'll warrant you do," said Mr. Munro happily. "Is it a nice house where you are? I assume you're in a house?"

"It's the queerest house you ever did see," Molly said. "The things that happen there!"

"I can imagine," Mr. Munro said. "And do you have to work very hard?" His plump, flushed cheeks screwing themselves into an almost sad smile that for the first time made Sara look at him not simply as a drunken nuisance, but as a person. He did look sad, behind all the noise and jollity.

"It ain't that bad," Molly was saying. "Not as bad as scrubbing floors in winter."

"The whore's eternal cry," Mr. Munro said. And again it was impossible to tell whether he was drunk or sober.

"We are *not* whores," Sara said coldly. "We work in a chop house. And a gaming room."

"Do you think I would look down on you whatever you were doing?" Mr. Munro said. "I know too much." He stared down at the pint of claret Toby was putting on the table in front of him. "Don't I, Toby boy? Don't I know too much?"

"You 'ead's bursting with it," Toby said. "Drink up and be 'appy."

"The only philosophy!" Mr. Munro cried. He lifted his pewter tankard and drained half the contents. He set it down and wiped his lips with his hand, still managing to give the movement a kind of polite elegance, as though there was a handkerchief there even if it was invisible. "I would need to be hard pressed to find an object of scorn before I chose whores."

"We ain't whores!" Molly cried. "We ain't, we ain't."

A man sitting at a nearby table, reading the *Times,* looked up and smiled. Sara nudged Molly with her elbow and whispered, "Shut up, for pity's sake. People are staring."

"When there are dukes to scorn, and princes, and archbishops! By God, I have a long list before I come to so much decency as whores! Do you know what I've been doing this day?" He peered at them across the table as though in the past seconds they'd moved farther away from him and he wished to be sure they were still there. "I've been writing a prayer!"

"A prayer?" Molly said, impressed. "You mean for parson to speak in church?"

"It might do many a parson good if he did speak it in his church. But I doubt if many will. However, *I* shall speak it. Let me read it to you." He began fumbling in an inside pocket of his coat, pulled out a sheet of paper, scanned it with his eyes screwed up, let it fall, and fished out another and then a third. "Ah, here we are. It is called 'Lord Southcott's Prayer.' "

"Lord Southcott—" Molly began. But he held up a commanding hand.

" 'Milord is in bed,' Milord's chaplain is to say aloud to the people. 'Pray do not disturb him!' And the people reply worshipfully, 'But the tears of the children are flooding the street!'

"And next the chaplain shall say, 'Milord is at table, pray do not annoy him!' And the response shall be, 'But the children are weeping. Oh, give us to eat!' "

Mr. Munro peered at them again over the top of his sheet of paper. " 'Milord is in church, pray do not awake him,' and the people shall reply in plain song, 'But the blood of the children is washing his feet.' And then the chaplain shall say, 'Milord's in debate, pray silence to hear him.' And there shall be no reply, for the children are dying, out there by the gate."

He laid his paper down beside his tankard and looked down it, and Sara saw to her astonishment that he was crying.

"That didn't sound like a prayer," Molly said. "Our Father an' Lord save us."

"Our Father!" Mr. Munro said with such savagery that his voice shook. "Suffer little children! By God, how they suffer."

He reached across the table and grasped their hands. "Do you think I'd dare to judge you, whatever you did? Or Snipe! Or anyone! In a world where children are whipped to work at four and five years old? Driven up burning chimneys to put out the fires? Brought down mineshafts before they can scarce toddle, to sit all day in the dark and never know it is day, while their mothers drag tubs of coal along the galleries, and the tiny children open and shut the ventilation doors for them, hour after hour, the water running over their feet in a black river? I've *been* there, I've *seen* them. I've seen the mills, I've heard the children clattering to work before dawn and staggering home after dark. And I've come back here and written, cried out to the Lord Southcotts and the Lord Liverpools and the great Duke of Wellington and the Castlereaghs and Cannings, 'You are murdering our children, they are dying, dying.' And they don't even hear my voice, except as a faint whispering of what they call sedition.

"And they have told me by their lackeys and their bully boys that I shall be put in jail for it if I continue to write such stuff. For they own the coal mines and draw profit from the mills and their crooked chimneys must be swept by children or their fine dinners might be spoiled, and the man who dares tell them that all this is wickedness is only fit for the company of thieves and murderers and poor starving whores. Perhaps they're right. In fact, I'm sure they are."

He bent his head and the tears ran down his cheeks and fell one by one onto Lord Southcott's Prayer.

"Don't get upset," Molly said unhappily. "Drink your wine. We've got to be going soon."

Toby had brought them their coffee and was patting Mr. Munro on the shoulder in a fatherly way.

There was an uneasy silence in the room as though the half dozen customers had all been listening. Indeed it would have been impossible for them not to overhear. Sara drank her coffee. She would have liked to touch Mr. Munro's hand and comfort him, but he had put both his hands up to his face and was rubbing his eyes. He began to laugh, emptied his tankard and gave it to Toby.

"Come my Ganymede, refill the flowing bowl with Father Luke's nectar, and let all be merriness and joy. What shall we do, my dears, with the great spread of time that lies before us, between this and the dark?"

"We have to go back to work," Sara said.

"Oh, aye. Work." He picked up his sheet of paper, considered it for a moment as though he was half of a mind to crush it into a ball and throw it away. Instead he refolded it slowly and put it into his coat pocket again. "And how is my pretty Snipe?"

"She's all right," Sara said. "We really do have to go back to work." She pushed away her half-finished coffee and made to stand up, nudging Molly to do the same. Mr. Munro hesitated, sighed and stood up to let Toby draw the table away and release them from their window seat. Toby set the freshly filled tankard down and Mr. Munro lifted it in salute as they squeezed their way out and past him.

"Give Snipe my love. My fond, fond love." He sat down heavily and stared after them, waving to them as they went by the window in front of him.

"He were funny," Molly said.

"I thought he was sad."

"Go away. You do think *everything* is sad. Oooh, look at that silk in that door there! Just imagine a frock made o' that!"

211

Chapter 17

Mr. Hunter came almost every night. Not for long, usually. Only long enough to stake a guinea or two and lose them, as though he were paying an entrance fee; to drink a glass of champagne, taste one of Maggie's summer pasties—fine slices of pheasant breast and bacon cut into thin shreds, baked in a thick wine sauce inside the pastry cups—to tease both of them, and Janet if she was there. Joke with Monkey. And drop a guinea into the top of Molly's dress, brushing his knuckles against her cheek, touching her ear, as though there were already an understanding between them and this was a ritual joke.

Sara stopped asking her about it, tried not to watch them together, Molly laughing, throwing her head back, showing her big white teeth, her bare throat, her laugh sounding like gold ringing above the noise of the gaming room. She asked Snipe about him, why a gentleman should come to a place like Monkey's. "Is it just to find someone like—"

"Lord love you!" Snipe said. " 'E don't 'ave to come to a place like this to find a dolly. God above, Mr. Hunter is a lord, 'e could 'ave any girl 'e looks at, near enough, just beckon 'em in the street, anywhere. No, 'e comes 'ere to mix with us, all of 'em do, the swells you sees comin' ere. They thinks it's marvellous, being 'ere with all the flash gents an' the bullies an' the 'ores an' the pickpockets. It gives 'em a thrill, see, what they can't get from anything else anymore. They ain't never been 'ungry, an' they gets bored with things. So they comes 'ere, an' we treats 'em just like one of us an' they thinks that's marvellous. An' Monkey puts 'is bloody great arm round 'em. An' they'd rather 'ave 'im do that than the king make 'em a sir. 'Cause they're sirs already, see?"

"I hate them," Sara whispered. "Hate them!"

Snipe looked at her, astonished. "What's up with you? Did you want 'im to fancy you 'stead of Moll?"

"I'd rather die."

"Get away."

"I would, I swear it."

"They don't do you no 'arm. In fact, they does us all a bit o' good' 'cause whilst they comes 'ere the Runners don't bother Monkey about the gamin' or nothing else much. That's one reason 'e lets 'em come. All their fathers is 'igh-ups, in Parliament an' that. 'S long as Monkey don't cheat 'em too much you won't never see a Runner come up them stairs. 'E don't even lock the doors. You go to the Parson's or Frenchy's place, an' you got to get through six doors all locked tight and with spy-'oles, before you can get near a table. An' then you gets robbed."

Sometimes the two young dandies came with Mr. Hunter, or others so similar they were indistinguishable, their cravats so splendid, so tight, thrusting their chins so high in the air it seemed impossible for them to see where they were going or to look down at the gaming tables. And the flash gents and the bullies, without appearing to be impressed, took the most careful note of every detail of their turnout, from the cut of a shoulder to the roll and curve of a velvet collar to the depth of a cuff to a skin-tight pantaloon that seemed to have the trick of never wrinkling even when its owner moved as carelessly as the young dandies did.

But Moses Gensch, or his brother Aaron, the favourite tailors of the flash-men, would never quite achieve the same results, that arrogant simplicity and sumptuous plainness. And the flash-men would never move like that. And without analysing it, Sara knew it, and felt humiliated by it without knowing why, and tried to leave the serving of Mr. Hunter and his friends entirely to Molly or Janet.

"You're downright mad, Sara Pownall," Molly said, tossing another guinea on her palm. "They do give a guinea like it's a shilling."

One night Mr. Hunter brought the man she'd seen in the rat pit, the square-set man with the chestnut hair and the sullen mouth, and again there was that odd impression of something familiar about him. He came into the gaming room as though he'd been brought there against his will, staring round not arrogantly, as the dandies did, but bored, and that seemed even more insulting.

She turned away from them to avoid Mr. Hunter's eye and let Molly serve them, as always, and as soon as they moved away from the door, she took a tray of used glasses and went down to the kitchen to spend ten minutes there washing them, and bringing up fresh wine. They were at the roulette table when she came back, Molly beside them, Mr. Hunter throwing on counters for her. She heard Molly crying, "Oh, I've lost again," as she passed near.

As soon as she could find an excuse she went down to the kitchen once more and found a stranger sitting there, very much at his ease, his boots stretched out towards the fire, his hat pushed back on his balding head, a strand of grey, wispy hair plastered carefully across the yellow scalp. Maggie fussing about at the oven, turning as Sara came in with an unnatural movement, a nervous tension that caught at Sara's attention immediately.

"Here she is, Mr. Brown, the lassie herself. Here's a gentleman as is waitin' to meet you, Sara, come ower here an' let Mr. Brown have a good look at you. She's a good girl, Mr. Brown, a good hard-working girl by all I've seen o' her, an' no nonsense with her."

"I'm glad to 'ear it," the man said. He had a flat, ugly voice, merely a dull rasping sound as though he grudged letting the words escape. "Come 'ere, girl, don't be frightened o' me." She came and stood in front of him and looked down into two small, mud-coloured eyes, set in a mud-coloured, almost shapeless face that made her skin shiver with instantaneous dislike. He had a bottle of the special champagne in a bucket of crushed ice on the floor beside his boots, and he was twisting a wine-glass in his fingers in a curious, dull caricature of a gentleman drinking. His lips had a dark mauve colour like half-cooked liver and he ran his tongue along them, slowly, as if the head of a toad was creeping out between two muddy stones, yellowish-white and horrible. She wanted to shut her eyes against the sight of that tongue.

"I 'ear you're a clever girl," he said.

She said nothing, stared at his tongue, forced herself to look instead into the small, muddy eyes, tried to control herself from shuddering.

"An 'ard-working clever girl."

"Aye, she's that, Mr. Brown. Keeps herself to herself. Not lazy like the rest of them." Maggie brought him a game pasty, smoking hot from the oven, holding it tenderly in a folded napkin. "Try one o' my pasties Mr. Brown, sir. 'Twill do ye good."

He took it without looking at Maggie or the napkin, his eyes still holding Sara's. "An 'ard-working clever girl as would 'ave the sense to keep 'er mouth shut if she knew something what shouldn't be talked about."

"Oh, aye, she's close, Mr. Brown, very close."

"A clever, 'ard-working, close girl what would know 'ow to listen for the right things?"

"Aye, aye, she would that, Mr. Brown. You just need to look at her to tell she's clever. That's why I recommended her to ye. T'other one's no more than a pretty blabber box."

"Now supposing I was to propose to you a little job of work what wouldn't interfere with your work 'ere. In fact, would depend upon it, eh, Maggie?"

"Oh, aye, Mr. Brown."

Sara looked round at Maggie, knew what was coming, felt sick and frightened and disgusted and at the same time held there almost more by the disgust than by the fear, as though it was part of a nightmare, knowing the end of it and still unable to move, to run.

"I don't want—I don't want any other kind of work," she whispered.

"Ah. But this ain't carrying, nor scrubbing, nor nothing 'ard. This is mental, ain't it, Maggie? In-ter-leckshul, so to speak. And of a very 'igh value. You don't want to say no to something before you knows what it is, my girl. That ain't clever. That ain't sharp nor wise."

"I know what it is. And I wouldn't do it."

He looked at her. There was a crumb of the game pie at the corner of his lips and the white toad head of his tongue crept out and gathered it, savouring the tiny flake of pastry.

"Oh," he said. "It's like that? Maggie 'as mistook you, 'as she? You ain't a clever girl after all?"

"I've never pretended to be clever."

"A stupid girl, eh? One that doesn't recognise a good friend when she meets one? Well, it so 'appens," he said, "that I needs a girl just at this moment, and just in this place. And if I can't 'ave a clever girl I shall 'ave to make do with a stupid one." He pushed the remains of the game pasty into his mouth and chewed it slowly, his lips opening and shutting as he chewed. Crumbs of pastry escaped. A dribble of mushroom sauce made a grey path down his chin and he wiped it away with his knuckle. While all the time the small, colourless eyes stared up into hers, not even with dislike or menace. Like a toad's eyes, fixed on a thing to eat.

"But I treats a stupid girl different from what I treats a clever one. A clever girl, I'm kind to 'er. Kind as a father. You ain't got any idea 'ow kind. But a stupid girl I 'as to be different." He had moved his right hand, was taking something out of his inside pocket. A short, leather-covered stick. He lifted the end of it, touched Sara's cheek. It was warm from contact with his body, warm and slightly greasy, and heavy as he let it rest against her face. She forced herself not to move, not to draw her head back. The mauve, greasy lips smiled, his cheeks creasing, like mud cracking open.

"You ain't never been nicked yet?" he said. "Ain't never been inside?"

When she did not answer, he pushed her cheek

216

slightly with the tip of his cosh, so that he turned her head away from him; he changed the position of the cosh to her other cheek and pushed her head back again to face him.

"I don't think you could 'ave been, or you'd know better than to be so stupid when a man like me makes you such a kind, generous offer o' work. I don't think you could ever 'ave." His hand moved like a snake; the cosh hit the flat wooden bench beside him with a thudding smash of lead against timber that made the bench dance on the slate floor, the Delft ring on the dresser and the table. The echoes died in the shadows. Sara felt her cheeks whitening, her throat locked.

"That's what 'appens to stupid girls," he said. "It's the only thing they understands. Now, as I say, I needs a girl 'ere, an' that girl is you. When you 'ears things, the kind o' things a man like me would want to know about, you tells Mag 'ere, an' she tells me. Or I comes to this kitchen an' you an' me 'as a little talk like we're 'aving now, an' you tells me everything I wants to know. *Everything!*"

She wanted to move, to look away; she thought she was going to faint simply from standing there in one position in front of him, staring down into that muddy, toad face, with its high yellow forehead and the quiff of thin grey hair plastered above it like something dead.

"An' I don't think you're near as stupid as you just been pretending. I don't think that at all. I think you're a girl what can learn. 'Old out your hand to us."

When she didn't move, he took her wrist in his hand, made her open her fingers. "Now," he said, "I 'ears that gypsies can tell fortunes in palms of 'ands. An' no doubt they can tell their own as well as others? Look down into that palm of yours and see what's there."

Against all her will she looked down, saw the dark rims of his nails, the grey fingers fastened round her wrist, her own fingers extended.

"Do you see there what they calls the line o' life? Now, if you was to go upstairs an' start blabbering about this little talk o' ours, that line o' life in your palm ought to be a very short one. Very, very short. Comin' to a miserable end almost immediate. An' it wouldn't need to be me what would shorten it. Ho, no. Them flash gents upstairs would see to that, because they wouldn't believe as 'ow they could trust you anymore. An' one morning very soon someone would find a sack floating down in the docks with you inside it. I 'opes you understands that? I do 'ope so."

He tightened his fingers, dug the grey-rimmed nails into her wrist. "Now, you 'ave another look at that pretty line. An' all them other lines what tells you what's going to 'appen to you. And just suppose you was so foolish as to 'ear things upstairs, or out there in that dining-room of a morning, an' not to tell me about it. Or tell me too late. Or leave out an important bit what would make all the difference as to me nabbing a nice forty pounder or missing 'im. Can you see in your 'and the kind of thing as would 'appen then?" He waited a second and then with that same snake quickness the cosh hissed in the air above her hand. She tried to wrench it away; he held her and at the last second checked the force of the blow, so that the cosh no more than fell into her palm with a small, ugly threat of pain, instead of pain itself. She shivered; he laughed, a hoarse rasping laugh, as though there was phlegm caught in his throat.

"You mind what Mr. Brown says to you," Maggie whispered. "I thought you had more sense than that."

"Don't be upset, Maggie," Mr. Brown said. "She'll learn. She'll learn. An' maybe she's thinking that if she tells me what she 'ears and I goes and nabs a lad at once on the strength of it, then very soon they'll catch on to what's 'appening and she'll finish down at Gravesend just the same. Oh, no, ho, no." He laid his cosh like a finger alongside his shapeless nose. "We ain't so foolish as that. Most of what you're going to tell me I'll know already because I knows a lot. A great lot, don't I, Maggie?"

"You do that, Mr. Brown, a great lot."

"An' what I don't know, I may not act on. Because we 'as our understandings, Monkey an' Maggie 'ere

218

an' me. We 'as our system and our code, don't we, Maggie?"

"Oh, aye, we do, we do that." All the time of the conversation Maggie had been busy at the fire or the oven, only turning to answer one of Mr. Brown's rhetorical questions, folding her big red hands in her apron, standing with exaggerated submissiveness to answer him.

"An' when I does act, I acts with discretion. Because discretion is my middle name, ain't it, Maggie?"

"You're a very discreet man, Mr. Brown, there's no one would say different."

"So you see, girl? On the one 'and, stupidity. Leading to a short un'appy life an' suffering very unpleasant accidents. Of the kind I've described. On the other 'and, wisdom. Cleverness and good sharp sense and obedience. And a 'appy, rewarding life with me for your good friend. And a girl needs a friend, don't she, Maggie?"

"Aye, she does, indeed."

"Now, mum's the word, mind. You run back upstairs and think over what I been saying, an' one day soon, a couple o' weeks or so, I'll come back 'ere an' see what you've gathered up for me. Or else you can send me word. But if in that couple o' weeks I 'ears— and I shall 'ear, you be sure o' that, I shall 'ear instant quick—if I 'ears you been blabbing . . ." He was still holding her wrist, and he tapped the cosh down across her palm again, harder than the last time, stinging the flesh with its still slightly warm, greasy weight of lead and leather. "It'll be Rest In Peace for you." He let go of her hand.

"An' one more thing. If someone else should come —a Mr. Lavender, say, or a Mr. Townsend—starting the same kind of talk that we've just been 'aving, you can tell 'em you're engaged. By me. Now, run along, my girl, an' let's 'ope for your sake that you're as wise as you're pretty."

He reached behind him for his champagne glass, held it out. Maggie hastened to refill it for him.

Sara stepped slowly back. He was no longer looking

219

at her, seemed no longer interested whether she was there or not.

"Take that tray o' pasties with you, an' not a word, mind."

She took the tray, turned, and went, slowly at first and then hurrying, stumbling over the bottom step of the stairs, almost spilling her load out of her hands, wanting to run. Anywhere. She heard voices above her, coming down the stairs—Molly's voice—and she knew that Mr. Hunter would be with her and wanted to run again. But there was no way to escape them, and she went on up to the first landing, where a lamp set in the window lit the staircase with a dull yellow glow.

Mr. Hunter just behind Molly, his hand resting on her bare shoulder, her head turned back towards him. Dawdling down the stairs like lovers. Mr. Hunter's friend some way behind them.

"Why, here's the gypsy!" Mr. Hunter cried. "Where have you been hiding, eh? This is the one I promised ye, Harry, come an' meet her."

"Let me by," she whispered, her voice failing, threatening to fail altogether, that feeling of her throat being locked, strangled. Mr. Hunter barred her way, smiling down from the step above her.

"You know who he is?" Molly cried. "Mr. Summers? He do be from Southcott Hall, his dad do own it, Lord Southcott his dad is, can you imagine? All the way from Thaxstone, from the hall! An' comin' here!"

He had come down another step, the light reached his face, and it was as though the captain stood on the stair above her, the same broad, square forehead, the blunt, half-ugly features, the hooked nose, the heavy clump of the mouth. She stared, held her tray foolishly, the pasties sliding. Mr. Hunter steadied it, laughed.

"Let the girl by," Mr. Summers said. "And let's get down. The damned air in there . . ."

The same voice. Essex in it and the marshes, the captain's burred growling when he was out of temper. And for a second he was really there. Looking down at her.

"Gad, you're an ill-humoured devil, Harry. Here's

220

the two prettiest girls in London and all you can think of is running from 'em."

She stood unable to move, the shock of that likeness still holding her, making her hands unsteady.

"Well, say somethin'," Molly said. "You look proper dazed. What's up with you?"

She tried to say something, and no sound came, and with an effort she pushed by them, found her strength, and went running up the stairs as though they might follow her, pull her back. She heard Mr. Hunter's laugh, Molly's astonished voice. "She do have the vapors tonight all right."

Dido was at the door of the gaming room, and he smiled at her as he always did, like a big brown dog longing to be touched and petted, but afraid to come too close in case he's cuffed instead.

"Where's Snipe?" she asked him. "Is she still here?"

His face flushed with the pleasure of her speaking to him, and he pointed to where Snipe was, at the rouge-et-noir table.

She took her tray round, trying to seem natural, unhurried, offering the pasties to the gamblers, her eye on Snipe, until she could work her way to her side. She held her tray at Snipe's elbow and whispered, "Can you talk to me? Over there?" She moved away, and after a minute or two Snipe followed her, said, "Where you takin' them pasties, Sara? Give us one, for Gawd's sake." And in a low voice, "What's up? You look as if you seen a ghost."

"There's a man downstairs," she whispered, "a Mr. Brown—"

Snipe closed her hand on Sara's wrist. "Sssh," and then, "The only good thing in this bloody place is the pies. Three quid I just lost. 'Allo, Scotchy."

Scotch Robert took a pie, grinned at Snipe, gave Sara the half-considering, half-respectful smile that all the regular customers gave her, thanks to Dido's watchful influence, and went on into the faro alcove.

"Don't tell me nothing 'ere. I'll see you upstairs in your room afterwards." She laughed as though they'd been exchanging gossip, and went back to her gambling. Sara stayed where she was, knowing that she

221

ought to move round, ought to behave as she always did. Was afraid that Monkey would notice, that Dido —And if they did? What did it matter? What did *any-thing* matter now? She stayed standing there in the corner by the long curtains of the bow window, a sudden burst of laughter from the faro table, the nearby whist players slapping their cards down at the end of a game—all the crowded room in front of her. And Mr. Brown's face, watching her, the leather cosh bending between his grey hands. She felt the weight of it still against her cheek-bone.

I must get away, she thought. *Tonight. Tomorrow.* At least she had money now. *And Molly?*

"You stuck or something?" Janet said. "I ain't got four 'ands, you know. Move round, for Gawd's sake. Give us a rest."

She moved mechanically, her tray emptied, and she stood again for a long time with the empty tray held out as though it were still full, until Dido came beside her, said in a low voice, "What's the matter, little *Pen*, little sister? Has anyone been bad to you?"

She shook her head, made herself smile at him, seem natural. But even that was less than natural.

"You needs to fill your tray."

She hesitated, saw him looking at her in growing astonishment, forced herself out of the doorway. On the landing below she stood for minutes before she could make herself go on down to the kitchen. But there was only Maggie there. She stared at her, and Maggie looked away, made herself busy with the fire.

"Well," Maggie said at last, "have you thought o' what Mr. Brown was sayin'?"

"I'll leave here," Sara whispered.

Maggie looked up at her from where she was stooping, the iron cinder rake in her hand. "He wouldn't let you get far."

"Who is he?"

"He's from Bow Street. One o' the runners."

"And do you tell him things?"

"I have no choice. No more do you, now."

"I'd die before I'd tell him anything."

"That's easy said, my lass." She raked the cinders

222

with a vicious rattle of iron against iron, a shower of sparks.

"Why did you tell him about me?"

Maggie straightened, her face gaunt with the shadows thrown upwards by the fire. "For Gawd's sake, ye poor wee ignorant lassie, do ye think ye can have a house like this without payin' a price for it? Never raided by the runners? Never bothered by anyone? This is part o' the price."

"It's a dreadful price."

"It's a ha'penny price, child. He doesn't want to go nabbin' every thief an' pickpocket you hear talking about the guinea they robbed yesterday. He just wants to know who they are, what they're doin', he wants to know everything that happens an' then, if there's too much trouble he knows right well who's responsible and he'll nab them then. An' no one'll know it was you that pointed the finger at them."

"Nab them when they weigh forty pounds?" she said bitterly.

Maggie looked at her in half-scornful surprise. "They've taught you that already, have they? Aye, mebbe that too. He has his living to earn the same as the rest o' us, an' him gettin' paid forty pound o' prize money for making one arrest is a great deal better for everyone, for us too, than him making four arrests for a miserable ten pound apiece. That way three goes free for the one that's taken. If a lad or a lassie does so much thievin' that they know the runners'll get forty pound for 'em, then if they've any sense they'll stop for a while, or go away north or into Wales or somewhere. They don't have to stay here."

"Neither do I."

Maggie shook her head sadly. "An' what would you do?"

She realised she was still holding the empty tray, looked down at it. "Why didn't you tell me you were—you were going to—" The shadows of the kitchen surrounding her, the fire—Maggie standing there, the red firelight against her apron, her bare red arms.

"Because you'd have begged and pleaded with me

not to. Do what he tell ye, lassie. D'ye think you're the only one? Every flash-house from here to Holborn an' back down to the river, they have someone that tips 'em the nod on everything. Wait now. There's someone coming. Take that tray o' punch up with you an' keep your mouth closed."

It was Molly; looking very pleased with herself, re-arranging the shoulder straps of her dress. Sara took the loaded tray, avoided looking at her.

"I'm starvin'," Molly said. "Is there a pie goin' free, Mag?"

Upstairs, the gaming room seemed more crowded than ever. The night went on and on, no one leaving, one o'clock, two o'clock, half-past. Endless. Until at last the crowd thinned, the croupiers began to yawn more openly behind their hands. She was collecting the empty glasses for the last time, Molly leaning against the wall, rubbing one foot against her calf, her eyes shut. Janet already vanished. Monkey with his iron cash box. No gamblers remaining.

They found Snipe in their room when they went up, fast asleep on their bed, her dress hanging over the back of the chair, the candle guttering in its tin saucer on the floor by the chimney-breast, its flame shuddering, threatening to snuff out as they opened the door. She woke as they came in and rolled forward to squat cross-legged on the mattress, wide awake on the instant, as if she could have continued the movement and run like a hare if it had been necessary. Sara closed the door and the candle flame steadied, Snipe's shadow dark against the sloping boards of the ceiling.

"That fellow Brown," Snipe whispered. "What'd 'e want?"

Sara told her, Snipe nodding her small golden head like a nodding doll, Molly listening open-mouthed.

"Bloody bastard!" Snipe said. "I always guessed Monkey was a bit in with them, you could only 'spect it, an' Mags as well. We don't never tell 'em nothing anyways. But I never thought of the girls working 'ere —Gawd. That little bitch as went sick before you come." She stayed hunched up on the mattress, her arms round her shins, her chin buried between her

224

knees. "It must've bin 'er what pointed the finger at Jim an' our mob. An' then she got scared an' run for it in case she was caught. So now 'e needs someone else. Gawd." She looked at Sara, then quickly away, as though already some kind of stain had touched Sara's face, and Sara put up her hand to her cheek, where the cosh had lain, and felt sick with shame and despair.

"You don't think I'd—I'd ever—"

Snipe looked at her. "I know you wouldn't," she said.

"I'll go away."

"Where can you go?" Molly whispered. "You did say Maggie warned as how he'd follow you."

"I'll go where he *can't* follow." She had sat down slowly on the end of the mattress, her legs seeming to fold under her. Molly kneeling beside Snipe, her dress and bodice undone, pulling them off, still staring at her.

"You don't understand," Snipe said, her voice sadly pitying. "There ain't nowhere 'e can't follow you. Not if 'e got 'is knife in you."

"What is she going to do?" Molly breathed.

"You'd best ask Monkey," Snipe said. "Maybe, I dunno, maybe if you were to jus' to *pretend* to be willin'? Till we could think of somethin'? 'E said 'e wouldn't come back for a bit?"

"A fortnight."

"A fortnight's a long time." She tried to laugh, did laugh. "Gawd, who knows where we'll all be tomorrow, let alone a fortnight? Monkey'll think of something." She rolled backwards, lay flat. "Ain't the pair o' you nice an' snug 'ere? I think sometimes—if I just 'ad a place what was really mine. Like this. What only me could go into. No one else never come there 'less I asked 'em. Can you imagine that? Lock the door an' you're safe, no bastard come near you. Just lie down and sleep. Oh, Gawd, I'm a fool, ain't I?"

She rolled up and forward again, catching her lower lip between her teeth. "I wonder if 'e's after me? Brown, I mean. 'E'd get 'is forty quid for me all right." She looked at Sara, her eyes nervous, unsure.

225

"You can tell things, can't you?" She tried to laugh again, pushed out her small, supple hand. " 'Ave a look for us, luv. Just—just to see what I got coming for me."

"I don't know what you—"

"Please," Snipe begged. "I knows you can. Dido said—"

"What did Dido say?" Her voice harsh with anger. She felt herself shivering, part anger, part something else. She hunched herself, clenched her arms against her stomach.

" 'E didn't say anything wrong! 'E just said 'e thought—'e didn't mean no 'arm."

"He had no right," she whispered. "He knows nothing about me. Nothing."

"But you do know 'ow? Don't you?" Snipe's eyes pleading, pleading, the shadows of fear behind them.

"I don't!"

"Go on," Molly said. "Look in the mirror for her." She leaned forward suddenly. "An' for me. Look for me, too!"

"Molly!"

"Where's the mirror?" Snipe whispered. "Does she look in it to see things?"

"She do see pictures there. Faces an' people an' things they be doin'. She learned it from old Missus Talbot." She looked at Sara, looked away guiltily, and said, "There ain't nothing wrong, tellin' her, is there?"

Sara shut her eyes, put the palms of her hands against them, hardly knew why she felt angry and at the same time afraid.

"Where's the mirror?" Snipe was saying, her voice urgent. "Tell us what you sees." Leaning forward, touching her hands, pulling them gently away from her eyes. "Please."

Molly hunted under the mattress, under the loose floorboard for Sara's bundle, laid it between them on the gray blanket. "Go on, Sara. Look for her, look for her, look for me, too. All of us!" Undoing the knotted scarf, finding the silver mirror. She drew it out slowly, dark silver, dark glass. A pool of darkness. Snipe leaned above it, bending her head so the gold ringlets fell forward, shadowed her small face, hid her eyes, which were staring down into the mirror as though it was a door into another world. Molly pushed the mirror closer to Sara's knees, bending forward herself, until their three heads were above the glass, golden, red, black, almost shutting off what small light there was from it, turning the surface darker still, only the shadows of their faces there.

She stared down into it. Not wanting to. Wanting to shut her eyes against it. And seeing that mud-grey face, that white, toad-head slithering between the thin, mauve lips. And saying—saying—She closed her ears against the flat, ugly voice, closed her eyes against that face, the mirror.

"Tell us," Snipe breathed. "You're seeing something, I knows."

"Nothing," she said. "I can't see anything."

"Tell me first," Molly whispered. "Tell me what'll happen to me with—with anything."

The three of them coming down the stairs towards her, Molly's head turned back to look at him, his hand on her shoulder, on the bare flesh beside her neck. And against her will, not wanting to see it, she saw a collar there, green jewels, gold, like a collar of green fire in the lamplight, and his hands caressing, touching, setting it there, cupping her face in his two palms.

"What is it?" Molly urged her. "What can you see?"

"A collar," she said, her voice harsh. "A green collar. Like a dog." She looked at Molly, tried to laugh, the echoes of Mrs. Talbot's voice still in her mind, in Molly's eyes looking at her, also trying to laugh, not be afraid.

"What kind o' collar?" she whispered, touched her neck.

"How should I know?" And the jewels burned in the shadows against that beautiful white throat, the velvet skin. "It will make you very happy," she said savagely.

"Jewels? Green jewels, Sara?" Such longing.

Bending over the mirror, not wanting to see that white, naked body, so beautiful in its nakedness, the green collar round the throat, and—and—Like screaming, like screaming in her mind, wanting to twist her head away, shut her mind to everything, sound, sight, not hear, not see. Her throat closing, closing as she tried to scream.

"Tell us!" Snipe's voice, Snipe's hand tugging at hers, begging. "Please. Tell us mine."

"I can't," she whispered. "I can't!" She looked at her, and Snipe's head was tilted sideways. "I *can't!*"

"What did you see?" Snipe breathed. She put up her own small hand to touch her neck, just below her ear, as if she knew, and her face was like paper in the candlelight.

"Nothing," Sara whispered. "Nothing." The candle danced their shadows on the wall. One shadow.

Chapter 18

It was the late afternoon before she could speak to Monkey. In the morning he was in the gymnasium with Dido and at dinnertime there were half a dozen people in and out of the kitchen and he was too busy supervising Ben and Maggie, or out in the front room grilling a steak for a favourite customer, for her to say anything to him quietly. And she was almost glad to put the thing off, afraid of what he might say and do.

But the dinner hours in the dining-room came to an end and they could eat their own meal and be free until the evening. She had wanted to catch him alone then, when the others had left the kitchen, but Dido and Ben were with him, and the three men went out of the kitchen together and back to the gymnasium. She followed them and stood watching for five minutes. Ben and Dido, tightening the ropes of the ring; Mr. Angelo, the fencing master who rented a corner of the gymnasium four days a week, mending the padded buttons on the ends of some foils; a couple of loafers in moleskins and the spotted neckerchiefs called belchers arguing about something.

One of Dido's sparrers coming in, the giant carter Hebbo, with his enormous shoulders and tiny head and an even tinier leather hat balanced on top of it. He gave Sara a small, shy, half-idiotic smile and touched his Newgate forelock.

Dido looked up and saw her, fastened the lower rope and also smiled at her, surprised at seeing her there because she almost never came into the gymnasium. She pretended to be looking at what Mr. Angelo was doing, picked up a foil, and bent it between her hands. Mr. Angelo went, "Tsk, tsk, tsk," and took it away from her, and the memory of Miss Hetty making exactly that sound was like a sharp pain. As though in that moment Lavender Cottage seemed a refuge, a lost safety.

She went closer to the corner of the ring where Monkey was leaning on the upper rope, testing it, and touched his arm. "I want to speak to you," she whispered.

He looked round at her, astonished. "Well, fer Gawd's sake, speak," he said, and saw her face and said, "You go an' speak to 'er about it then, tell her you can't manage." He turned away from the ropes and said in a lower voice, "What d'you want?"

"A man came last night," she whispered. "A Mr. Brown."

He put his hand on her shoulder like a weight. "Come back 'ere about five o'clock and I'll talk to you then." And louder, "Go on with you now, don't be afraid of 'er."

She went upsairs and Molly was waiting for her, her eyes round with waiting. "Where you been?"

She told her, and Molly sat up and tried to be

229

interested for a moment. And then, "Tell me about the jewels, Sara! Were they real, real jewels?"

"How do I know? Go to sleep." She lay down and refused to answer, pretending to be asleep herself and listening for the church clocks to chime. Three o'clock. Four. Five. She got up softly, leaving Molly asleep on her back with her mouth open and one hand lying curled across her bare breast. Even her hands seemed to have grown beautiful in the last weeks, now that she no longer scrubbed. She managed never even to wash the glasses and spent pounds on the creams Snipe told her about. Sara stood looking down at her for a moment and tried to remember her as she had been: the bones sticking out, the red hands and the chilblains, the smooth, full shoulders, the white throat, and the white hand lying with its fingers curved as though they were already grasping an emerald collar, filled her with pity—a sudden, irrational tenderness of pity. And then anger, so that she had an equally irrational urge to kneel down and shake her awake, make that pleased, sleeping, languid smile vanish.

She pulled on her dress, fastened it with nervous, hurrying fingers, kicked on her slippers, and ran down the stairs.

The gymnasium was full now, the carter and Dido sparring in the ring, a crowd of men round the ropes shouting advice, most of it in mockery of the carter as Dido slid under the great swinging arms and rat-a-tapped his gloves against the massive, rippling stomach like a wall in front of him. "Give 'im a facer, Hebbo! Darken 'is lights for 'im!" And Hebbo stopped to acknowledge the advice and Dido jolted him with a cross counter under the tiny jaw.

A cluster of dandies were round Mr. Angelo, the old man thin and rickety and wheezing, and his hand dazzling. One of Mr. Hunter's young men was lunging at him, grunting with fury, and the old man touched the blade aside effortlessly, tapping his padded point against the boy's shirt front, not even moving his feet. "You're too close to me, Sir Tom. Keep your distance. Distance, Sir Tom, distance an' time is the secret."

The crack of single sticks, a shout of "Blood, blood to me!"

The smell of sweat and stables; the men there looked as though they slept in stables, their clothes reeking of it. And brandy and tobacco. A few of the mobsmen were also there, watching Dido spar with Hebbo, but not many of them. It was another world from the gaming room. But even here Dido's protection hung round her like a cloak, and although she was the only girl in the room, no one did more than glance at her or smile recognition. She saw Monkey's bald, shining head and squeezed her way towards him, touched his arm. He came with her to the bay windows, where the two single stick fighters had their own crowd of onlookers, too absorbed in the sport to notice anything behind them.

"Tell us," Monkey said. He listened, looked round as she whispered, seeming merely to be watching the practise while she told him some domestic thing. He looked at her only when she had finished. "An' you don't want to do it?" She shook her head, began to say something, and he said impatiently, "For Gawd's sake, you thinks I likes it? Bloody leeches. Worse'n us, they are. But you got to play along with 'em. When 'e comes back, I'll tell you something to tell 'im, keep 'im quiet. Something what won't 'urt any o' my gents 'ere. Maybe send 'im after Darby for something, shake that old ratbag up a bit. You wouldn't mind that, would you?" He gave her a hard, probing look.

"I don't want—"

"Not even against Darby? An' if you don't 'e ain't going to leave you alone now."

"I'll run away."

"Run where you like. An' where the 'ell d'you think you'll get grub an' money like you gets 'ere? You run away from 'ere an' you'll come back on your 'ands an' knees in a month, starving. Or else you'll be in a 'ore 'ouse. What d'you think you are? A lady?"

"I'll find something."

A look almost like pity, almost affection, shadowed the white, battered mass of his face. "You're a nice

231

kid. Too nice for 'ere. But you won't find anything better. An' that bastard Brown is part of it. You do what I say. It won't take much to keep 'im 'appy. It's the *feeling* 'e likes. The feeling that 'e knows everything, that he can walk in that kitchen down there an' be a dirty-assed sort o' king in front o' Mags, an' frighten some poor slut with 'is cosh. That's what 'e likes. An' every now an' then 'e gets a bit of a tip about someone none of us likes much, who's done us a bad turn, maybe, an' 'e nabs 'im an' gets 'is prize money along with 'is wages, an' 'e's as 'appy as a rat in a jakes. An' the rest of us is left alone." He put his arm round her shoulders, walked back with her towards the boxing ring.

"Come an' watch Dido," he said. " 'E's going to 'ave a go with one o' the swells." He squeezed her shoulder. "It ain't the end of the world. You're too pretty to be miserable. Make the best o' things. You'll be dead long enough. 'Allo, Mr. Hunter, sir. 'Allo, Mr. Summers! Goin' to teach my poor Dido a lesson, are you?" He pushed Sara towards them. "You know our Sara, don't you? Ain't she a picture? An' following the fancy now. Ain't nothing to do with Dido, o' course, just 'as a liking for a good match." His arm holding her, heavy with good humour, cajolery. The two of them looking at her, Mr. Hunter quizzing her with amusement, Mr. Summers, already stripped to his shirt, bareheaded, his eyes indifferent, almost hostile as he looked at her, looked away.

She wanted to escape, but Monkey held her, the weight of his arm on her shoulders almost making her bend forward towards them. And the crowd was too thick, a dozen men crowding round them, whispering loud, obsequious admiration of Mr. Summers.

"So you're Dido's girl, eh?" Mr. Hunter said. "That's the secret?" He turned and called, "Dido!" And as Dido leaned across the ropes towards them, "Gypsy here belongs to you, does she?" She felt her face turn scarlet. Dido stared at them, tried to grin, his own face darkening. Mr. Hunter laughed and tapped her cheek, while the onlookers sniggered respectfully. She tried to run, and Monkey held her tighter, whispered in her ear, "Stay 'ere, girl, now you're 'ere. Don't make a bloody fuss."

"Put her up as the prize," Mr. Hunter cried. "The best man wins her! There you are, Harry. There's something to fight for!"

"Don't be such a damned fool," Mr. Summers said. He was ducking into the ring through the ropes, stripping off his shirt. Ben hurrying forward with the heavy leather gloves for him, fitting them on, Jim the hunchback and Hebbo in Dido's corner.

"Let me go!" she said to Monkey, and Mr. Hunter heard her and put his own arm round her shoulders, holding her between them.

"We can't have our prize escaping," he said. "And where's my Molly? Don't she like boxing too?"

She stood between them, savagely angry, not wanting to give him the satisfaction of preventing her from escaping, not looking at him.

"Well, don't she?" He touched her cheek with his knuckles, touched the lobe of her ear.

"Leave me alone," she said.

"Only for Dido, eh?"

"I am not for Dido."

"By God, ain't you then?" He looked round at her and against her will she met his eyes.

"I'm not for anyone," she said. "Nor is Molly. Why don't you leave her alone?"

"Because Molly don't *want* to be left alone, my dear." He touched his knuckle to her mouth. "And maybe you'll find you don't, either, under all that fierceness. Let's see which of 'em wins you."

They were already boxing. She tried not to look, heard the shuffle of their feet, the sudden stamp of a lunge, the men round them shouting, "There's a left! You got 'im, Mr. Summers!" And the smack of leather on flesh, gasp of breath, silence, shuffle of feet on resin, another shout, the drumming of body blows, and the creak and spring of the ropes. She had to look, could not prevent herself from looking, Monkey and Mister Hunter holding her prisoner against the ring, the men crowding, the smell of the resin, of close bodies, of stale sweat, the dust. Dido weaving, sliding, supple as a cat. Mr. Summers four square and solid. And again that unbearable likeness to the captain, the captain grown taller, younger, his grizzled hair grown thick and chestnut brown. Even his way of moving, a solid sturdiness, and then the quick strike of a blow, his left fist out like a sword thrust.

"Your Dido can move," Mr. Hunter said.

"There ain't no one moves better!" Monkey shouted over the noise of the crowd. "You'd think you was watching the Jew again. Move your feet, Mr. Summers, move your feet!"

Mr. Summers' ribs already darkened by dull red patches from Dido's gloves. Dido sliding in again, snake-streaking, and Mr. Summers gripping hold, trying to cross-buttock him, and Dido away, slithering, tapping out a long left in Mr. Summer's face, sending a thread of blood down from one nostril into his mouth. Mr. Summers wiped it away, grinned, came forward, trying to drive Dido into a corner, against the ropes, feinting to the right and, as Dido slid left, swinging with a back-hander like a hammer blow, catching Dido behind the head, sending him sprawling, and a roar of triumph from the crowd, "You got 'im, you levelled 'im, Mr. Summers, one for the swell!"

Dido scrambling to his feet before his seconds could move, sitting easy on Hebbo's gigantic knee while the hunchback brushed the resin from his gloves, sponged his face. Mr. Summers not bothering to sit, standing with his chest heaving, smiling with pleasure at Dido.

"Let me go!" Sara whispered.

"I thought you weren't his girl? Don't care to see him levelled, eh?"

They still held her, and the match began again.

"They ain't really fighting hard," Mr. Hunter whispered. "They ain't hurting each other, not with the mufflers on." And then it was over, no fall this time except for Dido going down on one knee in mock surrender.

"You're gettin' too good for me, Mr. Summers."

Mr. Summers ducked out of the ring, a towel round his bare shoulders, blood smeared on his cheek, his breath coming hard and fast, all the sullenness gone, his eyes almost happy.

"Ye'll be taking on Cribb next," Mr. Hunter said. "Ye had poor Gypsy here trembling."

Mr. Summers looked at her, the pleasure still alight in his eyes, his bruised mouth. "Ye don't need to worry about your fellow," he said. "He was playing with me, damn him."

"She says he's not her fellow. And you've won her now, Harry, fair and square. Hasn't he, Monkey? Don't he get the prize?"

"He does," Monkey said. "To the 'eavyweight prime Corinthian champion of this 'ere gymnasium room I presents 'is prize, to wit this girl 'ere, Sara, to be 'is till challenged for again, under the rules o' the fancy."

"Buss your prize, Harry!" Mr. Hunter cried. "Here she is!"

She ducked away, forced herself out from beneath his arm, Monkey's, pushed between the crowding men. One or two tried to hold her, but she was too quick, was at the door, running up the stairs, shouts of laughter behind her. In their room Molly was still asleep, lying rolled over on her side, her head pillowed on her arm, the same childish, enchanted smile, the same soft, greedy curve of the fingers lying now on the blanket.

Sara knelt, looking at her for a moment, put out a hand to her bare shoulder, touched, grasped hold, and shook it, gently at first, then fiercely, Molly groaning in her sleep, the smile fading, opening her eyes and staring in astonished alarm at Sara. "What is it? Wha's the matter? Is it late?"

"We've got to go away, Molly. Now. At once."

Molly stared, almost laughing in bewilderment. "Wha' d'you mean, Sara?"

As soon as she'd said it, she no longer knew what she meant. Except that instinct, that urge to run. To run and run, escape, lose herself in some new unknown place. And then? When it became known?

"It's—Monkey said I must tell, must tell Mr. Brown things."

235

"Well, if he said so, maybe you must." Molly yawned and stretched, shook her head to clear the sleep out of it. "Wha' time is it?"

"Don't you understand, Molly? They want me to be a *spy*."

"I know," Molly said, staring down at her knees. She said it, Sara thought, as though she didn't want to know. "But what else you goin' to do?" She looked up, and there seemed already to be a distance between them.

"That's why we—why I've got to . . ." She knelt there desolately, feeling more alone than if Molly were not there, and Molly seemed to sense it, put out her hand and touched Sara's arm.

"I'll ask Charlie about it," she said. "He knows all sorts of things an' his dad is a lord. Maybe he can do somethin'."

Sara shut her eyes, felt herself shivering at Molly's touch. "What do you let him do to you?"

"Do to me?" Molly laughed, throwing her head back, laughing full-throated. "Nothin' but kissin'."

"Just kissing?" Sara said, still not looking at her, and then turning on her, catching at her hands, tugging at them in a kind of desperation. "Molly! Molly! Do you think that's *all* he'll want for his guineas?"

Molly laughed again, as though she was laughing at a child's foolishness. "O' course it ain't all he wants. What do you think men are? But wantin' ain't gettin'. I told 'em plain, you don't climb the stairs till you've bought the house. I ain't rentin' rooms."

"How can you talk like that? About—about—"

"About wha'? Climbin' stairs? What do you think men want to talk about, 'specially in the dark with a maid?" Her laugh ringing happy as a golden bell. "Sometimes I think you're too foolish to live. Miss Hetty an' Miss Susannah teachin' you all them things didn't do you no good at all." She fell back on the pillow, stretched her arms, yawned again. "You keep sayin' you want to get away from here, go to Spain, go here, go there. How you goin' to get there by yourself? When the time comes I want to go off, I'll go in a carriage with horses, an' someone beside me holding

236

my hand an' swearing he loves me to death, an' when I gets where I'm goin', I'll have silk sheets to sleep on an' downy pillows an' a fire burning all night long. An' I won't get up till afternoon, never I won't."

"You don't know what you're saying." Even in her own ears, her voice sounded ridiculous.

" 'Course I know what I'm sayin'. I done my share o' scrubbin' floors with chilblains on my fingers. An' I done near enough my share o' carryin' trays up an' down here too. I want somethin' different to that before I die, an' I mean to have it." She rolled up and forward, hugged her knees. "Why not? You think they're different from us? That 'tis right an' fine for 'em to sleep soft an' easy, an' eat full, an' never scrub nor feel cold, but when we wants it, 'tis wicked?"

"It isn't that. It isn't that at all. It's—it's—" She let her hands fall, tried to laugh. And then, like a cry of despair, "You can't, you *can't!*"

Molly looked at her, no longer laughing, almost frowning, as if trying to think how best to explain something to a small, small child. "I ain't goin' to be like those girls that come here, you don't think *that*, do you?"

"What will the difference be?" Sara said bitterly.

"There'll be a lot o' difference," Molly said. "There won't be no Mr. Brown coming near me, threatenin' and bullyin', that's *one* difference."

"And when Mr. Hunter gets tired of you?"

"He ain't got me yet, to be tired o' me. An' when he's got me, maybe he'll be worryin' 'case I get tired of him." She threw herself back again, began to laugh. "Sara Pownall, you do say the most miserable things."

"We'd better get ready," Sara said. "It's nearly time."

"There you go! We don't need to get ready a good half hour yet. I just heard the clock striking. Lie here beside me an' we'll pretend we're ladies an' goin' to the opera with two beautiful men!" She caught Sara's arm, pulled her down, caught her round the neck, and held her tight against her. "I'm goin' to have everything," she whispered, "everything in the whole world. An' I'll give you wonderful things," she said, touching Sara's face, making her look at her. "I'll make you happy, in spite o' yourself. I promise you."

And as she felt Sara shivering, she held her closer still, stroked her hair. "Don't fret, little one," she whispered, rocking Sara in her arms. "Don't you fret. He won't come back for a long, long time. An' when he do, we'll have thought o' somethin', my Charlie'll have thought o' somethin' to fright him away. Don't fret, my heart. Your Molly'll look after you. Don't you fret."

Chapter 19

As the days went by, the shadow of Mr. Brown withdrew a little. She could almost believe that he *was* only a shadow, that he'd never come back, that he'd decided she would be useless to him. And she put off from day to day the idea of running away, gathering her money together with a kind of ferocity, as though the need for another guinea or two excused her doing nothing. And then she'd lie awake at four and five in the morning, hear the church clocks striking and think *Today. I must decide today.* And hear Molly sleeping beside her, hear her stirring as she stretched out and muttered something, would touch her, and think, *But he won't come today. Not yet.*

The third night Mr. Hunter and Mr. Summers had come back, with Sir Thomas of the fencing lesson, and she'd tried to avoid them as always, going to the faro alcove and staying there as long as she dared, watching the play, to give Molly a chance to serve them with whatever they wanted. And had turned back into the main room to find Harry Summers blocking her way.

She tried to move past him and he stopped her. "I wanted to speak to you," he said. She looked at him, the familiarity of the voice catching in her throat again. As though the captain was standing there. "I'm sorry for my friend's wretched joking of the other day. He has no judgement in such things."

She looked away, unable to say anything, scarcely hearing what he'd just said. She tried to say, "I must go," and pushed past him, shrinking away from contact with his arm, which he drew away just in time to let her by. For the rest of the hour that he stayed she felt him watching her, and she stayed at the far side of the room as much as she could, longed to escape to the kitchen and was afraid of what, of whom, she might find there.

That night in bed Molly scolded her, said, "You ain't got the sense o' a dragon-fly, why were you so rude to Mr. Summers an' he tryin' to be nice to you?"

"I don't want him to be nice to me. Go to sleep."

"You just think o' nothin'. You play up to him nice a bit an'—"

"Go to sleep!"

"He thinks you're master pretty, I promise. He's nice too when he don't look so cross."

"I don't want him to think anything. I hate them. I hate them!"

"Go away there! He just wants someone to make 'em laugh a bit. I told 'em about you wantin' to go poaching in his dad's woods an' you should have seen 'em laughin'! He said we were the strangest pair o' dollies he ever heard of. He looked downright happy for a bit."

"They didn't laugh about your father going poaching there," Sara said furiously.

Molly drew in her breath. "No," she said, her voice cold with hurt. "They didn't." And then like a cry of rage, "They didn't hang him for that!" She came onto her elbow, stared at Sara in the shadow light of the dawn, which was already breaking above the rooftops, filtering down through the grey skylight. "I can't go weeping all my life 'cause my dad was hanged. What good would that do? I got to live my own life the best I can, be happy a bit. An' if you weren't so stubborn foolish you'd be the same, 'stead o' goin' round like someone robbed your money. What did we come here for if you didn't mean to be happy an' jolly?"

She shook Sara, made her laugh against her will, and they lay down side by side, staring up at the skylight, at the sky above it growing pale. "We'll go shopping to Ma Casey's this afternoon, an' you goin' to find something downright beautiful to make their eyes pop when they see you tonight. I'm so sick o' seein' that one dress on you, I mean to burn it."

They went shopping and she had to buy a dress and a scarf to prevent Molly buying them for her, and they took a hackney coach to the park, Molly lying back on the musty, mouse-smelling leather as though it were her own phaeton and the cushions were silk. They had lemonade and cakes in the park, sitting outside the kiosk in the sun, watching the strollers going by and the distant riders along Rotten Row.

"Just imagine having nothing else to do, but come here an' be looked at!"

They walked round the edge of the lake and down to the Row until it was time to go back, and it seemed to Sara like going back into a prison as the streets closed round them again. She thought, *I must plan something. I have to decide what I'm going to do.* And she was furious with herself and Molly for the more than five guineas Molly had made her spend. She did not even want to put on the new white satin dress, with its blonde-lace trimming and its lilac satin ribbons and its gauze slip, the short sleeves caught up low on the shoulders with a satin knot.

"Put it on!" Molly said. "What'd you buy it for if you ain't goin' to wear it? You are the perversesest sort o' girl I ever heard of."

"It's cut too low."

"Sara Pownall! You don't put on that dress this minute I'm goin' to burn every stitch you got an' let you go downstairs in your shift. Put it on!"

She put it on at last and went downstairs to the gaming room, feeling suddenly as though she was naked, although in reality there was not much difference of cut between the new dress and the old. Only Snipe said anything about it, stroking the satin with admiring fingers.

"I daren't go back to Ma Casey's," she said. "I owes the old faggot too much. Lordy, I do miss my Jim."

The convict ship had at last sailed for Australia and Snipe had managed to see her Jim the evening it left, coming back from Gravesend the next day with her eyes still red and her face pinched.

"I wish I'd been caught with 'im," she said. And then, "No, I bloody don't. What's the good of *both* of us being dead?"

"But he isn't dead," Sara had said, trying to comfort her. "It mayn't be so bad when they get there."

" 'Ow many d'you think gets there? Half? If they're lucky. Or unlucky. I've 'eard gents say what knows about it that the real lucky ones is the ones what snuffs it on the ship."

She was gambling more than she used to, and with a kind of desperation in it now, as though it mattered to her much more whether she won or lost. That particular night Sara watched her lose five guineas in a row at rouge et noir, her eyes haunted as the croupier laid down the cards. Sara tugged her arm, whispered, "Snipe, come away from there," and Snipe looked at her blankly for a second as though she hardly understood what Sara was saying. Sara saw Mr. Hunter and Mr. Summers coming in, drew Snipe away with her towards the bow windows and the whist tables.

"You're just *throwing* your money away," Sara said. "You weren't even watching. He was dealing from the bottom half the time."

"Bloody bastard. Lend me a quid an' I'll try the roly-poly."

"I won't lend you anything, not for that. What's the matter with you, Snipe?"

"Nothing's the bloody matter with me. Just lend me a quid. I'll give it you back tomorrow." She looked up at Sara, laughed at her. "What you looking like that for?"

Sara fetched her the guinea, watched her stake it, win three guineas in two or three minutes, then lose them all. Snipe turned away from the table almost as though it was a relief. "There they bloody go, down the drain again. Oh, well." She nudged Sara gently. "One o' the swells is just about eatin' you with 'is eyes over there. You've struck it lucky, looks like."

She didn't need to turn her head to know who it was. "Let's go where he can't see us," she said.

"I'm going altogether," Snipe said. "Whyn't you want 'im to look at you? What a girl like you needs is one of them swells to take you out of 'ere an' set you up."

"I'll leave that to Molly."

" 'Least Molly's got a bit o' sense. Listen, see us tomorrow, will you? Tomorrow afternoon? Come out with me an' I'll show you something."

"I have to sleep."

" 'Ow can you sleep in that bloody attic afternoons like these? You must be bloody baked alive. Jus' come out and I'll show you something interesting. Bring Molly with you."

"Where are you going now?"

"To get your guinea back. Where d'you think?" Her eyes laughing, full of gaiety again.

"Snipe, don't, you mustn't! It doesn't matter about the guinea, you can have it."

"What d'you mean I can 'ave it? It's gone, ain't it?"

"I don't want it back."

"Don't be stupid. One dip an' I'll more than 'ave it back. A pity you can't never come down the Haymarket this time o' night. That's where the life is. Gawd, it's wonderful down there. Poor bloody Jim." She pulled away from Sara's hand, pushed through the crowd.

"Ain't you never going to talk to poor Harry?" Mr. Hunter said behind her.

She turned, and both of them were there, Mr. Summers looking angry. "Leave her alone, Charles, damn you."

242

"Now's your chance, Harry. Ask her about the poaching." He laughed and turned away from them. Harry Summers hesitated, seemed on the point of following him, and swung back to her.

"God damn it," he said. "I can't go on saying I'm sorry about Charles. What the devil are two Thaxstone girls doing in this place?"

Half a dozen answers came into her mind and all of them sounded wrong and pert or foolish. "A friend brought us here," she said at last, her voice so low he could scarcely hear her, had to bend forward closer.

"A friend?" He smiled oddly, and for that second it was as though the captain was there, and she had to close her eyes against the likeness. "And you were old Pownall's girl, eh? Poor devil."

She wanted to say, "He was my guardian," and at the same time did not want to tell him anything, only to escape.

"That was a damned dreadful business. And left you high and dry, eh?"

"Yes."

"Didn't he have sisters?"

"Yes." Her voice fading to a thread of sound. The crowd jostling them, laughing, chattering, a croupier calling. "One après. One après," and from the roulette table "Zero! Zero wins." *And in her mind the firelight, the captain leaning forward, cradling his tankard of mulled ale, staring into the flames.*

"I don't go down to Southcott much these days," he said. He laughed sharply, a harsh bark of laughter as if he was out of the habit. "And you wanted to go poaching?"

I would like to kill her, she thought. She said, "I have to go, people are watching us, I—"

"Let 'em watch. And what the devil would ye have done with a pheasant if ye'd caught one?"

"Do you know what happens to poachers?" She whispered. "If they're caught?"

"Of course I do. Was that what stopped you both?" He laughed again, and she turned away, pushed between two gamblers, forced herself into the crowd round the rouge-et-noir table, offering champagne until her tray was empty. When she came back from the kitchen with it refilled, Mr. Summers was gone.

Snipe came for them the next day at dinnertime, pushing a guinea into Sara's hand. "Hot from Ikey, the fence," she said, laughing. The worries of the night before seemed to have vanished, and she almost danced along the street between them, holding them both by the arms like a child with two grown-ups. "The size o' the pair o' you! It ain't natural. Gawd, I'd love to dress one o' you up as a swell an' we'd pull the breeches rig on some fat ol' bugger. I gives 'im the eye an' takes him up a dark alley, an' soon as 'e 'as 'is breeches down, you comes shoutin' 'What're you doin' with my girl you dirty ol' bastard?' An' the ol' bugger looks roun' an' I picks 'is pocket an' runs like 'ell, an' even if 'e catches on an' tries to run after me, 'e falls flat on 'is dial with 'is breeches round 'is knees."

"Snipe!"

"I'm only jokin' you, but, Gawd, it is a lark." She danced again. "I 'ates bloody men."

She took them to Regent Street to see the new shops and they stood outside Swan and Edgar's looking at the silks in the high, arched windows. "D'you see Scotchy goin' by?" Snipe whispered. "Don't let no one see you starin', but just look after 'im casual-like. See that girl with the feather 'at? She's 'is look-out, keeps watch for 'im. An' the girl behind 'er is the fanner—she brushes the geezer's pocket to see what's in't. Watch 'em work. Them two gents—them two together—is the jostlers." Sara and Molly and Snipe walked slowly up the curving pavement, past the half-finished buildings, an empty site, a new, just-complete house with empty windows, and ahead of them Scotch Robert's gang of girls and men and his boy walked casually, nothing to tell any innocent foot passenger they had any connection one with another, except for the boy holding Scotch Robert's hand like a dutiful, well-dressed son out with his father for a stroll, the two jostlers keeping just ahead of them, equally well-dressed in cutaways and pantaloons and fashionable top-hats.

"She's picked someone," Snipe whispered. "Watch the girl bheind 'er." If there'd been a signal from the look-out, Sara had failed to see it, and although she was watching for it, it was impossible to see what the second girl was doing, walking slightly faster, passing very close beside a stout old gentleman with an alderman's paunch and port-wine complexion, but not seeming to touch him, not seeming to do anything but change her reticule from one hand to the other, brush the sleeve of her spencer as though there was a speck of dust on it.

" 'E's got a wallet in 'is tail pocket, a thick 'un," Snipe breathed. "Watch 'em now." A strange kind of longing in her voice. A catch of excitement.

The two jostlers moving casually forward, talking together, not looking where they were going, bumping slightly into the old gentleman, raising their hats with courteous regret and the boy and Scotch Robert passing them, the boy's arms folded now, his hands hidden beneath his elbows, brushing close to the alderman's coat tails, going by, joining hands with Scotch Robert again, another girl, the carrier, overtaking Scotchy, turning away across the road between the carriages.

" 'E don't even know it's gone," Snipe said. "Give 'er 'alf a tick an' it'll be in Soho."

"O' course, I'd love to see 'is face when 'e finds out, but we'd better drift. You should 'ave seen us working. *Twice* as quick as that. I wonder 'ow much was in that wallet?"

"Snipe! It's dreadful!"

"Get away with you, it ain't dreadful. Where d'you think that ol' geezer gets all 'is money? 'E probably 'as poor little kids slavin' their guts out for 'im for threepence a week an' half starved along with it. It's just gettin' a bit back, that's all. The only dreadful thing is tryin' it by yourself, without a mob. You got to do everything yourself, an' if anyone twigs you, you 'aven't a bloody chance. I asked Scotchy to take me on, but 'e's afraid o' crossin' ol' Darby. An' Brown, too, I think. Darby 'as it in for me, proper."

"Because of us? Getting us away from them?"

"Nah, not really. Because of the money she owes
245

us. The day Jim was nabbed an' the others, I shoved all our stuff into their back yard. They 'as an 'ole in the back wall you throws stuff into if you're in an 'urry an' she pays you later. We always does it, same with Darby, any of 'em. But when she knew they was all nabbed 'cept me, she didn't want to pay up. Bloody old sow. Said all she could give me was twenty quid. An' there must've bin a 'undred quids' worth just in sneezeboxes an' clocks. We was still fighting about it the day you was there, an' that put the snuffer on it. I 'opes she dies o' the pox an' 'er bloody brother along with 'er."

They turned into Oxford Street, the crowds even thicker, a lavender-seller pushing bunches of sweet herbs into their faces, begging, a soldier with one leg and a ragged scarlet jacket playing the flute beside her, an ill-written notice hanging round his chest proclaiming *A wuonded Veteran of Waterloo*.

Sara bought a sprig of white heather from the girl, gave the veteran a shilling.

"You're too bloody soft," Snipe said. "If I weren't with you, you'd be robbed blind 'fore you got 'alf-way up to the park. Let's 'ave a look at the sharpers over there. See that feller with the little table? C'mon, Sara, you know their game better'n they do. Let's see if we can do 'em up."

The sharper was drawn back into the entrance of a narrow passage, ready to run if there was trouble; a small folding table with a moth-eaten green cloth to cover it set up in front of him and a pack of dog-eared cards. A thin, grizzled red-nosed man in a dirty stock and a narrow-brimmed hat, shuffling the cards, his eyes bright and hard as a sparrow's, searching his small audience for a victim. Half a dozen loungers watching him, grinning with contempt, suspicion, idleness.

"*Ladeez* and *gentlemen!* 'Oo will challenge 'is skill against the speed an' quickness an' sheer velocity of my 'ands? All you got to do, *ladeez* an' *gentlemen*, is to *spot* the ladee, just spot this 'ere little female queen of 'earts what you sees laid down there on the cloth. You sees 'er? You sees me turn 'er over? Just imagine turning a queen over, eh *ladeez, gents?* Wonderful things what you can do with cards, ain't it? Now, aside this 'ere queen, she's still there, look, there she is, lyin' down on her front waitin' for you."

The patter went on. Snipe nudged Sara. "See the feller suckin' the bit o' straw what looks 'alf-witted? That's 'is son. We can't do this lot, I knows 'em."

"Now, 'oo will put down 'is shiny gold guinea or 'is bright silver 'alf-crown in 'is effort to win a equal sum off of me? If you do win, you wins, don't 'ave no fears that Joe Smith can't pay you. 'Ere's my money bag, 'eavy with gold guineas for some clever lad." He saw Snipe in the background, "Or some clever lass to win off of me. That young lady there, 'ow 'bout you, miss? Trust a lady to find the lady. 'Ave a go, miss, sport your cash 'ere on the green table like the nobs an' duchesses do in their gambling 'ells."

"Done!" Snipe said, pushed her way through. Sara tried to pull her back and Snipe shook her hand away. "Shut up!" The small crowd made way, laughed, made rude whispering jokes about Snipe's feathered hat, her boldness. She laid her guinea on the table and the sharper matched it, shuffled the three cards again, laid them down faceup—queen, ten of spades, two of diamonds—slid them round and round, in and out. Sara followed the movements, which were like a ritual, identical to Pablito's, left to right, right to centre, centre out to left and immediately behind and back to right. In and out, apparently slowly. Usually, on one of those backward movements the queen would disappear up his left sleeve and the fourth card would come down from his right to take its place. But not this first time, the decoy time. The queen stayed on the cloth, came to rest in the centre.

"Now," the sharper said, " 'as the little lady made up 'er lovely female mind? There's courage for you, it takes a woman, a pretty little female woman like this girl 'ere, to show up all you sportin' gents, you bucks an' Corinthians what is just standin' there with your 'ands in your pockets an' suckin' straws. An' 'ere's this little golden-'eaded fairy what is ready to risk 'er precious 'ard-earned wages—Gawd, I'm a soft-

'earted old fool, but I 'opes she wins, I really 'opes she wins. Sure you can afford a guinea, love?"

"That one!" Snipe cried and stabbed her finger down on the middle card. Slowly, shaking his head in despair, the sharper put his own dirty forefinger beside hers.

"That one?" he said. "Oh, you're makin' a mistake, a terrible mistake, my dear. 'Ow about this one beside it? Why not try that one?" He looked up at the crowd, his nose shining with honesty. "I swears to you," he said, "upon my oath as a sporting gent what 'as never welshed on a bet in his 'ole life, that I don't know, I *positively* do not know which card is which. Except. *Except.* I am positive, I am reasonable positive certain and *sure* that it is not, is *not* the card what this poor young lady is risking her quid on. 'Elp her, someone, advise her. You, sir, you with the straw stickin' out o' your mouth, which card is which, sir? Or you, sir? Or you, ma'am? 'Elp this poor young lady not to lose 'er 'ard-earned week's wages at one awful blow."

"Show us the bloody card," Snipe said.

With one hand held dramatically in front of his eyes, as if to shield them from the tremendous disappointment he was about to inflict on her, he turned up the corner, half, the whole of the card, stared at it in disbelief, slapped it down face uppermost. "She wins," he said hoarsely, almost brokenly. "There y'are now. 'Oo would *believe* it? 'Oo would believe this little golden-'aired innocent maid would defeat the expertise of an old 'and like yours truly. But so it is, *ladeez* an' *gents*. She've won off of me fair an' square. 'Ere's your golden guinea, my dear, an' don't spend it all on riotous living!" He gave her the money and Snipe bit his guinea with quick practise and dropped it into her reticule.

"Now, 'oo's goin' to follow that young lady's money-winnin' example? You, sir, you looks a sportin' gentleman what knows 'ow to back your fancy with your money. 'Ow 'bout you, sir? Just watch the cards, *watch* the cards like that young lady did."

Snipe had pushed back through the onlookers to

rejoin Sara and Molly. The boy with the straw unobtrusively followed her. Snipe dodged round the far side of Sara, whispered, "See you up by the park gate," and was gone. She did not appear to be running but was simply gone round the back of a carriage, dodging past a cart that was unloading packages, into the crowds on the far pavement. The boy with the straw started after her, was almost run over in the middle of the road, hesitated, and came back muttering under his breath, his face scarlet with rage.

"We'd better go," Sara whispered. She drew Molly away; the boy stared at them furiously, caught Sara's wrist, and whispered savagely, "You were with her, you bloody big 'ore. Where's she gone?"

"Let go of me," Sara said, "or I'll scream."

"You 'ore, you pig's get! I'll kill 'er, you tell 'er I'll see 'er 'anged for this."

Sara pulled free from him, linked arms with Molly, and walked quickly away towards the park. "What did happen?" Molly said, running to keep up.

"They always let someone win first to make the others have a try. Only Snipe's gone off with their money."

"Serves 'em right," Molly said.

"I suppose so."

They found Snipe waiting for them at the top of Park Lane. "Was 'e cross?"

"He said he'll have you hanged."

"'E wouldn't 'ave the guts. An' 'e won't 'ave the chance anyway. I'm going off tomorrow. Going to do the fairs." She slid her hand into Sara's, looked up at her pleadingly. "Come with us, Sara? I wouldn't ask you to do anything you didn't like. Just for company. You could 'ave 'alf of everything I took. An' maybe we could try that rig." She jerked her head back towards Oxford Street and the sharpers. "You could do it better'n 'im with your eyes shut."

"Oh, Snipe," Sara said, and in spite of herself was almost tempted, felt sad because she knew it was impossible. Without so much as knowing why. Only that it was. As though her future was already *there*, decided, and nothing she could do would alter it.

Her voice with as much sadness in it as reproach.

"It'd get you away from Brown," Snipe said.

"I told Charlie about him," Molly said. "He said he'd have a think about it. What you mean doin' the fairs?"

"What d'you think I mean? Go thievin' o' course. Parsons an' farmers an' that. It's gettin' too rough 'ere, by myself. I near got nabbed this mornin'. You can't work it all by yourself these days. Let's go an' spend old Smithy's quid somewhere."

A child in a sailor frock bowled a hoop past them, but on this weekday afternoon the park was almost empty of people on foot. And up there by the Cumberland Gate there was no one at all. It was like the countryside. The noise of London fading behind them, the grass and trees sweeping away in front of them towards the distant villages, Kensington and Chelsea.

"Don't go," Sara said harshly. Scarcely knew why she said it. She stopped on the path and held Snipe's arm, half shook it. "Don't go."

"What you mean?" Snipe said. "I told you, I can't stay 'ere any longer. I'll get nabbed, I knows it."

"And you will if you go."

"Get away with that. Those country fellers, those chawbacons? Nab me? What you think I am? You ain't never seen me workin'. Look, let's go down the 'aymarket now, it ain't the best time, but we'll find something. Just you watch me workin'."

"Snipe!"

"Well, you don't believe me, so I wants to show you."

"Oh, Snipe, of course I believe you, it isn't that. It's just—Why don't you ask Monkey to give you a job? Like ours? He could do with another girl."

"You don't understand. It's all right for you, you 'aven't never done anything else, no one thinks any the worse of you for it. But I *bin* something. Our mob was the best there was, better'n Scotchy's, better'n Welsh Fred's, the best bloody mob there ever was. I go in there an' start servin' the mobsmen—" 'Ave a glass of champagne, Scotchy, 'ave a game-pasty, Fred' —they'd split their bloody sides. Every slut that goes there'd be giggling an' jeerin', 'Look what Snipe's doing now. Lost 'er nerve.' I'd rather go on the lag ship to Australyer.

"Why don't you find a man to look after you?" Molly said. She'd taken her slippers off and was walking on the grass in her bare feet.

"I don't 'old with men," Snipe said, " 'cept for Jim. No, I'll be all right. I'll see you in a month an' I'll 'ave so much rhino we'll start a bank with it."

They walked along the lakeside and over the bridge, the sun almost like country sun and the air clean. "I don't think I'll be here in a month's time," Sara said.

"Go away," Molly said. "I told you, Charlie'll think o' something. He do know everything about laws an' that; he did go to a school for laws. To Oxford."

They came to Rotten Row, watched the carriages and horsemen, riders bending down to talk lovingly to women riding in their open phaetons, lying back among white silk cushions, lap-dogs beside them or in their arms, parasols like pastel flowers twirling and tilting.

Three riders came towards them, a woman and two men, heads turning all along the row to see her. A pale blaze of gold under the tight green hat, the sweep of feathers. Mr. Summers beside her, an old man, stout and farmerlike in an old-fashioned bottle-green coat riding on her other side.

"There she is! 'Tis his ma!" Molly said. "Mr. Summers with his step-ma, an' that must be his dad!" The three riders passing them so close that Mr. Summers could have stretched out his riding whip and touched them. He saw the three of them, smiled slightly, inclined his head almost inperceptibly, raising his whip hand as though he were adjusting his hat. Molly waved, and Lady Summers turned her head in surprise, the pale, arrogant face taking the three girls in at a glance, hat to slipper to dress to beauty, as though she could have drawn their portraits from the one glance and burned the three of them. Younger than her stepson, twenty-five perhaps, arrow slim and straight in hunting green, tight velvet jacket, spreading overskirt, the toe of her boot showing beneath the wide curve of it. She said something to Mr. Summers and he bent forward as though answering her respectfully, Lord Southcott looking back towards the girls.

"You got 'im into trouble there," Snipe said, laughing. "What you go an' wave for?"

"Why not? I know 'em."

"Gawd, didn't she look wicked? C'mon an' let's 'ave a drop o' somethin'. We didn't ought to be down 'ere today anyway."

The next day she was gone. And it seemed to Sara that the evenings were even longer without her coming into the gaming room, to lose her money and curse about it and tell them jokes about her day. Two nights after Snipe left Mr. Summers and Mr. Hunter came again, beckoning them both. "I hear ye disgraced yourselves in the park?" Mr. Hunter said. "You owe us at least a dozen forfeits to make up for it, don't they, Harry? Gad, her ladyship was furious."

"I don't see why," Molly said. "Why shouldn't I wave to 'em? If 'twere the old king ridin' by, didn't I ought to wave to 'im neither?"

" 'Pon Honour!" said Mr. Hunter. "Portia made flesh! There's an answer for her ladyship, Harry. Tell her that one."

"And what's your answer?" Mr. Summers said.

"I didn't wave to you." She began to turn away from them as though someone was calling her for champagne.

"Damme, they're both a match for us," Mr. Hunter cried. "Don't go running off, give us a glass to drink your healths."

She gave them their glasses and said, "Someone's calling me," and made her way across the room, away from them, until she could escape down the stairs. She heard voices in the kitchen and she stopped, would have turned back, and Maggie called, "What's that? Janet? Sara? What is it?" And was standing in the doorway beckoning her. "He's here to see you," she whispered, and drew Sara into the kitchen, where Mr. Brown was sitting as though he belonged there, had never moved since the last occasion.

"Here she is, Mr. Brown. An' not a word o' anything out o' her mouth since you were here last, my oath on it."

"I'm very pleased to 'ear it," Mr. Brown said. "Come 'ere an' stand in front of me, miss, and let's 'ave a look at you. So you ain't said a word, eh?"

"That I promise you!" Mag said.

"Ah, but she don't promise it. Do you, miss?" He lifted his right hand, laid a grey finger alongside his nose. "From what I 'ears you been tellin' a friend as 'ow you was very upset and distressed at bein' asked to do me an occasional small service. Weren't you, miss?"

She said nothing, stared at him, her heart beating, thinking, *Why didn't I go long ago? It's too late, too late,* and at the same time knowing that it was not, that something had happened. A sickly sweetness in Mr. Brown's flat voice, in the ugly, liver-coloured smile.

"But we won't fall out about that, will we, miss? I didn't know, I didn't guess for one instant as 'ow you 'ad such 'igh-up important friends. Gov'ment friends! 'Ow could a poor 'ard-working man such as Mr. Brown know that, unless 'e was told? You see 'ow much a man in my position needs information? Information an' more information, that's the secret of success in life. No one can't 'ave too much information. Not if they knows 'ow to use it right. An' now that I knows, why, you an' me can still be the best o' friends, ain't that right? An' you don't need to worry your pretty beautiful head about a thing. Just as if our little conversation of the other night 'ad never 'appened. But you'll stay my friend, I 'opes? You'll say, if the occasion should ever 'rise, to one of your important friends perhaps, as 'ow Mr. Brown treated you with the 'eight of respect. An' as far as your other friends are concerned, your other friends in this 'ouse, I very much 'opes that you'll be guided by the path of wisdom and say nothin' at all. Nothin'. I do really 'ope so."

"Oh, aye, you may be sure o' that, Mr. Brown. Not a word she'll blab, I promise you."

"I don't understand what you've been saying," Sara

253

said. "What friends?" And knew that too, and did not want to know it, almost as though the remedy was worse than the disease. Mr. Brown laid his finger to his nose again, wreathed his lips into a still sweeter smile.

"Oho, there's discretion. I likes discretion, especially in a young female. I likes it very much. You'll go far, miss, I can see that. And I 'opes you won't forget Mr. Brown along the way. You never knows. You never knows what may 'appen in the future times, what vicissitudes may befall. You may need even so 'umble a friend as Mr. Brown. I 'opes not, but 'oo can tell? An' now, before anyone comes in, I'll take my leave. Your 'umble servant, miss. In case of need, which I'm sure won't arise, but in *case* of need, remember, Mr. Brown is your good friend. Your *very* good friend." He stood up and, before she could move back, took her hand, pressed it between his, a dry, limp grasp like something dead, bones covered by dry mud. He let go, was gone.

She stayed where she was, looking down at her hand, wanting to wash it clean.

"You have him well put in his box an' the lid closed on him," Maggie said. She seemed half pleased, half-vexed by it, looking at Sara peculiarly, as though not sure what to say. "You've—you've no hard feelings?"

"No," Sara said, "I'll take the tray." But when she'd taken it, she stayed on the stairs for a long time before she could make up her mind to go back into the gaming room, face them. What would she say to him? Nothing? Thank him? And the ugliness of what she must thank him for stuck in her throat like a knot. She waited until Janet came down the stairs and she had to go on up, pass Dido at the door, make herself smile at him, at someone else and someone else. And suddenly, only then, in that moment, she felt relief, realised that for the first time in days she could look at the people in this room without a shiver of horror, without the memory of Mr. Brown's small, muddy eyes, the feel of the cosh against her skin. And she stood still in the middle of

254

the room trying to believe that it was true, that he was gone, that he would never come back, never.

"Wha's up with you?" Molly whispered beside her.

"He came back," she said. "Mr. Brown."

"And what happened?"

"He's—He said I had high-up friends. That he was going to leave me alone."

"He did? He did truly? Ain't that wonderful! An' my Charlie must 'a done it after all, just like that, tellin' him to go off with hisself! Wait till I tell him, wait till I—" She was gone before Sara could stop her. And stop her from doing what? She felt again that lost, bound feeling she'd had in the park with Snipe. Of having no possibility of changing anything, of seeing something coming towards her out of the shadows, taking gradual shape. And nothing she could do could alter it. Like the faces she could see in the mirror. Seeing them against her will, wanting to see nothing. And the shadows moving. Taking shape.

She waited for them, saw Molly talking to both of them, Mr. Hunter looking up, shaking his head, saying something, Mr. Summers looking away. Molly beckoned her and she went over, her tray almost empty, sidling between the gamblers, Monkey catching her by the elbow, saying, "I 'eard 'e was 'ere."

"It's all right" was all she could say. Monkey squeezed her elbow almost affectionately, as though he, too, was pleased to think she had high-up friends, thought differently of her.

"So your problem's solved, eh, Gypsy?" Mr. Hunter said.

"I must thank you," she said, trying to make her words sound whole-hearted. "You've been very kind."

"Don't thank me. Thank Harry here, he did it. I did no more than act messenger."

"Then I must thank you," she whispered. "It's very very generous of you to have taken so much trouble."

"It was no trouble," Mr. Summers said. "Moll here says ye both knew old Margot Talbot in Thaxstone and that she's dead?"

"Gad, Harry, don't tell the girl it was no trouble! 'Pon my soul, will I *never* teach ye? Tell her ye ran

255

here an' there five days gettin' her out of her scrape an' promised your dear papa God knows what to bring him up to the mark. It was his papa, his lordship, that did it, ye know, so ye might as well thank me as Harry. When can I collect my forfeit?"

"You ain't collectin' no forfeits off Sara an' don't you think it."

"I have to go down for more wine," Sara said. "Thank you both for your kindness." She went by them quickly, afraid he would prevent her, knew that he was following even before he touched her arm. Half-way down the stairs. "Please," she whispered, "let me go."

"Damnation," he said, "I'm not Charles. I'm not going to ask you to pay for favours. What are you doing in this place?"

He stood above her on the stairs, looking down at her, his face with its almost habitual expression of sullen discontent, a barely contained anger. She wondered for a second what he had to be angry about, what more could he want than he already had.

"You can see what I'm doing," she said.

"That tone doesn't suit ye, ye know."

"I didn't mean to have any tone. I'm doing only what Molly and the other girls are doing. I'm earning my living."

"In a place like this?"

"There are worse places. If you think so badly of it, why do you come here?" She couldn't keep the anger out of her voice. "I don't mean to be pert," she said again, "I promise you. But I think there are many things someone such as you cannot understand. I've told you that I'm grateful, but now may I go down the stairs?"

"Not yet," he said. He put his hand on her shoulder and looked at her, his own voice half angry. "Ye're a damned strange girl. What happened to old Margot? Moll said something of her hanging herself in Urnford jail. What the devil did she do that for?"

"Because she was in a riot for bread, the one my guardian was killed in," Sara whispered. "Didn't you know about it? Don't you know about the men they

256

hanged? Molly's father with them?" She felt herself shaking, as though it was he who had had it done.

"I didn't know her father was one of them. She didn't—"

"Or that four of her brothers and sisters died of hunger? Do you know why the people rioted?"

"Some damned Jacobins stirred them up, poor devils."

"Your father's steward, Mr. Cameron, and Dr. Newall had the roadside grass ploughed up because they found two starving cows and a donkey and a pig daring to eat the grass of it! That's why they rioted. And they killed my guardian because they thought he was a spy, because they were afraid, and drunk and stupefied with dreams. Dreams of cheap bread and justice. And nineteen died for it! One old dear woman I loved killed herself because of it, to save herself from the shame of being hanged in front of a great shouting crowd of gapers. And eighteen were hanged. Eighteen men! Fathers, sons, brothers. Eighteen of them, twelve hanging side by side on the gallows, and twenty, thirty more transported, to die of fever half-way to Australia, and be luckier to die than if they reached there. For what? For what? For a few mouthfuls of grass for starving animals. For the hope of bread."

She stopped suddenly, shut her eyes, leaned against the wall, as though all was happening there between them, that ragged column marching, marching towards the solid barrier of the captain. And the echoes of her voice hung in her mind, harsh and arrogant, Mrs. Talbot's voice, and her shadow there with them, the folded paper in her hand. Emptying the dried seeds onto her palm.

"By God," Mr. Summers said. "I didn't think you had such passion in you."

"Let me go downstairs," she said dully. "What do you know of any of these things?"

"And she hanged herself? Dear God, I'm truly sorry. She was—she was my aunt's maid, many years ago. If my father had only known."

She turned away from him, ran down to the kitchen,

257

found a man and Janet in the passage fondling each other in the dark, pushed by them shuddering, heard Janet laughing. Had to listen to Maggie's talk of Mr. Brown, say, "Yes" and "No," and "Indeed, I am very glad," trying to smile.

All the remainder of the night she managed to avoid Mr. Summers, and when she and Molly were in bed, she refused to talk about him. "He do think you're the strangest girl he ever seed. 'Such a passion she do have inside her,' he kept saying to Charlie, 'such a passion you won't believe.' "

"Don't call him Charlie!"

"Lawd a' mercy, what's got into you? What else would I call 'im? A man do go beggin' a maid for kisses he do soon stop being mister an' sir! An' the more you scorn an' laugh at 'em the more he kneels down in front of you. I got 'im like a span'l dog beggin' his dinner, an' when I calls 'im Charlie he feels as how he's that bit nearer to gettin' it. But he's a long way off yet, I promise."

"Let me go to sleep."

"An' you could have Mr. Summers the same way, you give your mind to it. Lyin' flat down kissin' your slippers. 'Such a passion,' he kept saying. 'You should 'a heard her!' "

"Let me go to sleep!"

"You're right roused up, I can see that! Did he try an' kiss you?"

"I told him—" She stopped herself, turned on her side away from Molly, clenched her teeth in a spasm of anger that shook her body.

"What did you tell him?"

"Nothing." And she stayed silent after that, until at last Molly left her alone, angrily, turning her own back to Sara. And Sara lay unable to sleep, the shadows walking through and through her mind. Passion? And as though the word, the description had woken her, rather than the fact, she lay shivering with a cold fury that had scarcely any object. Certainly not Mr. Summers, nor even Mr. Cameron or Dr. Newall, or the judges at the trial, or anyone. As though behind them all there lay something that didn't have so much as a name, a shape—a dark, invisible force of cruelty and evil lying in wait. And gradually, as she sank into a half sleep, half dream, the force seemed to take on a shape, a face, and Mr. Brown's pale lips smiled at her, he laid his leather-covered, weighted stick against his nose, narrowed the small muddy eyes, seemed to be saying, "I can wait. I can wait forever."

Chapter 20

It was two days before he came to the gaming room again, and he spent an hour there, sipping champagne, watching the faro table in the alcove, before he tried to talk to her. She'd almost forgotten he was in the rooms when he came from behind the curtain and stopped her as she was going by.

"I want you to tell me about old Margot," he said. "But not here. Will you meet me somewhere? Tomorrow? Anywhere that you like. Moll says you're free in the afternoon."

"I told you she's dead. What else do you want to know?"

"Damnation, girl, it wasn't I that killed her! I'm sorry for it that she is dead. And I must write a letter to someone who will be still sorrier, who loved her more than you can have done, I promise you."

"How do you know how much I loved her? Let me go by. They're watching us."

"What the devil do I care *who's* watching? Do ye not owe me at least a minute's politeness?"

"I owe you more than that," she said. "I'm sorry.

But she was like a second—a second—She was the dearest friend to me. I do not like to think of the way she died." And as she said it, she felt her mouth shake with the longing to go on, to cry out aloud, "I killed her, I killed her, it was my doing that she died!" Tell him, tell someone, as though she could empty it out of her mind by telling it.

"I'm sorry," he said. "But the man I must write to loved her, too. A long time ago."

"She was your aunt," she whispered, "did you know that?" As if the pain inside her needed to hurt someone else, drag claws through flesh to ease itself. And it seemed to her that she was coming out of a long sleep in which the pain had been hidden, dulled, no more than an ache at the far back of her consciousness. And now she had woken, and it was burning inside her like a poison, agonising. "She was your father's half-sister."

He stared at her, began to answer her, and said nothing. She left him standing there, and when she came back a few minutes later to the same place, he was gone.

"You seem to have made 'im master angry," Molly said when they were going to bed. "What did you say to 'im?"

"I told him who Mrs. Talbot was. That she was his aunt."

"An' didn't he know? Maybe they don't like to think such things happen, not to lords' families, they don't like to think they got little ones running about that don't have no proper dads."

"I'm *glad* he's angry."

"Suppose he sets Mr. Brown back after you? What'll you do then, eh?"

She tried to laugh and failed, lay with her arms crossed over her breast, stared up at the dawn sky through the grey, dusty skylight, a pale glow of rose growing, growing, fading as the summer sky became day-bright and handsome above the rooftops.

"You best tell 'em you're sorry."

"I'm *not* sorry."

"You got to be sorry! Sara Pownall, what do you

want to see happenin' to you? I think sometimes if I weren't here to see to you you 'ouldn't know how to eat your meat. You tell 'im you're true sorry an' didn't mean to vex him tellin' 'im that." Shaking her, her face filled with concern and innocence.

"Oh, Molly," she whispered. "Why do things have to be the way they are?"

"What you mean? How *else* can things be 'cept the way they are? You say such queer things I think you're touched, sometimes."

But when he came again, the next night, he seemed to have recovered. She was talking to Dido when he arrived, and Dido went away from her so quickly, with such humility, that it hurt her to the soul; she felt even angry with him for his humility, his docile obedience, and she couldn't bring herself so much as to greet Mr. Summers, let alone tell him she was sorry for the previous night. And he said nothing about it, took a glass of champagne, glanced round as though he was hardly aware she was there. She wanted to turn away, and thought, *I must not be rude to him*, and then felt a sick shame for what her reasons were, tried to tell herself she owed him that much politeness, more. That it wasn't fear.

He swung on her suddenly and said, his face angry again, "God damn it, do what I ask. Bring your friend with you, anyone you like. What the devil d'ye think I want of you? Only meet me long enough to answer my questions. Will you do it?"

"Yes, I'll do it. Where do you wish me to come?"

"You choose the place."

"Do you know a coffee-house in Palace Way? Luke's Coffee-house? Would that do?"

"I'll find it. Tell me what time you shall be there and I shall keep you half an hour, no more, I promise you."

He left her alone after that, and she told herself, "I'll go alone. I'll prove to him—show him that—" What? Prove what? That she was not afraid? She brought Molly with her, ten minutes before the time, and they sat waiting while Toby asked them about Snipe and teased them about their new clothes in his tired voice. He seemed so like a friend, this place so kindly she wanted suddenly to cry with a strange kind of happiness and sadness; she wondered if Molly was right, if she was somehow touched in her mind, wondered if anyone else had ever felt as she did. The world now terrible, now dazzlingly, tenderly wonderful, heartbreaking. She thought of trying to explain what she felt to Molly and smiled.

"Well, least you're smiling a bit," Molly said. "The first time you says something wicked to 'im I'm goin' to pinch you so sore you'll shriek. You mind that. There he is comin' now. I wonder why he always looks so grim?" She waved to him through the window, half standing up from her chair to do it. "Charlie says he do hate his step-ma something fierce, an' she hates him as bad."

He came in, looked round him in something almost like surprise, as though he'd expected another kind of place, and came over to them, lifting his hat, looking towards Molly and then Sara with a slight smile that seemed to say, "So you didn't trust me after all."

He sat down and Toby came and took his order for coffee and went. Mr. Summers linked his fingers together and stared down at them for a long moment. "You asked me the other night," he said at last, "if I knew old Margot Talbot was my aunt. Yes, I did. I should have answered you then. But it isn't a subject we're fond of dwelling on."

"I cannot have an opinion about that," Sara said. "But if you tell me what you want to know, I shall try to answer you."

He was still looking down at his hands. "What I want to know is a strange thing," he said, "and perhaps you cannot answer it." He hesitated so long that she thought he'd changed his mind and wouldn't ask her anything.

"I said I'd try to answer. And Molly knew her as well as I did. We both loved her."

"Was she happy?" Mr. Summers asked. "That's what my friend will wish to know. You see how strange a question it is."

"Happy?" Molly said wonderingly. "Before all the

trouble came? O' course she was." She stopped and looked at Sara as though it had suddenly occurred to her it might not be true.

"How could anyone answer that?" Sara said. "Sometimes she was happy. Is it your father who wishes to know?"

"No. Someone else. It doesn't matter who. Someone who loved her and will be cruelly sorry to hear how she died. I'd like to be able to soften it for him if I can. He's an old man and hasn't much to make him happy."

"Then must you tell him anything?"

He looked at her in surprise. "Do you tell lies to your friends?" He waited and said again, "Was she happy? Did the people like her? The people round?"

"They were afraid of her," Sara said.

"Afraid?" he said, his eyes astonished.

"She was a witch," Molly said. And Mr. Summers repeated the word "witch" as he had "afraid," and laughed, half puzzled, as though he weren't sure whether there was a joke concealed in what the two girls were saying. "What do you—A witch! For God's sake!"

Sara looked at him, and the space between them seemed to grow so wide that it was difficult to make him out. She thought, *He knows nothing, nothing in the world. He owns it and knows nothing,* and she felt something close to pity, and then rage, and could have leaned across the table and struck him for his ignorance, his laugh, his smile of polite bewilderment.

"People came to her for medicines," she said, not looking at him. "She knew a great deal about such things."

"Ah," he said, "herbs and so on. I've heard them speak of it, I think. And they called her a witch for it? Poor old woman. And my uncle says that when she was a girl she was so beautiful she'd turn all heads as she passed by."

Sara locked her hands together against answering him, against savaging him for the condescension of "poor old woman." What did he *think* of? A witch out of his nursery books with nose and chin meeting and

263

a steeple hat? "Tell me what else you wish to know," she said.

"Only one other thing," he said. "Although I suppose there are a thousand things he would like to know. Did she"—he looked down at his linked fingers—"did she ever speak to you of someone? A man she had once—once known?"

He looked up at Sara and it was hard to tell whether he wanted to ask the question or had asked it against his grain.

"Yes," Sara said. And not meaning to say it, not even thinking of it before she said it, "Of an old man who sits in an empty room and stares. She spoke of him once or twice." Her voice harsh, coldly furious.

Mr. Summers tried to answer her and failed, separated his hands. "How much do you know of all this?"

"She did see 'im in her mirror!" Molly whispered. Sara turned on her, could have struck her, wanted to get up and leave them both sitting there. But if Mr. Summers had heard what Molly said, he showed no sign of it, or else did not understand it and let it go.

"I know she was your grandfather's child," Sara said, "and that if your father had lifted his hand, he could have saved her."

"He didn't know," Mr. Summers said. He looked away from both of them, and she wondered if he was lying or merely hoping that what he'd said was true. She thought, *He's sorry that he came*. But he looked at her again and tried to smile, and his face had suddenly a great sweetness in it, like the captain's, and she wondered, still wishing to keep her anger, whether his grandfather had begotten the captain as well as Mrs. Talbot, and was then sorry she'd thought of it. And Mrs. Talbot had had nothing of this man's face in hers. *Why am I angry with him?* she thought. *The only thing he has done that I know of is a kindness to me.*

"I'm very sorry," she said, in her own voice. "I have sounded angry, and I have no right to seem ungrateful to you. I'm very sorry. But perhaps you've never . . ." She thought then, *He lost his own mother at some time. Can I say nothing right?*

"Perhaps I have never . . ," he prompted.

". . . been inside a prison? Seen prisoners?"

"No, I have not."

"It has stayed in my mind."

"I don't wish to make you angry again," he said gently. "But if you would tell me that one thing. You say she spoke of—of a particular man. Did she speak kindly of him?"

She didn't answer him for a moment. "You will see more than I," Mrs. Talbot had said. "In this case." And all she had ever seen was that sad figure, staring, staring. And once, once, it had been as though she herself was in that empty room with him, going slowly, slowly towards him, drawn forward. Could see his face as though she needed only to reach out and touch him, knew how his yellow, withered skin would feel to touch. Could feel the heat of the room, stifling so it was difficult to breathe. And yet the old man was cold, wrapped in his padded velvet gown, and his eyes—only his unseeing eyes still really alive, dark with longing. She was looking into them, deep, deep into them, and felt terror, as though if she went too close the eyes would possess her mind, enclose it, and she would never escape from them; she'd had to make a tremendous effort to break their hold, break the image in the grey depth of the mirror, shake herself back into safety and reality. Mrs. Talbot had never asked her to do it again.

"Very kindly," she said in a dull whisper. "She thought often about him."

"Well, I'm glad of that at least," Mr. Summers said, making himself sound brisk, as if he half guessed at something and didn't want to know about it. "I wish he could hear you say that."

"Who is he?" Sara said, against her will.

He hesitated, looked down at his hands. "He is my uncle. At least, by marriage. He married my aunt." He looked at her and laughed with no humour in the laughter. "He's a very rich old gentleman and intends, he says, to leave me his fortune. So I'm very happy

265

to do him any small service of this kind." He looked far from happy, and it crossed Sara's mind, almost for the first time in her life, like a revelation, how much there lies behind other faces—as though she were surrounded by masks and behind each mask there stretched an echoing darkness, full of pain. She touched her throat, felt almost dizzy for a second, every protection stripped from her mind, and she thought that if anyone spoke, if anyone touched her in that second she would die. And then she managed to draw the reality of the room around her like a cloak and was safe again.

"Do you wish to know anything else?"

"I shall write him this evening and ask if there is anything more. You have been very kind. And now," he said, becoming another Mr. Summers, "you must let me play host. May I bring you anywhere?"

"Ain't you afraid your step-ma might see us with you?" Molly said.

And again, if Sara could've struck her, she would have. Mr. Summers' face clouded, became the familiar one of the gaming room, sullen with what she'd thought was boredom and discontent and realised now was a bitter kind of unhappiness. "My stepmother isn't likely to be in this part of the town," he said. He paid their bill and they went out with him. "Would you care to walk in the park a little?" he said. As though he were asking it of his sisters. And she felt a strange, unpleasant embarrassment, wondered if her clothes were the kind of clothes his sisters would wear, looked down at her dress. He'd given Molly his arm and was offering his other arm to her, a look in his eyes as if he knew what she was thinking.

They walked down three or four streets and passed the end of Glovers' Row where Madame D'Arblay's shop was. But there was no sign of anyone standing in the doorway. They went into St. James's Park and walked by the Long Water, looking at the ducks. "There is Old Jack," Mister Summers said, "the queen's swan." The bird sailed contemptuously away from them, a small girl trying to tempt him back with a piece of bread. "You'd best not go so near that big fellow," Mr. Summers said to the child. "Or he may pull you into the water and spoil your pretty clothes." The little girl looked at him as though he were mad and continued calling, "Swan, swan, come *here*," stamping her foot.

"Even if he does pull her in, I suppose someone will save her," Mr. Summers said. "Did any woman ever take advice, I wonder, unless it was bad?"

He bought them lemonade in the pavilion and seemed happy to sit with them while they drank it. No one seemed to think they looked strange in any way and Sara began to feel at her ease, to be content to sit there in the warm sunlight, her eyes half closed so that the trees made a green lacework against the sky and the figures of the passers-by; the others sitting near them on the wooden chairs were like silhouettes, the sun glittering, reflected from the windows of the round pavilion, from the distant water, from the glass in her hand. And she thought, *Suppose we didn't have to go back?* and realised with a shock what she'd been thinking and sat up quickly and said, "We shall be late. What time is it?"

"We got a mort o' time yet! She don't no sooner sit someplace than she wants to run somewheres else. I don't mean to go back till the last minute I must. It's nicer than t'other park here, more people."

"I like to hear Essex again," Mr. Summers said. "It brings back all my childhood." He spoke as though his childhood was infinitely far off.

They sat and strolled for another hour before he put them into a hackney coach and paid the driver for their journey. "I may see you tonight," he said. "Or else tomorrow night without fail. I've enjoyed our afternoon very much." He sounded almost surprised. He handed Molly into the coach, then Sara, held her hand for a moment and said, "We are friends at last?" She had to say yes and she was afraid he would kiss her hand, but he merely lifted it half-way, pressed her fingers slightly, and closed the door for her.

She turned to look through the little window in the back of the coach and he was already walking quickly along the pavement in his green coat, and it might have

267

been the captain. The same set of the square, wide shoulders, the same almost stamping stride as if he too were impatient to be somewhere else. The same tilt of the head, and again she wondered if the captain's mother or grandmother . . . She felt angry with herself as though the thought were a kind of disloyalty. How angry the captain would have been if he could have known such a thought could come to her.

"Did he wave to you?" Molly whispered.

"Of course not."

The coach lurched round a corner, threw them together. "Weren't he so nice? Just like we were ladies an' he were takin' us walkin'."

"What difference would it make if we were ladies?" Sara said, furious again.

"Well, you were the one as said I shouldn't have waved at him before. You do be master unreasonable at times, Sara, an' no one couldn't say different. O' course we ain't ladies an' it do make a silly lot o' difference with things like that. But I tell you something. We have a much better time o' it than ladies do. Even in Monkey's."

"What do you mean?"

"Charlie were telling me about his sisters, sittin' all day doin' embroidery an' readin' aloud to their mother or goin' visitin' old faggots because they're Lady This an' Lady That, an' yawnin' sick with nothin' to do day's end to day's end. Cain't even *think* about love case they gets pregnant, they don't even know how a maid do get pregnant, he said, they think it do come o' kissing."

"You seem to talk about very strange things with Mr. Hunter."

" 'Course I do. We talks about everything. He says I make 'im laugh better'n anyone he ever met. When he goes home he says he can't think of nothing but us an' the fun we all have. His dad's away in India or someplace an' he has to look after his ma an' his sisters and they drive him mad talking 'bout nothin' an' bein' so delicate they do faint if they hears a bad word. I told 'im he should bring 'em to Monkey's for a couple of weeks to get over that an' he laughed till he was near crying with it. 'Oh, I wish I could,' he kept sayin'. 'Oh, if only I could, poor wretches.' "

She looked at Sara, hesitated. "He wants me to go an' live somewheres."

The coach lurched again, was outside the chop house. The coachman called, " 'Ere y'are," in a sulky growl, as though in spite of Mr. Summers' payment, he thought it beneath him to bring such girls to such a place. They got down and Molly stuck her tongue out at him. "Mind your horse don't fall over," she said. "He couldn't get up again, the look o' him."

The driver shook his whip at her and they ran inside, were back in the dining-room, in their own world, and the park, the sunlight, the afternoon, seemed a thousand miles away, and Mr. Summers no more than a distant figure in a painting, the sun shining on his dark green coat, his white cravat. They went upstairs, and Sara felt as though she was tired already, before the evening had begun, and she imagined what it would be like to be able to lie down on the bed and sleep and sleep and think of nothing.

"You heard what I said?" Molly looked at her, half nervous, stripping off her gloves and bonnet. " 'Bout him wanting—"

"Yes, I heard."

"I didn't tell him I would."

Sara sat on the wooden chair, closed her eyes, letting her head fall back. "And will you?"

"You ain't angry with me?"

"Why should I be?"

Molly knelt down beside her, caught hold of her hands. "You promise? Promise you won't be angry if —if I were to—"

"What do you want me to tell you?" Sara cried, shaking Molly's hands away. "To be his lover, his kept woman, his whore? Sleep with him like his cat? What do you want me to tell you to do?"

"You said you won't be angry," Molly said sullenly. "I just tell you my secrets an' you go shoutin' an' snarlin' like old Dr. Newall or someone. I got a right to do what I like, ain't I? I don't have to ask your leave for it?"

269

"Then *don't* ask it! Go and do it! Be his whore. Get pregnant and come creeping to me to get you out of trouble. Let him keep you locked up in a room to play with when he's bored. Let him. Let him. And when he's tired of you, go down the Haymarket to find someone else. And someone else. And someone else. Only don't ask me to give you your license for it. Just go!"

Molly stayed kneeling, staring at her, shocked out of anger, simply staring at her white, savage face. Sara had stood up, was standing now with her back to the chimney, the rough brickwork against her shoulders, her eyes shut, her body trembling with rage, rage that had no reason, that she couldn't understand, didn't even try to understand, a shaking, mindless rage that was like terror, a black terror filling her mind. As though it wasn't Molly but herself, she could see herself lying on a bed, naked, and his face leaning over her, his hands, his hands—

"I'm sorry," she whispered. "I am truly, truly sorry. Oh, Molly!" She flung herself down on her knees beside Molly and tried to put her arms round her. Molly pushed her away.

"You do need to be sorry," she said. "I just say, 'Charlie did ask me if I would think to go an' live somewheres,' an' you go off like a rocket bursting. You don't have no call to shout at me like that an' I won't stay for it, I tell you."

"Oh, Molly, Molly, please. We mustn't quarrel. We've only got ourselves."

"That ain't true," Molly said. "Bein' friends don't mean you cain't know no one else. You ain't jealous?" she said, catching hold of Sara's hands again. "You ain't jealous o' me an' Charlie?"

"No," Sara whispered, her throat stiff so that it was hard to breathe, to shape the words. "No. How could I be? It's only—only that I'm frightened for you."

"You don't need to be afraid for me, Sara. I ain't goin' to go dollyin' up an' down the streets lookin' for a man to give me a guinea, I promise you that, not if I have to cut my throat first. Anyone as wants me'll have to do the lookin', I promise you that too,

270

an' I'd have to like 'im a master great lot before he'd do more'n look. An' if it's Charlie—well, I do like 'im a lot already, but I still ain't goin' to give 'im nothin' till I wants to, an' I'm certain sure what I'm doin'."

They made it up as best they could, kissed and held each other and went down to work. And all through the evening Sara found herself watching Molly as though she were a stranger, simply one of the hundred girls who came there to gamble, to spend an hour and lose a guinea or ten guineas before they went out again, back to the Haymarket or Regent Street, or the Argyle Rooms, to pick up another man and earn more to lose here tomorrow night, keep Monkey in his sweating happiness. *What will become of me?* she thought.

Mr. Hunter came, and she found herself looking towards the door for Mr. Summers and was furious with herself for looking, avoided Mr. Hunter. Half a dozen other swells arrived, led by Sir Thomas, filled the room with high-pitched Eton voices, cursing like stableboys in the belief that they were acting in a proper manner for the gaming rooms, making loud comments about different girls. Sir Thomas turned his baby face to Sara, needing to turn his whole body to do it, his neck held rigid by his *trône d'armour* cravat, his collar starched so stiff it threatened to cut off his ears.

" 'Pon honour!" he cried. "That's the one Harry fancies. Can't think why."

Dido was near to her and she saw his face flush crimson, the muscles bunch under his sleeves. She said to him quickly, "Come down to the kitchen with me, Dido, will you please? There are so many glasses to bring down." He would have taken the tray from her but she prevented him. "When we are outside," she said. She gave it to him on the landing and he looked so happy it was painful. He went down the stairs ahead of her and almost fell three times looking back to watch her following him.

When they were outside the kitchen, she took the tray from him and said hurridly, "Dido, please, I shouldn't have asked you to come down. Don't look at me like that."

"I'm sorry," he said meekly, lowered his eyes. "I know——" And then "Oh, *Pen*, why do you stay here?" He said it as though she were torturing him, and ran up the stairs again.

Chapter 21

The summer became heavier, the attic almost unendurable, even at night. A heat as unlike Spanish heat as muddy water from wine, a heat that made it hard to breathe, seemed to take the life out of her blood and bones. The sewer smells crept up through the house, hung like a fog in the stairways and under the roof. They slept naked and still sweated and woke tired.

"I'd love to be in Thaxstone now," Molly said. "Just lie in a field an' do nothin' an' breathe clean air. I feel I'm dyin', sometimes."

Even the gamblers seemed tired and the crowds thinned, though the hours were still as long. Monkey grew short-tempered, or shorter-tempered still, cursing Dido for not letting the young swells punish him enough when they boxed.

"One day I'll kill him," Dido whispered to Sara.

They were on the landing outside the gymnasium and there was a trickle of blood from under his left eye where a resined glove had grazed it.

"Go away from here," Sara said.

"I ain't got nowhere *to* go."

"You could make money boxing at the fairs, surely?"

"For someone worse than 'im? Maybe." He put his fingertips against his bruised cheek, the smear of blood, and she knew he was desperate for her to touch it, ease it for him, and could not. She knew what he wanted to say to her, to beg her to go away with him. Knew all the promises, everything that was in his mind, like seeing a page out of a book and reading it.

"I could not," she said. "I'm very sorry."

He looked at her and looked quickly away, half afraid and half accepting. "What are you seeing, *Hani?*"

"Nothing," she said. "Except the road." But she saw two roads. "Go away," she whispered, "think of the woods, think of the fire."

"It's a long time since I saw them."

"Go quickly. You'll find them again."

"What'll happen if I don't?" He looked at her with such humble longing that it was like a dog's humility, and it twisted her heart to see him at once so strong and so humble. And she saw him grown old, sweeping the cellar the hunchback swept, walking slowly along gutters in the winter cold, his shirt ragged and his face gaunt. Unless . . .

"Will I kill him?"

She shook her head. "No, you will not do that."

He seemed to be relieved and smiled at her. "You got to live where you can, 'ow you can." Sir Thomas and his friends came out of the gymnasium behind him. Sir Thomas clapped his shoulder. " 'Pon honour, you box well enough, but you should learn to block, fellow. You lack the science of it, you know." He didn't condescend to greet Sara.

She touched Dido's arm and it was trembling, the muscles shivering with self-control. "He's not worth thinking of," she said.

The next day, at dinnertime, Snipe came back. Sara was eating her own dinner, or at least pretending to eat, most of the others already gone, Molly lying back against the wall fanning herself with the flap of her apron, when the hunchback Jim came in and beckoned her. He always made a secret of everything, looking round him before he whispered the most ordinary things, and she thought at first that he was at the same business again, wanting to tell her that he'd caught a giant rat or that the water was rising in the cellars and to come and see.

"I'm too tired."

He came close, looking round in all the corners, at the fire, at Maggie's turned back, at Molly. "It's your friend," he whispered. "Your friend Snipe."

"Where?"

"Down in the yard."

"But why?" She stood up, feeling her heart pound with premonition, and followed the hunchback down the cellar stairs, out into the sunken yard, and saw Snipe standing there, leaning with her forearms against the wall, her face hidden. In rags.

"Snipe!"

Snipe looked up, straightened slowly, trying to smile, a faint glimmer of the old radiance there. She was filthy as well as ragged, as though she'd slept in ditches for a month, been rolled in mud. And she walked stiffly, very stiff and slow as she came away from the wall. Sara ran to her, flung her arms round her, and Snipe screamed, screamed like an animal for a second and then buried her face against Sara's breast to stifle the scream.

"Don't touch my back," she said. "I bin a bit unlucky."

"What have they done to you?" She held her by the arms, gently, tried to look at her, her bent face, tears of pain making lines in the dirt. "What's happened?"

"If you could let me lie down in your room for a bit. An' something to eat. I'll be all right." She tried to smile again. "Only I don't want none of the others to see me. 'Cept Moll maybe. I looks a sight, don't I?"

Sara took her upstairs, had to help her at every step, almost carry her, as if the effort of getting to the yard had taken the last of Snipe's strength. She eased her down onto the mattress, and Snipe lay on her face, sighed with happiness at the relief of lying down, of having a mattress under her. The back of her dress was stained with blood. Sara knelt down and began to unfasten it. She heard Molly come in behind her, catch her breath.

"Oh, Snipe!" Sara breathed. Someone had tied rags round Snipe's back, under the dress, and the rags were stiff with blood, blackened, like a crust, here and there an oozing of crimson. Sara knelt and stared down at it and felt sick with horror.

"Lawd have mercy," Molly whispered.

"I'll be all right," Snipe said. "Gawd, it's good to lie down."

"Stay with her," Sara said. "No. Come down to the kitchen with me. We'll have to heat some water. And I'll need some cabbage leaves. If Maggie has any —Oh, God, what have they done to her?"

When she came back upstairs again, Snipe had to support herself with an arm round Sara's neck in order to drink the warm milk Sara had brought her. She drank it like a child, a rim of white on her upper lip, sucking the milk greedily, not stopping until the mug was empty. "Oh, Gawd," she said. "You'll 'ave me blubbling in a minute. Why don't you laugh at me?"

"What happened?"

"Bloody chawbacons. Up bloody north. I dipped this geezer's wallet an' these fellers must 'ave seen me. They followed me out o' the fair an' I saw 'em and I ran for it. Only I didn't run bloody fast enough. Four of 'em, the bastards. They got me into this wood, see. An', an' then—" She tried to laugh and the tears ran down her face, made silver tracks in the dirt. Sara smoothed them away, stroked her hair. Molly came in with the water and Snipe stiffened.

"What're you going to do?"

"We've got to clean your back."

"Don't touch it!"

"But we must. I promise I won't hurt you."

"You don't know what you're talking about. You can't *touch* it without 'urting it. I can't 'ardly breathe without 'urting it."

"If you don't let me clean it, you'll die," Sara said.

275

She made her lie down. She had borrowed a razor from Ben and she began to cut the stiffened rags away, working more carefully than a surgeon cutting skin and flesh. Snipe still had to clench her hands on the pillow, sink her teeth into it.

It took an hour to ease the rags away from the flesh and five basins of warm water. Sponging, easing, waiting for the pain to die down again. Snipe fainted and they brought her more milk, and she lay as though dead, the tears running silently, her head not moving, until the pillow was sodden under her.

And when the rags were off at last, it was only the beginning. Long, crusted wounds as though an animal had clawed the length of her back until there seemed to be no skin left there, only dried blood and raw, putrefying flesh. Sara sent Molly to the apothecary for laudanum. "If only I had mandrake root," she said. "It would kill the pain quicker than anything." But the laudanum eased it, made Snipe lie half asleep, only shuddering now and then as the sponge touched her flesh. Sara laid the crushed cabbage on the wounds, which were not only on her back, where fingernails had torn the flesh open, but also between her legs, ragged gashes that had grown inflamed and poisoned, an ugly, burning red surrounding the still uglier yellow of pus, like great raw ulcers.

Snipe gave a long, shuddering sigh, half of pain and half of ecstasy at the cold kissing of the leaves, like putting out a fire. Sara laid the clean bandage across her back, bound it right round Snipe's thin body, no more than bones now, thin as a bird. Between her legs. Molly had knelt besides Snipe's head all the time, except when she was fetching more water, and the laudanum, holding her hands and whispering child words, "There's a brave little one, there's my heart." Crying herself.

The laudanum took its full effect at last, and Snipe slept, her body shivering in her sleep. It was almost time for them to go down to work for the night, and they got dressed as quietly as they could, leaving a candle burning in a saucer in case Snipe woke and was afraid.

Both Mr. Hunter and Mr. Summers came, near to midnight, and as he always did now, Mr. Summers waited until she went into the faro alcove and followed her, standing half hidden by the curtain until she was free to talk to him.

"I've heard from my poor uncle," he said when she came to stand beside him. She no longer troubled with the pretence that she was offering him champagne or a sweetmeat or anything else. It had become generally assumed she belonged to him, as Molly did to Mr. Hunter.

"He was greatly moved by what I told him. He begged me to learn all I could from you and offers you his thanks in advance for anything you shall tell me."

"I have told you most things by now." *Although not the things that mattered*, she thought.

"I must go visit him before the end of the summer. He lives at the world's end in Wales." He looked at her. "There are mountains. Like your Spanish mountains. You'd like them if you saw them."

And she knew as she had known with Dido what he wanted to say and was afraid of saying. Although with Mr. Summers "afraid" was the wrong word. Too courteous to say it?

"Ye're not looking yourself tonight," he said.

"I've had an unpleasant afternoon."

"Tell me about it."

She hesitated. "It's nothing," she said. "Merely a friend who'd had ill-luck." Someone called her and she left him; it was a quarter of an hour before he could talk to her again.

"Your friend? he said. "Is the ill-luck to do with money?"

He meant it so kindly, his face was so kindly as he said it that she felt ashamed of her anger, almost brought herself to tell him what had happened. "No," she said, forcing her voice to a neutrality. "She had an accident and Molly and I have had to care for her."

"I'm sorry," he said. He looked away. "You're a good girl." And still looking away from her he said, "You shouldn't stay in this place, you know."

"You've said that before."

"And it's still true."

"Have you a room to offer me somewhere? And an allowance? A place where you will come three afternoons a week? And—" She hadn't meant to be angry. And the passion of anger blocked her throat like a stone, made her whisper, her face gone white with rage. As though it was he who had raped Snipe, clawed her flesh open with his own bloody hands. She wanted to lay her forehead against the wall, beat on it with her fists.

"I have offered you nothing," he said.

She closed her eyes, tried to say that she was sorry, and could say nothing at all. She heard someone calling her, moved away from him, thought, *I've offended him utterly now. He won't talk to me again.* And tried to feel glad of it. When she'd emptied her tray, she went out and ran up the stairs to her room, opening the door softly. Snipe lay as they had left her, the candle almost burned down to its last inch, the wick grown long and smoking. She knelt down beside the pillow and took the sponge to wipe Snipe's forehead where the gold hair lay plastered against it with sweat.

"Bastards," Snipe whispered in her sleep. "Bloody bastards," and then "Oooooooh," in a long, shuddering whimper of agony as if they had hold of her again in her dream, had turned it to nightmare, her back arching and her fingers clutching Sara's hand. She lifted her face, her eyes blind with the laudanum. " 'Oo's there, 'oo's there?"

"It's me," Sara whispered. "Try and sleep, you're safe, just sleep."

Snipe's head fell on to the pillow again, her hand still gripping Sara's. She held it so tight that after a few minutes Sara had to pry the fingers loose to release herself. She went down the stairs and found them on the middle landing, outside the gymnasium, Mr. Hunter and Molly and Mr. Summers.

"She has just told me about your friend," Mr. Summers said. "I am truly sorry for her. It is a barbarous story."

"If they'd brought her up before the judge," Mr.

278

Hunter said, "she might have been hanged." He had his arm round Molly. Sara wondered suddenly what they talked of when they were together. "At least the poor girl will recover from this." He smiled consolingly.

"Charles, for God's sake," Mr. Summers said. "Will you allow us to give you anything for her?"

"No!" Sara said.

"Why not?" Molly said. "They want to give her something you shouldn't be stoppin' 'em. She don't have a stitch to wear down them stairs."

"She'll have what she needs," Sara said between her teeth.

"Well, she'd better give up picking pockets," Mr. Hunter said. "She obviously ain't much good at it."

"If you change your mind . . ." Mr. Summers took her hand to say good-bye, drew her towards the stairs that led to the street door, where Ben stood keeping it. "I want to speak to you," he said. He made her follow him half-way down. "Listen to me. Don't accuse me of things I haven't said. But if I were to find you . . . some employment? Would you take it?"

She said nothing, looked down at Ben, who was carefully pretending not to hear anything.

"Answer me! Would you?"

"I have employment."

"What kind, dammit? What do you think will become of you here? Does that poor creature lying on your bed upstairs not make you think of anything?"

"Yes," she whispered, turning on him. "She makes me think of a great deal. But what does she make *you* think of? Your sisters? Or just 'a creature,' like a dog dying in the gutter, a donkey flogged past its endurance? She's like a child—and—and four men— You should have seen her in that room upstairs, heard her laughing. And now she's lying on our floor like a dying animal, her back one mass of blood and pus, ready to breed maggots in if we hadn't cared for it. And you say, 'poor creature' and your friend laughs and sneers and you want to offer her a guinea for her pain. Will your guinea cure her?"

279

"No, it will not," he said angrily. "But it might feed her for a time and keep her from stealing again, so long as it lasts. Good God, did I make her a thief? And do you think of me as like—one of those—those ruffians—"

"Why do you think she steals?" Sara whispered. "What do you know of her? What do you know of anything? Before she was six years old her father sold her for a five-pound note. To a recruiter for a mill. For five pounds! A pound for each year of her age! To work fourteen hours a day and be beaten awake at the day's end in case she fell into the machinery and was killed or maimed. Or because the overseer liked to beat small children for amusement. *That's* why she steals. She ran away when she was eleven, when the same overseer tried to rape her, threw her down on a pile of waste threads and almost tore her body in half attempting, and now—" She put up her hand to her throat, felt it closing, closing, *heard the whisper, her mother's whisper, the terror in it, "Hush, hush, my darling, not a sound! They're coming!"*

"You must bring her to hospital," Mr. Summers said. "You'll make yourself ill nursing her. Please. Let me give you money. I'll have a doctor see to her; my father's doctor shall look to her himself. And when she's better, we'll think of something."

She forced the shadows away from her, came back to herself, the stairway. "I am so ungrateful to you. Please forgive me. But she wouldn't go into any hospital. And how do you think they'd treat her there?"

"At least let me send the doctor to her here."

"Molly has already been to the apothecary. She'll be all right with rest and food and the medicines we have."

"And will you not let me give you money for her?"

She tried to smile. "I think she would rather steal it from you."

"Then tell her I shall come one day with my pocket-book and she can try her skill." He took her hand and held it. "I wonder what my father would say if he

280

heard our conversation. At the moment his whole mind is engaged in drawing up a bill to make poaching a capital offence. He swears the world is falling into ruin from too much foolish tenderness with criminals."

"What must I say to that?"

"Nothing, of course. But, Sara, I beg of you, think of what I've said. My uncle, he is very old and long past doing injury to any girl, even if he would. He would give you a place."

"I must go back upstairs," she said. "Let me go."

"He would love you for Mrs. Talbot's sake. And very soon for your own, I know it. He has become the gentlest of old men and would ask nothing of you beyond—nothing at all but to make his blindness brighter for him. He even thought of it himself in his letter. I told him of you in mine."

"I must go," she whispered. "They're coming down to us."

"Molly's laughter on the stairs behind them, Mr. Hunter pleading for another kiss.

Chapter 22

It was three days before Snipe could sit up without being held and another three before she could walk. They bought a second mattress and let her sleep by herself and even then she woke them three and four times a night, or rather morning, with that terrible, shuddering cry of pain out of her nightmare of being raped. When she was awake, she never talked about it, tried to make jokes, and when she was able to move again, she cleaned the room for them, dusting things and tidying their bed. Sara came up one afternoon and found her kneeling against the chair, crying, rigid with the pain of a wound in her back that had broken open as she reached out to straighten a blanket.

"You must keep still," Sara said. "Lie down and let me see what you've done." And Snipe lay docile, like a hurt child, as Sara dressed her back, the scars gradually healing into long crimson grooves, horrifying, some of them still scabbed and crusted breaking now and then and bleeding afresh. Sometimes Sara sat for an hour holding Snipe's head in her lap, whispering to her, "Don't cry, don't cry," and staring at the brick chimney, at the curtain Dido had hung beside it for their clothes, at the cracked, splitting door, at the slope of the ceiling and the cobwebs Snipe hadn't been able to reach. Trying to imagine a world in which these things did not happen.

Molly helped with the nursing, spent pounds on buying Snipe presents, fruit and sweetmeats and cordials and a new bonnet and dress from Ma Casey's, never complaining at being wakened in the middle of her sleep. But Sara sensed an impatience, almost an irritation in her kindness, as though Snipe's helplessness and defeat made her angry. Or perhaps only afraid. And she waited day by day for Molly to tell her she was going, that at last her Charlie had made her an offer she could not bring herself to refuse.

But it did not happen until Snipe was almost well again. Both Mr. Hunter and Mr. Summers had come to the gaming room almost every night, even if only for a few minutes, and always brought something for Snipe, or at least Mr. Summers did and the gift was given as from both of them. A box of French handkerchiefs once, and a flask of perfume another time, or flowers, or fruit. And each time Sara wondered with a shadow of bitterness whether the gift was really for herself rather than for Snipe. But Snipe would sit up on the mattress surrounded by the flowers, or spreading out the lace handkerchiefs with so much delight that Sara felt wicked for not feeling more

282

grateful to him. She then wondered if that was also the intention.

" 'E's nice," Snipe said. "They both are. Gawd, ain't it queer? 'Is dad'd 'ave me 'anged if 'e could, e'd do it with 'is own 'ands and laugh doin' it, the old bastard. An' there's 'is little boy givin' me 'andkerchiefs an' sayin' e'll let me pick 'is pocket to get back into practise."

"That was only a joke, Snipe."

"I know, I know. What do you think I am? I wouldn't pick 'is pocket if I was starving. If 'e was 'ungry I'd pick pockets *for* 'im. You tell 'im that, make 'im laugh."

"I hope the occasion never arises," Mr. Summers said. "I think I should dislike being hungry. But please thank her for the intention."

Mr. Hunter wanted to go up and see her. "Have a look at your little nest. Gad, three such birds in one cage, eh?"

He tried to go up the stairs and Sara stood in his way, trembling with rage again and threatening to call Dido. "An' what the deuce d'you think your Dido would do, eh, Gypsy?" But he allowed himself to laugh and be pulled back down the stairs by Molly.

More than a week went by and Snipe stayed in the room, playing with her presents or sleeping. Sara tried to bring her down the stairs, to get some air in the courtyard or out in the street, and Snipe begged to be left in the room, began to cry again when Sara tried to insist. "I can't, I can't."

"But you must. You won't get well until you go."

"I can't."

Sara realised she was afraid of being seen, or not so much afraid as ashamed. She hid her face against Sara's dress and clung to her, saying, "Please don't make me. Please. Please."

Until at last Sara had to force her. "If you don't come down, I'll bring Dido up and he'll carry you downstairs."

"You wouldn't."

"I shall. Don't be so silly. Come down now."

"They'll look at me."

283

"No one knows."

"Everyone bloody knows. I bet it's been the biggest laugh they've 'ad for months."

"Well, you can't spend the rest of your life in this room whether people know or not. There's no one about now, only Jim doing the yard, and he saw you when you came back."

She brought her down, Snipe leaning exaggeratedly on her arm, pretending to be even weaker and more helpless than she was, and that was weak enough. The sweat poured on her face as she went down the stairs and they had to stop every few treads to let her rest. In the courtyard Jim rolled a small cask out into the afternoon sunlight and Snipe perched on it, leaning against Sara's shoulder; they stayed there for a quarter of an hour, Snipe's eyes shut, her face lifted, and her color did seem to get better.

"I must 'ave walked an' 'undred bloody miles to get back 'ere. An' now I'm near better an' I can't walk down the bloody stairs without 'elp. Funny, ain't it?"

They met Monkey on the way back up to their bedroom and he pulled one of Snipe's ringlets and said, "Poor bloody rat. Did they 'urt you much?"

Only Janet was unkind about her, saying that if Sara and Molly could work so hard for a stupid slut like Snipe they could do a bit more of what they were supposed to be doing, and she took to spending an hour at a time away from the gaming room and doing less and less in the dining-room during the endless mornings.

"I could kill her," Molly said. "Why don't you tell Monkey what she's doin'? Or not doin' rather." The next day she and Janet had a savage quarrel in the kitchen, and Maggie had to separate them and call Ben for help to take the iron frying pan away from Molly, Janet crouching white-faced and shaking behind the shelter of the heavy kitchen table. Monkey came down and slammed his fist on the same table, swearing that he'd get rid of the lot of them and that the first one that opened her mouth again he'd break her neck.

"You don't need to go breakin' my neck," Molly

284

said. "I'm goin'. I carried the last tray I'm carryin' up those stairs while she lies on her back with Tom an' Dick an' Harry on top o' her like London Bridge. If you don't want to make her work, then you best find someone to do her work for her, like we been doin'. But I ain't doin' it no more."

"You ain't bloody well going nowhere," Monkey shouted, and then at Janet, "You shut up snivelling, you whey-faced whore. God Almighty tries to get an hour's sleep an' you bitches start fighting. I'll smash your bloody teeth down your throat if you don't shut up, I'll give you to bloody Danser for nothing only 'e wouldn't take you. 'Oo wants to taste my belt?"

Three days later Molly went. In the afternoon, slipping down the stairs secretly, all her clothes bundled into a sack. She'd spent five minutes packing them, pretending at first that she was only tidying them away, and then ten minutes crying on Sara's shoulder.

"At least you should tell him you're going," Sara said.

"How can I tell 'im the way he carries on. Didn't you hear 'im t' other day, shriekin', and threatenin'? You tell 'im for me, he won't say a word if it's you as tells him."

Snipe watching them from her mattress, her eyes full of worry.

"You ain't goin' 'cause of me, are you, Moll? I'm near better, I ought to 'ave gone out o' this a long time ago, I didn't think—I'm in your way a lot, ain't I?"

Molly flung herself down on her knees in front of Snipe, began to throw her arms round her and caught the gesture just in time, held her face instead between her big hands. "It ain't you," she said. "O' course it ain't you. It ain't even that Janet, nor Monkey, it ain't no one, but me." She hesitated and after a second or two said in a swift rush of triumphant confession, "He's givin' me the most beautiful li'l place you ever seed, red curtains on the windows an' a great big bed like them shells you see with the pink things in 'em, all frothy with satin. He took me there to see yesterday afternoon an' I could a' just collapsed on that bed there an' then if he hadn't bin there."

" 'E'll be there the next time as well."

"Just to kiss my toes, mebbe. I got 'im so he don't know where he is, half the time, just dribblin' like a baby." She rocked back on her heels, laughing. "You got to come up an' take tea with me and we'll play ladies all afternoon. He's givin' me a maid to look after me! An' comb my hair an' wash my stockings an' make supper for us when he do come. He didn't want her at first, that's what we been arguin' about, days and days now. He said he didn't want no one spoilin' our little secret place an' listenin' an' pryin'. So I told 'im once I leave here I ain't never going to wet my hands again, 'cept with cream, nor carry no one's supper nowhere, let alone cook it. A' what does he think I'm goin' to do all day long, with no one to talk to, when he ain't there? So he's found her a li'l attic room at the top o' the same house where my rooms are." She spread out her arms wide and shut her eyes. "An' the bed full o' feathers, so soft you just sink in 'em like the marsh, down an' down."

"I thought you hadn't tried it out, yet?" Sara said.

"Only just pokin' it with my finger. Don't you fret for me, Sara Pownall. An' when I want to do something like that, I don't need some old black parson preachin' over me first. Do you think that do make it different?"

"I suppose it doesn't."

"I'd better be goin' if I'm goin' to. Oh, Sara! Why won't you act proper an' go to be happy with Mr. Summers, then I wouldn't feel so bad leavin' you."

"I'll help you carry your things down."

"I don't need no help with 'em. Just if you'd look an' see Monkey or no one ain't on the stairs."

They got down to the courtyard without anyone seeing them, except Jim, and he opened the street door at the head of the stone steps, and let them go out. Molly touched his hump and patted him; he grinned at her with his black teeth.

"Promise you'll come an' see me every afternoon? I got the address wrote down here for you 'case you forget where 'tis." She stood holding her sack of clothes, her dark blue French velvet bonnet tipped backwards on her red hair, her face filled with sadness. "I don't want to go now," she said.

"Then don't go."

"I'm just silly. I *got* to go. I want to, really. I don't know what I want, it do seem so long we bin here an' it's only a little time, after all, just the summer." She dropped her sack on the ground and flung her arms round Sara's neck and cried again and began to laugh. "Aren't I master foolish? Wait till you see my curtains, an' there's a pipe with brasses an' *I* won't have to clean 'em even. Oh, I'm so happy," she said, and cried more.

They heard sounds beyond the door, down below in the sunken yard, and Molly snatched up her sack and backed away from the door. "If that's 'im comin'! Tomorrow afternoon, mind!" she whispered, turned, and ran, hurried with long country strides in her blue sandals, the flounces of her dress dancing. Sara watched her until she was no more than a distant splash of white and blue at the far end of the street, half lost among the passers-by at the cross-road. Turning and waving. Gone. As though the last of Thaxstone had gone with her, the last of the captain, the last of . . .

Sara went down into the yard again, found Ben there with Jim, hurried by them before Ben could ask her anything, and went quickly back up the stairs to Snipe.

Only Mr. Summers came that night, and he said nothing to her about Molly or about Mr. Hunter, as though he knew how she must be feeling. And Monkey was so angry she had no time to feel anything very much.

"I'll 'ave bloody Brown after 'er, I'll kill 'er, the bloody great 'ore's slut. What the 'ell am I going to do? No bloody notice even. Not so much as workin' out 'er week's wages. When I gets 'er back I'll—"

Even Janet seemed frightened of him for the length of at least that night, and scarcely disappeared at all. The next day he brought Sophy in to take Molly's place, and found another girl for the daytime in the dining-room, a small, plump creamy girl from Devonshire who crept round for a week as though she expected to be raped at any moment, and then seemed slightly disappointed. She became Janet's slave, and Sara had the feeling she was alone against the other three, that they were watching her, resenting everything about her, from the fact that Monkey never shouted at her or threatened her, to her never going to one of the small upstairs rooms with any of the men.

The fourth day after Molly left, Mr. Hunter came to the gaming room himself, although only for long enough to deliver a furious message from Molly. "I am to tell you that she will never speak to you again, but that nevertheless you are to present yourself at her address tomorrow without fail, on pain of the Bow Street runners being despatched en masse to fetch you to her. And you're to bring Snipe with you. She wishes to know why you have broken your promise and are you angry, and—oh, a string more of deeply important matters that I have clean forgot, but no doubt she will ask them all again of you when you arrive."

"Shall you be there?"

He looked at her, his eyebrows raised in mockery. "Lud, is that the terror that has been keepin' you away? D'ye plan to join the Evangelicals, or are ye just not fond of men?"

"I couldn't leave Snipe."

"Well, dammit, bring her with you, as you are bid. And no, m'dear, I shall *not* be there, so have no fears of havin' to blush for anything. But don't fail her," he said, dropping his teasing tone. "She has sat four days expecting you, and cried so much the poor slavy is exhausted mopping her dry."

"Tell her I'm sorry," Sara whispered. "I did indeed mean to go to her but—"

"Then tomorrow," Mr. Hunter said.

Mr. Summers came later and took his usual glass of champagne and stood waiting for her by the curtain. "How is your patient tonight?"

"I'm to take her visiting tomorrow," Sara said. Strangely, she'd come to value these odd moments of

288

conversation and no longer cared what anyone might think of their talking together. He'd urged her twice more to think of going to his uncle in Wales, then abandoned the subject.

He said now, "I'm going to Wales myself in a few days. I shall miss my visits here. It's curious. I dislike champagne, and crowds and gambling, I'm not sure which I dislike the most. My father believes I'm obsessed by play."

"Do you tell him that you come here?"

"I don't need to. He has me watched."

"Watched?" she said, astonished.

"By a man like your friend Mr. Brown," he said indifferently. "As a minister, my father has whole gutters full of spies like Mr. Brown, and once you have spies you must give them something to spy on or they grow unhappy. It scarcely matters what. My father probably knows every detail about you as well." He spoke not with bitterness but with a kind of tired distaste.

"Shall you stay long in Wales?" She tried to sound merely polite.

"Shall you miss me?"

She hesitated and looked at him. "Yes," she said.

He smiled at her and the likeness to the captain made her close her eyes for a second. "What's the matter?" he said.

"Nothing."

"Will you tell me more about old—about Mrs. Talbot before I go to my uncle?"

"I've told you everything."

"Do you really think that's true?" He smiled again. "Molly has told me more of the reality of her in ten minutes of her nonsense than all your careful guardedness has told me in half a dozen conversations."

"What has she told you?" She held the anger back, controlled herself.

"You look your best when you're angry," he said. "Like my stepmother."

"I have to go," she whispered, but didn't move.

"I, too," he said. "My stepmother is giving a great reception tonight and I shall hear no end of the matter if I don't appear there before one in the morning. I shall dance with a duchess' daughter and tell her I've spent the first half of my evening in a gaming hell, full of thieves and wicked girls."

"And what will she say?"

"She will be jealous, poor wretch, and pretend to be shocked, and make up her mind that I must be converted to true Christianity."

When she came back to the alcove, he was gone; at odd moments for the remainder of the night she thought of him dancing with the duchess' daughter and tried to imagine what the daughter might be like and what it must be like simply to dance and not have to stand with a tray of glasses until half-past two and three o'clock in the morning and to be able to sit down when one wanted to. *I'm sorry for myself*, she thought, and tried to laugh but felt like crying.

The next afternoon at half-past three she brought Snipe in a hackney coach to Half Moon Street, and she felt her heart beating with an absurd excitement, almost fear, the whole length of the journey, Snipe staring out of the coach window at the streets as though she'd been away from them for half a lifetime. They knocked at the pink door and a tiny girl opened it, a girl even smaller than Snipe, about twelve or thirteen, in a lace cap and white lace apron over her pink dress, which looked as though it had been chosen to match the door. She had a small, pinched white face and button eyes, and curtseyed to both Snipe and Sara and called them "Mum." "She's expecting you, Mum. Mum." And before she could say any more or even close the door behind them, Molly came flying down the stairs, shrieking, "You came, you came. Ooh, I ain't goin' even to speak to you," and flung her arms round them, squeezed them, heard Snipe cry out with the pain and let go of her and kissed her, and half carried them both up the stairs, shouting, "Shut the door, Tib, an' fetch the tea, quick as you can."

Her rooms were on the first floor, a small rose-papered sitting room with a bow window overlooking the street and a glimpse of trees and the park across Piccadilly and behind it a small bedroom mostly filled with the famous bed, heaped with pink and gold and blue silk cushions, scattered with clothes, a black kitten lying in the middle of them thoughtfully sharpening its claws on a satin negligee. A wardrobe spilled more clothes out onto the carpet.

"You've got a kitten!" Snipe cried and picked it up, and the kitten scraped its claws down her cheek and drew blood. "Gawd above!"

"I found her in the street, ain't she beautiful? Charlie hates her, she scraped him in—I won't tell you where she scraped him, you should ha' heard 'im shriek." She fell on the bed laughing, spread her arms wide, and was buried in red satin and blue silk and down, the kitten jumping on top of her. She bounced herself up and down until the bed creaked and seemed in danger of collapsing. "An' what you think o' Tib? Ain't she a little sweet? Charlie wanted me to have a real old woman if I was to have one at all, but I found her in the orphan house an' just took her up an' kissed her she were so little. Oooh, Sara, what you think of it all, eh?"

They stayed all afternoon, Molly clinging to them to the last possible moment, crying and laughing when they left, and making them swear to come back the next day, to come every day, pressing a bottle of cordial and a basket of fruit into their arms at the street door, kissing them again and again, and tearing up the stairs to wave to them from her bow window, Tib standing in the doorway below, also waving, her eyes grown enormous with astonishment at how strange the world was outside the orphanage. Molly holding up the kitten, making it wave its paws at them.

"If 'e lets 'er down," Snipe said, "I'll stick a knife in 'im."

They walked home, wanting the air, although it was already late, Snipe casting a longing look down the Haymarket and up Regent Street. "Another couple o' days," she said, "an' I'll be back at work. I'll pay you for everything, Sara, I swear. You're the best pal I ever 'ad."

"Snipe!" Sara said. "You can't—you can't go and —do that again."

291

"What d'you mean?" Snipe said, astonished. "What the 'ell you *think* I'm going to do?"

They'd never talked about it all the time she was ill. As though they had both agreed that it must not be discussed. "You mustn't," Sara whispered, stopping her, making her look up into her eyes.

"Don't go puttin' your eye on me," Snipe said angrily, her own eyes frightened for a second, and then resentful, and after another moment trying to laugh, to make a joke of it.

Sara held the bottle of cordial against her breast, felt it like a cold weight of pain against her heart. "What do you mean?"

"What I bloody say." She hooked her arm under Sara's elbow, drew her along again. "Don't mind me, I'm nervous as a bloody cat from being indoors so long. Don't you worry about me. I think I'll go down to the Argyle tonight." She looked quickly at Sara. "Would you mind? I wish you could come with me."

"Of course I don't mind. Only—only you won't—"

"Gawd, are you mad? What you think the Argyle is? If I tried on anything like that they'd bar me for bloody life. No, I just want to see a bit 'appening, 'ave a chat an' a drop. It's a lovely place. Everyone dressed up to the nines, everything beautiful, an' all the swells there, an' I think, 'Just you wait, my lad, tomorrow down the 'aymarket I'll 'ave that sneezebox off you so fast you'll think it's been hit by lightning.'"

"Snipe, promise me!"

"Oh, shut up. You're like bloody—You're not, you ain't, I didn't mean that."

"Let me give you some money, Snipe. I've got so much saved up I don't know what to do with it. It's just lying there under the floor-boards."

"You leave it there."

She refused to talk about it anymore, trotted beside Sara with small dancing skips to keep pace with Sara's stride, complaining now and then about how fast they were walking. "You're like a bloody pony."

Monkey looked thunderous when she arrived a quarter of an hour late. Janet and Sophy and the new girl, Milly, who was eating her supper in the kitchen, looking up at her with sly dislike as though they had all been talking about her.

"We do 'ave a lovely time," Janet said. She was polishing glasses, Sophy putting them out in rows on one of the trays, ready to be filled when they were needed. " 'Ow's the 'ore?"

Sara stood looking at her for a second. She thought, *If I picked up that tray, if I smashed every glass on it onto the floor, what would they do?* And the temptation was so violent that her body seemed to shake with it.

"Mind she don't knife yer," Sophy said. "You can't never trust gyppos."

Monkey, who had been inspecting the first batch of pastries in the oven, straightened himself, slammed the iron rake on top of it. "You 'oring bitches," he said, his voice cracking on a squeaking pipe of rage, that from that gross head and body sounded not ridiculous but terrible. "You say one more bloody word to 'er an' I'll smash your face in with this, I'll brand you. Leave 'er alone."

"That wasn't what you was saying afore she come in," Janet said. "You said—"

Monkey crossed the kitchen, his feet like a dancer's, not seeming to touch the ground. He drove the hot iron rake towards Janet's eyes and she fell back against the wall, dropping the glass in her hands with a splintering crash onto the stone floor. She screamed "Don't, don't, I didn't mean it."

Sara caught his arm, hung on to it, and Maggie cried out like a wounded animal. *"Monkey! Don't touch her! Your own child!"*

"I'll touch her," Monkey whispered. "I'll skin her. Sweep up that bloody glass, you clumsy bitch, and you." He swung on Sara, shook her like shaking rain from his sleeve. "You get started. If you 'adn't been bloody late . . ."

All that night she felt Janet watching her, felt the hatred like something physical. She found herself waiting for Mr. Summers, half hoping he'd come, then hoping he wouldn't, as she thought of the eyes that would be looking at them if she stood beside him for a moment, the sneering. But he didn't come. Only Sir Thomas and two of his friends. She saw Janet talking to him, and all of them looking towards her, the men twisting their bodies round, peering down their noses in their dandies' fashion, Sir Thomas' pale, baby lips curving in a smile of malice. But she managed to avoid them and the evening came to an end at last and she ran up the stairs to see if Snipe was back and asleep. But there was no sign of her, and Sara stood in the middle of the floor, the candle she had just lighted quivering its smoking, crocus flame in her hand, the shadows slanting and moving on the walls and ceiling.

She realised that this moment had been in her mind all night, weighing on her, heavier and heavier as the night went on, and she'd stopped herself from running up the stairs earlier, had waited until—She felt her heart beating, the tightening of her throat. "Snipe," she whispered to the shadows. Without thinking of it, of what she was doing, she took the mirror from where it stood on a small shelf that Dido had made for her, held it, looked down into it as though she might find comfort there. And before she had time to look, before she realised she was looking, she saw Snipe running, saw her face white with terror, running like the wind. Only the dark and Snipe's white stricken face and that terror like a gasp of breath as she ran. And there was nothing in the mirror. It lay in her hands, reflecting the candlelight, and she stared down into it and saw nothing, except her own white face, white with the unreasoning fear for Snipe. What was she doing? At three o'clock in the morning. What time did the Argyle shut? Twelve? One? Surely long ago. She put the mirror away and went back downstairs to the gaming room, where Monkey was still counting the takings with Ben.

"Have you locked up yet?" Sara asked. "She hasn't come back."

"Dido's locking up now," Monkey said. "Three 'undred and forty-one, three 'undred and forty-two— 'Oo 'asn't come back? Snipe?"

"She said she was going to the Argyle."

"Well, let 'er bloody stay there," Monkey said. "I

bin meanin' to say to you, this ain't a bloody 'otel. 'Ow much longer is she going to stay 'ere? I wants to put Sophy in with you." He turned back to the counting. "Where the 'ell was I? Three 'undred and forty-three." The small piles of guineas, half-guineas, banknotes spread round him.

"Sophy?" Sara whispered. "Put Sophy in—"

"Gawd Christ!" Monkey cried. "Can't I even count the bloody take without some bloody slut interrupting? Right. Sophy. You tell that Snipe to find 'erself somewhere else. This ain't a charity 'ouse."

She turned and ran down the stairs, her mind blank with shock. Heard the rattle of the chain and bolts as Dido locked the street door. Heard Janet's low, fleshy laughter in the kitchen, the clink of a glass.

"Dido, Dido," Sara called. "Don't lock yet, wait, please, she hasn't come back."

"I got to lock up," he said. "Where is she?"

"I don't know. Oh, please, wait a little, let me look out."

The street empty. Dark. They waited five minutes, ten. Heard Janet going up to bed, someone with her, giggling and kissing on the landing above them. "I got to lock up," Dido said. " 'E'll go mad if 'e finds I ain't done it yet."

"Let me stay down here. If she comes I can unlock for her."

"She won't come now. She knows it'll be shut."

"Where can she be?"

They stayed together for half an hour in the dark, the door locked, Dido squatting on his heels as though beside a fire. She sank down into the same position, shut her eyes. She was so tired she fell asleep, dreamed that she was beside a fire, that the captain was there, she could hear him in her sleep. She woke and it was Dido moving, whispering.

"*Pen?*"

"Yes?"

"Nothing." After another moment he said, "She ain't going to come now. You go on up. I'll wait a bit."

When she tried to argue, he lifted her up and she

tried not to shiver as he touched her, not to draw away.

"Run quick," Dido whispered. He let go of her; she stood still for a moment and then ran. She stopped on the landing above him and turned back. His face was no more than a pale shadow against the dark mass of the door, staring up at her.

She lay down in her clothes, lay for an hour listening and fell asleep, and woke two, three hours later out of a nightmare of Snipe running in the wood, the men—fragments of earlier dreams twisting and jagged in her mind. Snipe screaming, screaming, the small, thin body twisting, struggling, held down. She started awake, listening, the daylight already a bright square of sky above her head, the sounds of traffic in the streets, iron cart tyres, voices. She stood on the small landing outside her door, listened again, crept down the stairs of the silent house, down to the street door.

The bolts were greased and slid easily but the chain rattled and she stood holding it, her body rigid, afraid that Ben, Maggie, Monkey might have heard her, might come out of their rooms to see who was there. Turn the lock. Ease the door open. And nothing but an empty street. A boy clattered past, saw her standing there, gave a jeering whistle. No one else. A cart coming, loaded with barrels, the two dray horses still fresh with the morning, tossing their huge heads.

The carter lifted his whip, called out a rude joke. She closed the door slowly, eased the lock back into position, and went up the stairs. She lay down thinking, *I should have stayed there, left the door open and stayed beside it.* She meant to get up and go down again. In five minutes. Less. Just to lie down for one more minute. But she fell into a well of sleep, woke to Maggie's hammering on her door, "Get up with you, are you dead?"

She ran down the stairs, no more than combing her hair and sponging her face, hoping to find customers already in the dining-room, someone she could ask if they'd seen Snipe. There was no one there, and it was eleven o'clock before a girl came yawning in for coffee and brandy, and said yes, she'd seen her in the Argyle just before midnight, talking to a man. "An old, fat buffer. I think she went off with 'im."

"Snipe? With an old man?"

"Why bloody not? What's so special about Snipe? Are you gettin' me that tot, for Gawd's sake?"

Twelve o'clock. One. Two. Half-past. Sitting down to her own dinner, unable to sit down for more than a mouthful or to swallow the mouthful. *I'm mad*, she thought. *Stark mad. She'll come back today, tomorrow, sometime. What does it matter to me? She's looked after herself all her life, why should I . . .*

As though she was unable to breathe or as though her breathing brought no air into her lungs. She pushed her plate away, went out into the dining-room again, went to the street door and stood there, gulping in the air that, if it wasn't fresh, at least smelled of other things than cooking. She stood there for five minutes, telling herself what a fool she was, and was turning away when she heard the sound of running. A swift pattering of feet like a bird running on a roof. She turned and saw Snipe half-way down the street towards her, looking over her shoulder, and it was the exact image of her dream, the turn of her head, the swiftness, the panting breath.

"Thank Gawd you're 'ere," Snipe gasped. "I threw 'em off. Quick, in the back."

She tried to stop her, without knowing why, but Snipe brushed past her, slid away from her hand, was through the dining-room like an arrow, into the kitchen, Sara behind her. "I got a bloody load o' stuff," she panted. " 'Allo, Mag; 'allo, Jan." She tugged Sara with her, out behind the kitchen onto the stairs. "You got to 'ide it for me, just till tonight." She was dragging things out from the depths of her inside pocket, which hung round her waist under her skirt. The glitter of a gold box, watches, a leather pocketbook.

"What have you been—"

"What the 'ell you think? 'Old your apron out, for Chrissake. 'Urry up."

She did as she was told without thinking, Snipe throwing the things into her apron until it sagged with the weight and she stood like a fool staring down into the small mass of gold and tooled Morocco leather and shabby, over-filled calf.

"Get up the bloody stairs with it. Listen, I'll be back round midnight, I swear to Gawd I won't leave you with it."

Janet's voice behind them. "What are you doing, what've you got there?"

Snipe pushing Sara's hands against her stomach, closing the apron like the mouth of a small sack, pushing Sara up the stairs. "Nothin', Jan, nothin' at all. 'Ow you bin?" And in a whisper to Sara, "I'm goin' out the other way, down through the cellars. See you tonight."

She was gone. Sara ran up the stairs, trying not to let the gold clink as she ran, in terror that Janet was following her, that—Trying to think, midnight, hide it, and then so furious with Snipe she missed her step and sprawled on her knees in front of Dido coming down.

"What's the matter, *Hani*? What's the 'urry?"

She wanted to tell him, could have spilled the contents of her apron on the stair tread at his feet and begged him to help, to run after Snipe and bring her back, but she only pulled herself together, said, "Nothing, nothing's the matter," and ran up past him into her room, pushing the bolt home, throwing herself on her knees by the mattress and opening the hiding place under it, scraping so clumsily at the edge of the loose board in her panic that she broke a fingernail.

She untied her apron, wrapped the things tight in it without even looking at them, stuffed them as far under the boards as she could reach, and then went to her door and listened. No one there? She drew the bolt, opened the door suddenly. Half expected to find Janet there. But there was no one. Not a sound beyond the ordinary sounds of the house.

She went back and sat on her chair, stared at the mattress, at the hidden place under the floor, at the door, the wall. *I'll kill her*, she thought. *How dare she do it? How dare she?* And then, *The fool, the fool, the stupid, stupid idiot.*

She sat twisting her hands together, listening for footsteps, her fury dying away and sheer terror taking its place. And then fury again, and then the terror. She wanted to go down to the kitchen, to find out if Janet, anyone, had seen what Snipe had given her, to see if they'd say anything, discover—But the kitchen would be empty, everyone would be asleep or in the gymnasium. She thought. *I could take them to Molly. She's expecting us, me. I could ask her to hide them, no one would imagine*—But she knew she couldn't. And the thought of walking through the streets with those things, even taking a coach, made her skin prick with fear. She tried to tell herself it was she who was the fool. *Why am I so afraid? Of what?* Snipe lived like this, day and night, and laughed about it. She'd lived this way herself when she was a child, with the captain.

But it hadn't been like this. They hadn't been thieves. And there had been the captain. Like holding on to a tree, a rock. Being sheltered by a wall. And everything like a game, play. Not like this.

She tried to lie down and could not. Where had Snipe gone now, where had she been, who had been chasing her? Snipe! Snipe! And the small wicked face, half wicked and half child, laughing, jeering, was in front of her eyes, like a ghost. She put out her hand for her mirror, drew it back, shivering. Lay down. *What's the matter with me*, she thought. She knelt upon the mattress, clenched her arms round her body, shivered as though the room was icy cold, and yet she was also stifled with the heat. *I'm going mad*, she thought, *it's because I haven't slept. I'm going to be ill*. And that too was a terror. *If I become ill*, she thought, *they'll put me out in the street*.

She lay down at last, almost fell asleep, half asleep for a few minutes, waking with a start, lying staring up at the skylight. There were clouds, the sky growing leaden with thunder, a summer storm. About six o'clock the storm broke; the rain lashed the skylight like hail, swept against the slates of the roof, eased. Thunder rolled; flashes of lightning lit up the room and ran jagged across the square of black cloud that she could see. Seemed to run down the inside of the sloped ceiling. Even behind her eyelids when she shut her eyes against it. Lightning and thunder crashed so close together that they were almost one. And then more distant, the thunder rolling away down the river, the rain coming again, a steady drumming, a soft, drenching heaviness. It was time to get dressed for the evening.

The evening dragged its length. There were far less customers than usual because of the rain, and for half an hour at a time she was standing idle with nothing to do but think about Snipe, about the things hidden under her floor, to tell herself for the hundredth time that she was mad to feel as she did, ridiculous. She had known what Snipe was from the first day, the first hour of meeting her. Was it different now because she'd seen what she stole? *I am simply a coward*, she thought. *I'm afraid. For Snipe. For myself. Of what? If anyone had been following Snipe, had known where she was going, they'd have been here long ago. In another two hours, an hour, I'll kill her*, she thought, *I'll take her by the hair and shake her till she screams. How dare she, how dare she!*

She began going half-way down the stairs, as though she were on her way to the kitchen for something, and stayed for five minutes at a time waiting, listening. Twelve. One. Only a dozen gamblers left. Half a dozen. Monkey with his cash box. And Snipe came in, drenched and breathless, laughing at her. "You look like I was a bloody ghost. 'Allo, Monkey; 'allo, Jan." Sliding her arm under Sara's, tugging at her, looking up with her eyes wide with innocence, laughing at her. "Are you mad at me? Come up an' give us the stuff an' tomorrow I'll pay you everything."

"I don't want to be paid."

"But I'll pay you just the same. 'Urry up, I'm goin' to bung it in Ikey the fence's dead box an' I'll collect off of 'im tomorrow dinnertime. Did you 'ave a look at it? If you wants one of the clocks—"

"I could kill you," Sara whispered. They were on the stairs.

"Get away with you. I'll 'ave you broke in yet. If you'd been working with me, I'd 'ave bin safe as the bloody bank. It's 'aving to carry it when you've nicked it that's the trouble. Get it for us quick."

Snipe standing outside her door, keeping watch. Sara drew out the bundle, gave it to her, still wrapped. "I'll give you back your apron tomorrow," Snipe said. Dropping the bundle into her deep front pocket, a muffled chink of metal. She patted herself, blew a kiss, was running down the stairs.

"Snipe!"

"What is it?"

"Don't go. Where are you going to sleep?"

"I'll be back in 'alf an 'our, tell Dido to wait up for me." Her footsteps echoing for a moment, vanishing. Sara hesitated, her heart thudding, ran down after her, called in a low desperate whisper, "Snipe! Come back!"

Heard her at the street door, laughing with Ben, who was down there, heard the door opening. *"Snipe!"*

She heard Snipe cry out, a frantic, frantic cry of terror, the scuffling of feet. Threw herself down the last dozen stairs in a scrambling, falling leap, was at the door beside Ben, out into the street. And four men there. Three of them gripping Snipe by the arms and body as she twisted like a trapped animal between them, the fourth watching, turning to look at Sara. Mr. Brown. Smiling. Lifting his hand to the narrow brim of his hat, the rain dripping from hat and sleeve and cape, shining on his grey face like silver, falling in a cascade from a broken gutter far overhead, splashing down into the street.

"Let go of her!" Sara cried, tried to throw herself against the three men, and Mr. Brown put out his arm, held her back.

"Ho, no," he said. "Ho, no. Put her in the van, Mr. Samson."

It was only then that Sara saw the black, closed van, the two horses, their heads hanging in the rain.

"Sara!" Snipe screamed, and suddenly stopped struggling, stood looking at her, her ringlets plastered against her white face, her bonnet torn off in the struggle, fallen somewhere. She looked at Sara with a kind of horror growing there like sickness, her eyes

301

widening. "You didn't," she whispered, "you didn't peach."

"Information received," Mr. Brown said. "Very good an' exact information. Get 'er in the van there, Mr. Samson, an' we'll all get out of the rain. You're gettin' wet, miss, you best go inside."

She stood, not able to speak, to move, Snipe still looking at her with that sick horror in her face. The van door opening. They lifted Snipe off the ground, put her inside like a thing, a parcel, as though she were already dead. *Snipe! Snipe!* The door closing, closed. The men inside. Mr. Brown with his foot on the step to climb up beside the driver. "Sleep well, miss. You can drive on now, Mr. Abbott." The whip cracking, the van creaking into movement, swaying.

"Snipe!" she whispered, stood with the rain pouring down her face, down her neck, inside her satin dress, her petticoat clinging to her skin with the wet. Ben caught her by the shoulders, tried to drag her back inside.

"You're gettin' drowned, love. You can't 'elp 'er now."

She looked at him without hearing what he said, without seeing him, shook his hand away and began to run after the van, calling, "Snipe, *Snipe, Sn-i-ipe!*" Ran so fast she caught up with the van at the corner, clung to it, almost fell under the wheels, got herself to the front, where Mr. Brown and the driver were sheltered by an oilcloth apron and hood, tried to catch hold of the apron, to tear it from them, to climb up and catch hold of the reins.

The driver struck at her with his hand and then with the handle of the whip, caught her on the shoulder so her arm went numb for a second and she fell, the wheels rumbling above her, grinding the edge of her skirt against the stones, missing her leg by no more than an inch. She lay face down in the mud and the van rumbled away, the iron tyres echoing, grinding inside her head. She got to her knees, stared after it, the pain still ringing in her hands, where they'd broken her fall. The tears ran down her face, mixed with the rain.

302

Chapter 23

The van disappeared and she knelt in the mud and rain as though she had lost all feeling, all power of decision. A man went by, sheltering himself with an umbrella, saw her kneeling there, and hesitated, then hurried on, staring back at her from the far corner of the street. A carriage came from behind her, the sound of the horses' hooves now ringing, now muffled on the road, the tyres rumbling. A voice shouted, "Get out o' the way, get out o' the way."

The horses went by her, tossing their heads and shying with fear of the white thing in their path. The hub of the rear wheel caught her shoulder, sent her sprawling towards the far gutter.

She got to her feet and ran, not knowing where she was running, calling, calling, "Snipe, Snipe!" and stopped when she reached the cross-roads, stared this way and that. The carriage that had just passed her was already small in the distance, its carriage lamps flickering yellow in the silver mist of the rain, in the blackness. She began to run again, with an aim this time, towards Piccadilly and Half Moon Street. Molly, Molly and Mr. Hunter.

It was like running in water, her dress plastered against her legs and body, clinging, her hair drenched against her forehead, getting into her eyes, her mouth. She thought of nothing except getting there. Two watchmen sheltering in a doorway cried out, "Stop, stop!" but only half-heartedly and she scarcely heard them. Past the Argyle, long since shut, a few hurriers-by, staring at her as she ran, an occasional carriage.

Half Moon Street. All the windows dark. Stumbling on the steps, hammering at the knocker. "Molly, Molly!" Hammering and shouting. A window opened across the street, a face stared out, shouted, "Stop that row! I'll call the watch!" She went on knocking and calling. Another window opened. Voices shouting at her.

Until at last a window opened above her head, and Mr. Hunter called down, "What is it? Who's there, damn you?" And then, astonished, "Sara? Is it you?"

She went on knocking even then, until he came down the stairs and unfastened the door to her, in his shirt and breeches. Molly at the head of the stairs behind him, holding a candlestick, sheltering the flame with her hand. She fell inside the door, clung to Mr. Hunter's arm, crying, "They've taken her away, they've taken her away, you must help me, you must."

"Gad, you're wet," Mr. Hunter said. "Molly! Wake Tib."

They got her up the stairs and Molly lit a lamp. "Mr. Brown," Sara gasped. "He's taken Snipe."

The water ran down from her body, spread out in a dark pool round her feet. Molly crying at the news.

"You'd best sit down and tell us quietly," Mr. Hunter said. He looked at the water gathering round her sandals and said, "On second thoughts you'd best stand where you are and Tib shall put something under you."

Tib came down rubbing her eyes and yawning, stared in astonishment. "Fetch towels," Molly said.

"And brandy," said Mr. Hunter. "Hot brandy and water. Now, tell me again."

"You must get her out," Sara whispered. She told what she could, trembling with impatience at Mr. Hunter's questions, at Molly's and Tib's attempts to dry her. "You must come with me *now* and get her out!"

The punch came and they made her drink it against her will. Tib still hopping round her with the towel, like a tiny bird trying to build a nest. Molly wanting to make her lie down, take off her sodden clothes.

"Leave me alone!" She caught hold of Mr. Hunter, shook him. "You've got to come now!"

"What the devil do you think I should be able to do if I did come out with you? Do you think there's a fellow sitting up all night in Bow Street waiting to let prisoners out when their friends come and ask for their release? Let Molly undress you and put you to sleep on the couch and in the morning— "

She backed away from him as though he was threatening to take hold of her and make her lie down by force. "You've got to come!"

"Damnation, girl. Come where? Do what? Even in the morning what the blazes do you think I can do? Say to the judge, 'She took these things, I know, but since she's a friend of a friend of mine, please don't take on about it'?"

"They'll hang her!" Sara cried. "I know it!" She put up her hand to her neck, touched it, as though a rope was there.

"You got to go with her, Charlie," Molly said. "If you don't go with her now, I won't be here come morning."

"The devil take you both!" cried Mr. Hunter. "What do you think the law is? Did I make her go out and steal God knows how many poor fellows' belonging? The prince himself couldn't get her freed as she is now."

"Mebbe he couldn't," Molly said. "But Mr. Summers can if you ask him. Him or his dad."

"Where is he?" Sara said. "Where does he live?" She caught Mr. Hunter by the arm again, shook him by it so violently he had to catch hold of the mantelpiece to steady himself.

"Deuce take it, it must be three o'clock in the morning!" He felt for his watch, looked at the little pendulum clock on the mantelpiece, and threw up his eyes despairingly. "D'ye never wind the damned thing? Tib! Tib! What time is it? Find my watch."

It was ten to three.

"God knows where Harry is. And wherever he is, he'll be asleep."

"Then wake him," Molly said. "We'll all wake him. If we do have to throw stones through his dad's windows."

They made her change into dry clothes first, took Mr. Hunter's umbrella, and sheltered under it in the doorway, Tib behind them, while Mr. Hunter stared up and down the street in the hopeless expectation of a hackney coach, cursing them both, and Snipe, and the rain and all the race of hackney men. After a minute or two they began to walk, and before they were half-way to Park Lane and Lord Southcott's house, the rain stopped and the moon came out.

"He won't be there," Mr. Hunter said. "If he sees his step-ma twice in a month it makes him ill, and he's seen her once this month already. But someone may know where he is."

The house was lit, with half a dozen carriages in front of it and Lord Southcott himself in the doorway saying good night to guests, footmen holding torches to light them down the steps.

"You'd best wait out of sight," Mr. Hunter said. "He will think I'm stark mad."

They waited by the park railings across the road, saw him speak to a footman, and then to Lord Southcott, heard the old gentleman's cry of "Charles, my dear fellow! What do you do here at this hour? Come in, my boy." Drawing him inside. They waited.

"What they doin'?" Molly said. Sara leaned against the railings, listened to the dripping of water from a tree, stared at the lighted windows. A woman passed across one of them. Lady Southcott.

"One day I'm goin' to have a house just like that." Molly caught Sara's arm. "She'll be all right. You'll see she will. Come morning we'll have her out o' jail and laughing an' eatin' her breakfast just like nothin' had happened."

Fifteen, twenty minutes going by. It began to rain again, a soft pattering of large, warm drops. The lights in some of the rooms went out.

"If he don't come back pretty quick, I'm goin' to

fetch 'im. What does he think we are, leavin' us here?"

Mr. Hunter crossing the road towards them. "Harry's inside," he said. "We are to go in."

"I'm near drownded," Molly said furiously. "What you bin doin'?"

"What the deuce d'ye think?" He was leading them not to the front door but to a narrow archway beside the house. A small door opened, a servant held a torch there, let them into a passage leading to the stables at the back. A side door of the house stood already open and the servant guided them up a narrow stairs and into a small, panelled room full of books. Harry Summers was there, standing beside a writing table.

He looked tired and angry and at the same time curiously amused, as though he'd half enjoyed his anger. "Here she is," Mr. Hunter said. "Shall we leave her with you?"

"I ain't leavin' her nowhere till Snipe is let go," Molly said. "An' don't you think I will. Are you goin' to let her out?"

"You see, Harry?" Mr. Hunter said. "You can't argue with them."

"You must help her," Sara said. She leaned on the edge of the table.

"That's easier said than done." He rubbed his hand on his jaw, smiled slightly. "There's not much anyone can do, except find her a lawyer and perhaps say prayers."

"If you came with me to Bow Street," Sara said, "they'd let her out." Her voice became uncertain as she was saying it; it began to sound ridiculous even in her own ears. Mr. Hunter laughed and Molly hissed with anger at him.

"Mr. Brown," Sara whispered. "He would listen to you—if you asked—told him to—"

"It wouldn't rest with Brown. Not Brown alone. Even if you were right." He shut his eyes and rubbed his fingers into the sockets. "You'd best sit down, all of you."

There were chairs against the wall. She sat on one

307

and felt suddenly that if she hadn't sat down that second she'd have fallen.

"Your dad can do anything he wants," Molly said. Mr. Summers laughed, stopped as sharply as he had begun and sat staring down at his hands. "If I could help. If. If my father could—" He looked up, cried out with a kind of furious amusement. "Do you know what you're asking? What you're asking me to ask him? He spends his life in government trying to make the laws more severe, swears to his colleagues that if they don't hang and flog and transport twice as many evildoers this year as last, and with twice as great severity, the whole nation will collapse in ruins. And you come begging for him to save a wretched thief out of jail who is twice been within a hair's breadth of a death sentence and has learned her lesson so ill that she's scarce recovered from her last adventure before she steals again. From what Charles tells me she must have stripped half Piccadilly before she was caught. And this is the girl my father is to save from hanging!"

"He's just *got* to," Molly said.

"If he were to do this," Mr. Summers said, looking at Sara, "you would have to do something in return."

Mr. Hunter laughed, and Mr. Summers looked quickly at him, his face flushing with anger. "Charles!"

"Shall I take Moll away and leave you to your bargaining?"

"What you mean?" Molly said. "What does he—"

"Dammit!" Mr. Summers shouted and then dropped his voice very quickly, as if afraid of their being overheard. "Will you let me speak?" He looked at Sara, the angry flush still in his face, his voice cold. "If I do this for you, you are to promise me you will go to my uncle in Wales. Will you agree to that condition? And to stay there." He waited and she said nothing.

"I will go," she whispered at last. As though nothing mattered any longer. Not even for Snipe's sake. Simply because she was so tired.

"Where's Wales?" Molly said. "What you want her to go there for?"

"Be quiet," Mr. Hunter said.

"I have your promise?"

"Yes." She seemed to have known always that this would happen, this conversation in this room. A shadow there beside her, another voice. Mrs. Talbot. *You remember! The road that you must follow.*

"I promise," she said.

"Then I'll do what I can."

"That ain't good enough. You got to give us a letter now."

"Be quiet!" Mr. Hunter said.

"We ain't leavin' here without something writ down for Mr. Brown to let her go."

"She can't be let go," Mr. Summers said. "She'll be lucky if she isn't still hanged. But some things can perhaps be done."

"Give 'em a note saying what I suggested," Mr. Hunter said. "That they charge her with receiving, not stealing. There's a better hope there." He turned to Sara. "Have you told me everything? She brought you the things, left them with you, and came back to collect them?"

"Yes."

"And only this girl Janet saw her hand them to you?"

"I think so. I am sure. Only Janet."

"Did anyone see you give them back to her?"

"No."

"And Brown was waiting for her? 'On information received?' "

"Yes."

"I think that's the line, Harry. All Brown needs to do is to tell this Janet to keep her mouth shut and to say he arrested the girl on suspicion of being in possession of stolen goods she'd collected from someone unknown in Monkey's house."

"What good'll that do Snipe?" Molly said.

"Because receiving is not so serious as stealing, and with a ha'porth of luck we can plead that she didn't know they were stolen. She thought they'd been lost at gaming, or pledges against debts or something. At least it gives her a chance."

"I'm not putting anything in writing," Mr. Summers said, "not for Brown above all. What time is it?" He

309

looked at his watch. "It's past four." He nodded at Sara. "Can she sleep in Half Moon Street? There's nothing we can do for a few hours. I'll come and collect her there at, say, half-past eight?"

He stood up and brought them down to the court-yard again. The same servant let them out.

"What was all that about?" Molly said. "We ain't done all this just to have her hanged for somethin' different to what she really done. Or just for a chance o' not hanging. A chance ain't near good enough, I can tell you that."

"I'm too tired to explain," Mr. Hunter said. "You'll just have to believe me. At the most she'll stay in prison for a few weeks while investigations are made. The investigations will come to nothing and she'll be let out without a stain on her frightful character. With luck she may even be let out tomorrow. Today. And doubtless she'll be arrested the day after tomorrow for stealing something else. She may then be hanged twice nightly outside my windows and I shall not so much as get out of bed to watch. I've caught the most frightful cold, I'm sure of it, and my mother and my sisters will be already certain that I'm dead or gar-rotted, or both."

"But *how'll* she be let out?"

"For the love of heaven, stop asking me questions and have Tib make us all some rum and eggs. If she hasn't had the sense to light a fire, I shall use her to light one."

Sara walked beside him as though she was already asleep, swearing to herself that she would not lie down, would not close her eyes until he came at half-past eight. She lay down on Molly's couch and was asleep before Tib brought in the rum and eggs, stayed asleep while Molly tipped the thick, sweet mixture down her throat, wrapped her in a velvet cloak and blankets, and put a warmed brick against her feet.

She woke at what might have been six o'clock, tried to sit up, told herself she would get up at once, get dressed again, imagined she was doing it, and fell back into a depth of sleep like a dark cellar, was searching, searching, heard Snipe's voice calling *"Sara! Sara!"*

Far away. Stumbling through the dark to find her and the voice farther and farther off, faint in the distance, vanishing.

"Miss! Miss! There's a gemmun, a gemmun waiting." Tib shaking her awake, the little, pinched, astonished face like an exhausted sparrow looking down at her on the couch. Mr. Summers coming into the room behind her.

"By God, the urgency seems to have vanished suddenly. Am I the only one awake?"

She sat up, pulled the velvet round her, still half lost in the dark of her dream, trying to think where she was. Snipe. Snipe! "Let me get dressed," she said. "I am sorry, I didn't mean to. Give me one minute."

"You'll 'ave to wait in the 'all, sir," Tib was saying. "There ain't anywhere else."

Mr. Hunter's voice calling from the bedroom "Is that Harry? Gad, is it morning already?"

"I'll get the breakfus," Tib said. She turned round and round, distracted, not dressed herself as yet, wearing one of Molly's shifts that came down to her feet, a too-large muslin cap, and a woolen shawl of Molly's round her miniature shoulders, making her look like a very small old woman. "I'll get everyone breakfus I serpose?" She seemed already to be a hundred years old, to have had the cares of these rooms on her forever.

It was only then, in that moment, that the thought of what she had promised came back to Sara, and she started towards him, almost dropped the velvet cloak, caught it, and said "Please, wait. Not you, Tib. Leave us for a minute, I want to—ask Mr. Summers—"

He turned in the doorway, Tib sliding under his elbow like an untidy shadow. "My promise," she said. "What—what does it mean? Why do you want—?" She looked away from him, felt her face, her throat burn. "I—I was so tired—"

"Do you wish to go back on it?" he said.

"I don't know what I—what should I do in Wales?" She took a step away from him, felt the cloak slide, grasped it tighter. "You must let me dress myself. I—" She turned back towards him, a despair of anger

311

in her voice that he was forcing her, not only to do what he wished but to seem ungrateful, to seem to care more for—And behind all that, something else that she would not allow herself to think of. "I hardly know what I'm saying."

"I think you do not know at all." He caught hold of her by the shoulders, twisted her round to face him. "Don't you realise the position you're in? That you have handled stolen goods, knowing they were stolen? Kept them? And gave them back to the thief? Gave them back wrapped in your own apron that some devil's bitch in that house will be able to identify? Why do you think you're still free, and not lodged down in Bow Street along with your ridiculous friend?"

"She is *not* ridiculous!"

He shook her so hard at that that the cloak fell out of her hands; she was naked in front of him and he turned away in such anger that she felt at first a burning shame worse than if he had stood and stared at her nakedness. And then fury, and then terror. Of —of—She backed away, closing her mind against the things that seemed always there, that sound of screaming, her mother's hand against her mouth, wanting to scream herself, choking, choking.

"Are you covered?" he said.

She knelt down beside the couch, gathered the cloak round her, a blanket. She stood up slowly, the anger coming back, against herself, against her stupidity and weakness. "Yes, I am covered. And I'll keep my promise. I'll keep my promise. I'm sorry for seeming to—"

"I thought you'd change your mind," he said. He turned round, still angry.

"It's not for that reason. *I'll* keep my promise because I made it. Now, will you let me get dressed?"

There were already the sounds of movement in the bedroom, Mr. Hunter shouting that he couldn't find something, that the room was like a blasted milliner's with all the fal-lals in it, a man couldn't find top boots in it let alone his stockings. And how the devil could he shave without his man? He flung open the door

312

between the two rooms and stood there furiously, in shirt and breeches, his hair dishevelled.

"Ah, Harry. Gad, have they left you standing? Oh, have I interrupted ye?"

"No," Mr. Summers said, clenching his teeth. "If there's anywhere else I could wait for you . . ."

Mr. Hunter nodded at Sara, grinned at the way she was standing, cloak and blanket held against her like protections. "Tib! Tib! Ye must run to my mother's house and tell my man that I'm not dead or lying drunk anywhere, and as soon as my mother wakes, he is to inform her that I slept perfectly and have gone out for an early ride in the park. What the devil are you doing in that preposterous garment, child? And that cap? Did you go down to the street door like that? God above!"

He came back into the sitting-room as Sara was putting on her petticoat, or rather Molly's, her own still lying in a sodden heap with the rest of her clothes, wherever Tib had put them.

"That looks vastly well," Mr. Hunter said. "Molly, you are to go out today with that child and obtain clothing for her that permits her to open the front door without scaring our visitors or having passers-by send for the watch. Vastly well," he said, turning his head towards Sara again. "Why the devil Harry should wish to send you to Wales—"

He closed the door and she finished dressing as quickly as she could and went out onto the landing and into the miniature kitchen, built like a swallow's nest at the back of the narrow house. Mr. Summers was standing in the middle of it, seeming to fill its entirety, drinking a cup of coffee.

"Her coffee is worse than her appearance," he said. "Where did they find her?"

"In an orphanage. I'm ready to go now. Shall we? There's no danger of our being late?"

"I've sent a messenger. He has told Brown already that we're coming, and Brown promises to meet us there and he'll do as I've asked him." He put the coffee down with a look of disgust. "I have a coach waiting below. We'll be there in plenty of time." He looked round the kitchen with the same almost-angry distaste that the coffee had roused in him. "Is your friend happy here?"

"I think so."

"Would you be?"

"No."

"You're a strange girl."

"There's nothing strange—"

"I didn't mean—" He broke off and laughed, the look of anger vanishing suddenly. "I'm quite looking forward to tormenting Brown. He's a most unhappy kind of man. I promise you we'll save your unfortunate friend." He smiled at her, seeming to make fun of her. "Although what we shall do with her afterwards, God in his wisdom knows. Will she steal again?"

"I am afraid so."

"So am I. Charles, why did you not find an orphan who could make coffee?"

"Apparently none of them can," Mr. Hunter said. "And Molly won't. I go home for mine usually."

"I will make it," Sara said. "If you're sure we shall not be late."

They arrived in Bow Street at half-past nine, a small crowd already there waiting for the vans to arrive from Newgate. Ragged women, mostly, waiting to see husbands or brothers or sons led out of the closed van and into the court rooms. A few men, some children.

Sara stayed in the Southcott coach with Molly, while Mr. Summers and Mr. Hunter got down to find where Snipe had been kept overnight. People stared at the coach, the coachman, the glistening horses, the coat of arms on the doors. At the two strange gentlemen going into Number Four across the road, up the stone steps. A dray pulled up in front of the Oyster House beside the court room, began unloading small barrels.

The two men came out again, crossed to the coach. "The clerk says she's likely to be across the road here," Mr. Summers said. He nodded towards the building beside them. The sign over the door said

"The Russian Hotel" and a larger sign above it advertised MEUX'S ENTIRE with a picture of what might have been a bear in the middle of the advertisement. "She would have been too late for Newgate, he said." He opened the door before the coachman could jump down to do it. They hadn't brought a footman. The ragged crowd stared still more, thinking that something was happening. Anything. The dray pulled away from the Oyster House and two boys ran after it, jumped on the flat tail board.

"Do you want to come in?"

"In there?" Molly said. As though already an enormous distance separated her from such a place. She got down doubtfully, Sara behind her and the coachman touched the brim of his top hat, closed the door with a soft, expensive sound of fine brass and silver lock and fitted, polished wood, and silk upholstery.

What does he think of all this? Sara wondered. *Of us?* And for the first time it crossed her mind just how much she was asking of Mr. Summers, and of Mr. Hunter. *And already I have tried to go back on my word*, she thought. There were no bars on the windows. Under the hotel sign was written Lodgings for Gentlemen.

"By Heavens, what kind of gentlemen?" Mr. Hunter said. "Gad what a stink." They went down a corridor. A man sat at the far end of it behind a hatchway. Fat, half asleep, starting awake as they came towards him, seeing well-dressed people and standing up in a tallow sweat of alarm.

"Yes, gents? What can I do for you?" Staring at Molly, at Sara, as though not sure whether they were ladies or prisoners.

"I have an order to enter," Mr. Summers said. "Was a prisoner Elizabeth Hargreaves brought in here last night? Or rather, this morning?"

"I'll 'ave a look at me book, sir."

"By Mr. Brown."

"Oh, yes, yes, a little small one, goldy 'air an' very wet. Yes, I got 'er safe, sir. Was you one o' the unfortunate gent'men what she robbed, sir? An' yer wants to hidentify 'er, sir?"

315

"We want to go in to speak to her. Please hurry."

The man came out from behind the hatch, his breeches undone and his belly hanging out like a great sack of lard. He tried to button himself, his unbuckled shoes slapping on the filthy floorboards, keys jangling on a huge iron ring as he took them down from a nail. "If you'll follow me, gents. An' the ladies want to come too? Mind the step, sir."

Another passage, stone floored. A door strengthened with iron straps. A grinding of lock and bolts.

"Get back with you, *get back*, blast you, it ain't court time yet. Visitors. You there, are you 'Lizabeth 'Argreaves? The gents what you robbed 'as come to identify you."

A stench of bodies, urine, rotting brick and timber, two barred windows so filthy they let in no more than a grimy twilight. A long bench against one naked, leprously plastered wall, a bricked up fire-place. Two buckets. Half a dozen prisoners there. An old woman, two men, a child, another woman. And Snipe, staring at them, not moving. Sara and Molly running towards her, stopping half-way.

"Snipe," Sara whispered. "We've come to help you."

As though despair fell from the walls, silenced everything.

"We'll talk to her outside," Mr. Summers said. The keeper began to protest and Mr. Hunter put a guinea in his hand.

"Outside with you. Double quick now. I'll be back for the rest of you soon enough. C'mon, don't keep these ladies an' gents waiting, damn you."

He pushed Snipe towards them. "I'm 'sponsible for 'er, mind. She got to 'ave the bracelets on. Come 'ere, duck, an' I'll put 'em on you."

"It won't be necessary," Mr. Summers said. "She won't run away. Come into the passage with us."

Snipe staring, from one to the other of them. A dulled whispering in the room behind them, the door thudding shut against it.

"Oh, Snipe," Sara whispered, held her. "You didn't think; you couldn't think. . . ." The small, thin body against her, crying.

316

"They bloody got me this time, 'ooever done it. I knew you was a pal."

"Listen to me," Mr. Summers said. He pulled her away from Sara, jerked his head at the keeper to leave them and go back to his hole. "You thoroughly deserve to be hanged and only one thing can save you. Listen carefully." He dropped his voice. "You didn't steal those wallets. You bought them in Monkey Palmer's gaming rooms, do you understand that!"

"*Bought* 'em? 'Oo from?"

"Someone you don't know. Keep your voice down. For God's sake, girl, if you knew what I'm doing for you. Just say what I tell you. And you will not be charged with theft, or pick-pocketing, but with receiving stolen goods, knowing them to be stolen. You'll deny that you knew any such thing, God forgive me, and you'll plead not guilty. There's a chance, a *slight* chance, that you'll be acquitted this morning. If you aren't, you will be remanded for further enquiries and acquitted later. I promise you. And if you're caught again, I shall—Dammit, shall I ever feel clean of this? Have I your oath that you'll never steal again?"

Snipe put up both hands to her neck, gave him a strange, crooked little smile. "I ain't got much choice, 'ave I? All right. Not—not even a little bit? Jus' now an' then?"

"Good God!" Mr. Hunter said. "I think we're wasting our time, Harry."

"I promise, I promise!" Snipe cried, clutched at Mr. Summer's sleeve. "I was only joking."

"It's an odd time for jokes," Mr. Summers said.

"You got to oath 'im proper," Molly whispered. "Swear on the book! I'll keep you, Snipe, I'll look after you."

"Oh, no!" Mr. Hunter cried. "Not as well as Tib."

"An' what a honour this is," a voice said behind them. "What a very great honour for such a 'umble place."

"Good morning, Brown," Mr. Summers said. "It's good of you to come so promptly."

The muddy eyes considering them all, the shapeless

317

face cracking, finding a shape, smiling. The colourless coat, which made him seem part of the passageway. The greasy hat. "Miss. Your servant, miss. Mr. 'Unter, sir. An' why wouldn't I come prompt, Mr. Summers, sir? Your father's son! An' such a gentleman as you are by your own rights! Why wouldn't I come prompt? An' 'ow is Miss Elizabeth 'Argreaves this morning? Slept well, I trust?"

Sara held Snipe's arm before she could answer, held her close again.

"We have told her," Mr. Summers said. He turned to Snipe. "You understand everything? You're to be most grateful to Mr. Brown. He's prepared to act with great generosity in this matter." The words came out of his throat like stones.

"It's my pleasure to be generous," Mr. Brown said. "Generous to a fault, I've always bin. It's been my worst 'andicap in life." There was a repulsive confidence about him, like a smell.

"Call the keeper," Mr. Summers said. "And have her put back inside."

"It will be all right," Sara whispered. Touched Snipe's hair. "We'll be there to see what happens."

She waited until the door closed on Snipe and went slowly down the passage after the others, Mr. Brown bowing, lifting his hat to show his bald, yellow skull, the smear of grey hair pasted across it, his voice rising in contortions of obsequious innuendo. "You may depend upon it, gent'men. Old Sir Nat 'as 'is tantrums an' 'is bad mornings, but 'im an' me gets on like a 'ouse-on-fire most o' the time, we 'as a werry close hunderstanding."

He went with his sidling swagger across the road, shouldering his way through the crowd of ragged suppliants, grown larger now, and disappeared into Number Four.

"Gad what a brute," Mr. Hunter said.

Sara touched Mr. Summers' sleeve. "I have been most ungrateful," she said. "I am truly sorry that you should need to—that I should have asked you—but I couldn't—there was no one else."

"Walk aside with me," he said. They went half a

318

dozen paces down the street, away from the carriage and the other two. "There are things about this that you do not understand," he said. "But if you do what you have promised, if you go to Wales and keep my uncle company, make him happy for a little time—he will not live much longer, I think—then you will have repaid me." He clenched his fists, made a gesture as though he was going to lift them in the air in anger. "I never felt so vile in my life." He put his hand on her shoulder. "It isn't your fault. You have only wanted to help your friend. Perhaps I can explain one day. There are the prisoners coming, I think."

They had turned back towards the carriage, and she saw a van stopping outside Number Four, a long, black, closed coffin of a vehicle drawn by four sad horses that seemed in mourning. The crowd was gathering round the back of the van, struggling to get closer. A warder getting down, men coming out of Number Four, forcing the crowd back, women shouting, "Are you there? Are you there?" And then names of the prisoners as they stumbled out down the folding steps of the van into the daylight. All of them chained. Pushed up the stone steps of the court-house, the crowd following, struggling in the doorway.

A few moments later officers, Mr. Brown among them, going across to the Russian Hotel to fetch the prisoners from there. Sara shut her eyes, then opened them again for fear of missing Snipe, for fear of her not being there, of Mr. Brown tricking them in some hideous way. But she was there, looked round for them, lifted her now manacled hands in a cheery wave. An officer pushed her so that she almost fell on the steps.

"They're to take her first," Mr. Summers said. "Shall we go in?"

Again that smell of packed bodies, dirt, a strange, rancid smell of grease as though somewhere in the house a kitchen did nothing but burn wretched food. A clock as dusty as the windows. Five past ten. Dock, witness box, a railed-off dais at the far end of the long, crowded room. A screen hiding something. What? A crowded tangle of people coming, going, whispering,

319

writing, impossible to understand. Where was the magistrate? She had expected a court room like the Town Hall in Urnford. What was happening? She tried to ask Mr. Hunter and he said something she could not hear. More whispering, a door opening, a voice rapidly pattering something aloud, rattle of people standing, sitting, those of them that had chairs, Mr. Brown beckoning someone. Snipe. Almost hidden by the rail of the dock. Where was the magistrate?

"You are Elizabeth Hargreaves?"

"Yes."

She could understand nothing of what was happening. A voice from behind the screen, old, rusty, the words indistinguishable. Louder. "Plead, girl. You must plead guilty or not guilty. Which do you plead?"

"Not guilty, Milord."

Mr. Brown talking. "I 'ad reason to believe, on information received from a third party . . . appre'ended . . . I 'ave since learned—I understand the prisoner to be of unblemished previous character, your honour. The possibility exists, your honour, that this 'ere matter arises from an altercation between this female and another female that may 'ave sought revenge in this unfortunate manner. The goods are unidentified, your honour. The prisoner claims as 'ow she bought 'em in good faith. She 'as never been suspected of receiving before, no, your honour. Yes, your honour. The third party what laid the information 'as refused to testify, your honour, an' now claims uncertainty. Thank you, your honour."

"Case dismissed. Next case."

Snipe staring round her, her eyes unbelieving. Mr. Brown pulling her down out of the dock, pushing her away, his face twisting into its version of a smile, the lips writhing as though they'd been tasting wormwood, but a wormwood to be followed by a golden draught.

Snipe fumbling her way towards them, still not believing she was free, afraid to run, hurry, in case they dragged her back. Realising suddenly that her hands were still manacled. Mr. Brown unlocking the handcuffs, writhing his smile again, whispering something to her.

Sara pushed her way towards her, caught hold of her, wanted to cry, to laugh, to crush the thin, dirty, child-body against herself. Molly dragging them both out of the crowded room into the passage, the street. The coach waiting for them, the coachman impassive on the High Street, his cockaded hat shining in the sunlight.

"Gawd," Snipe said, drawing the air into her lungs as though it was a long time since she'd breathed. "I thought I was booked for Tyburn Fair." She hung on Sara's arm. "If I could only bloody steal something for you to pay you back. D'you think 'e really meant it, I wasn't to go nicking no more?"

"Yes," Sara said. "He did."

The others came out behind them, and they went across to the coach.

The coachman had got down, was holding the door open for them, his face unreadable. No more to be read in it than had been already there at the first sight of this street, this poverty. As though he was no more than looking down at mud that threatened his shining wheels, his paintwork, his glistening coachman's boots and smooth grey livery.

"Where are we going?" Snipe breathed, looking at the coachman as though she felt more fear of him than of Mr. Brown.

"Get in!" Sara said. Lifted her inside. Molly behind them, the two men. The coach moving, harness creaking, ringing, small boys running behind. Snipe held her hand.

Three

Wales

Chapter 24

The brake lurched, the off wheels hung over the edge of the track, mud sliding from under them, and Sara looked down a hundred feet of broken rock and scree to a white lace of water in the gorge below them, thought, *We're going to fall*, and gripped hold of Snipe, preparing to jump if the brake leaned one fraction farther beyond the edge. The wheels found stone again, gripped, the driver cursed his horses in Welsh, and Mr. Summers cursed the driver in English.

"Oh, my Gawd," Snipe whispered, for the fiftieth time since Bettws-y-Coed. "I should 'ave stayed in jail." Black mountains. Rock. Heather. White rushing streams. Summer sky.

"It's all right," Sara said. "He must travel this road every day."

"There 'as to be a last day for everyone, and per'aps this is 'is."

"I'm more interested in whether it's ours," Mr. Summers said.

A bird hung far above them, lay on the wind, black against pale blue. Sara felt as though for the first time in months, years, she was breathing true air. Every twist of the mountain road like a memory. She wished that neither of them would talk, almost that neither of them were there, that she could be alone, walk up this twisting track alone. Or ride. If she closed her ears to the creaking of the wheels, half closed her eyes, she could seem to be in the mountains, long ago and

324

think, *He is there, walking ahead. I'm safe.* Or hear the steady fall of hooves in the dust. Only the real heat of the sun not there, on her neck, her shoulders. Like a burning weight. She wanted to lift her face to it, close her eyes against the burning on her eyelids. Round the next shoulder of the mountain to find a camping place. Rough grass, low bushes to cut for kindling, to lie on the warm rock.

But the air here was warm enough, the last of summer. To climb down to that stream, bathe their feet in it.

"This is called the Place of Eagles," Mr. Summers told them.

"The bloody eagles can 'ave it."

"You're the most wretchedly ungrateful girl I ever encountered," Mr. Summers said.

"I ain't ungrateful. I'm frightened. Is there really a real 'ouse where we're going?"

"No. We're going to live in a cave with a bear. Where the devil do you *think* my uncle lives?"

"I 'aven't seen a 'ouse for hours."

"Shut up, Snipe. If you say one more word, I shall throw you down there."

"I 'aven't said anything."

"Snipe!"

They had come to the pass, a narrow saddle between the mountains. The track tilted down into the high neck of a valley, great shoulders of mountainside below them, a cup of green, the silver flash of water, a lake. Mr. Summers pointed. "There's the lake now."

It vanished as the road went down towards it, a blue ridge of rock and heather hiding it, and it was another ten minutes before it came in sight again. They seemed to have been travelling forever. The mail coach for a night and a day and another night, until it had become difficult to remember when they had not been travelling in it, jammed between other passengers, breathless in the heat of it because a woman with a small baby could not endure having the window opened. And the clerk on his way to Ireland, endlessly boasting about "His Grace's urgent business," and the fat man also on his way to Dublin to sell ribbons, who smelled of brandy and got drunker and drunker as the night continued, continually taking nips from his brandy flask "against the sea sickness. 'Orrible rough it is, they tell me." Oxford. Birmingham. Shrewsbury.

"Oh, Gawd, not Shrewsbury, I ain't gettin' down 'ere," Snipe had said and had stayed in the coach the whole half hour they had been allowed to stretch themselves while the horses were changed, whatever her memory of Shrewsbury had been. *Was this where it had happened?* Sara wondered. But she hadn't liked to question her about it. Mr. Summers travelled on top with the driver, and she had longed to ask if she could as well but had been afraid to ask him anything after the one enormous achievement of bringing Snipe. It had taken an hour, his first amusement turning to fury, and then to a cold rage as he realised how determined she was. Threats, appeals to her promise, to commonsense, to Snipe herself, who had sat white-faced and mute in the corner all the time of the argument.

"You promised!"

"I'll keep my promise. I only wish to bring her with me."

And Snipe had seemed half-a-dozen times on the point of destroying everything by whispering that she didn't *want* to go, opening her mouth to begin saying it until Sara caught her eye with such ferocity that she stayed quiet. Mr. Summers had guessed it without her need to say anything.

"She doesn't *want* to go to Wales, Goddammit. You're not her keeper!"

"Nor are you mine. I want her to come. And I don't want her to stay here and be hanged. What do you think she'll do if we leave her here?"

She had won, and he had even shown good grace in giving way, laughing about it in a helpless fashion. "If my father should find out," he said. "And my uncle. What shall I tell him?"

"That you have brought him *two* amusements instead of one," she said against her will, her voice becoming harsh.

"You're a damned strange girl," he said, looking at her. They'd hardly spoken after that, beyond the few necessary words of the journey. And after Shrewsbury, into Wales, Llangollen, Corwen. The ostlers speaking Welsh between themselves, a difference in the faces, darker seeming, sharper cut. And the small stone houses and the fearsome road that they were rebuilding, great piles of stones alongside it. And at last Bettws-y-Coed and the sudden emptiness of the narrow, closed valley as the mail coach trundled and rumbled on towards Bangor and Holyhead, leaving them at the inn. They had to wait there for an hour for the brake to be got ready that would bring them to Llyn Owain and Mr. Gifford's house, and she had walked up the road for half a mile to stretch herself, while Snipe trotted beside her, protesting that she was mad, where was she going, why weren't they sitting snug inside with Mr. Summers 'aving a drop of something?

"Because I don't want to sit anywhere with Mr. Summers."

" 'E fancies you, Sara. 'E fancies you a lot."

"I don't want to be fancied by him."

He had followed them along the road after seeing to the hiring of the brake and brought them back, and although there had been nothing but courtesy in what he had done, it had seemed like the action of a jailer. And for all the twelve miles over the mountains towards Llyn Owain she had thought, *If I was alone*. And had accused herself of ingratitude, and thought it again, more and more strongly as the feeling of Spain came back to her, of the breadth of the sky. As though she was going somewhere she wanted to go, towards something she had known was waiting for her for a long time. And he would destroy it.

And yet but for him she would not be here, Snipe would—*I am wicked*, she thought. Felt so ashamed she could almost have touched him, taken his hand to show her gratitude. *Not*, she thought, *that he is very likely to want me to take his hand.*

He had told her very little more about his uncle, and almost nothing more of what she must do when they arrived. "Amuse him. Tell him things. And as for the rest, why, I suppose there will be things for you to do. How should I know? I know only he wants you with him."

"There's the house," he said.

The green meadow, the lake, was spread out in front of them as the road turned a corner, and the cliff fell back to become no more than a rough slope. A grey house was set on the far side of the lake, against the enormous curtain of the mountains. Grey stone, with narrow windows flashing in the evening sun, stone chimneys and steep slate roofs, trees behind it and to one side, and a long terrace and a lawn between house and lake.

"And there is Dinas Owain!" the driver was saying, pointing not at the house, but at the mountainside above it, where ruins jutted up from a shelf of rock, like rocks themselves. And the expectation was so strong that it choked her. Was knowledge. She knew the house, the lake, the lawn and terrace, the ruins hanging above it like an eagle's nest, knew what she would find inside the house, thought, *He is waiting, he is waiting for me to come*, and the voice inside her head was not her own but Mrs. Talbot's voice, her eyes seeing, looking with harsh arrogance at what she once had almost owned, had walked away from on foot without looking back, up that winding track behind them. The sense of pain, of a wound, an agony of pride and anger and bitter love.

I am gone mad, she thought, swaying on the rocking bench of the brake, on the broken leather of the hard cushion. She had to clutch the rail to steady herself. And saw with Mrs. Talbot's eyes, as though she was Mrs. Talbot, her own self driven back into a corner of her mind, possessed, that harsh force devouring her. She put up her hand to where the iron ring hung at her neck, gripped it through the cloth, clenched her mind against the threat of being overthrown, and was drained of strength and safe and emptied and chilled with such a desolation of sadness that it was like drowning in black water, ice cold and terrible. But not herself drowning. Only an echo of that mind that had walked away from this valley, how long ago? A tall woman in a grey cloak.

It was gone. She was looking at a pleasant house beyond a small, bright lake, a fringing of brown reeds at one end of it where the water must grow shallow.

"Is this where we got to live?" Snipe whispered in a small, frightened voice. "What will we *do*?"

A driveway that was no more than wheel tracks in the meadow led away from the road towards the house. The road itself continued on down the valley, disappeared among rocks, where the valley closed again. They were at the terrace, the front door, getting down. A manservant, women, an old gentleman in black saying that he was Mr. Gifford's butler, that Mr. Gifford would be most happy to hear that they had arrived, had scarcely been able to sleep for expecting them. But they would no doubt wish first to be brought to their rooms. The house was most honoured to receive them.

"Us?" Snipe said. " 'E mus' be daft."

They had hung back as Mr. Summers was greeted and he beckoned them forward now and presented them. "This is Miss Sara Pownall, whom I have mentioned in my letters. And this is her friend, Miss Elizabeth Hargreaves." No shadow even of dryness in his voice, and Sara felt again a pang of self-reproach at her ingratitude. The butler inclined his head. Snipe bobbed. Sara held out her hand and the butler took it. "You are welcome," he said. He had thin, silver hair, the skin of his face stretched tight over fine bones, parchment yellow. His hand old. "My name is Pritchard," he said. "You are welcome here."

She lived through the next hour as though it would never end, one moment longing for the end of it, for the knock on their door that would summon her to Mr. Gifford, and the next moment so afraid of its coming that she felt her throat closing. Pacing up and down by the window of the room they'd been given, high up in the house, but not an attic, not a servant's room. With two small windows looking out over the valley. Strange windows with stone frames and square, leaded panes each pane no bigger than her hand. A wide, handsome bed, a stone fire-place, rugs, chairs, a great wardrobe set into an alcove of the stone wall, the walls themselves panelled to the height of her head and above that merely painted white. The white ceiling crossed by heavy oak beams, grown black. The fire burning.

"It will grow cold in an hour's time," the butler had said. "You'll be glad of it." The woman who had helped them up with their small amount of luggage spoke only Welsh. An old, strong-looking woman, no taller than Snipe, looking at them out of sharp brown, questioning eyes. "I shall come for you in an hour's time if that is agreeable?" the butler said. "Rhonwen will bring you warm water and a dish of tea."

"I'd rather 'ave a pint of something," Snipe said, but only when both butler and woman were safely gone. The water came, and the tea, with oatcakes and butter and honey on a silver tray, set with silver. Snipe sat by the fire looking at it, holding the jug of milk in her two hands and stroking the metal with her fingertips.

"It ain't real silver?" she whispered, almost as though she wished it wasn't. And she drank her tea and ate her oatcake and honey as though she were afraid of touching the cup and the plate. When she'd finished, she went and lay down on the bed.

"Aren't you going to wash yourself?" Sara said. There was no answer. Snipe was already asleep, as though she'd been knocked unconscious by the tea and the warmth of the fire, lying with her mouth open, a tiny sound of breathing in her throat, like a bird ruffling its feathers. Sara covered her with the quilted eiderdown and stood by the window looking out. Had this been her room? Had she looked out of this window? She began walking up and down, from one window to the other, the light changing on the grass, the meadow, the surface of the lake. Growing wine-gold with evening. And the sadness of the house drew round her like a cloak of shadow, out of the stones, while the logs burned in the grate. What had happened? Why had she run from here, left this house?

And there seemed to be an echo of that familiar voice, saying, "Help him, do not be afraid." No longer bitter. Walking from one window to the other, now content to wait, now impatient, then fearful again, as though everything had led to here. She held the small iron ring through the muslin of her dress, shut her eyes, leaned her forehead against the stonework of the window. A knocking at the door. She went to it and the butler said, "He is waiting for you if you will come."

A long corridor. Down broad stairs. A wide, mahogany door. She felt cold, shivered, wanted to close her eyes against the room as the door opened. The windows already curtained against the evening, a fire burning but the room almost dark. And stifling. The heat of it flowing out the door. The shadow of a man sitting, wrapped in a dark, thick robe. Nothing else in the room.

"Go close to him," the butler said. "Take his hand."

She went very slowly and the man lifted his head. Heavy with flesh, the ruin of a face. Blind eyes. Searching for her, the yellow hand lifting from the velvet lap. Cold. She took it and the fingers closed, touched, drew her closer.

"Speak to him," the butler said.

"I'm Margaret's friend," she whispered. "I've come to stay with you."

"You have her voice," he said. He lifted his other hand, felt for her face, touched her mouth with his fingers, felt her jaw, her cheekbones, eyes, and forehead. Felt her hair. "Tell me how she died," he said.

Chapter 25

His fear of death was overwhelming, horrifying. Like a dreadful sickness of the mind. Not always, not all the time. For hours together, a whole day, he would seem well enough. Ready to be amused, to be nursed and cared for. To listen to Sara reading. He loved her to read to him in French, which he himself spoke well, with a low, careful accent, shaping each word in isolation as though he held it in his mind like a small jewel, considering it. Or he would make Snipe come to him and sit at his knee and talk while he fondled her head.

Snipe was so frightened of him at first that she couldn't speak without her voice shaking, and he seemed to know that and to be almost pleased by it; he sat for a half hour at a time merely touching her ringlets and saying, "I'm too old for you to be afraid of me. Many years ago, oh, *then* you might have been afraid." Until at last she could sit there quite willingly and she began to talk to him about things she'd never told even to Sara or Molly. About her childhood, before she was sold into the mill and the apprentice house, and how she'd escaped and made her way back to London.

Sara came in one morning and found her telling the old man how she'd learned to become a thief. "They 'ung a bell on this coat, see, an' you 'ad to pick the coat pocket without ringin' the bell."

"I'm glad you brought your friend." Mr. Gifford

said. "She's a good child." And later that night when Sara was alone with him he whispered, "If one could only become innocent again, as that child is," and held Sara's hand in his cold, shaking fingers and whispered still lower, "Can you imagine what it is to know you are damned?"

"No one can know that. No one." But she scarcely knew what he meant, no more than echoes of Dr. Newall's leaden sermons in her imagination, the lath-and-plaster Evangelicalism of Lavender Cottage.

"Hold my hand," he said. "It's so dark and so cold. Tell me again, promise me as you hope to be saved, that she didn't curse me? Please."

She tried to tell him. Felt his hands trembling, plucking at hers. "You will make yourself ill," she said. "I've been brought to you to help you. Not to make you ill."

"You were brought? You felt that? That she—that she brought you to me?" He touched her face again, the cold finger-tips against her mouth, tracing her lips, her chin.

"Mr. Summers, your nephew, it was he who brought me."

"But you meant more than that. You meant—I felt it. From the first moment I got Harry's letter! I knew. Have you the Ronsard there? Read to me, read those lines again."

She lit the lamp and knelt beside him, the book resting on his lap. *"Quand vous serez bien vieille, au soir à la chandelle . . ."*

"You have her voice." He found her hand, lifted it against his face, and she felt the tears run on her fingers, and they, too, seemed cold. "We loved one another," he whispered. "More than my soul I loved her. She was so beautiful." With an old, slow movement he drew her head against him. "And I think that you, too, are beautiful," he said. "They tell me so. They tell me you are like a gypsy girl. But tall and beautiful and very proud. Is that how you are?"

"I am tall at least."

"She was like a young tree in blossom. Does that seem foolish to you to liken a woman to a tree? When

333

I saw her first, I knew. The first moment. Before I married. I thought, 'She is like the morning.' A maid! A servant girl on the stairs, waiting to attend me to her mistress. And I knew in that instant that I was about to do something that would injure me all my life." He gripped Sara's head against his old, soft body, the cold velvet of the gown. "And beyond. And beyond! You cannot understand that, child. How could you, you are so young?"

"Why did you never send for her? After she left here?"

"I did."

"And she never answered you?"

"No." He sat quiet for a long time, holding her, the fire burning now bright, now dying, the lamp flickering. And gradually such coldness in the room that it was like death. Pierced through her thin dress, into her bones. She began to shiver, could not control the shivering. The flame of the lamp seemed to wither in its glass, die down, as though the room was walled with ice. "She is here," he whispered.

She tried to say, "There's no one here," and could not, closed her eyes, felt that shaking of her mind. "You must not," she whispered. "Be at peace. Lie still." And she saw the burned hut, the still reflection of the water. The grass had grown already over the scars of burning, the flowers had spread themselves. Honeysuckle had begun to clothe the chimney. "It is love," Mrs. Talbot's voice said. "It is love that brings me." Held his hands, tried to warm them against her breast.

Behind them the door opened, the butler came in with Harry Summers, and the kitchen boy behind them carrying more coal. "Are you well today, sir?" Mr. Summers said. He came and stood beside them while Rhonwen rebuilt the fire.

"You've found me a treasure for my old age," Mr. Gifford said. "Do you think she'll stay with me?" Touching Sara's head and face, as though his hands were saying, Do not mind my words. He's a stranger to us.

"I trust she will, sir. I'm not so sure of her friend."

"We must hang up a coat for her, with a bell on it," the old man said. "Has she told you of that?"

"No," Mr. Summers said, "she hasn't."

That night when they were in bed she asked Snipe what she'd done to upset Mr. Summers, and Snipe looked at her with huge blue eyes in the candlelight. "Done? Nothing. Nothing."

"You did something. I know it."

"I just said—I just said 'e 'adn't got no right to punish you for what I done, that's all. An' he got cross. But only a bit."

"He hasn't punished me. And you had no right—"

Snipe joined her small hands together as though she was begging and looked very mournful and then wicked. "Well, I think it's a bloody punishment. 'Ow long are we going to stay 'ere?"

Sara tried to be angry with her, felt for a second as though she were Miss Susannah faced by rebellion, felt almost a dart of sympathy. She got Snipe by hands and hair and shook her, pretended to stifle her in the pillow and then cuddled her like a cat. "What am I going to do with you?"

"I'll be good," Snipe whispered. "I mean to be good, every morning. Only—'alf of 'em can't even speak the bloody king's English. They're 'eathens."

"You must learn to read," Sara said. "And then you can read to him too."

"Read!" Snipe cried. "Are you mad?"

"Well, you can learn to keep house. You don't even know how to make tea."

"I don't *want* to make bloody tea."

"Well, we must find something for you to do or you'll—"

"I'll be all right. I promise. I ain't ungrateful, I swear I ain't. Only I never been anywhere like this, it's like being 'aunted."

It was the butler who found her something to do, almost by accident. He seemed to think of her as a child and was always giving her glasses of milk and asking if she had changed her slippers since she came in from the terrace. And that next afternoon, as though he'd been waiting to do it until he was sure

335

she was worthy of the honour, he brought her and Sara up the stairs to a room filled with dolls and a great doll's house full of miniature furnishings.

"You may play with them if you're very careful of them," he said to Snipe. And instead of laughing, Snipe stood looking without making a sound. Looking and looking. Dolls in dresses of the previous century, like ladies of the court, in panniered skirts of silk and taffeta and satin, with high, powdered wigs above their wax faces, their courtly smiles. French ladies. Gentlemen dolls in cloaks and uniform and cockaded hats. Dolls dressed as children, as babies. A doll dressed as a queen. Another as a king in a blue velvet cloak, with golden fleur-de-lys on it.

"That is her majesty, Queen Marie-Antoinette," Mr. Pritchard said. "And that is her poor king. You may touch them. Go on. Don't be afraid. Mrs. Gifford loved them and would like to think someone was playing with them again."

"Did she never have children?" Sara said.

"These were her children, Miss."

Snipe knelt in front of Marie-Antoinette, put out one hesitating finger, touched her ivory silk skirt, the ribbons, the shepherdess's crook. "Could I 'old 'er?" she whispered. She took the doll up as though it was the most delicate of children, held it between her hands. "And the 'ouse," she whispered. "Gawd above."

They left her there, and she had to be fetched down to her dinner. She ate hurriedly, her eyes lost in the thought of the dolls waiting for her, and vanished up to them again. Sara went to the window and looked down the valley. *I must find my own dolls*, she thought. Each afternoon she walked by the lake or down to the road and along it to where their valley ended. That afternoon she'd promised herself she would climb up to the ruins. She'd seen very little of Mr. Summers. He ate by himself in the great dining-room while they ate in a small room near their bedroom that Mr. Pritchard had had re-arranged for them as both dining-room and parlour, deciding for himself apparently what their rank in the house should be, neither servants nor guests. As for Sara's duties, they were never stated. Mr. Pritchard simply brought them to pass, escorting her to his master at the appropriate times, letting her understand when she was free and when she must wait to be called. Finding her the books she must read to the old man, marking the passages he would most want to hear. French poetry, and English poets of the seventeenth century, John Donne, Lovelace, Milton sometimes—More and Browne and Shakespeare and the Bible. The heat of the room making her head swim until the words shimmered on the page, and against her will her voice would become drowsy, whispering. And she'd stop reading, stay looking into the fire as if it had stolen her senses, and he'd stroke her neck and hair, sit holding her against his knee as though he was content simply for her to be there.

Until Mr. Pritchard or Mr. Summers would come in to them, bringing the old man his broth and watered wine for supper, or the news of what Mr. Summers had been doing that day. Visiting the farms that belonged to the estate, usually, or the woods farther down the valleys, with the agent, Mr. Parry. He spent most of the evenings going through documents about two law cases concerning the estate and sometimes had questions about them to ask his uncle. But on such occasions Sara would offer to leave him alone with Mr. Gifford, and he never prevented her from going.

He treated Sara politely whenever they met, there or elsewhere in the house, but he seemed to have drawn back into formality, as though he was determined she shouldn't think he'd had any motive in fetching her there beyond his uncle's welfare. It began to weigh on her a little, and she wondered if she'd offended him beyond explanation on the morning of Snipe's acquittal.

Snipe had no reserves about the matter at all and treated him as she treated Mr. Pritchard and everyone else except the old gentleman, with a cautious, birdlike friendliness that always seemed on the brink of impertinence and yet never quite became impertinent. As though she was protected from herself by innocence.

"I am beginning to understand why you like her," Mr. Summers had said. "I'm glad we rescued her, in spite of—"

"In spite of—"

"Oh, nothing. I'm glad, that's all. She's too childish to be punished for anything."

She thought of that now, looking out of the window of their parlour-dining-room, the remains of their meal on the table behind her. She had tried once or twice to help with such things as clearing their own meals away, but it had not been allowed. And there seemed to be so many servants in the house, it would have been pointless. Besides those who lived in the house —and they alone should have been enough for one old gentleman and three visitors—there were still others who came there every day from the small farms hidden here and there about the mountainsides. She guessed that anything she did for herself would deprive some other girl of needed shillings and schooled herself simply to ask for what she wanted, and to leave even their bed unmade and their clothes lying here and there, to be put up and folded and cared for. She'd begun to learn a few words of Welsh and said "Good morning" and "Good evening" and "May we have some hot water please" in Welsh to Rhonwen or whichever of the girls she came across in the corridors or down in the great echoing kitchen where she was never allowed to stay for more than a moment. As though the kitchen belonged to their Welsh dignity and must not be invaded.

She felt the house press on her, and went to their bedroom to put on half-boots and a spencer, and quickly down the stairs and out onto the terrace. Clouds drifted. Three sheep had strayed from some-where and were beside the lake, a boy driving them away from the lawns with shrill cries of "Hu! Hu!"

She began looking for the path she'd been told led to the ruins, found it behind the house, and began to climb. Within a few yards she was sorry she'd put on her jacket and took it off, felt even her dress cling round her like an encumbrance, and thought longingly of the time when she'd been dressed in a shirt and breeches and could run like a boy. She looked back over the dark grey rooftops and stone chimneys of the house and saw the garden boy running, his bare legs flashing brown-white against the bright green of the grass, the dark silver of the lakeside. The sheep galloped away from him, divided, one turning back with sheep's obstinacy, beginning to browse again as soon as it thought it was safe. "Hu, hu, hu!" The boy running, growing frantic. She wished she'd stayed to help him, could have stayed. Stood watching for a moment, the valley spread out, the mountains lifting, unfamiliar from this new height.

She began to climb once more, moving quickly, falling into her pace of long ago, and realised that she'd been saving this moment, this climb, like a glass of wine, while she prepared her mind for it, walking deliberately down there on the level ground. As though this moment might not come again, mustn't be grasped too soon. Was it still too soon?

I will not turn and look again until I'm by the ruins, she thought. She began to hurry. The sun was warm, beat gently off the rocks. A bird cried in the silence, a harsh raven-croak of loneliness. The sky was turquoise, with fleece clouds like the sheep below. The ruins just above her. She turned the corner of a rock and he was standing by the remains of a doorway, waiting for her.

"I've been watching you climb," he said. "I never saw a girl climb a mountain path before."

"Perhaps you haven't visited many mountains?" she said, trying to make her voice polite. The moment seemed to die, to wither, like finding the cherished glass of wine gone sour.

"And what is your friend doing? Elizabeth?"

"She's playing with some dolls that Mr. Pritchard found for her."

He began to laugh and stopped himself. "Do you think you can be happy here?"

She'd gone to the edge of the rock shelf and was looking out over the valley. "I'm very grateful," she said. "I'm afraid I don't show it enough."

"I didn't ask you for that reason. You don't have to be grateful."

"I must be. Twice over. For Snipe and for myself. And I shall be happy here. I intend to be."

"And you are only seventeen? You have learned a great deal in a short time."

"Is it a thing to do with age? To be happy?"

"No. But to intend to be happy, that is wise." He'd come to stand beside her. The house was very small below them, clear-cut as a toy against the green grass in front of it, the lake no more than a silver mirror. The boy had chased the sheep as far as the road. "I wish I could intend such a thing."

It was as though they were back in the gaming rooms and he was standing beside her by the curtains of the alcove.

"Why did you come to Monkey's house?" she said. "You never seemed to like it much."

"Charles thought it'd do me good."

"And did it?"

"We should not know each other if he had not." He laughed abruptly. "I don't mean to make fun of you," he said. "I'm very glad to know you. And Molly. And your appalling little friend. And Dido. I used to look forward to the evenings, I swear it." He stopped and she thought, *He's waiting for me to answer him.* She tried to answer, and say, "I also looked forward to them," but she couldn't say it.

He turned to her and said, "Can you imagine what it's like to wake up in the morning, to be woken up by a valet with a razor and hot water and the newspaper and to lie there wishing one hadn't woken? And to think, 'There are sixteen hours ahead of me before I can lose myself again?' A German poet has written a whole book about it, and I can experience it in a moment."

"But do you have nothing to do?"

"The things I have wanted to do are not proper for Lord Southcott's only son. And the things that are proper I have not wanted to do."

"But your father's estate—"

"Southcott? Cameron sees to that, and if I went

340

down, I should have either to agree with him, which I cannot imagine myself doing, or to disagree with him and make my father unhappy."

"Perhaps," she said, not looking at him, "your father deserves to be made unhappy about certain things." The sheep had begun to follow the boy back towards the house.

"You have no—" he began and stopped himself. "Of course you have a right," he said. "I'm sorry. What do they think of him? In Thaxstone? The poor people, I mean, the labourers?"

"Can you wish me to answer that?"

"He truly believes he is loved," Mr. Summers said. "He goes down once a year and they light a bonfire for him on the green, and the women send up turkeys and chickens to the hall as gifts."

"Will he go there this year?" Her voice sounded even drier than she meant it to and she saw his face tighten.

"He's much engaged in government business. He may not find the time." He turned to her again and tried to laugh. "This is a strange conversation to have with you on a Welsh mountainside. We should be romantic. I should be taking your hand and telling you how beautiful you are." He was smiling, but with a stiff awkwardness in the smile.

She said very quickly, "You promised to tell me something. Why it was so—so hard for you to save Snipe. Why you felt so—you said 'vile'?"

"Damnation, has a man not a right to feel vile, dealing in perjury and the perversion of justice, and by means of such a creature as Brown? Isn't that enough reason for you?"

"No, it isn't. We learned a great deal about such things in Monkey's house. Some of the runners make half their income by perjury, and most of it on behalf of gentlemen. Or is that another of the things your father does not know?"

"How dare you!"

She thought stupidly for a second that he was going to strike her and shut her eyes against his hand. But he turned away and leaned his hands against the wall

341

of the ruined tower, pulled a stone from it. He came
back and threw the stone over the edge of the rock
shelf they were standing on, and there was a long
moment before it struck the path below and lost itself
in the heather.

"I am very sorry," she whispered.

"I should not have come here," he said. "I heard
you say two days ago that you intended to climb up
to this place. I waited here for an hour yesterday until
I saw you walking down by the lake and knew you
would not be coming, at least then. And I've been
here an hour today."

"Why?"

"Why do you think?"

"Please, please."

"Is it so terrible for a man to want—to—"

"Yes."

"Am I so frightening?"

She wanted to run, was held there by—by what?
Gratitude? Obedience? Fear? She felt herself shivering,
put up one hand to her throat, and stared at him.

"Goddammit," he said. "Do I look like a monster
to you? I thought—I thought at one time that you
were beginning to find me tolerable."

"What do you want?" she breathed.

"What does any man want?" he shouted, and then
dropped his voice and said, "Nothing. I told you I
wanted nothing from you, not gratitude, nothing except to come here. And you have come here and that
is an end of it." He made to catch hold of her hand
and she drew away, without meaning to, and her
foot slipped and she was half over the edge of the
rock and falling before he caught her, dragged her
back. "Goddammit," he cried, "are you trying to kill
yourself?" His face white, he pulled her back towards
the ruin.

"I will tell you something," he said furiously. "I will
tell you what it meant to me to help your friend." He
stopped, looked away from her, still gripping her
wrists. She wanted to free herself and was ashamed
to. "You asked me once," he said, "if—if my father
knew that Mrs. Talbot was one of those to be hanged."

"You don't need to tell me anything," she whispered. "I know."

The fingers tightened on her wrists until it became painful, and she was glad of it, glad to think of her wrists and the small pain in them, and not of the man who held them. Of his father. Of—

"What do you know?" he said. "How?" He began to shake her, not roughly but with an intensity that was like fear. "Did—my uncle—does he—"

"No."

He let go of her, tried twice to say something, and whispered finally, "Tell me what you mean."

"Your father knew," she said harshly. She shut her eyes, felt her throat lock, felt a shaking of passion, hatred, put up her hand to the iron ring, and could not find it for a second. "He knew I—Let me go," she breathed. Had she said "I"?

"Tell me!"

She found the ring, closed her hand on it as though she was going to tear the cloth of her gown. Regained control of her mind. Her voice. "Your father knew that Mrs. Talbot was to be hanged. And was glad of it," she whispered. "Or did he pretend?" Her voice shook again. As though a bird was stooping above her head, its wings spread, to fasten its talons in her flesh, grip and possess her. Possess her inmost self.

"What are you saying?"

"He was afraid," she whispered. "For thirty years he was afraid. That she would inherit all this, that your uncle would die and leave it to her, would rob him of his hopes."

"You're mad!" he breathed. "Mad and—"

She leaned against the stone of the tower, the shadow gone. Looked at the valley, at the distant, hidden farms. "She didn't want them," she said. "She wanted nothing from him except to be honoured. You would still have inherited everything when he died. Except the little that would have kept her. Your father didn't need to be afraid of her."

"How do you know these things?" he said. He took hold of her again and held her upright against the wall. "She told you? But not the truth," he said, his voice savage. "She wanted everything. Everything. My aunt's place. She took that soon enough. And after that, everything. When my aunt died—"

"And how do you know these things?" she said. "Did your father tell you them?" As though they were enemies, their shadows twisted together, locked and struggling. "Let go of me, you're hurting my arms."

He hesitated, let go of her, and swung away. "We're being fools," he said. "It's all so long ago. And she's dead now, and my father—" He put his hands up against his face, his eyes. "He didn't know," he said in a low voice. "I swear before God." And stopped, as though he realised himself the futility of his words. "Do you think I care whether I inherit from my uncle or not?"

"I have no right to say anything."

"My father is a bitterly unhappy man. I don't think he knows how unhappy. My stepmother is like a sickness with him. Half the time he grovels to her and half the time he is so ashamed of it he could shoot himself. And I must say, 'Yes, ma'am,' to a golden bitch with a jewel case for a heart who is six years younger than I am. My father wakes in terror in the night that he will die soon and that I will throw that woman into the gutter where she belongs and drag his money back out of her hands. His whole soul's chained to her, and if he knew what she is! But he does! He does! That's the worst of it! And he tells me that when my uncle dies, I shall have half a million from him and will I swear to him on my oath as a son that I'll leave her with what she has."

"And do you swear?"

"No. And never will. I will break her like a stick for what she's done to him. I put him off, make a jest of it." He beat his fists softly against the stones on either side of her head, laughed. "Such a pleasant jest. Your Mrs. Talbot was happier." He touched her face. "And I've waited here two days for you and now I spend the time telling you secrets about my stepmother. Do you not remember your own mother at all?"

"No," she whispered, remembering her. The red

skirt. Remembered suddenly her dancing, the stamping of her bare feet. She felt sick with fear, wanted to run from him, and couldn't move. The fire burning and the red skirt like a huge flower, turning and turning. She had clapped her hands. That had been the night before. "They killed her," she said. "The soldiers killed her. And then he came."

"Who came?"

"The captain. He rode into the village and found me there."

"You said once that I was like him."

"You are."

"I—"

She twisted away from between his hands. "I must go back."

He reached out and caught hold of her. "You must not." He looked at his own hand holding her, his face with that look of anger in it that seemed directed at no particular thing and at the same time at everything. "I didn't mean to say any of this, or do this, or come up to this place, or speak to you beyond 'Good morning' and 'Good night.' I swore to myself in London that I meant nothing but to please my uncle. I went on swearing it from London to here. What have you done to me?"

"Nothing."

"You have done it to my uncle, too. He dreams about you." He let go of her and spread his hands as though he was demonstrating to her that she was free. "You have inherited her witchcraft, I think." He tried to laugh. "It's just as well for both of us that I'm to go back to London tomorrow."

"Tomorrow?"

"Yes. Are you glad of that?"

"Why do you wish to think me so ungrateful?"

"Because—" He took hold of her again. "You look as though a spark would set you blazing," he said. "And instead of that you are made of ice. It is unjust. And Charles is so damned smugly happy with your Molly, as though God created Half Moon Street for no other purpose. When we first saw the two of you in Monkey's, we tossed a coin for you and I won. Is that not funny?"

"You tossed a coin?" she whispered. Felt her face burn with anger.

"Well, Charles did. He made me call heads or tails and I called heads, to keep him quiet. I even won you again, afterwards, from Dido. Do you remember?"

"I remember."

"And do I still get nothing for all these victories?"

She turned and ran down the path, rounded the corner of rock, and was twenty yards below him before she remembered she had left her jacket by the wall. She looked up and he was looking down at her.

"I have left my spencer."

"Then you should—I'll bring it down to you. Please wait."

She waited and he came slowly, as though he wished not to make her afraid, holding her jacket across his arm. "Have I made you angry?" he said. "Telling you that we tossed a coin?"

"No."

"I must come back in a month's time," he said. "Will you—I swear I meant to say none of this, not even to think of it—but will you *think* of it? When I am away?"

"You mean, that you called heads and won?"

"You said you weren't angry."

"I am not."

Clouds had come, there was the feel of rain in the warm air, a breath of cold. The small lake was leaden grey.

"The doctors say my uncle will live a few months. The winter perhaps. No more than that. If you stay with him so long, I shall give you a gift that may keep you free of—of concern for a little while. But then? What will you do then?"

"I shall go to Spain."

"To find a burned village? You will not find even a grave there. And when you have found it?"

"How can I tell?"

"I would bring you to Spain."

"Your uncle brought Mrs. Talbot to India."

"You have no right to make fun of me."

"Do you think that is making fun?"

"Why are you bitter with me?" He stopped and held her arm. "God above, I've done nothing but—"

"You've done nothing but kindnesses, I know."

A drop of rain fell between them, like a coin.

"And I would do more. So much more that it would be hard for you to imagine. You should have your own house. If you wished your wretched Snipe to stay with you, you might have that too. I would give you so much you could be secure forever."

She tried to answer him, knew he was misunderstanding her silence. Almost laughed, felt the blood burning in her face, in her throat, and scarcely knew why.

"I know you mean it well," she said at last. "It's—it's only that I don't want such a thing."

"What the devil else could I offer you? What will you *do*? Marry someone like Dido? Bear him children in a garret somewhere? Or go from here as a servant into some other house, with a letter from my attorney recommending you as honest? God above, Sara, think! Think of the future!"

"I do think of it. Sometimes. Are these the only possible futures?"

"Not quite the only ones. But the others do not bear thinking of. What would have happened to you if I'd left you in Monkey Palmer's? With Brown?"

"I should have run away."

"Where to? Where the devil to? Spain? For God's sake, be sensible. Am I so terrible? I am not old, nor diseased, nor cruel, nor more than ordinarily bad-tempered. You shall have your own carriage." She began to run from him again and reached the house just as the rain began.

Chapter 26

It was late autumn when he returned. Long, golden mornings, and the afternoons turning to rain and storm clouds, dark before evening, an hour before sunset perhaps, the sun breaking the cover of the clouds and a last echo of summer reaching them, still and beautiful and sad. Silence, and dark red berries on the hawthorns, and brown gold leaves on the few trees of the mountainside, the bracken fading.

He came back in one of those half hours of evening sun, in the same brake, and she went out onto the terrace to greet him, with Mr. Pritchard and Rhonwen and another of the maids and the garden boy, Elfed. He avoided her eyes as he jumped down, and made something of a formality of greeting everyone, of being greeted by Mr. Pritchard. "And how is my uncle?" and "Do you all find yourselves well?"

It was only when his portmanteaux were being taken in that he looked at her and took her hand again and said, "I am glad to be back." As they walked into the house he said, "Would you join me at supper, perhaps? I've asked Pritchard to give me something in half an hour."

"I will come and sit with you if you wish."

He stared at her at that and said half angrily, "Is that my answer?"

"I meant only to be polite. Snipe and I have our supper together at six o'clock."

"Yes, yes, of course. Snipe." He made himself smile

348

and said, "I must go and pay my respects to my uncle. And then I shall be glad if you will sit with me. Do you permit yourself to take a glass of wine out of her company?"

"If you invite me to do so."

She was already waiting for him in the dining-room when he came down. A bleak, unused room, dull portraits hung in it of undistinguished Giffords and Delaneys and Clives. A few objects from Mr. Gifford's years in India: a golden box set with rubies, an Indian sword lying on the stone mantelpiece, its hilt and scabbard equally extravagant.

He had changed his linen and his coat and looked as apologetic as he ever did. "No sooner am I here than we are exchanging sharp words. No one should speak at all at the end of a journey until they have washed and put on a clean shirt. Are we friends again?"

"Of course."

He held her chair for her. "I think our dining-room is pleasanter," she said. "I don't envy you."

"And how is Elizabeth? Are the dolls all broken?"

"By no means. She has taken over one of the stable lofts and made it into a dolls' theatre. Elfed and his father made scenery for us. We have the Haymarket and the Argyle Rooms and the Alhambra. And also the Court of Denmark, now. We're preparing a dolls' version of *Hamlet*, but it's not quite ready for the public yet."

"Good God. And who is your public?"

"Why, Mr. Pritchard, Rhonwen, Myfanwy and the other maids, Elfed and his father, and Gwyn the kitchen boy. We've had distinguished visitors too. We are making a royal box for Mr. Parry and his wife and daughters."

"And may I use it?"

"We shall be honoured."

Mr. Pritchard came in with Rhonwen, carrying a tray of cold meat and wine.

"I hear you have theatricals here," Mr. Summers said.

"Indeed, sir. And take much pleasure in them." Mr.

Pritchard poured wine for Sara and set another log on the fire and left them.

"You have transformed my uncle, too," Mr. Summers said, lifting his glass to her. "He tells me he does not know how he endured living before you came."

"It pleases him to hear French poetry again."

"And more than that." He put his glass down so hard that wine spilled. "Do not play with me. I've thought of nothing this past six weeks except our last talk and this moment now. I have sat in a theatre beside Charles and his Molly and not known what play we were looking at. I have been to Monkey's gaming house again and lost ten guineas without knowing whether I was playing faro or roulette or rouge-et-noir. I have looked round and seen dark hair and thought, 'She is there!' I have—What have you done to me? I am thirty-one years old, a grown man, and you have turned me into a schoolboy. I even understand my father." He got up from the table and stood with his hands on the mantelpiece, staring down into the fire. "Have you an answer for me?"

"My answer," she whispered, "my answer is no. Why do you torment us both?"

He banged his fists down on the stone, rattled the gold clock. "I have asked you too quickly, God give me patience. I've travelled two days and two nights and have scarcely slept. I've thought—tomorrow—and then today—and then in one more hour. I will not allow you to answer me yet." He turned round, shut his eyes, and put his hands against them. "I'm to remain here for a week, or ten days. I shall wait until—"

He came to their stable-theatre and watched the dolls' tableaux and rehearsals. He spent his days with Mr. Parry or the attorney from Bangor, Mr. Roberts, a small, fat, glistening man with cheeks that seemed to have been polished like red apples and who was Mr. Pritchard's cousin's son. They, too, came to the tableaux to hear Snipe announcing, "Wot you're about to see is a dreadful crime bein' committed in the 'Ay-market at midnight of a winter's night. This 'ere is a terrible garrotter what strangles 'is victims an' leaves 'em lying naked in the gutter. An' this 'ere is the garrotter's mate, what picks on the poor victim. You see the mate liftin' 'is 'at to give the all clear. An' this 'ere is a honest pickpocket girl what is goin' to save the victim's life."

The pickpocket girl was Marie-Antoinette and the victim King Louis.

"Good God above," said Mr. Summers.

"Hush," Sara whispered.

"Wonderful, wonderful," cried Mr. Roberts when the performance was done and Marie-Antoinette had married King Louis to live happily ever after, Scotch Robert in a kilt having given Marie-Antoinette away. "A true artist she is, the little lady, another Mrs. Siddons come to Wales just to please us. Fancy now that you have your own theatre here in this valley!"

Mr. Summers was to go the next day. "I must talk to you," he said as they walked back from the stables into the house, leaving Snipe and Elfed to put the dolls away and see to the darkened theatre. "Will you take supper with me tonight?"

"I cannot."

"Goddammit, why can you not?"

"Because, for one thing, Mr. Pritchard would not allow it."

"Damn Pritchard! If I wish it—"

"And for another thing I should not allow it."

"You will drive me mad!" They were outside his bedroom. "At least come into my room for a moment where there aren't three maids and a boy listening round every corner. What do all these servants do all day? One cannot turn round but they are underfoot." He opened the door and made her go in.

"I should not be in here."

He set his back against the door. "But you are in here and you are not leaving until I have my answer. And a fair, sane answer."

"You have it already."

"I will not accept such an answer. There's almost nothing you cannot have. Perhaps I shall wake one day and realise that I have lost my mind, been bewitched. God, I am worse than Charles and he's bad

351

enough, doting and puling like a schoolboy with a dancer, but I am gone out of my wits entirely. Why the devil did Charles ever bring me to that damned place?"

He came away from the door and caught hold of her.

"Let me go."

"I will not."

He held her by the shoulders, kissed her suddenly, harshly, hurting her with the violence of it, and she felt her mind go dark with terror, felt such terror that her knees gave, she was falling, she could hear the screaming, her mother's long shuddering scream as the soldiers caught her, dragged her away. Running from her hiding place, herself screaming, and the soldier turning, lifting his musket, crashing the butt of it down against her forehead. And still the screaming as she fell.

"What is the matter?" he was saying. "For God's sake, what have I done, what's wrong with you?" Chafing her hands, her face. She was lying where she had fallen, sliding out of his grasp onto the floor. "God, I did but—What's the matter with you? Shall I call a—Do you want water?"

She lay still, looking at him with hatred. She tried to say something and could not say a word, her mouth opening, no more than a sound whispering in her throat.

"I'll get you some water, brandy. God above, shall I call a woman to you?"

She had come to her knees when he brought back the water and his travelling-flask of brandy. She let him hold the glass to her mouth. The brandy burned her, shocked her back into the present moment.

"Let me go now," she said. "Or do you want more payment?"

He opened the door for her without a word and they said nothing more to each other, weren't alone together to say anything until he was leaving the next day. They stood in the morning sunlight while the brake was turned and loaded with his luggage: Mr. Pritchard; Mr. Parry; Mr. Roberts, who was to go with Mr. Summers as far as Bettws-y-Coed; and Snipe and half a dozen of the servants.

"I have a word to say to you about my uncle," Mr. Summers said. "Would you walk aside with me for a moment?" They walked the length of the terrace before he said anything. "Am I forgiven?"

She did not answer him.

"Is it so terrible that a man should kiss you? Suppose you were ugly and no one wished to? Would not that be truly terrible?"

"I have not thought of it. I do not care to be handled."

"God's teeth, you're an impossible girl. I should like—I should like to—" He stood and controlled himself. "I would give you one of the farms here if you wished," he said. "You should have the income of it for life."

"The brake is waiting for you. Mr. Roberts—"

"Damn and blast them both. Do you wish us to be enemies?"

"Of course I do not. Haven't I told you enough that I am grateful?"

"God curse your gratitude. Damn, blast." He took off his hat and seemed about to throw it onto the ground. "I can't come here again until the spring. I must go to Germany for my father, and may God cure me of you in the interval. But if He doesn't—Sara, Sara! If you knew what my life is, you'd be sorry for me. May I not hope for anything? Even friendship?"

"Of course."

"When you say, 'Of course' like that, my heart sinks like a stone. You'll have me writing love letters to you next."

"Will you give all my messages and love to Molly?"

"Damn Molly. Yes, yes, of course. Why the devil aren't you like her?"

"You should have called tails."

He shut his eyes for a second and then laughed, not very successfully. "I should never have told you that. Well, it is good-bye again. If fate is good to me, I shall meet some dear plump blue-eyed fräulein in

353

Germany who'll drive you out of my head. If you wish me well, wish that for me."

"I do indeed."

"How can you?" He swung away and went so quickly towards the brake that she was left behind, and he was already mounted on it beside Mr. Roberts when she came close enough to say, "Good-bye."

She watched the brake creak and rumble away down the gravelled drive that swiftly became no more than the rutted track through the meadow, the scythed stubble of the hay grown with flowers again, gold and blue and white and red, like coloured stars. The distant road, the lake, the mountains.

The servants went in and Snipe. Mr. Parry got onto his horse and rode away. Mr. Pritchard said to her, "If you would go to Mr. Gifford now? He feels sad when guests leave and would be glad of comfort."

She went into the dark, heavy room with its drawn curtains and its firelight. Cushions were always left for her beside the old man's chair, and the books she might need were on a shelf fastened to the wall where Mr. Gifford could not stumble against it. She had used to put the cushions away each day in case he caught his foot against one of them, but he'd insisted they be left beside him. "I touch them when you aren't there," he said. "They have your warmth in them."

"Is he gone?" the old man said.

She came and knelt down beside him. "He will come back."

"And you said 'no' to him."

She moved under his hand and saw him smiling.

"Do you think I didn't know? What did he offer you?"

"Gifts. Security."

"I would have given her much more than that. If I had known. If I had known what age is like. Blindness. I should have married her in spite of all of them."

"How did they prevent you?"

"I wanted a title. I wanted things that had happened in India forgotten. And I never received the title." He laughed with a dreadful self-mockery. "Do you know yet how base men can be?"

"Don't think of it. She has long ago forgiven everything."

"It is easier to forgive others than oneself." His hands tightened round her. "Hold me," he whispered. "It's so cold." He stroked her face, his fingers slowly growing a shade warmer from her skin. "One does a base thing and it seems nothing. No more than all men do. And through the years it grows and grows in one's mind like a tree of evil, darkening everything. First my poor wife. Then Margaret. And before that in India—worse, far worse—and yet it's those two who lie on my mind until I think I shall go mad. Hold me closer, child. Put your hand here against my heart. We used to sit like this, by this fire. She knelt so straight. She never wanted to betray my wife. And my wife so sickly, so alone. We sat here and I would stroke her hair and her throat. Like this. Can you imagine that I was handsome? Full of strength? And I knew so much of love-making. I learned it in Bengal. It's an art with them and I could touch a woman's throat like this and her lips would open and I could breathe such sweetness into them that she would weep for me."

His hand stroked her throat, stroked and fondled, and she felt her eyes closing, her own lips opening. But not of her own will. Stroking, stroking, touching a nerve beneath her hair at the nape of her neck, another under her jaw. As though he were sending her to sleep. She lay against his knee, felt his heart beat under the palm of her hand, against her forehead, lay with her face buried in his lap, and he stroked and stroked and she was half asleep, her body now shivering, now quiet, and her mind filled with colours as though a brilliant bird was spreading out its wings. Green fire, crimson, dark blue and orange. The dark green of trees, a river flowing, brown water; flowing, flowing; and she lay, Mrs. Talbot lay young and ivory smooth, ivory slender, filled with love; lay on cushions staring at the arching of the dark green forest trees. And for a moment Sara half imagined it was her own

355

body shivering, trembling as he touched her; almost longed to be naked also like that other long-dead, long-vanished girl who had lain by that Indian river naked, ivory-naked on the silk cushions and the Persian carpet spread on the starred grass.

"My love's breasts are two flowers," an echo whispered. From so far off, so long past a time. When? Where? She felt the warmth of the forest, of the dark earth, the river; heard the river, heard the birds high up in the hidden vault of the trees; heard the monkeys that cried like children; heard the rustling of the leaves; felt a dark emptiness longing to be filled with love. Whose emptiness? Whose love? And in her own resisting mind felt a depth of pain that all she could offer to these long-dead lovers was her pity for them, her tenderness.

"Make me warm," the echoes breathed. "Only make me warm." And "My love," the echoes answered. "My love. My love."

I am asleep, she thought. His fingers stroked the soft skin beneath her ears, touched the pulse of her neck, tried to fill her mind with dreams.

"Is not tenderness enough?" she whispered. "Pity?" And felt his cold tears on her hands.

Chapter 27

"My great fault it is, frankness," Mr. Roberts said. "A dreadful handicap in a lawyer, I've known it always and fought against it, but what can a man do against his own nature? And so I am forced to tell you, forced against my own interests, you see, to tell you that you need have no fear in the world of them, not a tremolo. Bound in brass that will is, girded in brass and iron such as the forces of Midian may prowl round to their hearts' content and do no harm to it, though they might have the lord chancellor himself at their head and throwing his old Woolsack at it. Iron bound and brass locked like a strong room in Caernarvon Castle."

But she was afraid. She listened to Mr. Roberts' would-be reassurances with half her mind, the other half straining to hear the sounds of the brake, or of a carriage, that would announce they had arrived. Who would come with him? His father? Or only lawyers?

She sat very straight at the head of the long table in the dining-room, looking out of the nearest window at the autumn landscape. Winter. Spring. Summer. And now another autumn. A year since she had seen him. Two furious letters. And then nothing, until these last weeks and the stream of letters. From him. What would he say now? What would he do?

"Let him rage furiously!" Mr. Roberts had cried. "Slanders and defamation! I shall be here taking them down, my dear, every word! And then we shall see what we shall see! Then we shall see if a little gibbering—that was the word was it not, gibbering? Gibbering is it? I shall gibber him!—a little gibbering Welsh attorney may not play David to the Goliath of his great London wigs and gowns. Balm to my soul that would be, Mrs. Gifford dear, balm in Gilead. But I must be frank with you. My great fault it is, frankness."

What would he say? Not that she was afraid for herself. She looked down at her hands resting on the silk-smooth mahogany. The black sleeves of her mourning gown.

"And I must tell you another thing, which I have been afraid to tell you, my dear. On my recommendation it was that Mr. Gifford divided the estate in two halves and did not give all to you as he wished. 'Mr. Gifford!' I said to him. 'Look at it like a dear sensible gentleman! What will they do if you leave everything to Mrs. Gifford and not a penny piece to Mr. Summers, who lies awake at nights expecting a great fortune? What will they do? They will come and make poor Mrs. Gifford's life impossible, impossible they will make it, with writs and torts and vexations to fill that lake out there in the valley, and the valley as well. No life at all will she have if you do that, for there will be nothing to restrain them, and greed and hatred to drive them on, like hornets and gadflies upon the haunches of cattle. They will prowl about her in the darkness, like the Amalakites; they will set upon her by day. No, no, my dear,' I said to him, 'do not do that. Be guided by wisdom, take advice from the serpent, be cunning to do good. Leave half to each and let it be made clear as crystal to them by the will and testament that I shall draw up for you that not a chance do they have, not a fragment of a peradventure do they have, to upset such a document, and that instead they risk the loss and wasting of that half of your substance which is offered to them should they reach out ungodly and avaricious hands to steal from the widow that which is hers. No, no, Mr. Gifford dear,' I begged him. 'Better that she be secure in the possession of half—' " His voice rolled past her ears, bright with joy.

"They are coming!" she breathed. She felt her throat contract, tighten, forced her hands to lie still, herself to remain where she was. She saw the carriage climb up from the meadow toward the terrace, vanish out of her sight again. The carriage black and heavy and somehow even more threatening than if it had been merely the brake from Bettws-y-Coed and Elwyn the Brake driving it. She heard it come to a stop. They would be getting down. Pritchard opening the front door, standing on the steps, waiting.

My heart will burst, she thought. She wanted to close her eyes. Held herself still as iron.

"You aren't angry that I gave him that advice? I would lay down my soul on the carpet before your feet rather than think you were angry with me. Death it would be to me, I promise you."

"Of course I'm not angry. It was wise advice. Mr.

Gifford discussed it with me the same day and I was very pleased with what you had done. Moreover it was just."

"He told you? You knew of it already? Oh, my soul, and I've been tormented with the fear of telling you."

"They're coming now!"

The door opened. "Mr. Summers, ma'am, and a Mr. Hatton."

"Show them in."

She stood up, her finger-tips on the table, her face white as marble against the black velvet of her mourning. He came in carrying his hat crushed under his arm, his face impassive, like a stranger's; Mr. Hatton thin and elegant behind him, bowing, his smile also thin and elegant and watchful, and condescending.

"If you will sit down," she said.

She sat herself, and after a hesitation Mr. Summers took the chair that Mr. Pritchard had drawn out for him. Mr. Hatton sat down carefully, parting his coat-tails, looking sideways at Mr. Roberts, at the spread of documents in front of him. He primmed his mouth as much as to say, "Can the creature even read then, I wonder?"

"Let us come to the point at once," Mr. Summers said. "I have made a long journey for this charade."

"Charade!" Mr. Roberts said happily. "Charade, does the gentleman call it? Note that, Mr. Pritchard, remember it, if you please. Charade!"

"God above," Mr. Summers cried, "this is intolerable. First you will not come to London to see me, but drag me here two hundred and fifty miles to repeat to you something that I have already told you by letter: that all this damned folly has no more substance in law than——" He put his hand up to his cravat and dragged at it. "I'm prepared——"

"No substance in law?" Mr. Roberts crowed. "No substance, is it? Oh, oh, let us see proofs, let us hear chapter and verse quoted, precedents cited, my dear."

"Will you tell that fellow to be quiet?" Mr. Summers said. "Or must I?"

"If you've come here only to abuse us," Sara said, "you must expect unwelcome answers. And if you truly believed what you said, you wouldn't be here. Neither would Mr.—" She allowed herself to pause before adding the name Hatton, with a slight questioning in her tone that raised a dull flush on Mr. Hatton's cheek-bones. Mr. Summers controlled himself with a visible effort. "I told you in my letter," he said, "that we can discuss this matter calmly."

"I *am* calm."

"Dammit," he cried, "so am I. Good God, it couldn't even have been a true marriage! What birth certificates did you produce! What documents? From where?"

"Invalid," Mr. Hatton murmured. "Not a doubt of it but it must have been invalid."

"Do you hear that, Mr. Pritchard! Slander, that is, defamation! An attack on Mrs. Gifford's honour as a woman, upon her chastity! Oh, I have noted it down, verbatim, verbatim!"

"Will you be quiet?" Mr. Summers shouted. "Merciful God, how much more have I to endure from you? And tell your—Pritchard, you can leave us."

"Oh, no, he cannot. Oh, no, my dear, he is a witness, a most necessary and vital witness to what is said, and the moment all is ended I shall have a draft of this conversation ready here for him to sign as being a true representation of all that has been spoken. Oh, yes, my dear, we are not such fools as you may think."

Mr. Summers spread out his hands on the table, closed them into fists, staring down at them with his face draining of blood. "I came here to be generous," he said. "And in spite of what—in spite of—" He gathered himself, looked at her, his face darkening again. "I repeat the offer I have already made to you. You may have a small house for yourself, any one of the cottages on this estate or in Essex that you think suitable. You may have enough money to keep you respectably. You may call yourself Mrs. Gifford."

"I *am* Mrs. Gifford."

"Sara!"

"I am Mrs. Gifford. We were married with the full knowledge and approval of the bishop, by his own

360

chaplain, by his own license, in full knowledge of all my circumstances and after correspondence with Dr. Newall of the parish in which I last resided. You may challenge my marriage where and how you wish. I think your House of Lords is too occupied with the prince regent's marriage to spend its time attempting to upset mine."

"I would give ten thousand pounds to take you and thrash you," Mr. Summers whispered. "Twenty thousand."

"Threats of violence!" Mr. Roberts cried in ecstasy. "Oh, Mr. Pritchard, not a word must you miss of all this. Oh, I could not have hoped for it, not in my dreams of salvation I could not!"

"Mr. Summers, I beg of you," Mr. Hatton whispered.

"Marriage?" Mr. Summers said furiously. "You call it a marriage? To an old, blind, dying man? To cozen and cheat and trick him into fondness."

"Cozen! Trick! Cheat! Oh, delightful, perfect. Go on, my dear, spread out the net before your own feet that you may stumble and be caught up in the toils of it!"

"Mr. Summers, I pray you, I had your promise as we came here that you would not—"

"God's teeth, Hatton, will you be quiet? And I brought her here! I tell you, Sara, you have five minutes in which to accept my offer of a compromise."

"You call that a compromise?" Sara said. "Is that the well-bred term for it? I am left by my husband—by my husband—this house and the land and nearest farm attached to it, and two hundred and thirty thousand pounds invested in the funds, as my widow's portion."

"Widow?" Mr. Summers said, his voice breaking. "You—you—"

"Mr. Summers, I beseech you, I beg of you," Mr. Hatton said, catching hold of his client's arm in his despair.

"Let me recall to you Clause Eleven!" Mr. Roberts cried. "Clause Eleven of Mr. Gifford's last will and testament, of which a copy has been duly furnished

361

to you as an interested party! 'If any beneficiary shall challenge—' "

"Damn you, Roberts! Let go of my arm, Hatton! God above!" He leaned back in his chair, with his eyes shut, gripping the table's edge. "Sara. I swear to you I meant to be—but you have provoked me in such a manner—" He swallowed. "Let me talk to you alone. If that man says another word in my hearing, I cannot answer for myself."

She held her own hands together and looked at them. All her fear was gone. She felt almost amused. "Very well," she said. "Mr. Roberts? If you would walk with Mr. Hatton in the garden for a little while? And if you would bring us some wine, Mr. Pritchard, and some tea? I should like tea now, I think."

"Oh, Mrs. Gifford, dear, it would not be my duty to leave you! And after such threatenings! Such talk of thrashings and violence! I could not answer to my conscience."

"I do not think he will be violent, Mr. Roberts. And you will be no more than outside the windows. Show Mr. Hatton the children's garden."

"Children?" Mr. Summers whispered. "You—you are not pretending—"

She looked at him, truly amused now, and waited until they were alone.

"It is worse than witchcraft," Mr. Summers said. "It is devilish. Devilish." He spread his hands on the table, looked round the room. "You are scarcely eighteen, it is no more than a year since I brought you to this house as a—as a—"

"Are you so greedy for another fortune that you must grudge me my share of this one?"

"Greedy?" He cried, astonished. "I? Greedy? God in heaven, girl!" He put up his fingers to his cravat again, tugged it so hard that the knot loosened and the cravat fell open. He tried to re-knot it with trembling hands, and she wached him, smiling, the certainty growing in her that she had won, that he knew she had won, and that all this journey and shouting was no more than a last threatening, after the lawyers had realised they could do nothing. That the will truly was bound in brass and iron and triple-locked as Mr. Roberts claimed.

"If we are to talk of greed," he said and stopped, as though he were gasping for air. "Crying, 'Do not touch me, do not make me swoon away by such a violent offence as trying to kiss me,' and a month later crawling into an old man's bed like a female viper."

"I shall have to call Mr. Roberts back."

"Sara! Sara! All right, I was a fool, a blind, stupid, trusting fool to leave you here and must pay a price for my folly. But two hundred and thirty thousand pounds. And this house! And the best farm of the entire estate! What will you do with it all? I mean if—even if—"

"I think your lawyers have already told you that you have no case? Am I not right? You were no blood relation to my late husband."

"Sara!"

"There is no similarity between this case and that of your stepmother. There perhaps you may dispossess her as you please, I know nothing about it. But if Mr. Gifford had wished it, he might have left his whole fortune to me entire and undivided. He left no living blood relation. He wished to do it, to make me his sole heiress. Was set upon it, and the more so when I told him my plans for using anything that he left to me."

"What plans?" He half stood, sat down again.

"You may see if you wish. But I am telling you something. The only reason that the will gave half the estate to you was by my entreaty. And Mr. Roberts' advice. We both thought it wise. And I thought it just."

"Did you, by God? Did you?"

"Come with me and see my plans. There are only seven of them at the moment, but there will be many more, I hope."

"Seven what? Stop playing with me, Sara. You shall have—you shall have fifty thousand pounds, I swear it. A London house. But you cannot expect to keep all this. You cannot! It isn't—"

"And you would come and visit me in my London house? Three evenings a week perhaps?"

"*Sara!*" He banged his fists on the mahogany. "You wouldn't even know how to—how to use so much, how to look after it."

"I shall have advice. And I have invited you to see how I intend to use it. Come." She stood up and offered him her arm, and he was obliged to take it.

"They are in the stables at the moment. I told them they must be very good and quiet because a kind gentleman was coming to see their new home."

"What are you talking of? What have you been doing?" He stood still in the hall and she drew him on towards the passage leading out to the rear courtyard and the stables.

"I have been gathering children," she said. "I've told you, there are only seven at the moment."

"Seven?" he shouted. "Seven children? Are you gone mad?"

"I don't think so. They're quite small children, and very glad to be here."

"What children?" He had stopped again in the courtyard. They could hear the children's voices now, laughing. "What have you—where do they—"

"We find them in London," she said. "Or rather, Mr. Munro and Dido found these for us. Dido is to come here soon, to help look after them, but Mr. Munro will go on looking for more children for us. They're quite easy to find, you know. The doorways seem to be full of them on any night you care to look. But perhaps you have never done so? You should ask your father to look sometimes. But doubtless he's too busy when he's in London."

"You're mad," he whispered. "Raving mad."

"I don't think so. When you see a child cold and hungry and naked and afraid, it is quite a natural thing to wish to take care of it. Come and see for yourself and tell me then if we are mad." She led him into the stables and up the loft staircase, which had been made both strong and broad with shallow treads that small children could manage easily.

The children sat on low stools watching the theatre

play, the movements of the dolls as Snipe manipulated them. "This is 'Amlet," Snipe was saying. " 'E's an orphan like us, but very rich an' 'e lives in a palace. An' this is the wicked king what killed 'Amlet's dad."

She stopped as Sara and Mr. Summers came in and all the children turned round and stared.

"You must stand up," Sara said, "and make your curtseys. This is the kind gentleman I told you of, who is very glad for us to have this house to live in and all the fields round. Tell them how glad you are, I beg of you."

She felt his hand shaking on her arm, gripping it hard. The children spread out the skirts of their white dresses, ducked their heels. Like a row of seven dolls, not much bigger than the dolls upon the stage.

" 'Allo," Snipe said.

Mr. Summers whispered something and turned and went hurriedly down the stairs.

"He's very, very glad," Sara said. "And now watch the play."

THE BEST OF BESTSELLERS
FROM WARNER BOOKS!

 A Warner Communications Company

Please send me the books I have checked.

Enclose check or money order only, no cash please. Plus 35¢ per copy to cover postage and handling. N.Y. State residents add applicable sales tax.

Please allow 2 weeks for delivery.

WARNER BOOKS
P.O. Box 690
New York, N.Y. 10019

Name ....

Address ....

City .... State .... Zip ....

_____ Please send me your free mail order catalog

THE BEST OF BESTSELLERS
FROM WARNER BOOKS!